...this
...nd you're going to put the past
...side and let me."

"Put the past aside?" She jerked out of his hold and took a step back. "It's not that simple, Nolan."

"I didn't mean it like that," he corrected. "I know we have unresolved issues, but for now, we need to work on your current situation."

"Fine. What's your miraculous plan?"

Pepper stared back at him with those wide, expressive eyes. This was the same woman he'd fallen in love with as a teen, the woman he'd thought he'd spend his life with and the woman who had carried his child. Yeah, they had quite a bit left to hash out between them and throwing this bomb onto that already smoldering fire was only going to complicate matters further.

Nolan closed the space between them. "We're getting married."

* * *

Claimed by the Rancher
is part of The Rancher's Heirs series—
Loyalty and family mean everything to these
Texas men and the women who tame them.

CLAIMED BY THE RANCHER

BY
JULES BENNETT

First Published in Great Britain 2017
By Mills & Boon, an imprint of HarperCollins*Publishers*
1 London Bridge Street, London, SE1 9GF

© 2017 Jules Bennett

ISBN: 978-0-263-92824-2

51-0617

Our policy is to use papers that are natural, renewable and recyclable products and made from wood grown in sustainable forests. The logging and manufacturing processes conform to the legal environmental regulations of the country of origin.

Printed and bound in Spain
by CPI, Barcelona

National bestselling author **Jules Bennett** has penned over forty contemporary romance novels. She lives in the Midwest with her high-school-sweetheart husband and their two kids. Jules can often be found on Twitter chatting with readers, and you can also connect with her via her website, www.julesbennett.com.

To my plot angels for this story:
Elaine Spencer and Melissa Jeglinski.

One

The bell on the door to Painted Pansies chimed, and nerves danced in Pepper Manning's stomach. Opening a shop with her one-of-a-kind paintings and unique fresh floral bouquets had been on her bucket list for some time. She might be a drifter, a free spirit of sorts, but her creativity—her ability to make something from nothing—was what really drove her.

Coming back to Stone River, Texas, however, would take some master creative skills. She would certainly be making something from nothing—a business, a home to call her own. Pepper had always loved this town, so it made sense for her to make this the place where she started the next chapter in her life.

Besides, time was not on her side.

If she hadn't had anyone else to think about, she could've chosen a different town to settle into, but in five short months, she'd be a mother.

A *single* mother with no one else to turn to for support.

Pasting a smile on her face, Pepper stepped through the doorway from the back room and her entire world came to a halt.

The man standing at the display of cheery tangerine roses had Pepper gripping the edge of the door frame. That profile, the black cowboy hat, those narrow hips she'd once known so well…

No. This was too soon. She needed more time. How could she be thrust into her past already? Though she'd been in town a month, this was her first day launching her brand-new business.

She'd assumed he most likely still lived in town because of his family's ranch and vast holdings, but she hadn't geared herself up to face him just yet.

Would she ever be ready to face the man who broke her heart at the most vulnerable time of her life? The man she'd been so certain she'd be spending her life with.

Before she could muster up some generic greeting, Nolan Elliott's gaze swept around the shop and then landed on her.

The flare in his eyes calmed her somewhat, as he was plainly just as stunned to see her as she was to see him. He quickly masked his emotions as he took a step toward her. She sighed despite herself. Apparently some things never changed.

"Pepper."

That low, sexy drawl of his hadn't changed over the years. He still managed to make her toes curl with that piercing blue gaze and those strong, broad shoulders. And that mouth. He'd done plenty to make her squirm with that mouth, too.

"I had no idea you were back in town."

Thankfully, the tall cash wrap separated them. Pep-

per stepped forward, leaning her hands against the edge.
She needed a little support.

"I've been back about a month," she replied. Small
talk, she could do that. "I took a few weeks to make this
place my own, so this is my first official day open."

He glanced around again, and she hated how she
waited to get his approval. She'd given up letting Nolan
Elliott have any control of her mind or her heart years
ago when she left town…or so she'd thought. Yet somewhere deep inside her lingered that young, naive girl who
thought this man was her everything. She knew better
now, but that didn't mean she couldn't appreciate how
undeniably sexy he still was.

"This is a nice store. Good location, too."

The old two-story brick building had belonged to her
grandparents decades ago. They'd never sold it and her
free-spirited, nomadic parents had no interest in staying.
Granted, she didn't necessarily want the building, either,
but with her funds at an all-time low, she had no choice.

"I assume you're in need of flowers? Or were you here
to look at the paintings?" she asked, hoping to move this
process along because having Nolan this close, where she
could see him, inhale all that tantalizing masculinity…it
brought back an onslaught of feelings she just couldn't
handle right now.

"Flowers," he replied easily, as if he wasn't torn up on
the inside. Clearly the memories weren't threatening to
strangle him like they were her. He'd pushed her away
and obviously moved on without a second thought. "But
this artwork is exceptional. I remember how much you
loved painting."

He *should* remember because she'd tried to teach
him…and that had ended up a disaster with paint all
over them, which led to the best shower sex of her life.

Well, the only shower sex, but regardless, the experience had been epic.

Nolan examined another canvas with bright flowers before bringing that heavy-lidded blue gaze back to her. He tipped up his black cowboy hat, a familiar move she'd seen him do countless times. Only he wasn't the same cowboy he'd been when she left. Now he was a big, broody, powerfully built man, hotter than she'd ever thought possible.

Being a member of the prestigious Elliott clan didn't hurt him, either. Gorgeous and wealthy were a lethal combination. He'd been both of those when she'd loved him before, but that had nothing to do with how fast and hard she'd fallen for him. He'd been so much more than her boyfriend, her lover. He'd been her very best friend and she'd thought her soul mate.

After she left, she'd wondered if it was all real, if her emotions were just those of a guileless young woman who hadn't any life experience yet. Unfortunately, she'd done too much thinking since she'd been gone.

Pepper wasn't sure what all he'd done in the past few years—she'd purposely distanced herself to keep the pain at bay. She did know that, despite his privileged upbringing, Nolan had wanted more out of life than ranching. He'd been determined to help others. And it was that damn career goal that had ultimately been the catalyst that ripped them apart.

Nolan's lifelong dream had wedged its way between them and had him choosing his unknown future over her. Over their family.

The Elliotts were one of the wealthiest families in Texas, probably the country. Pepper had loved their home on Pebblebrook Ranch. She'd once envisioned a life there, a life with Nolan and their baby. The two of them had even designed a home together and she'd thought for sure they'd live happily ever after surrounded by puppy dogs and rainbows. That was how naive she'd been, because she'd never once considered that something could rip them apart.

But something had and all of those dreams had been stripped away, leaving her with nothing but a shattered heart.

Nolan moved back to the display of roses, giving her a full visual of those tight jeans over slim hips. Pepper closed her eyes, took several deep, calming breaths and willed the memories to go away. She was trying to rebuild her life, not get swept up in the darkest moments of her past.

She'd known she'd come face-to-face with him eventually. Heck, she'd even played out the scene in her mind. But nothing had prepared her for the crushing reality of the actual moment.

"Roses are too typical for a first date."

Pepper swallowed. Of course he'd be shopping for a lady... Why else would a man come into her shop? And she wasn't stupid. Nolan was a very attractive man, a rich rancher to boot—what woman *wouldn't* want to go out with him?

Still, why did she have to be privy to his wooing tactics? That was just more salt in the wound that had never healed.

But she'd opened this business for a much-needed fresh start, and she needed it to be a success. Which meant she had to cater to all clientele so she could start making money. No matter who walked through her door.

Pepper pulled on her professional panties and squared her shoulders. "What type of lady is she? Does she have hobbies? That can tell me quite a bit about a person, if I know her interests."

And if this faceless woman had an interest in Nolan, Pepper already knew enough...and she hated her with a fiery passion.

Nolan turned toward her once again. "She works at the hospital with me. I'm not sure what she does outside of that."

Her heart hitched in her throat. So he had fulfilled that dream of becoming a doctor after all. He'd followed through and now had everything he'd ever wanted. Nolan was the type of man to never let any obstacle get in his way...no matter who he hurt in the process.

"I assumed you'd still be ranching at Pebblebrook." She hadn't meant to let that thought slip out.

"I help out when I can. That's definitely Colt's area of expertise." Nolan crossed his arms over that powerfully broad chest, and Pepper had to force her eyes to remain on his. "I'm a surgeon at Mercy Hospital, so my schedule can be crazy at times."

A cowboy and a doctor? Did he have to up that sex appeal by telling her this? No doubt this woman was a cute little perky nurse. She probably also had a perfect waistline and could fasten a pair of size-two jeans.

Drawing in a deep breath, Pepper smoothed her tank over her round abdomen. The most comfortable things for her these days were her long flowy skirts and her tanks. Anything that stretched along with her belly.

"Okay, then. Let's not do roses," she suggested. "What about a variety of colors in a bouquet? I have a few options over here with some tulips or some with daisies. Tulips are classy. Daisies are more fun."

She moved from behind the counter and started for the

front of her shop. But she'd taken only a few steps when she heard Nolan's swift intake of breath.

That past she'd hoped to never face again had officially hit her square in the face.

Nolan prided himself on control and the ability to think on his feet and hide his emotions. For a rancher and skilled surgeon, there was no other way to live.

But seeing Pepper Manning with a baby bump had knocked the air right out of him...as if seeing her after ten years wasn't enough. She was still just as breathtaking as he remembered. Then again, their sizzling physical attraction and sexual compatibility had never been the issue.

No...those aspects of their relationship were beyond compare. He exhaled roughly, rubbing a hand across his stubbled jaw, as the memories assailed him. His fear of commitment at such a young age and the pregnancy and subsequent miscarriage were what had ultimately torn them apart. It had all been too much, too soon, and to say he hadn't handled things well would be a vast understatement.

But he'd been afraid. That fear had spawned his actions and he'd been too prideful to admit it. Ultimately, he'd let everything go in an attempt to save himself. He'd never forgiven himself, but he sure as hell didn't want to dredge up all of that now. He'd moved on, and it was obvious Pepper had, too.

Even so, having her so close yet being unable to reach out and touch her was difficult. She personified beauty, and she'd captured his heart once, so long ago...but he wasn't sure that man existed anymore. The miscarriage had broken something inside him that had never fully healed.

Pepper was clearly stronger than she'd been years ago. Her beauty was just one of the things he'd loved about her. Her inner strength was definitely another. But seeing her now, ready to move forward with a child, only proved she'd handled the situation better than he had.

She had always wanted a family; he'd always wanted to be a surgeon. Dreams they hadn't discussed because they'd been too caught up in the euphoric throes of young love. The type of love that naive couples felt could carry them through anything. Obviously that had turned out to be a bold-faced lie.

His eyes raked over her again from head to toe. How could she be just as stunning, just as vibrant, as ever? Her curves were still as alluring, her breasts fuller than before due to the pregnancy, and her long mahogany hair still hung like silk over her shoulders. His hands itched to feel those exquisitely soft strands gliding through his fingers.

Nolan cursed himself for allowing the past to rush up and assault him, but Pepper had always managed to wield control over him like no other woman before or since.

Now he couldn't help but wonder if there was a husband or significant other in the picture. Not that it was any of his concern, but…was there? Despite everything, he found himself wanting to know everything that had transpired since she'd left. He had zero rights to her life, but that didn't stop the intrigue from creeping in.

Pepper clasped her hands together just below her abdomen, the bangle bracelets jingling on her arms. She'd always had a thing for jewelry, he remembered fondly. Then her dark eyes suddenly held his as if she dared him to make a comment. Nolan hardened his jaw. He'd never backed down from a challenge before and he sure as hell wasn't going to let the unbidden memories overpower him now. He'd come too far, had everything he ever wanted. Every bit of angst that settled between them was from a different time, a different life.

He'd literally given up everything to be where he was today. There was no looking back, no time to dwell on the regrets that always seemed to be just below the surface.

"Congratulations," he said, offering her a tense smile.

For a fraction of a second, her eyes narrowed. But then she nodded. "Thank you."

Those memories might be from another chapter in their lives, but they'd left so much unresolved. He'd gotten angry, broken things off, she'd left town…and that was pretty much the end of it.

Stubborn male pride had kept him from searching for her, and with his money he could've hired anyone and found her in record time. But he hadn't. She'd left to get as far away from him as possible, and like a fool, he'd let her go.

They'd said some hurtful things after the miscarriage, things he continued to cringe over when he thought about them. But the damage had been done; they'd strayed too far from the blissfully in-love couple they'd once been.

Nolan didn't see a ring on her finger, but that didn't mean anything. Regardless of the fact he shouldn't care, he wanted to know more. He was just getting reacquainted with an old friend…that was all, he reassured himself.

Though at one time they'd been so much more.

"Where are you living now?" he asked casually.

"Upstairs, actually. It's a small apartment, but perfect for me, and it saves money."

Perfect for me. That told him all he needed to know about a man in her life. There wasn't one. Instant relief swept through him, which was hypocritical considering he was here to buy a gift for another woman.

Still, Pepper had a story and he wanted to know every detail.

No! No, he didn't. He was here to get flowers for his date and that was all. Then he would head home and catch some sleep. After a traumatic night in the OR, he needed to regroup. Maybe he'd take his favorite stallion out later for a ride so he could unwind and think.

His dinner date would certainly revive him. Nolan had asked this particular nurse out months ago, but their schedules had just now lined up.

"How far along are—"

"This bouquet would be perfect." She cut him off. Clearly, he was not welcome in her personal space. "There's a few peonies, roses and lisianthuses."

"I'll take it. Go ahead and pick out another bouquet."

Her dark brow quirked as she shot him a side glance. "For tomorrow's date?"

He bit back an oath. This unexpected reunion needed to come to an end. No good could possibly come of it, no matter how irresistibly drawn he still was to this woman. Need he remind himself that *he* was the one who'd let her go? He'd thought at first that might have been a mistake, but over time, as he grew up, he'd realized it had been the right thing to do.

They had been ripped apart by grief and they wanted different things. He had no right to be carrying a torch for her after so long. Even if, in all honesty, seeing her pregnant hit him in a way he couldn't quite explain.

"Actually, Colt's fiancée's birthday is in two days."

Pepper's features softened at the mention of his baby brother. "Oh, sorry. I didn't mean—"

"It's fine." He reached forward, taking a premade pink vase with blooms of all sizes and colors. "She'd love this one."

Silence settled between them and Nolan couldn't pull his gaze away from hers. They were practically strangers now, but he knew those eyes. They'd always been so expressive and now was no different. He'd never met anyone else with eyes such a mesmerizing shade of dark gray. Pepper was definitely one of a kind.

Weariness reflected back at him now, though, and he couldn't help wondering what she was facing right now. She was alone, and that tidbit of information didn't sit well with him.

There were too many parallels to the last time he'd seen her, so it was impossible not to be swept up in nostalgia and bittersweet memories.

Pepper was all woman now, however. There was a level of maturity, almost an underlying stubbornness, that hadn't been there before. The defiant tilt of her chin, the rigid shoulders, as if she dared him to bring up the past. Fine by him. He was all for living in the here and now… He just hadn't expected to do it with her back in Stone River.

"I honestly didn't expect to see you this soon," she muttered. "It's harder than I thought."

Nolan swallowed…that guilt he'd been so good at tamping down suddenly threatening to overcome him.

"If this is too difficult—"

"No." She shook her head. "We've moved on. It's fine, just…different."

She pushed her dark, satiny hair back with her hand, those bangles jingling again as she pasted on a smile. "Is this all you need? Two bouquets?"

"Give me your favorite painting," he added impulsively. "It will be the perfect gift for Annabelle."

"Colt's fiancée?"

Nolan nodded. "She's quite the cook and she has twin daughters, Emily and Lucy."

Just as he'd hoped, Pepper's smile widened. He hadn't anticipated the punch of lust to his gut, though. What the hell?

This smoldering attraction was not welcome. Not. At. All. Memories were one thing, but layering in this fierce, unwanted need was simply not smart. Damn his libido.

"Sounds like Colt is a lucky man."

If a man wanted a family, sure. Colt and Annabelle were perfect together and had found solace in each other during a tough time. When Annabelle's father had literally gambled away their home to Colt, the two had sparred for a while before realizing they were crazy in love.

Love worked for some people, not for Nolan. Saving lives and being his own boss were more than rewarding as far as he was concerned. He'd tried the whole relationship thing with Pepper...and look where that had gotten him.

All he needed to do was continue on the way he had: dating, working, living day to day...ignoring that niggle of emptiness that crept up and choked him on occasion.

Nolan was more eager than ever to get to his date. He'd booked reservations at the classiest restaurant about an hour away and if things went as planned, he'd have no trouble taking her back to her place after. Because no woman ever went to his home. Ever. That was his sanctuary, a space he'd built on the back of Pebblebrook for privacy. That house held a special place in his heart and the reason why was standing right in front of him carrying another man's baby.

After glancing at his purchases spread out on the counter, Nolan pulled out his credit card. Once he had the items paid for, he slid the painting beneath his arm and grabbed the two vases. "Thanks, Pepper."

She folded her hands on the counter and nodded. "You're welcome. Be sure to tell your friends where to get gifts for their ladies."

"I definitely will." He swallowed hard, deciding to go ahead and tell her what was weighing on his mind. "I'm sorry. I know I said that a long time ago, but..."

Her lids lowered for a second. Then she blew out a breath and met his gaze again. "It's over, Nolan. I'm focusing on my baby, this new life I'm rebuilding. I can't look back."

Rebuilding. How many times had she done that since he'd left her? Pepper had always been such a vibrant woman, always happy and smiling. The loss of their child had dimmed her spark, and the way he broke things off had doused what little flicker of light had remained. He'd often wondered over the years if she'd ever found joy again...or who she'd found it with.

More potential heartbreak was definitely something he couldn't and didn't want to deal with. The risk was too great to even entertain such thoughts.

They'd both done exactly what they'd set out to do. He was damn happy being a doctor and a rancher. And his bachelor status would remain intact. He was getting ready to help Colt gear up to open Pebblebrook as a dude ranch, so any spare time he had was taken.

"I wish you the best," he stated, the blasted guilt settling heavy in his chest. "See you around."

"Yeah, see you," she said softly.

With one final nod, Nolan headed out the door. He couldn't get out of Painted Pansies fast enough. Sleep deprivation could cause a man to start thinking about things, decisions he'd made and everything he'd given up to seek success.

But Nolan didn't have regrets on the path he'd taken. He did regret hurting Pepper, though, so much it cut him to the core. At one time he would've done anything for her, but in the end, they'd wanted different things and he couldn't be what she wanted.

Nothing had changed since then, either. He'd opted not to have a family after they lost their child. He wouldn't say he shut down exactly, but he'd certainly reevaluated what he desired in life and he knew for certain he wished never to go through that kind of anguish again.

Nolan carefully set the arrangements on the back floorboard of his SUV. This quaint shop Pepper had was perfect for her. For as long as he'd known her, she'd had a flare for art and creativity. She'd been a dreamer, one of the things he'd loved most about her.

Without looking back to see inside the wide storefront window, Nolan forced himself to move forward. Wasn't that what he'd always done? Pushed onward, no matter what was going on internally. That was what made him one of the best doctors around. He could compartmentalize his feelings and turn them off when needed.

The jumbled emotions he had after seeing Pepper were absolutely not something he was ready to face...no matter how attractive she still was. So he'd shut those feelings down, just like he had the last time he saw her.

Two

The aftermath of this date was quite the opposite of what Nolan had initially planned. But cutting the evening short had been his idea...and he was still second-guessing his decision.

He'd taken his date home and dropped her off with a lackluster kiss good-night. In hindsight, he could've put more enthusiasm into the kiss and should've been whisking her off her feet and to the nearest bed. Unfortunately, he hadn't been in the right frame of mind for a sexual romp or even dessert. He'd feigned not feeling well, when the reality was, he'd spent his entire night envisioning another woman.

Damn it. Pepper had barely stepped back into town and now he was totally off his game. Well, technically, she'd told him she'd been back a month, but he'd only seen her this morning. Bottom line...he'd not had any heads-up on her return. Clearly he'd been too busy working to familiarize himself with the latest gossip running amok in Stone River.

But deep down, he knew *nothing* could've mentally prepared him for how he'd feel when he saw Pepper after ten long years. Hell, he wasn't sure he could even put a name to it.

Nolan found himself heading toward Painted Pansies before he recognized what he was doing. Why was he even on this road? This was quite a bit out of the way of his home on Pebblebrook Ranch.

Thankfully, he was off tomorrow, because he knew he'd be up all night trying to figure out why in tarnation he was getting so—

What the hell?

Nolan saw the flames in the distance, but as he got closer, he realized they were shooting out the top-floor window of Pepper's building. They were small and only in the front, but nonetheless, fear gripped him like nothing he'd ever known.

In his line of work, Nolan was used to making life-and-death decisions under pressure. But this felt different, like a vise around his chest. With adrenaline pumping, he quickly dialed 911. Then he pulled off the road, rattled off the address, and raced from his SUV toward the back of Painted Pansies.

As he rounded the corner, he saw Pepper attempting to crawl out the window and onto the roof of the back porch.

"Pepper!" he shouted. "The fire department is on the way. Climb onto the roof and I'll help you from there."

She threw a look over her shoulder, and Nolan's heart clenched. Pepper's face was filled with pure terror and she held one hand protectively over her abdomen. He couldn't think about that right now; he couldn't focus on the fact she'd lost one baby already and was most likely petrified as she tried to get out of this situation without causing harm to her unborn child.

All that mattered right now was getting her away from this fire. Nolan heard the approaching sirens and relief trickled through him.

"Come on," he urged. "You're almost to the roof."

Cautiously, she let go of the window ledge and crawled on her hands and knees over the roof until she reached the edge. She stared down at him as if she was afraid to jump.

"I'll catch you," he told her as he extended his arms. When she hesitated, he felt that adrenaline surge. "Pepper, come on."

"I can't fall," she cried.

"You won't," he assured her, knowing he'd never let her get hurt. "I promise."

And now was not the time to analyze the fact he'd hurt her immensely once before.

Sirens grew louder, but Nolan didn't take his eyes off her. She eased closer to the edge and gave him another look, and he nodded, silently pleading for her to trust him.

It seemed like slow motion, but Nolan knew the time it took her to let go and fall into his arms was only a mere couple of seconds. He cradled her against his chest and ran back to his SUV. His pulse continued to pound fast, but not from carrying her. Pepper didn't weigh much; she'd always been petite. His work as a part-time rancher demanded he be physically fit, so even pregnant, she wasn't putting a strain on his muscles.

"I can walk," she told him breathlessly, but her arms encircled his neck as he crossed the street.

"And I can carry you. Did you get hurt? Inhale too much smoke?"

Pepper shook her head. "No. I was getting ready for

bed when I smelled smoke and came out of the bathroom to see the front curtains in flames."

A chill coursed through his veins. What if she'd been asleep? What if she hadn't gotten out in time? What would she have done had he not been driving by? Would anyone have been around to help?

She trembled against him, and he instantly recognized the shock. The fire truck pulled up and in an instant the firefighters were working on the flames, which still seemed to be only in the front of the second story. An ambulance arrived right after, and Nolan swiftly carried her over.

"I'm Dr. Nolan Elliott." He addressed the two EMTs who came around to open the back of the ambulance. "I don't believe she was inside long, but I want her to have oxygen and be taken in immediately. I'll follow and get her admitted."

"I don't need to be admitted," she argued, but Nolan ignored her protest. She wasn't in charge here.

"She's pregnant," Nolan went on as he stepped up into the back, still holding her in his arms. He lowered her down onto the cot. "How far along?"

Her dark eyes met his and he had to ignore everything that had happened between them up until now. She was a patient. He had to compartmentalize.

"Pepper?"

"Seventeen weeks. Nolan, I don't think—"

"Oxygen," he said as one of the medics climbed in on the other side. "I'll meet you at the ER entrance."

Pepper gripped his arm as the oxygen mask was placed over her nose and mouth. She pulled it aside and shook her head.

"I don't need you there and I don't need to be admitted," she insisted. "I wasn't in the apartment that long. I'm not coughing and I'm not light-headed. I'm fine."

"And you're positive your baby is?" he retorted.

Her eyes narrowed but he didn't care if he angered her. In his years at Mercy, he'd seen it all and he wasn't taking a chance with Pepper and a baby…not again. Even though this wasn't his child, he wouldn't risk it.

Damn his desire to protect her.

"I'll go get checked out, only for the baby." Her hold tightened on his arm. "But you're not coming. I don't need you there."

Nolan stared at her another minute but didn't say a word. Finally, he met the gaze of the medic and nodded. No way was Nolan going to let her go alone. No matter what Pepper wanted, right now someone was going to look out for her and her child.

And it seemed he was the chosen one.

"This is ridiculous."

Pepper realized her argument was in vain. But as she sat in the passenger seat of Nolan's extremely flashy SUV heading up the drive to Pebblebrook, she also knew she had little choice but to go along with his plan.

Well, actually, he hadn't planned, more like *steamrolled*. After he'd shown up at the hospital, despite her repeated requests that he stay away, he'd informed her he'd be taking her to his house to rest because it was nearly two in the morning and she couldn't go back to her apartment.

Her apartment. The one place she was going to try to set down roots, to build a life for her baby.

Yet here she was pregnant and temporarily homeless until she found out what damage had been done by the fire. Oh, and she was back with the one man who'd crushed her heart and her spirit and turned his back on her when she needed him most.

It went without saying that she'd had better days. Like the day she'd broken her arm in two places after she'd gone hiking and attempted to climb a vine over a ravine. Even then she was having a better time than she was now.

"I don't want to stay with you."

Nolan grunted and continued up the drive. Pebble-brook was exactly like she remembered. Magnificent, with rolling white fencing flanking the drive, the three-story main house was adorned with porches extending across the top two floors. The stables, which were nicer than most homes, brought back memories. Memories of spending evenings in the hayloft, riding horses over the acreage, sharing hopes and dreams.

They'd failed to discuss the one dream that had ultimately come between them, but that was water under the bridge. Pepper firmly believed everything happened for a reason... If only she could figure out why she was here now with Nolan.

"You tell me a logical place to drop you off in the middle of the night and I'll consider it."

Pepper crossed her arms and continued to stare out the window into the darkness. She really didn't care that she was acting like a child. After all, who could blame her? She was tired, scared, worried of what the future would hold for her as a single mother. Once again she'd gotten tangled up with a man who wanted nothing to do with a family or her. But at least this time she hadn't been in love.

Although she didn't need a man to complete her life or to help her raise the baby, she was sorry this child would never know his or her father. But Pepper was confident her child would be loved and cared for and would never feel the void.

"That's what I thought," Nolan muttered when she failed to answer him. "Now, you need to quit being stubborn and just relax for tonight."

"Stubborn? Relax?" Pepper whipped around in her seat. "I'm not stubborn, you jerk. You pushed your way into the ER—"

"I actually flashed a smile at the charge nurse."

Rage boiled within her. "Just because you work there doesn't give you the right to steamroll me into agreeing to this."

"I didn't steamroll anybody," he said as he made a sharp curve in the drive. "I merely stated that you could be admitted or come home with me. Those were your two options whether you liked them or not. You have no other place to crash tonight."

Pepper scowled. As if she needed the reminder. She'd been racking her brain trying to work out what had happened in her apartment. She'd been burning some new melts she'd made that afternoon, but she was positive she'd turned off the warmer before she got into the shower. Hadn't she?

"I won't be your charity case so you can feel better about yourself over how you treated me in the past."

There. She'd laid it out there. Pepper didn't want there to be any question about where they stood. Because the truth was, she'd moved on. And the fact that the sight of Dr. Nolan Elliott made her weak in the knees and brought up so many unforgettable memories, both bad and good, didn't mean anything. She was a different woman now. And he was a different man.

But the way he wanted to come to her aid warmed

something inside her…something she couldn't afford to let herself feel ever again.

"I'm not doing this out of some warped sense of redemption, Pepper," he told her. "I have seven bedrooms and nine bathrooms. Stay here as long as you want until you make alternate arrangements. I won't even know you're there."

Yeah, but *she'd* know *he* was there. Did he truly believe she'd be comfortable on his turf? And why on earth had he built such a huge home when he was single? Had he married after she'd left? Pepper had purposely distanced herself from him and not doubled back to find out what Nolan had done with his life. She didn't want to know if he'd found another woman, created a life with her, had children. Because as hard as it was to admit, she feared that if he'd gone forward and had a family, she wouldn't have recovered from the crushing blow.

So, one night together was more than enough. Besides, she had more important things to contend with than licking old wounds. Like figuring out where to go if her apartment was a total loss. She only prayed the fire department was able to spare her shop because there was no plan B for income.

"I'm only staying tonight because I'm exhausted."

A two-story stone home came into view and Pepper's heart clenched with sorrow. Granted, it was dark, but the spotlights illuminated the incredible home enough to send her falling back into yet another memory.

This was the dream home they'd planned together. Everything from the stone facade to the thick wood columns leading up to the second-story porch. And if he'd stuck to the original plans, those doors on the top floor led straight to one impressive master suite, with a matching master suite at the other end of the hall.

He'd gone through with every plan they'd made…and he'd done so without her, as if she'd never had a place in his life at all.

Pepper covered her abdomen with her hands as Nolan pulled into an attached four-car garage. Of course each bay was filled with another impressive vehicle. A work truck, which looked fresh off the showroom floor, a sporty car and another SUV. Why did one man need this many cars and this large of a home?

Pepper wasn't a shrink, but she also wasn't naive. Clearly Nolan was trying to either compensate for something or fill a void in his life, and she was pretty sure he didn't need to overcompensate for anything.

And now, to add fuel to the fire, she was spending the night with the one man she didn't want to be attracted to, *shouldn't* be attracted to. But there was no denying Nolan was still just as sexy, just as powerfully commanding in that irresistible way that made her breath catch in her throat and her palms grow damp.

"You built our home." The words slipped out before she could stop them and now they hovered in the air between them.

"It's the only home I ever saw here," he replied.

Pepper turned in her seat. The garage lights lit up the interior of the SUV and she preferred when things were dark. From this angle she saw too much—and she worried what he'd see when he looked back at her.

She started to ask him more but decided none of his life was her business. He'd made that abundantly apparent, and she needed to remember that. Just because he'd rescued her from her burning building and hadn't left her side since, didn't mean he wanted to revisit their past. And she had too much on her plate to even think like this.

Clearly, she was exhausted.

"Pepper, I—"

"Just show me to my room." His blue eyes met hers, and Pepper held her breath. He still had the power to make her tremble without so much as a word. "I'm tired and need my rest. I have a big day tomorrow assessing damage and talking to the insurance and fire department."

He gave her a clipped nod. "I'll go with you."

"You're not going with me." Did he really think she needed someone to hold her hand?

She took in his dress shirt, his dark jeans, and realization slammed into her. Pepper closed her eyes and pulled in a breath. "Your date... I hope this didn't ruin anything."

"I'd already dropped her off when I was heading home."

For reasons Pepper didn't want to delve into, she was glad to know the recipient of the mixed bouquet went home alone.

"Well...if I didn't say it earlier, thanks."

Nolan stared at her another minute, his eyes dropping to her lips for a half second, but it was all she needed to know. He was affected by the fact they'd been thrust back together, albeit temporarily—it had made him leave his date.

Maybe coming back to Stone River hadn't been the best idea, but she was all out of options at the moment. All she had to do was get through this night and then she could make a concerted effort to dodge Nolan Elliott at all costs. Because she wasn't sure she could resist the temptation if she had to spend too much time with him.

Three

Despite how insistently Pepper protested, Nolan joined her the following morning at Painted Pansies to assess the damage. He used the excuse that he had to drive her, but he wouldn't have let her face this alone regardless.

The apartment wasn't a total loss, but she would not be living there anytime soon. Thankfully, the store wasn't harmed, but an electrician needed to come out to double-check things because the fire marshall was sure the spark that started the fire had come from the outlet her warmer was plugged into.

Nolan had already contacted someone and expected him shortly. Pepper wouldn't like that he'd taken over, but someone had to because she looked dead on her feet.

And, okay, maybe some of that past guilt was spurring his actions, but he knew that top-notch contractors could get things done quicker than she could if she were left to her own devices. There was no reason she should wait on insurance to get their act together, because they were notorious for being slow, and Nolan was just offering his aid. Money meant nothing to him and he could see that Pepper could use a break.

Pepper walked around the shop and into the back room. Nolan took in the window display with large canvas paintings and the flamboyant bouquets in various heights. Everywhere he looked, there was vibrancy, color, life. He knew Pepper had always envisioned something like this, but she'd been such a free spirit, wanting to travel the world, he'd never really thought she'd set down roots anywhere.

Of course, once upon a time, they'd planned on settling down together. They'd designed a house when they were so young and tossing one dream after another out into the wind, hoping they would catch.

Regret tightened the corners of his mouth. Some things just weren't meant to be, because when faced with reality, he hadn't been able to take charge. The death of their unborn baby made him too wary to consider going down that path again.

When someone tapped on the glass of the front door, Nolan jerked around. A middle-aged couple stood on the other side and he shook his head and pointed to the closed sign.

Behind him, Pepper let out a gasp.

Nolan glanced over his shoulder. "You know them?"

Her eyes remained fixed on the door as she nodded and pressed a hand protectively over her stomach. She'd thrown on one of his T-shirts and still had on the same shorts from last night. Her hair had been washed but left down to dry in long, silky ringlets. Desire pulsed through him. He knew exactly what that hair felt like between his fingertips and draped over his body, but now was not the time to get turned on. Still, his fingers itched to touch those luscious locks again, to see if they were just as smooth as he remembered.

"Want me to get rid of them?" he asked.

The tapping grew louder, more persistent.

"They've already seen me." Pepper raked a hand through her hair and finally looked his way. "I hate to ask this, but can you stay? I'm exhausted and this could get ugly. I know we're not necessarily friends or anything, but—"

"I'll stay."

Whoever these people were, Pepper wasn't happy about seeing them.

She crossed the store and placed one hand on the knob, the other on the lock. Throwing a look over her shoulder, she caught his eyes again. "Their son is the father of my baby. I've only met them once."

A sense of unease roiled through him. Of course, he knew nothing about the father of her baby, other than the fact he was obviously not in the picture at the moment, but his parents showing up here from…wherever it was they were from was probably not good news for Pepper.

He bit back a curse. Why was he sticking around? Whatever Pepper had going on in her life was *her* concern, her business. He should be at Pebblebrook helping Colt with the ranch or coming up with things he could do at Hayes's house. Hayes was one of his other brothers, and he would be home from his deployment overseas in two weeks.

With four Elliott boys, there was always someone in need of a helping hand. Nolan hadn't seen Beau, Colt's twin, in nearly a year. He'd been too busy shooting one film after the next. That must be the life he loved out there in LA, because he rarely came home.

The flick of the lock pulled Nolan's attention back to the moment. Pepper moved back and opened the door.

The couple swept in like they owned the place. Nolan was instantly on alert. He didn't like to stereotype, but he figured he had these people pegged. Expensive clothes, flashy car on the curb... He knew how much that car was because he'd had one, as well, and sold it for an upgrade. The way the woman looked condescendingly down at Pepper had Nolan taking a step closer, his protective instincts kicking into high gear.

"Mr. and Mrs. Wright. What are you doing here?" Pepper asked.

"We didn't have a number to reach you, but Matt told us where you were moving to and we heard you opened a little shop in Stone River." Mrs. Wright glanced around the shop, her nose snarled as she turned back to Pepper. "Is this typically how you come to work?"

"I'm actually not open today." Pepper cast a worried look to Nolan. "We're doing some minor renovations."

The couple glanced to Nolan but immediately dismissed him. Most likely they figured him for the hired hand. That was fine. He wasn't here to make friends or to give a good impression. He was here for...what? To support Pepper, although she didn't want it and he had other things he really needed to be doing.

"Can we talk privately?" Mr. Wright asked quietly.

Pepper crossed her arms over her chest. "You can just tell me now."

"We have some...devastating news." Mrs. Wright swiped at her eyes, and Nolan knew that expression. He'd been a doctor long enough, had seen grief too many times to count. He took another step toward Pepper but resisted the urge to reach out and touch her. He wasn't sure what the Wrights were going to do and he didn't want to show his hand this soon and reveal that he and Pepper had a past. They didn't need to know.

"Matt had a heart attack two nights ago," the woman whispered as if speaking through the tears clogging her throat. "He didn't make it."

"Oh…no." Pepper reached a hand out for support and Nolan grabbed it right away, the worry for her far outweighing the need to keep his distance. "But he was so young," she murmured in disbelief.

Again, Nolan knew from experience that age meant nothing in the medical field.

"I know he told you he wanted nothing to do with this baby, but we do." Mr. Wright wasn't quite as emotional as his wife, and he seemed to be ready to get down to business. "We want full guardianship rights for the baby now that our son is…is gone.

"What?" she whispered, her eyes widening in shock.

"We're filing for sole custody. It just… It makes sense given how stable we are and the financial backing we can provide."

Pepper's hand tightened in Nolan's. "No, you can't do that. I don't even know you. Matt paid me. He gave me money to leave him alone and to invest however I wanted for the future of the baby, provided I never contact him again. He signed his rights away right before I left…"

Pepper seemed to be rambling out of fear, and Nolan knew in that second he'd do anything to keep this baby in her life. Forget what happened between them years ago. Pepper needed someone in her corner and he damn well wasn't going to leave her to face these vultures all alone. He owed her that much at least.

His chest constricted with guilt as realization struck. This Matt guy had treated Pepper like she was a burden… the same way Nolan had done years ago.

"Matt's gone now," the lady sniffed. "And we want to raise our grandchild. We've already contacted our team of attorneys."

"What?" Pepper gasped.

"We aren't questioning your parental skills, but we feel the child would be better off with us," Mr. Wright reiterated. "We know our rights. We're determined to have a DNA test done to prove we're the grandparents. You have to be realistic here and see that we're more financially stable."

Nolan wrapped his arm around Pepper, which drew the attention of the other couple. "Pepper isn't going to discuss this any further without talking to her attorney. If you'll leave me your lawyers' information, I'll be sure to have someone contact them."

Because he had his own team on retainer and he would be calling them before the Wrights pulled away from the curb.

Mrs. Wright's eyes narrowed. "And who are you?"

There was no good way to answer that question and it was none of his concern anyway. "The contact information, please, and then you can go. Neither Pepper nor I will be discussing this any further without our attorneys present."

Beneath his touch, Pepper trembled. If she could hold it together long enough for him to usher them out the door, she could break down all she wanted later. Nolan just needed to get her alone.

Mr. Wright gave the name of a high-powered attorney in Houston. Nolan knew his team was better, more ruthless, and there was no way this couple would take Pepper's baby. Not as long as Nolan was in charge…and he had every intention of seeing this through.

Between the fire, the renovations and now this, Nolan

didn't see himself pulling away from Pepper anytime soon. Which was fine in the grand scheme of things. He owed her more than he could ever repay. So somehow he'd just have to find a way to resist temptation and keep his hands to himself.

Nolan released Pepper long enough to open the door and gesture for the Wrights to leave. "Don't call or come back. Someone from my law firm will be in touch."

"Pepper, don't push us away," Mrs. Wright said over her shoulder. "You're carrying the only piece of our son that we have left."

Nolan closed the door and slid the lock back into place. Pepper continued to stare at the spot where the older couple had just stood. He gently gripped her arm and guided her toward the back room, where he eased her down onto an old wooden chair at the desk as he propped his hip along the edge.

"What am I going to do?" she muttered aloud as she continued to stare at nothing in particular. "I don't have an attorney and I can't compete with them anyway. Their money, their power. I can't let total strangers have custody of my baby."

She never once looked up at him as she rattled off her concerns. But Nolan was taking all of this in. He leaned down over the desk, bracing his weight on his hands.

"Look at me," he demanded. "I pay my lawyers a hefty fee. They'll be on this case today and we'll make sure they don't take your child."

Pepper blinked, sending a tear spilling down her cheek. "I used all the money Matt gave me to invest into this place. I wanted a secure future."

A wave of fury surged through him. He hated this guy. Who the hell paid a woman to leave him alone?

Shame seized him once again. How had he been any

different? He'd pushed her away with his actions, his harsh words. He'd been hurt from the loss of their baby— a baby he hadn't realized he'd wanted until it was gone.

"My team will take care of this. I'll put the call in now."

Pepper shook her head. "No. I'll handle this. I'm not leaning on you or anyone else."

While Nolan admired her determination, he wasn't about to argue with her idiotic logic. He shoved his hands in his pockets and rocked back on his heels.

"You have enough on your plate with this building and you said your funds were tied up here. How can you pay for an attorney? A good one you don't have to second-guess about whether he's doing what should be done to secure your child's future with you? How are you going to do that?"

Pepper's lips thinned as she shrugged one slender shoulder. "The same way I've gotten along these last ten years without you. I'll find a way."

He jerked in a breath. She was hurting, he understood that, but the jab she delivered had no doubt been bubbling below the surface just waiting to come out. He deserved that, but he wasn't about to stick around for more verbal punches.

"My contractor is due here any minute to get an estimate ready for your insurance. I'll have my attorney call you today, too. Don't hold back with either guy and don't worry about the money."

"Says someone who's never worried about money," she muttered.

Nolan pulled his phone from his pocket. "I'm trying to help and then I'll stay out of your way. It's clear you don't want me around. I get that, Pepper, but I won't let you deal with all of this on your own."

Pepper tucked her hair behind her ears and nodded. "Fine. But I want an itemized list of all the charges so I can pay you back after the insurance kicks in. I may take a while, but I won't be indebted to you."

He wasn't getting into that now. But Nolan had no intention of taking a dime from her. She needed to be stress-free, to concentrate on this pregnancy and a healthy baby, not worry about her new business and a looming custody suit.

To keep the peace, he merely nodded and then headed toward the back to talk to his contractor. He wanted everything done right, sparing no expense. And a few upgrades wouldn't hurt in the apartment, either. Nolan wasn't certain what it looked like before, but he planned on personally seeing to it that it was all up-to-date, with state-of-the-art appliances, whatever it took to ensure Pepper had everything she needed to live comfortably.

It was the least he could do. And, yes, guilt spurred his actions, but so what. He was a different man than he was ten years ago.

Except that part of him that still desired her. Damn it. After all this time of not seeing her, having her this close wasn't something he'd prepared for. She was sexy as hell, her figure a bit fuller from the pregnancy, but she was breathtaking. The fact she wore one of his T-shirts was even more arousing because he recalled many other occasions when she'd wear his shirt...only his shirt.

Nolan headed back to the ranch, determined to work out his frustrations on the farm. But first he needed to call his attorney. There was no way in hell those people were going to take Pepper's baby. Nolan would make certain of that.

Four

Pepper ended up opening her shop later in the day. There was no reason she couldn't work and she wanted to get her business up and running. She needed to be open to the public during peak hours, and thankfully, this old building was nestled right in the hustle and bustle of the small town.

Maybe if she spent some time on a painting to keep her mind occupied, that would help. Making something beautiful out of a blank canvas always calmed her nerves and right now she needed calm. Between the obvious stressful events of the fire and the contentious visit by the Wrights this morning, she was still reeling over the fact Nolan was so eager to offer help.

Throwing money around was the easy part, though. Perhaps that was the only way he could clear his conscience. Pepper didn't want his guilt to spawn his actions. If he wanted to help, she'd rather it be because he actually wanted to, not because he was trying to make amends for the past.

As Pepper set up her easel in the back room, the shop's phone rang. She glanced to the ID, but didn't recognize the number.

"Painted Pansies."

"Ms. Manning?" the deep male voice asked. "This is Jason Davis. I represent the Wright family."

Pepper gripped the edge of the table and slowly sank into the chair. Her heart clenched as fear squeezed it like a vise.

"Is there a time you and your attorney can meet with us?"

Pepper's mind raced. She hadn't even talked to an attorney, had no idea if Nolan had even called anyone yet. This was all so fast, so unexpected, she had no idea what to do.

"Mr. Davis, I'm not sure when we could meet." She hoped her voice sounded strong and confident, considering she was shaking like a leaf. "I'm speaking with my attorney today and he will be in touch."

She hoped.

"My clients are willing to offer you a generous amount—"

"I won't be bought or bullied, Mr. Davis. My lawyer will be in touch."

Pepper hung up, tossed the phone from her jittery hand and attempted to pull in a deep breath. She wasn't sure if she wanted to scream, cry or run away and never look back. Maybe all of the above?

No. She wasn't running. She'd left once before and had circled right back. She would stay and fight. This was where she'd put her roots down, where she'd raise her baby and grow her business. The decision had been made of necessity, but she'd chosen to stay because of her connections to this place.

Pepper had no idea who Nolan's attorney was or if he could even fight, but there was no way she was going to just hand over her child.

A pang of sadness swept through her. She did feel terrible that Matt was gone. He wasn't a bad guy. They'd been more friends than anything and he hadn't wanted to be a father, but she wasn't about to give his parents a replacement child. They might argue they had superior finances, but didn't that just prove they were more concerned about money than the actual welfare of their grandchild? Who would be heartless enough to want to rip a baby away from its mother?

Pepper shot off a text to Nolan asking about his attorney because she needed to speak with him ASAP. When the bell on her door chimed, Pepper sucked in a deep breath and forced herself to relax. She had customers she needed to tend to. Reputation was everything and she couldn't be in a bad mood with the public.

How simple would this all be if she could just lean on Nolan and use his power and influence to make the chaos and fear go away? She wanted her baby, her fresh start at life…and she wanted to seek solace in those captivating blue eyes of his.

Unfortunately, she couldn't turn to him, because they weren't over what had happened. They'd dodged the feelings, the hurt, the anger…and she'd left.

But she'd moved on. She'd grown up and she wouldn't give in to temptation no matter how kind and supportive he was being. She knew what it was like to get her heart broken by him.

Right now, though, she had to be a businesswoman. She'd deal with Nolan later.

* * *

Oh, the irony.

Nolan still couldn't believe the conversation he'd had with his attorney, but the suggestion kept rolling through his head. At first he'd laughed, then he'd been appalled at the crazy notion, and now the idea had taken root and he could think of nothing else.

He had already spoken to his contractor and was told the renovations to the apartment could be done in two weeks. Pepper wouldn't like what he had to say, but Nolan wasn't backing down. She'd have to see that what he was about to present to her was her best option. Temporarily, of course.

Just as he pulled in front of Painted Pansies, Pepper turned her open sign off. She met his gaze through the large front window and stilled. Nolan knew she'd put up a fight, but this time, where she was concerned, he was holding his ground. He could do this and not lose himself in her. This was about making up for the past, not reigniting an old flame.

No more running…for either of them.

Those protective instincts had kicked in the moment he'd seen she was expecting and alone. Now with the fire and the custody case looming over her, Nolan had every intention of slaying every one of her dragons.

Remorse drove his thoughts, his actions. He refused to delve into all the reasons why he couldn't let her do this on her own.

As soon as he entered her shop, he flicked the lock on the door. Pepper stood behind the counter as if she wanted some barrier between them. Nonetheless, that wouldn't stop him from doing what he'd come to do.

And if he didn't broach this now, he'd talk himself out of it because this crazy idea embodied every fear, every doubt he'd ever had when it came to Pepper. Their crackling attraction aside, this was a risk he'd never thought he'd take again.

"I'm surprised you opened today," he told her.

She glanced down to her register and pulled out receipts. "I have to make money. The fire didn't do damage down here and I was able to salvage a couple of outfits that happened to be in my clothes dryer and were unscathed from the smoke and water."

He made a mental note to get her more clothes. Another thing she'd most likely balk at, but too bad. He wouldn't ask. If he had them purchased and delivered, she'd have no choice. Right?

"Did you have a productive day?"

Pepper blew out a sigh and finally stared up at him. "Did you stop by for small talk?"

Those piercing gray eyes were no less affective than they'd been a decade ago. She managed to touch him with just a look. And how she still had that power over him was beyond his comprehension.

Adjusting his hat, Nolan crossed the room and rested his arm on the top of the counter. "Not at all, Pepper, but I figured it was best to play nice because what I have to say may not put you in the best mood."

"I'm not in a good mood anyway, so why don't you just spit it out."

His eyes raked over the scoop neckline in her simple tank, his gaze heating at the sight of the thin cotton molding perfectly to her full breasts. She had on those bangle bracelets again and some long earrings in a variety of colorful stones. Her silky dark hair was still down from when she'd showered at his house, and all he could think of was how to get her back there again.

The image of her wet, naked, soapy in his oversize

shower with the rain-head spray cascading down her gorgeous curves had him getting extremely hot and uncomfortable. Damn it, he still wanted her. There was no reason to even try to deny such a fact.

He had no right to her, but that wouldn't stop him. Pepper would be his again…at least temporarily. The ache he had for her had nothing to do with the past and everything to do with an all-consuming, burning need he hadn't expected upon seeing her again.

"You aren't seriously going to look at me like that," she stated, crossing her arms over her chest. "I can't be fooled by your charm."

"You're still just as beautiful," he drawled. "Makes a man want to admire the view."

Pepper shook her head and focused back on her receipts. "I'm immune to you now, so just say what you have to say and go."

Adorable that she thought things were that neat and tidy between them. They'd never been so structured. Back in the day, they'd been wild and young and free. Then life had thrown hurdles in their path and they hadn't survived the fallout. Now they were back to square one and nothing about this situation was simple.

"You never answered my text," she said tersely as she sorted the slips of paper. "If you don't want to help, that's fine. But if you could pass along the name of a good attorney, I'd appreciate it. The Wrights' lawyer called me and I had no idea what to say—"

Nolan was around the counter and taking her shaky hands in his as she rambled on. "Breathe," he commanded. "Just calm down and tell me exactly what their lawyer said."

Pepper removed her hands from his and flattened them

over the papers. She dropped her head between her shoulders. "Just give me the name. I don't want you involved."

Too late for that, he thought ruefully. If she didn't want him interfering now, she'd be really ticked when he dropped the ultimate bomb. He'd gone further than just reaching out to his law firm.

"I already spoke with my attorney earlier—he's on it. I was at the ranch helping Colt, so I didn't get to text you back, but I have this all under control."

With her hair curtained around her face, Nolan couldn't make out her expression, but he knew she was exhausted. Most likely she also felt defeated and/or cornered.

"Pepper, I'm only looking out for you and you're going to have to let me. I'm not trying to make this more difficult."

"Can you look at this from my perspective?" she asked as she slowly turned toward him. "Can you imagine finally having your entire life planned out only to have it crash down all around you, then have to come face-to-face with your past and pretend nothing happened?"

Nolan grabbed her shoulders, hauling her against his chest. Pepper's head tipped back as she stared up at him with wide, tormented eyes.

"You think this is easy? Seeing you again, knowing you're carrying another man's child?"

Nolan hated that he wasn't more in control, but there was no way he could lie to her, to himself. The fact she was pregnant again gutted him and reminded him exactly what he'd given up.

"I'm going to help you through this and you're damn well going to put the past aside and let me."

"Put the past aside?" she jerked out of his hold and took a step back. "It's not that simple, Nolan."

He rubbed his hand over the back of his neck. "I didn't mean it like that," he corrected. "I know we have unresolved issues and there is so much that needs to be put to rest, but for now, we need to work on your current situation. I need you to hear me out."

Pepper rested one hand on the counter and propped the other on her hip. "Fine. What's your miraculous plan?"

They'd reached the part of the conversation he'd rehearsed over and over again, but he had a feeling no matter how he delivered this, she would refuse. He expected, and deserved, no less.

"My contractor said your apartment would be ready in two weeks." There—laying some groundwork for his defense was probably best. "You can stay with me until then."

When she opened her mouth to argue, because she would without a doubt have a snappy comeback, Nolan held up a hand. "You have nowhere else to go and my house is plenty big enough. Besides, I'm on call and at the hospital so much you won't even see me most of the time."

That seemed to pacify her as she shut her mouth and nodded.

"What about the attorney? Does he think he can help? Because I can't lose this baby, too."

Too. That simple word said so much, yet left even more hurtful, accusing words hovering in the air between them. They would have to face that dark time in their lives eventually. Yes, they were two totally different people now, but he'd destroyed her and he would somehow, someway, make this right. Then he could move on once and for all—guilt-free.

But first things first. For now, Pepper and her child were his top priority.

"You're not losing the baby and I'm doing everything I can to make this less stressful for you," he informed her.

"Their attorney wants to meet with me and my lawyer."

She bit her lip as her chin quivered. That sight alone was like a punch to Nolan's gut. What kind of people came after a pregnant woman? Granted, this was their grandchild and their son had just passed away, so they were understandably grieving, but there was a better way to approach seeing the baby. If they wanted to fight dirty, Nolan would spare no expense because he wasn't about to let Pepper carry this burden all on her own.

"We will all go meet with them," he said.

His heart kicked up because there was no more dodging the rest of this. Not only did he worry how she'd take this, but he would be lying if he didn't admit he was hesitant because of his own sanity. Could he really go through with this?

Pepper stared back at him with those wide, expressive eyes. This was the same woman he'd fallen in love with as a teen, the woman he'd thought he'd spend his life with, the woman who had carried his child.

Their bond ran deep, but even if that didn't exist, he would find her sexy as hell. Her fiercely independent attitude was just an added layer to the enticing allure of this new Pepper Manning. Damn if he didn't admire her for moving on and doing exactly what she wanted.

But he'd caught her looking at him. Raking her eyes over him as if she was struggling with that same internal battle.

Yeah, they had quite a bit left to hash out between them and throwing this bomb onto that already-smoldering fire was only going to further complicate matters.

"You're not going with me," she told him with a stubborn lift of her chin. "I'm still not so sure about this whole idea of moving in with you for two weeks. There has to be somewhere else I can stay."

Nolan closed the space between them. "You'll be staying with me because we're getting married."

Five

"Married?"

She couldn't have heard him correctly. Because there was no way in hell she'd marry anyone right now, especially Nolan.

"My attorney said if you were married, that would be another bonus for our side."

Our side?

He explained this as if they were discussing a side order at a fast-food restaurant. How could he be so calm? This wasn't some joke or a test-drive on a car. This was real life—*her life*. There was a baby involved and Pepper refused to bring a child into such an unsteady world.

"I'm not marrying you." She turned back to her receipts, not that she could think about her sales right now, but she needed something to do with her hands. "And if that's the only way your lawyer thinks we can win, then I'll seek my own legal representation."

Nolan's hand covered hers. The strength, the warmth, that familiar touch had Pepper closing her eyes. These pregnancy hormones were already out of control, and adding a dose of this potent man was not helping.

Those devastatingly attractive good looks aside, he seemed hell-bent on helping her. How could she let him get close to her again? She didn't trust him. But more than that, her body still responded when he was around and getting in deeper with him now was a chance she didn't think she could take.

Was he aiding only out of guilt?

Honestly, at this point, she'd take his guilt and help if it meant holding on to custody of her baby. Money was one thing, but...marriage?

"Listen to me." Nolan's low, matter-of-fact tone demanded she hear him out. "I know the irony of this is hurtful, but if we show we're married, that we are making a life for this baby, it will look better in court."

Pepper stared at his large hand on top of hers. "I don't want to go to court. I don't want to be in this position at all." She tilted her head to glance at him out of the corner of her eye. "I want to get my business growing, have my baby and be left alone."

Beneath that black hat, Nolan's sharp blue eyes held her in place. "Sounds like a lonely life."

"Maybe being lonely is what I'm after," she countered with more bite to her tone than she'd intended.

She pulled in a deep breath, instantly filling her nostrils with his masculine, woodsy cologne or aftershave or just plain Nolan. He didn't smell like he'd worked on a ranch most of the day. He smelled *amazing* and Pepper was having a difficult time concentrating. Her traitorous heart beat wildly in her chest. He stood so close, smelled too tempting, and that touch was all too familiar.

Pepper sighed. She wanted to be angry with Nolan for the rest of her life, but she had grown since she'd left. If she gave in to this physical attraction now, she'd be going backward. She'd come so far during their time apart, but she was having trouble differentiating what she should do from what she wanted to do.

"The Wrights are going to come after you with everything," he added. "There's no way to sugarcoat this. They're going to look at your background, your work ethic, your finances, your boyfriends… Everything in your life will be used against you. Let's cut them off before they gain any momentum and perhaps they'll back off."

Pepper eased around, her swollen belly brushing against his taut abs. "Why are you doing this? What's in it for you?"

Nolan stared back at her, completely void of emotion. She wanted to know his angle, to understand what he was thinking, but as always, he was holding everything inside.

With no more energy for a verbal battle, Pepper gathered her receipts together and shoved them all into her bank bag. She'd look at them later.

"I'm not marrying you."

As she started to move around him, he grabbed her elbow. That firm grip sent a burst of arousal rushing through her. One touch, that was all it took. How did he do that?

Pepper refused to meet his gaze. Having him this close and constantly touching her that way was too much to deal with on top of everything else.

"Don't do this," she whispered.

"I'm not giving up, Pepper. You need me, whether you want to admit it or not. The marriage would be temporary, long enough to untangle you from this mess. We'll get an annulment after."

Meaning they wouldn't consummate their marriage. Wow, this proposal just got more and more romantic. Her heart was all aflutter.

"I won't be married to a man who has girlfriends on the side to appease him."

Nolan's eyes dropped to her lips. "I'm more than happy to let you appease me, but that would put a damper on our annulment."

Pepper didn't want her body to tremble at the picture he painted. She knew all too well what an amazing lover Nolan was. And he was trying to wear her down. If she wasn't careful, he'd succeed.

"We're not getting married, so *that* puts a damper on this annulment."

She slid from his grasp and headed into the back room. She'd never gotten around to that painting she wanted to start earlier. Her blank canvas stared at her, just waiting for her to transform it. She could really use the stress reliever, but right now she didn't have the time or the energy.

All day she'd wondered where she would stay tonight. She could technically sleep in her bedroom upstairs. The damage was mostly contained to the living room and kitchen. But it still smelled like smoke and she shouldn't be inhaling that.

"You know this is the only way."

Pepper cringed as Nolan followed her. "I'm sure I can think of something."

There *had* to be a plan B. She refused to believe otherwise. What kind of example would she set for her child if she perpetually depended on someone else to help her out of a bind?

"Is that so?"

His smug tone had her stilling, but she kept her back to him.

"Because if you marry me, you'll have that much more leverage over them. We have a past, so nobody will think it's a lie. You have nowhere to go, Pepper, and you know firsthand that my home is more than large enough. You never have to see me."

But she wanted to. Even after all this time, with all that remained between them, she wanted to see him. She had that damn flutter whenever he was around. He captivated her on a deeper scale than before, despite all the alarm bells clamoring in her head.

"As I mentioned before, I'm at the hospital most days," he went on. "Come home with me and we'll sort it all out."

Pepper pinched the bridge of her nose as resignation sank in. She was out of options and knew it was pointless to keep fighting the inevitable. "I'll come home with you—for now—but no more talk of marriage."

She turned to face him, realizing he was so much closer than she'd thought, she lost her balance as she tried to step back. He reached out to steady her, clasping her arm with one hand and molding his other hand over her rounded belly. That instinct to protect her and her child warmed the area in her heart he'd left so cold, so broken.

How did she resist these feelings when he kept trying to infiltrate her defenses?

"I'll drive you," he rasped, still holding on to her. "First we're going to stop and buy you some clothes and whatever else you need."

"I don't need clothes. I have a few things upstairs— just let me grab them."

Nolan shook his head and drew his hands away. "They smell like smoke. This is nonnegotiable."

Pepper glared at him. "I'm not about to be bullied into anything, not by you and not by the Wrights."

The edge of Nolan's mouth quirked into a half grin. Damn if that wasn't sexy with the combination of those cobalt eyes and dark lashes.

"Good," he replied smoothly. "I'd hate to think you were letting people walk all over you."

Pepper couldn't help but roll her eyes. "Oh, please. Like you don't love this power trip you're getting by backing me into a corner. I'm not the same girl you hurt, Nolan. Nothing will happen between us ever again, no matter if I'm under your roof or not."

That smirk turned into a full-fledged smile. Damn him. Something inside her shifted—maybe it was pregnancy hormones or maybe she'd just gone mad. Regardless, Pepper was going to take full advantage of this opportunity. She'd lost so much, too much, and if Nolan was determined to help, then she'd take it. On her terms… which meant she may have to ignore her fears and give in to this preposterous marriage plan.

"But I'm willing to discuss some arrangements," she added, playing this out through her mind as the plan molded together. "You're paying the contractor for the renovations, which we agreed on, but I also know you're going overboard and not just putting things back the way they were."

Nolan merely nodded and remained quiet…still with that smug grin and mesmerizing gaze boring into her beneath his Stetson.

"And I'm sure you have your attorney pushing everything aside to help me with this case, which I appreciate." Guilt was a powerful tool. Pepper didn't like to play games, but if he thought this would somehow vindicate his actions, then she'd let him. "I'll live in your house.

I'll marry you in name only. We won't sleep in the same room. We won't consummate the marriage."

The muscles in his jaw tensed and his lips thinned, but he finally said, "Fine."

"And you'll not be buying flowers for any more cute little nurses or any other woman. This marriage may be temporary and for pretenses only, but I won't have you unfaithful. The last thing I'd need is for word to get out that you're cheating on me."

He never took his eyes off her. Pepper wasn't sure what he was thinking, but if he truly wanted to help her, this was how he could do it.

"I already proposed something similar," he stated as he took a half step forward until he came toe-to-toe with her. "But I'm not sure you'll be able to stay with me and hold up your end of the deal with not consummating the marriage."

When he leaned closer to her ear, Pepper's breath seized in her chest.

"You remember exactly how it used to be," he whispered roughly. "And you'll start to wonder what we'd be like together now. Are you sure you can be in the bed so close to mine and not slip down the hall in the middle of the night?"

Pepper shut her eyes, imagining just that. It would be so easy to give in to this attraction, because she couldn't deny that physically she wanted him. Those weren't old feelings, either. Nolan Elliott was one sexy doctor, cowboy, knight to the rescue...even though his armor was tarnished.

Regardless, she *would* have this marriage annulled. Therefore, they had to keep their clothes on and their hands off each other. There was too much at stake to let sex screw things up. The entire situation was going to take a giant leap of faith on her part because if she didn't keep her heart guarded, she feared how she would be at the end of this farce of a marriage.

Pulling in every ounce of strength and courage she possessed, Pepper backed up until she bumped into the table her casel sat on. Straightening her shoulders, she stared directly at him, refusing to be intimidated by that intense blue gaze.

"The marriage will be quiet, at the courthouse and only temporary. As soon as this case is cleared up, you and I will get this annulled just as quietly. I'm only agreeing to this because my baby comes first and I need my life to be secure before I bring her home."

"Her?"

Pepper shrugged. "I actually have an appointment with a new obstetrician next week and I'll be finding out the sex. Don't get distracted. This baby is not your concern—you made it clear a long time ago that you didn't want that family life."

"As long as you're in my house and married to me, you're both equally my concern."

Pepper hated that she was accepting his charity, because that was what it boiled down to. But she had to be realistic. She'd used all of her funds from Matt to open Painted Pansies. Thankfully the building had already been in her family. Still, she'd had to pay for new flooring, lighting and decor, and all the start-up costs that went into a brand-new business.

Acceding to the inevitable, Pepper smoothed her hair behind her ears and stared up at Nolan. "So, when are we getting married?"

Six

"You may now kiss your bride."

Nolan rested his hand on Pepper's side as he leaned in, but she turned her head just enough so that his lips brushed against the corner of her mouth.

So that's how this would be. She was sticking to her guns and freezing him out. Fine. He could wear her down. Because she was his wife and he fully intended to get her into his bed before all was said and done.

In a swift move, he framed her face and tilted it to capture her lips. He'd be damned if he started this marriage without kissing his bride.

He didn't care if this sham of a union ended in a divorce or an annulment. The final result would be the same and that was all that mattered to him. His biggest struggle now was the fact he burned with desire for his wife.

He wasn't looking for a ready-made family, but he wanted Pepper. No matter what had happened in the past, no matter that she was expecting another man's baby, his attraction for her hadn't diminished. If anything, the fierce need he had for her was stronger than ever.

Today she wore her hair down with soft curls on the ends. Her short, simple white dress had flowy sleeves and fit over her abdomen to show off her gently rounded belly. She had on her bangles again and a pair of fat gold hoops. The little gold sandals on her feet were just as simple as everything else.

Yet Pepper took his breath away. He didn't want this pull any more than he wanted this marriage. But he owed it to her to help her out of this mess that she had become ensnared in. Having her in his home would be trying because he never brought women to his house. That was his sanctuary, his safe haven from the stresses of the outside world. He was putting literally everything on the line for her.

Pebblebrook was his life when he wasn't at the hospital and that was a part of himself he wasn't willing to share. His career, his need to serve others and make a difference, overrode anything else.

Once their child died, something in him had switched gears and turned him completely away from any type of commitment. That was a level of heartache he simply couldn't experience ever again.

He was the oldest of the Elliott boys and there was a self-imposed expectation to do great things. While he loved the ranch, he'd always wanted to achieve more. But it wasn't always that way. There was a time he'd wanted a family, but once Pepper left, he'd started focusing on his career goals, throwing himself into the next chapter of his life so he didn't have to revisit the past.

His father had told him he worked too hard and wasn't

enjoying life. He had enjoyed it with Pepper, but fate had had other plans for both of them.

Nolan extended his elbow to escort Pepper from the old office building at the courthouse. Not the most romantic setting, but then again, romance had no place here.

"Now what?" she asked as they stepped out into the thick Texas heat. "Do you need to call your attorney?"

He assisted her down the concrete steps toward his SUV parked out front. "I notified him last night. But he needs more information from you and we will have to meet with the Wrights and their lawyer."

Nolan opened her car door, but she turned to him instead of getting in. "Thank you. That sounds ridiculous, but you're going out of your way for me and my baby. I know this is some way for you to make amends for the past, and honestly, nothing can change that, but I need this plan to work. I can't lose my child."

Every primal instinct in him wanted to protect her, to shield her from everything trying to drag her down.

Unfortunately, she wasn't his. This brief marriage would end as soon as he felt she was safe—and he'd spare no expense when it came to legal fees. He'd fight for her because she deserved this second chance at fulfilling her dream of having a family.

"You won't lose this baby," he assured her, taking her hands in his. "I have a hectic work schedule over the next few days, but I'll set up a time with my lawyer when we can both meet with him."

Once they were on their way back to the ranch, the irony of their circumstances fully hit him. He was bringing his pregnant wife back to a ranch house they'd designed years ago. Only this wasn't his baby, this wasn't his forever bride, and there would be no honeymoon phase.

"You don't have to check in with me." Pepper finally broke the silence as he pulled into the drive. "I don't have to know your every move."

Keeping that wall of defense firmly in place was her coping mechanism. She couldn't let this get too personal, or any more personal than it already was. Her heart had to come out of this unscathed.

"I know this isn't how you planned your life going once you came back," he told her.

He waved to Colt as he passed the stable. There would definitely be some explaining to do, but he'd get to that later. He'd been so preoccupied with helping Pepper he hadn't even told his brother she was back in town, let alone that he'd married her.

When Nolan had taken Annabelle her flowers and painting for her birthday, Colt hadn't been home. Nolan was guaranteed to take some flack for this, especially since Nolan had given some to Colt when he'd been messing with Annabelle by blackmailing her into getting the adjoining property.

It wasn't that long ago that Annabelle was Colt's neighbor and fighting to keep her land. Then nature took its course and Colt ended up falling in love with not just Annabelle, but her precious twin girls, too. Now their properties were legally joined.

Pebblebrook was now in the third generation of ranching, but Colt was the backbone behind the operation. Their father had long dreamed of expanding and opening a dude ranch, but he now suffered from dementia and was living in a nursing facility. Nolan visited as often as he could, sometimes even in the middle of the night after his shifts. He'd stop in and sit by his father's bed and, in the peaceful quiet, remember the man he used to be.

What would he think of Nolan marrying Pepper under these circumstances? When everything fell apart ten years ago, his father had been disappointed that Nolan had let Pepper go.

He'd made a mistake, one he could never rectify, but he was starting fresh now. And once this marriage was over, they'd go their separate ways and he'd be guilt-free. In theory that sounded amazing, but he didn't think things would go quite that smooth.

"I was hoping to avoid you completely," she replied, jarring him from his thoughts.

Nolan glanced toward her, noticed her staring down at the pewter-and-diamond ring he'd slipped on her finger moments ago.

That ring had been his mother's. Since Nolan was the oldest, he'd gotten it when she'd passed. With the last-minute marriage, he'd opted to get this out of his safe and give it to his temporary wife.

Pepper didn't have to know where the ring came from, because she would read too much into it. She didn't have to know that years ago he'd planned the perfect proposal with that very ring, but the pregnancy happened, then the miscarriage, and he'd withdrawn from getting too close and opted to throw himself into his career.

He hadn't been there for her when she'd been grieving and she'd left Stone River before they could settle things. It was still for the best that she'd gone, though. After the miscarriage, they weren't the same couple they'd once been, and they sure as hell weren't the same now that they'd been apart.

"You can still avoid me," he told her as he maneu-vered into his four-car attached garage. "Take the bedroom on the opposite end of the hall. It's another master suite and nearly identical to mine. That's where I had all your clothes delivered anyway."

He'd been tempted to have them put in his closet, but there was no reason to make this more difficult for Pepper. Besides, he came and went all hours of the night and he wanted her to be able to feel free to move about his house. Having her here wasn't easy, though. She infiltrated his space, putting his heart at risk once again. The pull was tough to fight because he couldn't even pretend he didn't want her. But he had to attempt to keep some control over his emotions.

"I have a pool, so feel free to take advantage of that anytime."

Pepper laughed. "You're going to make it hard to go back to my apartment when all this is done."

Nolan grimaced.

"Wow, you still have that same look." She gripped her door handle and jerked it open. "Don't worry. I'll still leave when this case is over and you can go back to the life you chose."

Like hell. Did she think he'd be untouched by this whole marriage? Did she honestly believe he'd just go back to his old ways now that she'd reentered his life?

Before she could exit, Nolan grabbed her arm and leaned over the console so his face was within a breath of hers. "You have no idea the life I want. You know the man I used to be, so stop telling me what you think you know."

Her eyes widened as her tongue darted out to swipe across her bottom lip. Nolan was barely hanging on and she wasn't helping. She had no clue the power she still held over him...he hadn't realized it himself until he'd seen her vulnerable and alone and being verbally attacked.

She still did something to him, something deeper than just physical attraction. Maybe it was that protective instinct overriding common sense, because he shouldn't want to keep touching her, but he couldn't stop himself. Hell, he didn't *try* to stop himself.

"I didn't get to properly kiss my bride at the ceremony. I want privacy this time."

Pepper's eyes widened a second before he captured her mouth beneath his. He cursed himself for being such a fool, as if passion and desire could erase years of hurt and emptiness.

But she tasted so sweet and when she opened for him that Nolan was lost. Again, that power she had no inkling she held was dragging him under. Relinquishing control had never been an option, but right now he had no choice. Pepper was drawing him in deeper and deeper. They'd been married for thirty minutes…there was no way they'd make it weeks, or even months, without tearing each other's clothes off.

Nolan drew back but slid his hand up to gently cup the side of her face. Pepper's lids slowly opened, feverish desire staring back at him. But she blinked a few times, as if pulling herself back from the moment.

"Don't do that again," she whispered.

"No?" His thumb stroked along that lush bottom lip. "Because it sure felt like you wanted me to not only do it again but take you inside and finish it."

Pepper whipped away from him and rushed out of the car, slamming the door on anything else he was about to say.

He winced. Well, that had gone about as well as he'd expected. He actually hadn't even planned on kissing her.

Okay, that was a lie. He had planned on kissing her, often actually. Why did he have to keep fighting this desire? Maybe he should take her to his bed, convince her to finally give in to what they both wanted. She wasn't immune to this sexually charged energy between them, but she was resisting it with everything she had. Maybe a little seduction was exactly what they both needed. And maybe he wanted to see if things were just as good as he remembered.

But wooing her into his bed would take careful planning and finesse. After all, that kiss had completely backfired on him and it was apparent he needed to up his game. He had to prove to her that their attraction couldn't go ignored…the question was, how?

Nolan raked a hand over the back of his neck and figured he might as well go talk to Colt and let Pepper cool off…or think about that kiss, because he sure as hell would.

Pepper stared around her bedroom and tried to calm her breathing. Even taking in the beauty of the room with the four-poster king-size bed, the sheers surrounding it and the double doors leading onto the balcony did nothing to settle her. She'd appreciate the aesthetics later.

She wasn't sure what she needed to get control of more—her anger or her desire.

How dare he just kiss her like he had the right? Like she wanted him to?

No. Nolan Elliott did whatever the hell he wanted, just like he always had. Did he honestly believe that now that they were married, she'd be in his bed? Not likely. Arrogant jerk.

Pepper slammed the door to her bedroom. Childish to go around slamming doors, but she wasn't quite sure what to do with all her emotions right now. She truly feared if she started crying, she might never stop. If she thought it would help, she'd throw something, but then she'd just be even more indebted to him than she already was. Besides, she wouldn't give him the satisfaction of knowing he had such a powerful hold over her.

Life was so much simpler when she traveled from place to place, taking odd jobs and then moving on to another city. No ties, nothing to break her heart all over again.

Yet she'd circled right back around and landed on Nolan's doorstep…literally.

Pepper crossed the spacious room and headed toward the double doors of the most impressive walk-in closet she'd ever seen. Complete with an island in the middle, this spacious room was every woman's fantasy. The island was full of shoes tucked in each divider. Along the top was jewelry all laid out on display. Hanging in her closet was a variety of clothing, still with the tags dangling.

Slowly, she took a step forward. She trailed her fingertip over the simple jewelry. Colorfully beaded bangles, long, simple gold chains with delicate charms, oversize earrings. It was like the man knew exactly what she'd pick out. And he did. He knew her better than anyone because he'd been the only person she'd ever let that intricately into her life.

Even though all those years had separated them, Nolan was so in tune with her…and that was what scared her the most.

Pepper turned toward the clothing and started pushing hanger after hanger aside, each piece made for her growing belly. Neatly stacked in the shelves along the wall were pajamas, bras, panties.

Part of her wanted to relish in this moment. The other part wanted to tell him her forgiveness couldn't be bought.

But the biggest part of her was still stuck on that kiss.

She'd be lying if she said she hadn't enjoyed it. Nolan had always known how to kiss to make her feel alive, to make her want so much more than just his mouth on hers. Being held by him again, kissed by him again, only proved her emotions had never died. No, they'd just been lying stagnant for years and were now flooding to the surface.

Pepper spun in a slow circle, still amazed at how Nolan had managed to pull all this off in such a short amount of time. No doubt he paid someone a hefty sum and when he snapped his fingers, his employee immediately complied.

She sank onto the cushioned bench across from the floor-to-ceiling mirror. How had her life landed her right back where she swore she'd never come?

When she met Matt in Houston at a party of a mutual friend, they'd immediately hit it off. The attraction had been there, but they didn't have the same life goals.

They'd enjoyed each other's company, both in bed and out, and when she got pregnant, she'd known he wasn't going to get down on one knee or anything, but she really hadn't expected him to be so cold about it, either. The way he threw money at her to extricate him from the situation had stunned her at first, but she didn't want anyone in her baby's life who didn't want to be there.

The fear of this custody issue was becoming more and more real. Pepper spun the ring on her finger, glancing down to the sparkling stone. Ten years ago she would've given anything to have Nolan place a ring on her finger. She would've supported him in his journey to become a doctor, to be a part-time rancher, to save the world because that was what he'd been destined to do.

But he couldn't save their relationship. He hadn't even tried, yet he was bending over backward to save her now.

Did he have regrets? Of course he felt remorse for the obvious hurt he'd caused, but did he lament letting her go? Had he thought of her over the years and wondered how their lives would've been had she not miscarried? Would he have eventually come around and seen that a baby wasn't the end of life as they knew it and he could still have it all?

Or what if he'd stuck by her side through the pain and anguish of losing a child? Would they have grown stronger and maybe gone on to have more children?

Pepper cursed herself for getting caught up in that nostalgic what-if game. Sliding a hand over her belly, she smiled when she felt the slight shift beneath her palm. She actually loved being pregnant. Pepper relished each and every moment, knowing how fortunate she was to get a second chance at motherhood, and had even welcomed the morning sickness. She hadn't had that the first time.

The mere thought of Matt's parents taking her child away brought on a whole new level of fear. Surely no judge would award custody to them. Their money and their attorney were her biggest barrier, however. Pepper knew she was no match for that.

So she'd play the dutiful role of Mrs. Elliott if that meant she'd keep her child. She'd sell her soul to the devil himself if that ensured her a life without worry that her baby would be ripped from her arms.

Pepper came to her feet, staring at all the brand-new items just for her. She might not have sold her soul to the devil, but she wasn't too far off the mark. Knowing Nolan, she had no doubt he'd go out of his way to make sure she was comfortable, without a worry, and he'd take on everything to make her feel secure.

Between the sweet gesture and the touching and kissing, he was proving to be a perfect husband. Damn it. She didn't want this marriage to feel real or right or anything else, for that matter. She wanted to count down the days until they were done, but right now she didn't even want to think of the end.

In other words, Nolan was going to make it extremely difficult not to fall in love with him all over again.

Seven

Nolan had barely stepped foot in the stables when Colt came out of one of the stalls muttering beneath his breath.

It was late and all the workers had already gone home, but Colt was happiest right here with the horses. Well, that was where he used to be the happiest. Now he was pretty cozy with his fiancée, Annabelle, and her twin girls. They made the picture-perfect family.

Nolan's boot scuffed against the stone walkway between the stalls, and Colt jerked his head up. With a flick of his finger, he tipped his hat.

"Hey, man. Not out saving lives this evening?"

Nolan shook his head. "Too busy getting married."

Colt started to reach for the door on the stall and froze. "Excuse me?"

"I got married today."

Colt's eyes went to Nolan's hand, but he held up his

ringless finger. "I don't have a band. I probably should get one."

He'd been so worried about Pepper having one that he'd not even thought of getting a wedding band for himself.

"What the hell are you talking about?" Colt exploded.

The reality of the day settled in and Nolan crossed to one of the benches on the wall between the stalls. He sank down and rested his elbows on his knees, suddenly feeling the weight of the world on his shoulders as he glanced down wearily at his boots.

The constriction in his chest seemed to tighten even more, like a vise grip around his heart. He'd pushed Pepper away so long ago, had been so harsh and cold to her because of his own uncertainties and fear. Yet here he was married to her and she was up at his home right now awaiting his return.

Everything had happened so fast in the past couple of days he wasn't even sure he believed he was actually married.

"Pepper is back in town," he mumbled, as if that blanket statement explained everything. "She's in a bind, so we got married."

Nolan glanced up to see the reaction on his youngest brother's face. Colt merely leaned against the stall door on the opposite side of the walkway and gestured for him to continue.

"Care to fill in the giant gap in between her coming to town and you saying 'I do'?"

Blowing out a breath, Nolan eased back on the bench. "She opened a new shop in town. That's actually where I got Annabelle's present for her birthday. I went in and had no clue it was Pepper's store. She's pregnant."

"Oh, hell," Colt muttered. "Are you all right?"

Nolan nodded. Did he have a choice?

"She was living in the apartment over her store," he stated. "It caught fire the other night. I've got Wayne working on it now, but then the grandparents of the baby came to confront her when she was already down. Their son had a heart attack and passed away."

"Damn. I take it Pepper and the guy weren't together anymore?"

Shaking his head, Nolan added, "He paid her a lump sum for support and asked to be left out of the upbringing."

The silence that followed that tidbit was a bit uncomfortable.

"Now his parents want custody," he went on. "They're a pretty powerful family."

"We're more powerful."

Nolan met his brother's determined gaze. "We are," he agreed. "My attorney joked that if she were married, there would be even more leverage for her case. So—"

"You jumped in to play white knight to make up for past sins."

Colt's tone wasn't accusing, more understanding, and Nolan was thankful he didn't have to explain. Apparently love had softened Colt, because a few months ago his brother would have been tearing him up for getting involved with Pepper again.

When Nolan and Pepper parted, his family hadn't kept their feelings about it to themselves...or rather their feelings about the reason why they parted. Nolan's defense had fallen on deaf ears. He'd been set with a plan of fulfilling his dream of becoming a surgeon, marrying Pepper and traveling with her during his off time.

But then they had lost the baby and their world had imploded around them.

"She's going to be living with me until this case is resolved."

Colt's brows shot up. "And you think this is all going to go that smoothly?"

"It has to."

Colt crossed his arms over his chest and shrugged. "You probably don't want my opinion—"

"Not at all."

"But you two haven't seen each other in years and you're already torn up. How do you think this fake marriage is going to play out?"

Good question, one he unfortunately had no clue how to answer. He hoped like hell he'd be working most of the time. Having Pepper so close yet so unobtainable would be pure torture. He wanted her with a desire that had nothing to do with the past and everything to do with the independent, beguiling woman she was today.

But she'd made it perfectly clear she wasn't interested. Did he actually believe she'd fall back into bed with him? No, but that didn't mean he wouldn't try. Everyone had a weakness and he fondly remembered every single one of hers.

"My house is big enough," Nolan explained. "And I've got double shifts coming up. I'd say for the most part we'll avoid each other."

Colt snorted and pushed off the door. "Keep telling yourself that, bro."

He would, because as much as he wanted to seduce his bride, he also knew she was vulnerable right now. He might be a doctor, but his bedside manner left something to be desired. He wasn't much on comforting or offering words of wisdom.

Added to that, there was too much at stake. Getting

back in so deep with Pepper had potential to reopen old wounds he'd hoped would never be exposed again.

Something inside him had been damaged when Pepper left. If he had it to do over, he'd…hell, he didn't know what he'd do. They were both so different now, yet the familiarity…the aching want and need…was still simmering beneath the surface. Now they were thrown together, on borrowed time, but after this marriage they'd go back to being single. And he'd be in this big, empty home he'd built with no wife, no family. That was what he wanted, right?

Hadn't he said something to Pepper about a lonely life? He was the poster child.

Nolan rose to his feet. "Hayes will be home next week."

"I went by to see Dad earlier and told him. He was having a better day but wasn't sure who I was."

Their father was in and out of touch with reality—more out than in. But some days he recognized his sons. He often recalled their names but never put them with their faces.

"He remembered Hayes, but he thinks we're all in grade school," Colt added somberly.

"Maybe once Hayes goes to see Dad he will be having a good day. I'd hate for him to come home and catch him at a bad time for the first visit."

Hayes had been overseas for over a year now. He was finally getting out of the military and planning on farming for the time being. His house was back on the east side of the ranch and was the original Elliott home. It needed some renovations, but Nolan figured his brother would work on that as a way to keep busy because he wasn't the man he used to be. That much had been evident the last time he was home from a tour of duty.

"I've already blocked off some time next week," Nolan said. "I plan on being around more the first few days he's home."

"Good. He won't like us hovering, but he's always different when he's home and trying to acclimate back into the civilian world."

Colt fell into step beside his big brother as they headed out of the stable. "Did you come down to ride or to tell me about your marriage?"

"Both." Nolan pulled in a deep breath and glanced up at the orange-and-pink-streaked horizon. There was nothing like a sunset on the ranch. "But I'm going to head home. I can't keep avoiding this marriage."

Which meant neither could she.

Pepper had soaked in the oversize garden tub and enjoyed the wide window overlooking a portion of the ranch. Pebblebrook was the most beautiful piece of land she'd ever seen, and she'd done quite a bit of traveling.

She loved it all—the lush green grass, the brook winding through the property, the livestock dotting the horizon, the ever-present cowboys who worked here. The Elliott men were big, strong, handsome guys, but the stable hands were something to admire, too. They were in their forties, but farm life kept them in great shape.

Feeling more relaxed, Pepper slid into a simple sundress. She wouldn't mind continuing her evening of leisure by having some lemonade on the porch swing, but Nolan was around here somewhere. She wasn't quite sure she was ready to face him after that kiss.

If he didn't keep his hands and his lips off her, she didn't know if she'd be able to stop herself next time.

Pepper opted to take a stroll through the house instead. After all, shouldn't she get the lay of the land since she was now Mrs. Elliott? She wanted to see the finished product of their vision. They'd discussed so many details, yet this all seemed so new. Never once had she stopped to consider Nolan might actually go ahead with the plans they'd made.

When they'd played around with house designs, they'd discussed their future. Having kids had been a nebulous dream, but the realistic side of life had kicked them when she miscarried, ultimately driving an immovable wedge between them.

Pepper's heart tightened as she made her way down the wide hallway. Nervous about creeping through Nolan's house, she toyed with the foreign ring on her finger. Everything was so fresh yet so familiar. She'd seen these plans on paper, but had he changed much from their original vision?

She poked her head in the other bedrooms on this floor. They were all simply decorated in that muted, classy style. No doubt he'd hired a decorator to complete the home—a job she would've taken on had this been her place from day one. She would've splashed more color on the walls, accented with patterns and textures. And rugs. Mercy, this place needed some life.

After she closed the door on the last guest room, her eyes were drawn to the end of the hall where Nolan's master suite called to her. Her pulse quickened. Should she go inside? She had no rights here and he'd not given her the green light to explore.

Then again, she hadn't given him the go-ahead to kiss her, either, but he hadn't waited around for permission.

Squaring her shoulders, Pepper crossed the hall and didn't hesitate when her fingers closed over the knob. She turned it beneath her hand and opened the door. Her eyes instantly landed on the massive king-size bed occupying the middle of the floor, as if taking center stage.

A wide wall of windows with double doors in the middle to the patio took up the far wall. The room was identical to hers except for the layout of the decor and furniture.

An image of the two of them entangled in those sheets as they watched the sunrise flooded her mind.

Pepper moved farther into the room, transfixed by the fictitious scene. Her body responded, from memories of his touch or from the recent kiss, she wasn't sure. But this room smelled like him, all woodsy and masculine. The dark furniture screamed wealth and the navy bedding was so simple, yet she could see Nolan spread out with his sculpted shoulders and—

The bathroom door opened. Pepper jerked her gaze from the bed to the man in the steamy doorway. A man who wore nothing but dots of water glistening over taut skin stared back at her.

He propped one shoulder against the door frame as if he didn't care at all that he stood before her completely naked. Granted, Nolan had nothing to be ashamed of. If she'd thought that body was spectacular before, it was now a work of art.

"Decide to consummate the marriage after all?" he drawled.

His question pulled her attention back to his face. Her entire body heated at the way he stared back at her. So much raw desire and want and need, and with her hormones all over the place, she was barely hanging on.

"I—I was just looking around."

Nolan moved across the room, never taking his eyes off her. Pepper's heart kicked up as she tipped her head back to meet his gaze.

"In my bedroom, Pepper?" he asked in that low, husky tone.

There were too many things to take in all at once: the fresh, crisp scent from his shower, the heat that seemed to radiate off his bare body, the fact that said bare body was now inches from hers and the way he continued to look at her as if she were already his.

If he touched her now, she would not be responsible for her actions. She couldn't even lie to herself and pretend to be strong. No matter what her mind said, her heart yearned desperately for him.

"I was just looking around and—"

"When you say looking around, you mean at my bed? Because I saw your face. Were you daydreaming? Maybe about forgoing this agreement not to sleep together?"

Pepper willed herself to get control of this situation, but it was rather difficult when someone like Nolan was so…everything. He was overpowering, demanding in that confident, primal way.

"Whatever thoughts I have or don't have are none of your concern."

He trailed a fingertip up her bare arm, over her collarbone, and down the V of her dress. She couldn't suppress the tremble.

"I'd say they're very much my concern when I'm standing here naked and you're imagining yourself in my bed."

Eight

Nolan didn't care that he was pushing her. She'd stepped into his domain, so he considered her free game. Those wide eyes never wavered from his.

Undoubtedly he could spin her around and have her on his bed. He wasn't giving up on seduction, but he also wanted to be respectful. He'd ultimately started this marriage process as a way to give Pepper the family she'd always wanted. There was no point in rushing things. He had time to take her to bed because she wasn't going anywhere anytime soon.

"This was a mistake." She turned to go but stopped and glanced over her shoulder. "I'd rather do this on my own than have you mock me. Yes, I'm attracted to you—that was never our problem. So, if you want to revisit the past, I suggest you start opening up about why you abandoned me after all we'd been through."

Nolan didn't get a chance to respond before she strode from the room. He grabbed a pair of shorts that were folded on top of his dresser and hopped into them as he headed down the hall. He caught her bedroom door with a firm grip a second before she could slam it in his face.

"You want to talk about the past?" he said, storming into her room. "What do you want me to say, Pepper? That I handled things poorly? That I—"

She whirled around, her face flushed. "I don't know what I want! Apologizing won't change anything and I know we're different now, but…"

Pepper reached up and rubbed her forehead. The way she squeezed her eyes shut had Nolan rushing forward. She swayed slightly.

"Pepper."

She opened her eyes but didn't focus on him. Alarm shot through him, but that turned to full-on terror when she collapsed. He reached out just in time to keep her from falling to the floor.

The doctor in him kicked in, but the man who cared for her threatened to take over. What the hell had caused her to pass out? Was something wrong with the baby?

He scooped her up in his arms, then gently laid her down on her bed and smoothed her hair back from her face. Her face was still flushed and a sheen of perspiration covered her forehead. He rushed to the bathroom to get a cold cloth and then came back. After placing it on her forehead, he checked her pulse. Strong and steady.

The stress must be getting to her. The fire, the custody issue…him. He hadn't made things exactly easy for her by goading her. If something happened to this child, Nolan would never forgive himself. *Pepper* would never forgive him.

Her lids fluttered, and Nolan eased down on the bed beside her. She opened her eyes and glanced around the room, then blinked and focused in on him.

"You passed out," he told her. "Don't try to move, darlin'. Just lie here a minute."

Her hands went to her stomach.

"I caught you," he informed her. "Have you fainted
before with this pregnancy?"

"One other time," she admitted, taking the cloth from
her head and attempting to sit up. "I'm okay. I think I
just need to eat."

"You haven't had dinner? You can't be that careless
at a time like this. You're already under too much pressure and that's not good for the baby."

She glared at him. "Really? I wasn't aware of the obvious."

Damn it. He was still panic-stricken and beside himself with worry from seeing her go down, and now she
mocked him. Perfect. Just perfect. Wasn't this some wedding night to remember?

"No, I didn't eat. I took a bath to relax me and I was
going to go downstairs and find something when I decided to take a tour."

"To my bedroom."

Her eyes turned to slits. "Your ego is out of control. I
wasn't even aware you were home, so don't flatter yourself."

She might not have been aware he was home, but when
he'd stepped out of his shower buck naked, she hadn't
made a move to leave his room or to avert her eyes. That
in itself spoke volumes.

"Stay here. I'll bring up something."

"I can get it."

Nolan stood up and stared sternly down at her. "No.
You'll stay right here."

"I'm not playing the roll of the dutiful wife."

Placing a hand on either side of her hips, Nolan leaned

down. "Darlin', you're far from dutiful where I'm concerned. But you're in no shape to go downstairs and cook. I'll get something quick and bring it back. Stop arguing."

As he turned to go, her softly spoken words stopped him. "Why are you doing this?"

He prided himself on being truthful when at all possible. Casting a glance over his shoulder, he replied gruffly, "Because I wasn't there for you before. This may not be my child, but I have to make it up to you somehow. I'm sorry I left you to handle the grief alone, but I'm trying to do right by you now."

"Actions from guilt won't erase the past," she countered.

"No, but I'll be damned if anything is going to happen to you or your baby. No matter what I have to pay for the custody dispute or how I have to care for you here, I'll do it."

He turned and walked out before he could say anything else that would betray his emotions. He wasn't quite sure what to even label them, but once words were said, they couldn't be taken back. So Nolan opted to remain quiet and concentrate instead on caring for her.

Pepper was his wife, which meant right now her child was his. No, not literally, but in his view, they were his to care for, to protect. This wasn't the best mind-set to be in, but considering the choices that had been made thus far, this was where he stood. He couldn't deny he wanted her with him. And that went beyond merely wanting to shield her from harm. He wanted to see if that old spark, the one that still simmered between them, was real.

He already knew the answer to that.

Maybe he should take some time off in addition to the days next week. He had more than enough saved up and with Hayes coming home from overseas, now would be a good time to take a break. Besides, someone needed to look after Pepper, whether she wanted to admit it or not. And, heaven help him, he was the only man for the job.

Five days had passed since she'd fainted and she'd purposely taken better care of herself. She didn't want to rely on Nolan any more than necessary.

He'd worked the next three days and then informed her he'd be off. Wonderful. Just what she needed. Time alone with her husband wasn't something she was exactly looking forward to. The temptation was much too strong.

As Pepper pulled into the drive of her temporary home, she glanced to the black-and-white images lying in her passenger seat. Images of her baby boy.

Nothing could spoil this day. She'd been counting down the days till she found out the sex of her baby. Now that it was confirmed she was having a boy, she wanted to focus on getting ready for her son's arrival. A wave of anticipation rippled through her as she envisioned getting back to her apartment and setting up a fun nursery with paintings she'd done herself. Maybe she'd put a mural on the wall over his crib.

But then reality set in. The contractor wasn't done with her apartment and she wasn't going to be living there anytime soon anyway. She'd yet to hear from the attorney and everything in her hoped the Wrights would just drop this case.

That was wishful thinking.

Colt led his horse from the stable as she passed by. Since she made eye contact, she threw up a hesitant hand in an awkward wave as she drove on. Odd to just wave as if they were truly family or friends. She hadn't had a face-to-face conversation with him since being here.

Granted, he was busy and, well, she was doing everything she could to avoid bumping into her husband.

She stayed after at her shop to paint and make new arrangements to replace some that had sold. So far Painted Pansies was thriving. Mostly people strolled through to see what the new shop had to offer, which was fine. She hoped they'd come back and tell their friends, drumming up more business.

Maybe she should plan an open house. Something after hours for those who worked. Definitely something to consider. A glimmer of hope coursed through her for the first time since she'd moved in. She knew that focusing on positive aspects of her life was what would help her get through this tumultuous time.

Eventually she would have her life just the way she'd dreamed. But she had to tread carefully here because giving in to her attraction to Nolan would only derail her plans.

Pepper parked in the driveway and went into the house through the garage door. All of Nolan's vehicles were in the garage, but that didn't mean he was home. He often went out on his horse or four-wheeler and lately he'd been at Hayes's house making sure everything was ready for his brother's return. She preferred when he was out because he tended to hover whenever he was nearby. Not that she was unappreciative…he had truly gone above and beyond to make her feel comfortable. He had his chef come in every other day to make up meals so Pepper didn't have to do a thing. She even had lunches prepared so Pepper could take them to work.

Nolan had thought of everything, but they'd still not resumed their heated conversation from the other day. Would he apologize for how he'd treated her? He was obviously a different man now. Perhaps becoming a doctor had changed him, or maybe her leaving had. Of course, that was her broken heart talking.

When she'd left, she'd waited for him to reach out, to call her back and tell her they'd work through everything and they'd be all right. That never happened and she'd finally had to push through the pain and realize that life without Nolan was her new reality. She'd made plans without him—she wouldn't upend them again. Doing so would only end in more heartache for her and her child.

Pepper hung her purse on the hook near the back door and clutched her baby's pictures in the other hand. Maybe she could get a little frame to put them in. She couldn't wait to see her son's sweet face in person and cuddle him in her arms.

The back patio door opened and Nolan stepped in. The spacious kitchen and eat-in breakfast area separated them, but those bright eyes still zeroed right in on her.

"You're getting home pretty late," he commented as he yanked his hat off and wiped his forehead with the back of his hand.

Pepper straightened her back and tipped her chin. "I wasn't aware you were keeping tabs."

"My contractor called and said you'd talked to him when you left the shop almost two hours ago."

She moved farther into the kitchen and stopped at the large center island. "Well, I had something to do after work. I already told you going into this marriage that it was on paper only. I'm still my own boss."

He propped his hat back on his head and crossed the room, coming to stand across from her. His gaze drifted to the ultrasound images in her hand.

"You were at the doctor?"

Pepper nodded.

"I would've gone with you."

Surprised he'd even mention such a thing, she merely shrugged. "Didn't cross my mind to mention it. That's not something you ever wanted to do before."

The muscles in his jaw ticked as he continued to look at the pictures. "We've already established I'm a different man."

"A man who wants kids in his life?"

Those bright blues came up to meet her gaze as silence surrounded them.

"That's what I thought," she finally murmured.

He reached across and slid the pictures from her hand. As he unfolded the long strip of paper, he studied the ultrasound shots.

"A boy," he muttered. "Congratulations."

"Thank you."

He laid the photos back on the counter and looked at her again. "I heard from my lawyer today. We have a meeting set up for tomorrow morning with the Wrights and their attorney."

Fear clutched her heart. "I was hoping they were going to let this drop."

Nolan came around the counter and took her hands in his, forcing her to face him. "No matter what you and I have been through, or how we feel now, I won't let your child get taken away. I've got the best attorney in the state on this and I'll call in a whole damn team if need be. Let me handle this, Pepper. You focus on your baby boy."

In theory that sounded nice, but in reality this was her battle to fight. Unfortunately, she didn't have near the impressive bank account that Nolan did. So as much as she wanted to stand on her own two feet, right now she needed his help. She just wished it hadn't come at such a high price.

Why did he have to seem so caring, so concerned with

her emotions? She couldn't emotionally afford to have him so invested. Financially, she'd take all he could offer in order to keep her child, but anything too intimate or personal could possibly destroy her once all was said and done. Because in the end, they would part ways.

"I just want all of this to be over," she told him, not caring that she was vulnerable. There was only so long a person could be strong and she was almost at her breaking point.

"It will be soon and then you can get on with your life," he assured her as he cupped her cheek, stroking his thumb across her skin.

He sounded so confident and she hoped he was right. If she only had an ounce of his certainty, it would go a long way in easing her mind.

But with the impending meeting in the morning, there would be no relaxing until she saw what she was up against. Maybe after talking with Nolan's attorney herself, she'd get a clearer picture.

She sighed despite herself. As hard as it was to admit, the fact that Nolan insisted on coming with her and sticking by her throughout this entire ordeal filled her with a measure of comfort. She wished she could be angry with him, but how could she? Yes, he'd treated her badly years ago, but he was truly trying to make up for it now. Pepper knew he still cared or he wouldn't be going to so much trouble. Even with his guilt, there was a level of concern and it warmed her, made her wonder what type of man he was now.

And maybe she wanted to get to know this Nolan a bit better. The prospect seemed terrifying. The risk to all of this temptation was almost more than she could bear. But the intrigue was there…and she'd already been pulled in too far to back out now.

Nine

"I didn't know you used to live in Montana and Oregon."

The meeting with the attorneys and the Wrights had gone about as abysmally as he'd thought it would. Nolan had sat by Pepper's side as everyone discussed the custody of her unborn child. The more he listened, the more he realized the Wrights were indeed going to fight dirty.

Their attorney brought up Pepper's frequent moves over the past ten years. The only upside to the whole debacle was that Nolan discovered quite a bit about her, courtesy of their extensive background check, and appreciated the insight to her life. Although, he wasn't too keen on the way they made her sound so unstable. Having known her for years, he understood the way she used the adventure as a way to cope with her grief.

"Both were beautiful states." She continued to stare out the window of his SUV as he headed toward her shop because she insisted on working. "Other than Texas, I think Oregon was my favorite place to live."

"You love it here?" he asked, surprised.

Pepper shifted in her seat, smoothing a hand down her pregnant belly. "What's not to love? The small-town feel with the big-city attractions. All of the farms, the old homes, and the architecture. Not to mention all the little shops and parks. Stone River is a beautiful town."

He gripped the wheel tighter. "Would you have stayed?"

Silence settled heavy between them. He should've kept his mouth shut and not said a word. But he'd always wondered. If she hadn't gotten pregnant, had a miscarriage… if he hadn't acted like a jerk because he was overcome with grief, would she have stayed? Would they be living in his house on Pebblebrook for real as a married couple?

"I would've done anything for you," she murmured.

Nolan swallowed the lump of remorse. He believed her. She'd have stayed even though she wanted to go travel the world. He hadn't been able to see it at the time, but now he knew the truth. She'd have done anything to make him happy, to stay together. He was the one who hadn't held up his part of the commitment.

Relationships weren't always fifty-fifty, with each person giving fully of themselves—a life fact he'd discovered the hard way. At least, that was what his father had always said, and Nolan's parents had had an extremely successful marriage.

He didn't even think before he reached across and slid his hand over hers. "I'm sorry that was difficult back there."

"Not your fault." Pepper blew out a sigh and changed the subject. "I think we stunned them with the marriage announcement."

Nolan smiled. "That was the idea."

They'd explained that Pepper had come back to her hometown because she and Nolan had reconnected. Not a total lie. Nolan had stayed by her side, offering her support and comfort as she was given the third degree on why she moved so much, why she held so many jobs and why she thought this new venture into entrepreneurship would be the thing to keep her grounded.

The fact that he was a doctor didn't seem to impress the Wrights. If anything, they looked ready to attack him, too. Nolan didn't care what they did. His record as a surgeon was impeccable. He was the top general surgeon in the entire state and if they had the balls to dig into his financial records, they'd find he could buy them out five times over if he wanted.

So, no, he wasn't afraid of them and he hoped like hell they knew who they were up against, because they were going to lose.

"I have to go into the hospital," he told her as he turned into the lot behind Painted Pansies. "The next three days will be busy. I have twelve-hour shifts, so don't look for me at home during normal hours."

Pepper gathered up her purse from the floorboard. "Does a doctor even have such a thing as normal hours?"

"Not at all," he chuckled. "I'll have a couple of the ranch hands drop your car off to you so you can get back home."

He pulled up to the back door and before she could get out, he squeezed her hand to get her attention. "I wasn't lying when I told you everything would be all right."

Her dark eyes met his. "I want to believe that."

The way she looked at him, with so much hope, twisted something deep inside him. Yeah, he'd slay all her dragons, but then he couldn't help but wonder if he'd be battling himself. His hands were dirty, too, when it came to hurting Pepper.

"Will you be okay at the house alone? You remember how the alarm system works?"

Pepper nodded. "I'll be fine."

Damn it. For the first time since he became a doctor, he actually dreaded going into work. But he knew he had a full schedule of surgeries and there were always emergencies that occurred with patients.

"I don't like leaving you."

That revelation came as quick as the words spilled from his mouth. He wanted to spend more time with her, and that was a dangerous thought.

Pepper's brows rose. Yeah, he caught the irony in that statement, too, but he meant it.

"Promise me you'll eat regular meals," he ordered.

"I can take care of myself, Nolan."

She tugged her hand free, and he hated the lost connection. He didn't want her to withdraw. He wanted her to hold on to him, to allow him to gather her close and soothe her worries away. How could he continue to help her if she insisted on guarding her heart? He couldn't blame her, but damn it, he was trying. He wasn't going to stop reaching for her, touching her, kissing her.

"Pepper…"

She gripped her purse in her lap. "I really need to get the shop open. I promise everything will be fine."

Unable to stop himself, he leaned across the console, curled his fingers around the back of her neck, and brought her mouth to his. He brushed his lips over hers, shocked when she parted for him.

Threading his fingers through the hair at the nape of her neck, Nolan tipped his head to capture more of her.

The kiss was quick yet left him wanting more as he

eased back just slightly. Part of him wanted to keep kissing her, but he refrained. Maybe if he kept giving her a taste of what they could have, she'd come to him of her own accord. He knew he could have her begging.

"What was that for?" she breathed against his mouth.

"I won't deny myself what I want anymore."

Her body trembled beneath his touch. "And that includes me?"

He nipped at her lips once more before releasing her. "Have a good day at work and don't hesitate to call Colt if you need something. He knows I'm working and he's right there on the property."

Pepper stared at him. No, he wasn't answering her question; she already knew what he'd say. Hell, yes, she was included in that statement. He wanted her—he knew it was unsettling, risky, but he'd eventually have her in his bed...or wherever else he could take her.

Both times he'd kissed her, she'd melted against him and kissed right back. There was no reason they had to deny themselves what they both wanted.

"You're making this difficult for me," she stated as she opened her door. "If you want to kiss me, fine. But don't push, Nolan. I'm not strong enough to fight for my baby and resist you, too."

She hopped out of the SUV and headed to the back door of Painted Pansies.

Well, damn. If that didn't give him hope, nothing would. She was just as achy as he was. He knew Pepper and there was no way a woman that passionate would be able to resist him. Not that he was God's gift to women— he wasn't that arrogant. But he wasn't naive, either. They had unfinished business between them whether she was willing to admit it or not.

A smile played on his lips. Pepper had no clue that

after these three days were over, he'd be home for a bit. He never took vacation and with Hayes coming home, Nolan wanted to be there.

Maybe he'd just surprise her.

Nolan pulled away as soon as Pepper was safely inside. Yeah, he'd surprise her. Wouldn't she just love that?

After having the ranch to herself for a few days, Pepper had completed and sold several paintings with six to spare and had a few rather profitable days at the shop. With each customer who came through, she had to explain the noises overhead. All of the hammering and sawing was music to her ears, however. Most of the townsfolk knew of the fire and were quite sympathetic, which added to sales.

As soon as she got out of this awkward marriage, Pepper planned to be back in her building, where she could live and work while raising her baby. Because *she* would be the one to raise her son—there was no other option as far as she was concerned. Having strangers get custody wasn't even a possibility she wanted to entertain.

For now, she needed to remain as calm as possible if she wanted to keep her blood pressure under control. Her son's health came first. Everything she was doing was for him. Through each step of this pregnancy, she'd had fears. So many memories of her first pregnancy swirled around in her mind, the roller coaster of emotions from the excitement to the anger, then the loss and the emptiness— -the broken heart.

Pepper stepped back and tipped her head to the side as she examined the new painting she'd done last night when she couldn't sleep. Between her demanding pregnancy bladder and all the worries of the future, she'd barely gotten a few hours. And that wasn't even touching on all the swirling thoughts in her head regarding her new husband.

Once she'd started painting, she'd become lost in the moment. The soft strokes of coral and pale gray looked so much better in Nolan's living room of navy and white. That old ugly black-and-white picture he had really needed to go. He might be a bachelor—or he used to be—but that didn't mean he had to live in a constant state of bore.

Pepper had already put a bright watercolor painting in her bedroom. She needed the yellows and oranges to brighten up all the beige. *Beige.* Who the hell chose that color to decorate with? Why be so mundane?

So far she'd added three paintings to his home, and the third one was propped on his dresser in his bedroom. Also a dark, somber room done in navy and dark wood, so she went with something bold and bright to spruce things up. Various shades of reds and golds ought to make his domain a happier place.

Not that she figured he'd say anything. A man like Nolan didn't care about decor, because she knew him well enough to know he'd hired interior designers to have his home done but he'd most likely told them to keep it neutral.

Neutral. Just the word made her cringe. If she'd lived here from the beginning, the words *beige* and *gray* wouldn't even have been in the mix. Each room would've been its own showpiece. There was so much possibility to liven things up, but this wasn't really her house and she couldn't exactly transform everything. But a few of her one-of-a-kind paintings couldn't hurt.

The furniture and decor all over the house had been chosen with a man in mind—dominant, bold, rich.

From the automatic lights and blinds to the indoor-and-outdoor pool and even a megatheater room, everything was so grand. He had deviated slightly from their master plans years ago, but only to make this place even more larger-than-life. Because when they'd first tinkered around with house plans, they'd still been in that dreamy stage of their love affair. Pepper never actually thought she'd have a master suite with a sweeping balcony to overlook the land but it sure had been fun fantasizing about it.

Dreaming with Nolan had been her favorite hobby when she was twenty years old. Making love by the brook that ran through the ranch had been another of their favorite pastimes. With an estate this vast, there were plenty of areas to find privacy for young lovers.

It wasn't difficult to imagine her life here. Had she not miscarried, she and Nolan would've still built this amazing home on his family's estate. She wondered how he lived here all alone, though. Did he even go in half the rooms of this massive home? Had he thought of her as he built this place? As he designed the master suite?

No. She wasn't going to get caught up in the fantasy life she could've had or the fact that she still craved Nolan. He may be different than the boy she left behind, but he was also very much the same. And try as she might, she still wanted his touch, even if it was only temporary.

Pepper padded barefoot back through the house, the dark hardwood floor smooth beneath her feet. A gentle kick in her belly had her rubbing a hand over her tank top and smiling. She loved every moment of feeling her little boy move. Every time he shifted, she wanted to freeze that moment. As excited as she was to hold him, she would miss this wondrous feeling.

She headed back to the living room and surveyed the three paintings still waiting to find a home. She could put them in the shop, but she already had so many and she didn't want the small retail space to look cluttered.

"What the hell are you doing?"

Pepper swiveled around, her hand over her chest as her heart quickened at the intrusion. Nolan stood behind her with his hands on his hips. Dark hair all disheveled, lips set in a thin, hard line and jaw clenched, he was clearly pissed about something.

"I didn't hear you come in," she stated breathlessly. "Care to tell me why you're angry with me?"

His hand gestured toward the painting over his fireplace, then to the ones resting to the side. "Are you redecorating?"

So much for him not noticing. "I, uh, thought—"

"Did you think about the paint chemicals?" he added, his voice rising.

Pepper had no idea what had put him in this mood, but she didn't have to stick around to listen. "I use the best paints and in a ventilated area. I also have a mask I wear, not that it's any of your concern," she huffed. "And if you hate it so much, I can easily take down the paintings and put your boring, lifeless art back in place. It's clear some things never change. Whatever Nolan wants, Nolan gets."

She turned on her heel, marched across the room and carefully lifted the painting from the nail. With unshed tears, she cursed herself for getting too comfortable. Over the past three days she'd been alone here, she'd begun to think of this as her place...which was a terrible mistake.

Firm hands gripped her arms, and Pepper stiffened as she gripped the painting. "Don't," she whispered. "I don't want to argue."

And she didn't want to see that look in his eyes again, the one that was clearly disapproving of her getting too cozy in his home.

Ten

Nolan didn't mean to take his piss-poor mood out on Pepper, but he'd just been totally caught off guard. He was used to coming home to a quiet, empty house after work, unwinding by riding his horse Doc or hitting his workout room with the punching bag and free weights. Plus, he'd nearly lost a patient tonight and he was still turned inside out about the whole ordeal. He'd lost patients before, but now that Pepper had come back into his life, this particular experience only made him remember so vividly the time when they'd lost their baby.

"I didn't expect to come in here and see that you'd re-decorated," he explained in a milder tone, as if that somehow made up for the way he'd greeted her. "Something wrong with my artwork?"

Reluctantly, he released her so she could turn to face him. When she didn't, Nolan curled his fingers around her shoulders and eased her around. There was a tiredness in her eyes, one that he hadn't seen before…one he didn't want to see again.

No matter what he'd been through on this last shift, Pepper came first. His *wife* and this child had to take top priority. At this point he wasn't even questioning why he'd allowed this faux family to overtake his life. There were too many reasons to list—and none he wanted to address.

"Your walls are boring." She raised her chin up in defiance, as if silently daring him to argue. "I'm sure you paid a ridiculous price to have this place decorated, but it's putting me to sleep."

He didn't even try to stop himself as he reached out to swipe the pad of his thumb beneath her eye. "You're not sleeping enough."

She blinked, her long lashes brushing against the tip of his thumb. Cupping her cheek, he felt his chest tighten when she leaned just slightly into him.

"I'm in a new place," she explained, those dark gray eyes holding his. "I'm trying to adjust to my surroundings."

"You've traveled all over and adjusted. Why can't you just put your feet up and relax?"

Pepper offered a soft smile. "You know the answer to that."

Yeah, he knew. The same reason he'd been so worked up about coming home, knowing he'd be off for the next few days…which he still hadn't informed her of.

"Have you heard from anyone regarding the case?" he asked, dropping his hand but remaining close enough to touch.

She shook her head. "Not a word, hence all the new paintings."

Nolan couldn't help but smile as he glanced to the new

addition to his living room. "You always painted when you were nervous or worried."

He recalled a few times when they'd been dating and she'd gotten anxious about something, no matter how minor. Some people reached for pills to combat anxiety— his Pepper reached for her paintbrush.

"I did more than the six I brought home," she stated with a shrug. "I put several in the shop and most of them sold."

"That's great." He was so proud of her for opening her shop and already showing that she was going to make it successful. "Business has been good, then?"

He suppressed a smile. Okay, so he *may* have been chatting up her new shop a bit to folks at work. He'd mentioned it casually to his male coworkers in case they needed flowers or a gift and had also told several of the ladies in his department where they could find one-of-a-kind paintings.

"Better than I'd expected, but I know that will die down once the novelty wears off."

Nolan glanced to the stack of canvases on the ottoman. He crossed the room and lifted one up to examine the colors. The vibrant image seemed to jump out at him and he looked closer at the fine details she'd added to each stroke. The variations of tones, then the bold shades that demanded attention.

"I doubt the novelty wears off," he returned as he laid that piece aside to survey the other two. "These are extraordinary."

Nolan turned back around, surprised to see a slight blush creep up her cheeks. "You have to know how talented you are."

"It all started as a way to relax and take my mind away

from reality. I know I have a gift, but when I hear someone I care about tell me…"

Her eyes widened as she jerked her gaze to his. Yeah, he'd caught that slip. Apparently she didn't want him to know just how much she still cared or that declaration wouldn't bother her so much.

At least he wasn't the only one worried about what to say or how to act.

He strode across the room, never taking his eyes from hers. "We have to have complete honesty, Pepper. I know you care for me. I could feel it when you kissed me."

"You kissed me," she corrected.

"And I plan on doing it again." As often as he could, actually. "But my stance hasn't changed since you were here last. I'm not looking for a family."

Pepper folded her arms over her chest, which only aided in pushing her breasts up. He wouldn't be so trite as to stare, but damn, she looked good.

"And you think that because I'm staying here, I won't be able to resist throwing myself at you?" she asked, her tone mocking. "In case you didn't know, I have quite a bit on my plate at the moment. As much as your ego would love for me to fawn all over you, you're not high on my priority list. And as for more kissing? That's not a good idea."

Nolan moved toward her, pleased when her eyes widened. When his chest brushed against her forearms, she immediately dropped her arms to her sides.

"None of this is a good idea, yet here we are."

Those dark flecks in her eyes drew him in. She was an enigma and he was fighting a losing battle…even so, he couldn't surrender. They were different people now. If she hadn't come back and turned his life on its head, he'd still be going along just like he always had. And he was just fine with that…wasn't he?

"You didn't have to marry me," she reminded him. "This was your idea. I would've found a way to keep custody of my baby."

"I'm sure you would've, but this way is easier."

Pepper's laugh filled the room. "Easier? Being married to you and living in a house we designed is definitely *not* easier. I'm temporarily living the only real dream I ever had and I know in a short time, it will all be ripped from me once again."

Nolan clenched his jaw as he reached for her. Settling his hands on her shoulders, he forced himself to face this emotional beast head-on.

"This isn't the same as before," he countered.

Pepper nodded. "You're right. I'm going in with my eyes wide-open. I know the outcome. I appreciate all you're doing for me, Nolan, but every bit of this stings and I can't help how I feel. You wanted honesty, and that's it. Being here with you is hard."

Since they'd first seen each other only days ago, things had become so intense so fast. He needed to lighten the moment, to show her that they could live together and get through this without always throwing the past out in the open like a weapon.

"Are you too tired to go somewhere?" he asked.

Pepper's brows drew in as she gave him the side eye. "Depends on where."

"The old Pepper wouldn't question me. She'd just jump at the unknown and the idea of an adventure."

With a soft smile, she let out a sigh. "Fine. Lead the way, but nothing too adventurous. I'm carrying precious cargo these days."

As if he could forget. That rounded stomach, her new voluptuous figure, the reason they'd married...and the fact this was another man's baby.

Nolan had to face the truth that the crux of his entire bad mood lately was that fact alone. Jealousy had never been an issue with him, but Pepper was different. She was special.

And eventually, that was going to be a problem because these weren't past feelings he was having. Everything he craved now was the new Pepper, this vibrant woman who was made of steel yet had such a vulnerable interior.

Nolan took her hand and led her from the house. The sooner they eased the stress and relaxed, the better. There was a fine line he was hanging on to…and it was about ready to snap.

Pepper entered the dark stables and waited at the doorway while Nolan stepped in and flicked on the lights. She couldn't suppress the gasp. She hadn't forgotten the beauty of the old stone barn, but she'd been gone so long the place had been out of her mind.

The stone pathway leading between the stalls stretched to the other end of the stables. Each stable was separated by sturdy, thick wood beams and an occasional worn wooden bench. Old industrial wheels had been turned into modern chandeliers that were suspended from the vaulted beams.

There was no expense spared on this masterpiece and the horses were no different. Pepper knew the Elliotts kept only the best stock. They offered stud services, as well. Everything about this farm, from the horses to the men, dominated. There was no denying Pebblebrook Ranch was remarkable.

Nolan turned back to her. He'd transformed from a doctor in scrubs to a cowboy complete with Stetson and tight jeans in the span of minutes. Now he stood before her so much like the boy she used to know. But Nolan was all man, filling out his dark blue shirt with muscles that nearly pulled at the seams.

"I know you're not supposed to ride, but I thought you might like to see what we have. You always used to love coming down here."

She had. And every time they'd come down, they'd ended up in the loft overhead. There was nothing sexy about the smell of a stable or the straw on your back, but when she was with Nolan, nothing else had mattered.

Over the years she'd imagined him here, tending to the horses, working on this beloved ranch. This was his life and he was good at it. A burst of jealousy speared through her that she hadn't shared this part of his life when she'd dreamed for so long of being here.

The baby stirred in her belly, and Pepper placed both hands over her bump, wanting to capture every single moment.

Nolan's eyes dropped to her stomach. "Is he moving?"

Pepper nodded, reaching for him. "Want to feel?"

His gaze jerked to hers as he stilled. This entire situation was so foreign to her she had no idea how to react. But she couldn't lie that disappointment didn't spiral through her. She really had no one else to share these joyful moments with. And not that Nolan was her real husband or even her best friend, but he was here... He'd volunteered to be here. She just wished...

Did it matter? She'd had so many wishes over the years and she should know by now that none of them came true.

"It's okay." Pepper offered a smile she wasn't quite feeling. "I didn't mean to make you uncomfortable."

The awkward silence had Pepper smoothing her tank down her belly, causing her bangles to clang against each other. She took a step to move around Nolan and head toward the stalls. Before she could take the second step, however, his big hand snaked out, landing on her abdomen, stopping her instantly.

That strong, warm palm made Pepper's breath catch in her throat. Tipping her head to the side, she met those deep blue eyes beneath his black hat. He turned slightly, placing both hands over her abdomen as he kept his eyes locked on to hers.

Pepper didn't move, didn't breathe. Nolan had completely mesmerized her by his sheer masculine power, his silent command for her to let him do this. And she wanted his hands on her. She wanted him to be part of her life, not in the temporary way, either. There was no lying to herself anymore. She was growing more attracted to Nolan. Her need for him had nothing to do with the past and everything to do with the man he was today.

"He's an active little guy." Nolan's smile widened as he glanced down to his hands. "Is he always like this?"

"Lately. It almost feels like he's flipping at times, but I know he's not. My ultrasound showed he's exactly where he should be and his heart rate is perfect. He's the size of a can of soda."

Nolan laughed. "Amazing."

"I'd think a doctor wouldn't find something like this so remarkable."

Nolan's hands shifted when the baby slowed. He searched for the movement, but Pepper wasn't about to tell him the baby had stopped wiggling.

"I don't deal with babies and definitely not pregnant women. But even if I did, you're different. You could never be just a patient to me."

Pulling in a deep breath, Pepper closed her eyes and willed herself to remain in control. Part of her wanted to give in to the weakness and throw her arms around him, lean into him and let him carry her over this life hurdle.

But the independent woman inside her demanded she deal with this head-on. There was no future here, so there was no reason in letting her mind, or her heart, wander into forbidden territory.

"You can't say things like that to me." She opened her eyes and backed away slightly. "Now, show me your horses, because I've missed this simple life."

He didn't move; he just continued to stare at her as if seeing her for the first time.

"You're beautiful like this," he murmured huskily. "Fuller figure, hair down, desire in your eyes. I always pictured you back here. I wondered if you'd ever return."

Pepper's heart clenched with each word. Marrying him might have sounded like the perfect solution in theory, but now that reality had set in, she wasn't sure she could continue. She wanted too much.

Before she could tell him they needed to keep focused on why they were forced together, Nolan closed the narrow space between them. His boots shuffled against the stone, breaking the tense silence.

"Tell me you haven't thought of us since you left."

Pepper's resolve crumbled as he loomed over her, looking down into her eyes with such...raw desire.

"Nolan—"

"Tell me," he demanded. "I see how you look at me. I feel you trembling now beneath my touch. You want me as much as I want you."

She did, but her feelings, her *wants*, didn't matter.

"I want you," she admitted, not surprised when her voice cracked. "I thought of you, of this ranch, every day for years. But then everything faded. I moved on. You moved on, too."

Banding an arm around her waist, he thrust his other hand into her hair and tilted her head back. "Or maybe we haven't."

Nolan captured her mouth, sending every single doubt and red flag to the back of her mind. In the fury of motions, his hat fell with a soft thump to the ground.

All Pepper could feel, all she could concentrate on, was this potent man who overtook every single emotion.

His hard body lined up perfectly with hers—just like she remembered. Even with her baby bump, it was like they were made for each other...and part of her still believed they were.

Nolan gripped her hair, pulling just enough to send another burst of arousal through her. Not only was he commanding, he knew exactly what it took to turn her on.

Pepper grasped his biceps and returned the kiss, opening further for him. She couldn't deny herself this pleasure. Didn't want to. She'd already had so much taken from her and for these few stolen moments, she was going to be selfish and damn the consequences.

Nolan tore his mouth from hers to rain kisses along her jaw, down the column of her throat. Pepper arched her back, giving him full access. He tugged at the scoop in her tank, managing to pull her bra to the side, as well, exposing one breast. When his lips closed over her heated skin, Pepper cried out and reached up to clutch the sides of his head.

Her entire body lit up from within. But if she didn't put a stop to this, there was no question where they were heading. She tingled all over and it was difficult for her to remember why this wasn't the smartest move.

"Nolan." Why did his name come out like a pant? Maybe one more minute, that was all she needed. Then she'd stop him.

Those talented lips traveled back up until he feasted on her mouth once again. Pepper pressed herself against him, needing to feel more, wanting to rid herself of these clothes and—

No. That was exactly the opposite of what she should want.

She pushed away from Nolan and his spellbinding kiss. As she took a step back, then another for good measure, she tugged her tank up and made sure she was fully covered before she looked him in the eye.

But when she did, there was so much staring back at her. Beyond all the passion and arousal, though, was one emotion worrying her most. Determination. She knew without a shadow of a doubt that Nolan wasn't done with her, that this was only the beginning...and she'd let this happen. She'd wanted it.

"Don't say anything." His stroked his thumb across her bottom lip. "You're not sorry this happened and you don't regret it. You can't lie to me, darlin'. I can see everything in your eyes."

That was precisely what she was afraid of. It never mattered what she said or did—her eyes always revealed the truth.

"Maybe I'm not sorry and I don't regret it," she told him, trying to ignore that tingle shooting through her. "But at this point in my life, I am not looking to revisit the past or even get swept into an affair."

"I'm your husband."

As if she could forget. The unfamiliar band on her finger was a constant reminder of the decision she'd made in order to attempt to secure her baby's future.

"In name only." The reminder wasn't just for Nolan. "I know a man like you..."

Smoothing her hair away from her face, Nolan

flashed her a naughty grin. "A man like me? Please, keep going."

"A healthy, virile man will find this difficult, but we can't... I can't..."

He covered her mouth, softly, possessively, with his. Feathering his lips over hers, he rendered her speechless once again. Pepper turned her head, causing his lips to land on her cheek.

No matter if his kisses were rough and demanding or soft and sweet, Nolan had the same impact on her as if he'd stripped her bare. The man was too potent and she was sinking deeper and deeper into a place she feared she'd never recover from.

"Did you bring me down here to seduce me?" she whispered.

His warm breath fanned her skin, causing even more chills to course through her. "Baby, when I seduce you, I won't worry about the location."

Pepper filled her lungs and turned around, taking a minute to gather her thoughts. Her body betrayed her because she wanted nothing more than to whirl back around and have Nolan finish what he'd started.

She rested a hand over her belly as her son shifted. The reminder was all she needed. He came first; nothing else mattered. Not the past, not her present internal battles...nothing.

Pepper glanced over her shoulder. "Are we going back to the house or are we here to see the horses?"

Nolan's deep gaze was just as potent as his touch, but Pepper raised a brow, silently informing him she was in charge.

Nolan reached out, grabbed her hand, and led her toward the farthest stall. But Pepper still didn't let her guard down. As long as he insisted on touching her, she was going to have to keep giving herself pep talks. Nolan was a force to be reckoned with. .and he knew it.

"This is Doc."

Nolan pointed to the stallion with deep chocolate eyes and a glossy chestnut coat. He was absolutely beautiful. Pepper reached for him, running her fingertips along his velvety nose.

"He's magnificent," she murmured. With his head tilted slightly, Doc seemed as if he was looking right at her. "He's a gentle horse."

"He is," Nolan agreed, patting the stallion's neck. "We understand each other. I ride him every day that I'm off. Sometimes I need a longer ride to decompress, but on occasion I take him out and see what he can do."

Pepper smiled, glancing to Nolan. "You take turns being in charge."

Adjusting his hat, he let out a bark of laughter. "I suppose, though he thinks he's always in charge."

"Much like his owner?" she quipped, turning to face him. "Sounds like you two are a perfect match."

The fans blowing through the stable sent Pepper's hair stirring around her shoulders, just slightly, but enough to tickle her bare skin. She reached back and fisted it, pulling the thick strands over one shoulder. Nolan remained quiet as he seemed to be taking in every move she made.

When the silence became too much, she stilled. "What?"

"You look good here at Pebblebrook."

The soft tone, the way the muscles in his jaw clenched, Pepper knew he hadn't meant to let that slip out. She tried not to allow the words to penetrate her heart, but how could she not? She'd gotten a sneak peek into his most private thoughts.

"I haven't brought another woman here." He continued stroking Doc's neck, then patted his head before he resumed stroking again. "Never seemed right."

Pepper wasn't sure what he wanted her to say, so she kept quiet. She wasn't going to deny that knowing he hadn't brought other women here thrilled her. She had no right to those emotions, but she could always blame it on the pregnancy hormones...right?

"What are you doing tomorrow after work?" he asked.

Stunned by his sudden change of subject, Pepper shrugged. "I'm not sure. Why?"

A mischievous grin spread across his face. "I have something for you."

Pepper patted the horse's nose once more before fully turning to face Nolan. "I'm afraid to ask."

He reached out and brushed her hair off her shoulder. With a featherlight touch, he trailed his fingertips along her jawline.

"You don't have to be afraid, Pepper. Never of me."

His voice held such conviction, and she wanted to believe him. But she knew all too well that there was no way to avoid heartache...and Nolan's name was written all over it.

Eleven

For the first time since Pepper opened her shop, she was anxious for the final customer to leave. But this particular older lady was becoming a regular. She had discovered the woman was a widow of five years and had a fondness for fresh flowers in nearly every room of her home. Pepper was all too willing to feed her addiction.

She purchased three arrangements and one of the larger paintings and, thankfully, stayed only ten minutes past her regular closing time. With a sale like that, Pepper would gladly work overtime. She'd just turned the closed sign around and flicked the lock on the old glass door when the shop cell phone rang.

Figuring it was someone asking the hours, which was the most common phone call, Pepper crossed the shop and reached over the counter for the phone.

"Painted Pansies."

"Pepper, this is—"

"Mrs. Wright," Pepper stated. Her heart kicked up as she rubbed her abdomen and prayed for strength. "You're supposed to go through my attorney if you need anything."

"I know that, but I wanted to talk to you as a mother."

Pepper gripped her phone so tight her hand started shaking. "I don't think this is a good idea—"

"You don't have to say anything," Mrs. Wright hurried on. "Just listen for a few minutes to what I have to say."

She closed her eyes and rested her elbow on the counter. Before she could reply, the older woman clearly took the silence as the green light to continue.

"I just want you to put yourself in my place," she started, her voice quivering. "I've lost my only child and there's a part of him that will live on. I want to be part of my grandchild's life. I know you don't know me, but you have to agree that my lifestyle and finances are in far better shape. Don't you want that for your child?"

It took every ounce of tact for Pepper to keep from exploding. Yes, she wanted a great life for her child, but money and a staid home life weren't it.

"From one mother to another, let me tell you this." Gathering her strength, Pepper pushed away from the counter and paced her shop. "You of all people should know what it's like to have your only child taken from you. Is that really what you want to do? This child needs his mother. I never said I would cut you out completely— you assumed and took it upon yourself to come at me. If you have anything else you need to say, call my attorney. Don't contact me again."

Pepper disconnected the call and held the cell phone to her side. Her whole body trembled and she had no clue how she was going to make it through this custody case. Her sanity could handle only so much and she truly needed to remain stress-free.

After taking several deep breaths and counting backward from fifty, Pepper had reined in her anger and fear...somewhat.

She went to the back and pulled a large painting from her overstock. She needed to straighten up the shop just a bit before leaving. With so many sales today, she had several holes in her displays. Restocking nightly was a wonderful problem to have and it kept her busy. For a few minutes at least, she could keep her mind on doing what she loved.

Nolan had mentioned a surprise for her and between the phone call and gearing up to face him, she needed to do something that was just for her. She was so thankful for this shop, for the talents she possessed that gave her the ability to make a living out of her passions.

It wasn't that long ago that the idea of settling down would have made her twitchy, but now she was thrilled. When she'd left before, she'd been nervous, scared. Then she'd gone and traveled so much and felt so free she hadn't given settling down another thought.

Now that she was back, though, she knew this was the perfect place to set down roots. She wanted her baby to experience the beautiful small town with a large-city feel. The farms, the parks, the amazing school. Everything Pepper had ever loved was right here in Stone River.

Everything and everyone.

She finished the displays and realized she couldn't put off meeting Nolan any longer. She had no idea the surprise he had in store, but if it involved his talented lips or roaming hands, she wasn't sure she had the willpower to keep telling her husband no.

When the back door opened and clicked shut, Pepper

pivoted toward the rear of the store. Who was coming in the back door, which she had locked? The contractor had already left for the day.

Nolan stepped through the opening as if he owned the place—but a man like that dominated anywhere he went. Her heart was no different.

"Did you just get out of work?" she asked.

He continued to stalk toward her with that devilish gleam in his eyes. "I didn't work today. I'm actually off for several days."

Pepper tipped her head to the side and crossed her arms. "Something you failed to mention."

With a careless shrug, he flashed that killer smile. "I was busy doing other things."

"Like trying to get my clothes off?"

His eyes raked over her from head to toe and back up. "When I want your clothes off, darlin', they'll be off. But I didn't want you to get stressed about me being home. I actually took the time off since Hayes is coming in soon. Plus, I thought I could help you."

Pepper narrowed her gaze. "With what?"

"Nothing as naughty as what you're thinking," he assured her with a low, masculine laugh. "I'm taking you to pick out baby things."

"Baby things?"

"Furniture, bedding, clothes. Whatever you want for the baby. Everything, actually, since I'm guessing you haven't bought anything."

Stunned, Pepper blinked, trying to imagine the cost this would be. "No, you don't have to do that."

"You're right, I don't. But I'm going to and you can either come with me and pick out what you want or take the chance with me getting things on my own. I admit I don't know one stroller from the next."

She stared at him, realizing he was completely serious. Emotions overwhelmed her, as the burning in her throat was a telltale sign that she was about to lose it.

"Oh, no." He reached into his pocket and produced a handkerchief. "No tears."

What man carried around a handkerchief? Why did he have to be so incredible when she desperately needed him to be a troll? If he were a troll or a conceited jerk, it would be so much easier to leave him in the end.

But as things stood now, she was sinking further and further into the perfect role of Nolan Elliott's wife… and she loved playing that role. It was what she'd always wanted.

Pepper took the cloth and hiccupped. "Since when do you carry these?"

"Since you started crying."

She dabbed her eyes. "Damn you for making me want to be selfish and take you up on your offer."

"It's not selfish," he corrected, taking the handkerchief from her and gently swiping her cheeks. "You're going to be a wonderful mother. I'm just helping to make the transition easier."

"I don't want you doing this out of guilt."

Nolan dropped his hand and closed the space between them. "I'm doing this because I care for you, Pepper, and I want to give you something to be happy about. For a few hours we're going to forget the case, the renovations and the fact you want me as much as I want you and are fighting it every step of the way."

Pepper opened her mouth to argue, but he put his finger over her parted lips.

"Let's not waste time denying the truth."

She shoved his hand away. "I'm not denying anything,

but I should tell you that Mrs. Wright called me earlier. We need to let your attorney know."

Nolan's face hardened, the muscles in his jaw tensing. "What did she want?"

"To talk to me, mother to mother." Pepper shook her head and released a sigh. "I'll tell you about it later. I want go look at baby things and forget everything else like you suggested. I need some retail therapy in the worst way."

"At the expense of my credit card?" he asked, raising his dark brows.

"Hey, you offered. There's no woman that would turn down a shopping spree on someone else's dime."

With a bark of laughter, Nolan wrapped an arm around her shoulders and started heading toward the back exit.

She stopped just before they reached the door. "Thank you, though. Seriously. I don't know what I'd do without you."

"I have faith in you, Pepper. You would've gotten through this just fine. But as long as I'm around, you won't have to do it alone."

She knew all of that but worried for the day when he wouldn't be around. Because their time together was slowly ticking to a close and eventually he would move on…just like last time. Despite the close bond they were forging now, the end was inevitable and she needed to remind herself of that in an attempt to avoid getting hurt… if such a thing was even possible.

Nolan stared at what used to be his spacious living room. Now the open space was adorned with bags and boxes, a high chair, some portable sleeper he forgot the name of, and piles and piles of clothes. There was also a plethora of rattles, teethers and bibs.

He'd honestly had no idea what he'd been in for when

he suggested going shopping. He figured a crib, some diapers, a stroller, and they'd be outta there. After all, how much stuff did one tiny being need?

Pepper's hands covered her belly as she surveyed all the paraphernalia. Then those gray eyes turned to him and the widest smile spread across her face. And that was when he realized he'd spend three times this amount to see that light back in her eyes. She'd been like a whirlwind going from aisle to aisle in every store he took her to. She'd had the sales clerks fawning all over her.

"Did we go overboard?" she asked innocently.

"Not if you're having quintuplets."

Her nose scrunched as she glanced around the room again. "I did kind of go crazy, didn't I?"

Considering they still had custom-ordered furniture to be delivered in a few weeks, maybe. But he didn't care. Once she'd started, she'd gotten on a roll and he wasn't about to stop her.

"Nothing wrong with being excited. You should see Annabelle and Colt with the twins. Colt is over the moon for those girls. He bought them matching cowgirl boots and hats. They can't even walk yet."

Pepper's eyes went big. "Cowboy boots. Why didn't I think of that?"

"There's still plenty of time," he laughed.

"What if he's not with me when it's time to buy his first pair?" she whispered in a stricken tone.

Heaviness settled in his chest. He'd bargain with the devil himself to make sure she kept her child. He was already working on plan B, but he hoped the Wrights came to their senses before he had to resort to desperate measures.

Nolan crossed to her and pulled her against his chest.

"You will be with your son for all of his firsts. You can't keep letting doubt steal your happiness."

Pepper clutched at his shirt and sniffed. He knew this wasn't all pregnancy hormones. She was legitimately afraid of what the future held.

"Do you trust me?"

When she didn't answer, Nolan eased back and tipped her chin up with his thumb. Misty eyes met his and another punch of guilt hit him in the gut. Of course she didn't trust him. He was still trying to prove to her that he wasn't the man he used to be.

"I won't let them take your son," he vowed. "I know we haven't exactly tackled the past, but you have to believe I will make this right."

Pepper blinked away the tears and attempted a smile. "I believe you'll try, but even you can't play God, Nolan. No matter how much money and resources you have. Ultimately, this will come down to the opinion of a judge. The picture the Wrights are painting of me isn't a flattering one and on paper they are a better choice."

"Like hell they are." He framed her face between his hands to make sure she kept her focus on him. "You can take some time to feel sorry for yourself, but then we're moving on. We're staying positive and we're going to fight this battle together. I married you so you'd keep your son."

Damn it. He cared for her, didn't she see that? After all these years, all this heartache and elapsed time, he cared too damn much and it was tearing him apart.

"I have just as much at stake here, too," he went on, unable to keep his mouth shut. He'd curse himself later for exposing his vulnerable side. "I'm opening myself to the past, seeing you pregnant again, part of me wishing that child was mine."

Pepper's mouth dropped as she continued to stare up at him in disbelief. "You don't mean that," she murmured.

"I don't say anything I don't mean. I want you, Pepper. I want you with a fierceness that didn't exist before. I want you to trust me with everything…and that includes your body. I want more than you just taking my name. I want you in my bed."

He didn't give her a chance to answer. Nolan slammed his mouth over hers, wrapping his arms around her waist to secure her perfectly against his body. He'd think about the consequences later. For now, however, he wanted her with a fiery passion that nearly consumed him. If only he could convince her to let that blasted guard down and allow him in.

Pepper hesitated for all of two seconds, the longest of his life, before she threw her arms around his shoulders and threaded her fingers through his hair.

Nolan scooped her up and carried her to the large leather sectional. Without looking, he swiped a hand over the packages, sending them clattering to the hardwood floors.

"Nolan," she panted against his mouth.

"Don't stop me," he all but begged. Wait, he didn't beg. He'd *never* begged. But he was damn well going to if she put the brakes on.

"I need you," she whispered.

He gazed into her eyes, saw that desire he'd been feeling staring right back at him. Those three words were the sweetest he'd ever heard.

"You'll have me," he promised.

Twelve

Pepper didn't care about all the reasons she shouldn't do this. She didn't care that they were about to consummate the hell out of this marriage. Nolan's lips and hands continued to torment her in the most delicious ways. Everything about this moment was so familiar yet so new. They were different people now but so very much reminiscent of the young lovers they'd once been.

In a flurry of hands and clothes, Pepper found herself beneath Nolan. Her bare back against the leather, his weight settled between her thighs. He brushed her hair away from her face, dropping heated kisses along her jawline.

Pepper arched her back, needing more, aching for a touch and a passion only this man could provide. Her husband. She was about to make love to her *husband*.

"I don't have protection," she confessed, hating to discuss this in the midst of things, but it was necessary.

Resting his weight on his forearms alongside her head, he met her gaze. "I'm clean, Pepper. You're the only other woman I've not been careful with and I have regular blood work."

"I'm clean, too."

She wasn't about to get into how she became pregnant because of a condom malfunction. Now wasn't the time to bring that story to light.

Pepper wrapped her legs around Nolan's waist, locking her knees behind his back. The silent plea for him to join their bodies worked like a charm. Nolan slid into her and everything else ceased to exist. *Finally.* That was the only thought that entered her mind. She was finally back where she belonged.

Nolan shifted his weight and stilled. "Am I hurting you, darlin'?"

"No." She trailed her fingertips over his taut, muscular back. "You're perfect."

And he was. Perfect now, perfect in her life, perfect as her husband. But she refused to delve into the fact that this was all temporary. She was holding on to this moment, this man.

Nolan's weight pressing her into the sofa was absolutely glorious. His strength, his determination to make her his top priority, was even more arousing than nearly anything else. He cared for her, whether he wanted to admit how deeply or not. The way he touched her with such exquisite tenderness, the way he moved with her, caressing her and raining kisses all over her face and neck…it was abundantly clear that his feelings went far beyond just that of a physical relationship and marriage of convenience. This entire ordeal was anything but convenient.

Nolan's warm breath tickled the side of her neck as he

rested his forehead against hers. Pepper was barely holding on—she didn't want this to end, didn't want to face the other side of their intimacy. But her body had other ideas. The faster he moved, the more Pepper lost control, until she finally could hold out no longer.

Her entire body tightened as she clutched his shoulders. He whispered something in her ear, but she couldn't make it out. Every part of her trembled and before she could come down from her high, Nolan followed. He arched back, the muscles in his neck straining, his shoulders tense as he tried to keep his weight off her. Even now, she was his number one thought.

Pepper stroked her hands up and down his back as his breathing started to slow back to normal. When he eased up, she pressed her palms flat against him.

"Stay here. You're not hurting me and this feels too good."

Once he got up, they'd have to talk or wallow in awkward silence. But she wasn't ready for either option at the moment.

"If I'd known shopping for baby things was all it took to get you naked, I would've done this on day one."

Pepper laughed. So much for the awkward silence. "That's not why we ended up here. I'd say it was inevitable, even though that annulment is going to be impossible now."

He lifted his head and flashed that killer smile. "Baby, I could've told you that. There's no way I can be with you again, especially in my house, and not have you."

"This could complicate things."

"It could if we let it." He shifted once again, somehow flipping them to where she straddled his lap and she found herself looking down into his deep blue eyes. "We're adults, we're married, we know this is temporary. Why can't we just enjoy each other for as long as it lasts?"

He made the situation sound so simple. But her heart was already tumbling and she had no doubt that she was going to leave at the end of this ordeal with a heartache. Would the pain compare to the last time? She had no clue, but she truly didn't want to be so broken. It had taken her literally years to recover.

"Don't worry about tomorrow," he told her quietly. His hands settled over her belly. "This little guy is all that matters and I'm here to make sure you both get what you deserve. And that's a lifetime of happiness."

A lifetime without Nolan in her life. Once he saw that she was secure, he'd move on. He'd go back to being married to his work. He'd made no promises beyond helping her keep her baby and she should be grateful. She *was* grateful, but she was also greedy. Now that she'd slept with him, she feared walking away wouldn't be an option, and Nolan wasn't about to make this marriage permanent.

Which brought her right back around to that heartache she didn't want. A little too late to be having regrets, she reminded herself. She needed this marriage, needed Nolan, and her feelings didn't matter in the long run.

When he slid his hands up her abdomen and over her breasts, Pepper let the worries go for now. It was getting late and her husband clearly had other plans…

The pounding on the door jolted Nolan from sleep. In a tangle of arms and legs, he quickly realized he and Pepper hadn't moved from the couch. Apparently they'd worn each other out.

With a quick glance, he saw that his wife was still asleep. Her dark lashes lay against her creamy skin, her slightly parted mouth sorely tempting him to ignore the knocking and remain right where he was...taking full advantage of those lush lips.

Pepper stirred, and Nolan quickly untangled himself. He wanted to get to the door before the uninvited visitor woke her.

Scanning the room, he finally spotted his boxer briefs and jeans. He danced from one leg to the other down the hallway, and he'd just gotten the jeans zipped when he reached the door. He quickly flipped the lock and jerked the door open.

"Oh." Annabelle jumped back, a hand over her heart. "I thought you were home, but..."

She raked her eyes over him. "I'm so sorry. I didn't realize you'd still be in bed."

Nolan propped his forearm on the edge of the door. "It's okay. Late night."

"Winnie made extra rolls and a casserole for you."

It was then he noticed the large basket in her hand. Damn it. He didn't want to be rude, but he also didn't want her coming in and risking seeing Pepper wearing nothing but bedhead and whisker burn.

"I can take it." He reached for the basket, but she eased it to the side and raised her brows.

"You don't want to introduce me to your wife? We're sisters-in-law, so I really should get to know her."

Nolan combed a hand through his hair and groaned. "She's—"

"Right here."

He cringed at the sound of Pepper's sexy, sleep-roughened voice behind him. Risking a glance over his shoulder, he got an eyeful of her. Even with her hair in disarray, her face void of any makeup, and her curvy body wrapped in the gray throw he kept on the sofa, Pepper was truly the most beautiful woman he'd ever seen.

"I'm so sorry." Annabelle stepped over the threshold, forcing Nolan to move back. "I just assumed Nolan would be at work and I'd get to sneak a visit with you privately."

Nolan closed the door behind her—apparently they were getting company whether he wanted it or not. He loved Annabelle like a sister, but he wasn't quite ready to share Pepper with anyone just yet.

"So you thought you'd come quiz my wife and get in some girl talk?" Nolan asked, reaching to take the basket.

Annabelle flashed him a sheepish smile. "Maybe."

"Well, let me throw some clothes on," Pepper said. "We can kick Nolan out and get that talk in. I'm so excited to meet you. Mostly I'm excited to have another female around."

Annabelle sent him a wink as she strode on into the house. Fantastic. Despite being a man who didn't want to get sucked too far into this family lifestyle, he'd slept with his wife, forging an even deeper bond, and now his soon-to-be sister-in-law was fostering her own special connection with Pepper. And that bond would be worse because women stuck together. So if he did anything wrong or hurt Pepper in any way, Annabelle would naturally side with Pepper. Then she would tell Colt, and Nolan would have to hear about it from his baby brother.

The inevitable snowball effect already gave him a migraine.

One thing was for sure, Nolan didn't want to stay around for this little meeting. He had a few days off and he intended to get back to his roots and enjoy some old-fashioned manual labor. No doubt Colt would appreciate the extra hands.

Besides, this would give him some space to figure

out where to go from here. Turned out he wasn't done with Pepper. Not by a long shot. They'd consummated their marriage, but he wanted more. More of Pepper in his life…and in his bed. This marriage might be in name only for the sake of her unborn child, but as long as they were man and wife, he fully intended to use that to his advantage. He doubted he'd get too many complaints from Pepper if that satisfied smile on her face this morning was any indicator.

He couldn't wait to get back and have her all to himself again.

Thirteen

"I should apologize about barging in, but I've been dying to meet you."

Pepper laughed, appreciating the woman's candor. "These cinnamon rolls smell delicious."

"Yeah, Winnie is a master in the kitchen."

Pepper sat down across from Annabelle. Once Nolan had left—more like made tracks getting out of his house—Pepper had led Annabelle out into the enclosed patio room. The mouthwatering aroma of the fresh pastries had reminded Pepper just how hungry she truly was. Last night had…well, it had been nothing short of amazing and magical and all of those euphoric adjectives that came to mind when describing the best sexual experience of her life.

"And she didn't want to bring these and check me out herself?"

Annabelle laughed as she tore apart a gooey roll. "She said she remembers you from when you and Nolan were together before. She said she always liked you and I could take a turn coming. But be warned. She's preparing more food for tomorrow and will be here to pay you a visit."

"I'll be fat by the time this marriage is over." She smoothed a hand down her swollen midsection. "Well, fatter."

"You're stunning." Annabelle's brows rose as she twisted the diamond engagement ring on her finger. "So you're only married for the baby?"

Why lie? It wasn't like they had to pretend to be in love. Love didn't exist, not for them, anyway. No matter how much Pepper felt for Nolan, she knew better than to hope for a happily-ever-after with him. She was a grown woman, a realistic woman, and had her eyes wide-open.

"I just want to keep custody," she explained, pulling apart her roll. "The father of my baby passed away, something I didn't know until recently, because we had parted ways before I even found out I was expecting. He paid me a lump sum of money as his way of support and wanted to be left out of the upbringing."

"Sounds like a jerk," Annabelle muttered. "Sorry. Go on."

Pepper put a bite in her mouth and nearly moaned as the flavors exploded on her tongue. This might be the best thing she'd ever tasted.

"They're amazing, right?" Annabelle said around her own bite.

"I can't even find words," Pepper groaned. "Where was I?"

"Discussing why your marriage is going to end."

Pepper took a sip of her juice and ripped off another bite. "Nolan and I have a history. I don't know what all Colt has told you."

"He pretty much gave me all the details of the past."

That made this conversation a bit easier. "Then that brings you up to speed on why this is so awkward for us now. I mean, those old feelings are there, but then there's so much going on and we definitely aren't the same people we used to be."

Annabelle reached across the table and patted Pepper's hand. "Honey, life knocks us all down, but it's those feelings deep down, those that you can't ignore, that pull you through."

Pepper drew in a shaky breath. She didn't want to count on those feelings that lived deep inside her. Those were the ones that scared her, the ones that kept her up at night and made her wonder.

"Well, I've got so much going on right now I can't even think about my feelings for Nolan."

"You love him." Annabelle's matter-of-fact tone had Pepper stilling. "I saw it in the way you looked at him. He loves you, too, or you wouldn't be here."

"Oh, I'm not so sure about that," Pepper laughed, trying to lighten the intense mood. "He's a player. That much I know for sure."

"Maybe so, but he's never brought another woman here. Colt said he's been very adamant about that. He thinks of this place as some type of sanctuary, someplace he can escape everything and be alone. His job is demanding and so is the ranch."

Pepper waved a hand in the air before diving back into her roll. "He married me to help me out of a bind... that's all. It would've looked rather silly for us to live separately. Besides, my apartment had a slight fire. It's getting renovated now."

Annabelle quirked a brow and smiled. "But he didn't

have to do anything, did he? He could've let you deal with everything on your own."

No, no, he didn't have to step in, but guilt often made people do things they otherwise wouldn't. Pepper wasn't going to keep defending her position, because she was exhausted and Annabelle clearly had stars in her eyes. Of course she was happy, engaged to an Elliott brother and raising twin babies. Her whole world was perfectly in place. Pepper wanted to visit there for just a bit. What she wouldn't give to have just one day of pure bliss and no worries...

"Let's not talk about my crazy life," Pepper said. "I want to hear about your girls. Nolan said you have twin girls. I bet you're tired."

Annabelle laughed. "It's challenging, for sure. But they're so sweet and fun."

"I'd love to meet them."

"Of course." Annabelle took a drink of her juice, holding on to her cup as she swirled the liquid. "They're with my dad right now. I didn't know if I should bombard you with my zoo for our first meeting. I didn't want to scare you in case I liked you and wanted to be friends."

With a laugh, Pepper leaned back in her seat and shook her head. "Please. I'd love to be bombarded by babies. I have no idea what to expect and I'm terrified."

"That's understandable," the other woman told her with a sympathetic smile. "Why don't you come down to the main house and you can meet them? Unless you have something else you're doing this morning."

Pepper smiled, feeling like she was making a new friend, and one she desperately needed. A female ally could quite possibly be the outlet she needed to get through.

Because in a few hours, Nolan would be back and

they'd have to talk about last night. She wanted to know where they'd go from here. She didn't want to play that female card and ask for a label on their relationship— this complicated mess was too chaotic to try to define. But she did feel that she deserved to know what he was thinking and feeling.

And she'd be sure to guard her own emotions until she knew. Getting a broken heart from Nolan Elliott once in her life was all she could handle.

"If you slam one more thing, I'm going to make you leave."

Nolan gripped the brush, ready to fling it back into the bucket, but caught himself. He'd been in a pissy mood since leaving his house. Probably right about now, he figured, the women were knee-deep in gossip, and he'd wager a bet that every topic had his name on it.

He scowled, wishing Annabelle had never shown up at his door with those damn cinnamon rolls. The last thing he'd wanted was to leave Pepper after their incredible night together. He'd wanted to stay, to take her upstairs, and do it all over again. But would she welcome this new twist in their relationship? Or would she put the brakes on because she didn't want to get too attached? He knew Pepper well enough to know she led with her heart.

When he'd first left, he'd been in a great mood, thinking of last night and how happy Pepper had seemed. But then reality settled deep and now that devil on his shoulder was putting negative thoughts in his head.

He thought he'd grown since they'd been together last. He'd believed he could sleep with Pepper without getting more involved. But he'd been a fool. The daydreams he had about her, about this marriage, were all too real… and all too consuming.

Damn it. He didn't want to hurt her, but he wasn't about to turn back. He wanted his wife in the most basic, primal way a man wanted a woman. And now that he'd had her again, all that passion they'd shared before came rushing back and he refused to let it go after he'd had a taste.

"Bad night?" Colt asked, stepping into the doorway of the stall. "Or are you mad because Annabelle interrupted something?"

Nolan grunted. "Shut up."

"You're the one who got yourself into this mess. Don't get grouchy with me."

Nolan tossed the brush into the bucket anyway. "You think I don't know how I got into this? I had little choice, though."

Colt hooked his thumbs in his belt and shook his head. "You don't believe that any more than I do."

Nolan didn't know what to believe. Right now he was too keyed up about last night to worry about too much more. Having Pepper back in his bed, so to speak, was all he'd wanted, a temptation he couldn't resist. But now that he'd had her, he wasn't so sure he wanted her to be anywhere else. Of course, then there was the whole issue that he didn't want to be married with a family, yet here he was. He'd *volunteered* to put himself in that exact position.

Nolan patted Doc's side. He needed a good ride, but he'd groomed his stallion instead. Doc needed some downtime today.

"All I know is she's turning me inside out, but then I think, this is not my cross to bear."

"Are you sure about that? Sounds like years of guilt have caught up with you."

Nolan blew out a breath and turned to face his baby

brother. "I can't turn back the clock. I'm not the same young jerk I was, but I'm honest about what I can give. She knows I'm still not wanting a family. We're taking it day by day, I guess."

Colt merely raised his brows but Nolan didn't care what his brother thought, or anyone else, for that matter. He had enough of his own turmoil to deal with.

"You're playing house with a woman you were once in love with who's pregnant and back in town for good, and you think you can be this calm about it?" Colt snorted and tipped his hat back on his head. "I'll play along with your delusions if you want. Besides, I'll get all the details from Annabelle when she comes home later."

Growling, Nolan pushed passed his brother. He headed down the stone walkway between the stalls and ignored Colt's obnoxious laughter. Surely Pepper wouldn't spill everything. Of course, there was no hiding the fact Annabelle had gotten them out of bed, or off the couch, as the case may be. That would be enough fuel for Colt to assume that Nolan was falling into this whole married-bliss phase.

Nolan refused to let that happen. Yes, he might want to be physical with Pepper, he might be doing all of this to help her, and fine, he might be a tad jealous that she carried another man's baby, but he didn't want to settle down for real. Wasn't his life busy enough? He was perfectly fulfilled without adding more. Being a doctor and a rancher was full-time. Adding a child into the mix would only spread him even thinner and that wouldn't be fair to an innocent baby.

"You still picking Hayes up from the airport?" Nolan asked as he grabbed a blanket. He planned on taking out Lightning, Colt's stallion.

"That's my horse," Colt stated. "Use your own."

"Mine needs to rest and you haven't taken Lightning out yet." Nolan ignored his brother's protest. "I need to get away and think. I'll do a perimeter check of the fence line."

"Running from your problems didn't work so well the first time you were with Pepper. What makes you think it will this time?"

Nolan tossed the blanket over Lightning's back and smoothed it out. "I didn't come down here to ask your opinion. I came to work, to ride and to give the women time to talk about us and do their nails…or whatever the hell else they're doing."

Colt laughed. Bastard. Nolan wasn't in the mood for jokes or laughter. He wanted to wallow in his dark mood because the more he thought about last night, the more he was conflicted. He wanted to go back to the house and take Pepper to his bed and forget the world existed.

Nolan fixed the saddle in place and threw a glance toward Colt. "I'll bring him back in a few hours."

"Why don't you let me and my guys do the work and you go back home to Pepper?"

Nolan led Lightning outside. Colt followed behind. "Why don't you focus on your own woman and leave mine to me."

He mounted the stallion and kicked him into a gallop. Nolan could get work done and hopefully clear his head. By the time he got back home, maybe he'd have all the answers. Most likely he'd still be confused, but he was sure of one thing…he'd still want Pepper in his bed. That would never change. It was just what they would do outside the bedroom that he had to worry about.

Fourteen

Nolan slid his cell back into his pocket and breathed a sigh of relief. Well, somewhat. His PI had dug through the Wrights' dirty laundry and discovered something useful. If that family was going to fight, he was damn well going to come back at them full force.

He couldn't wait to tell Pepper. She needed something positive to focus on right now and discussing the case, in a positive way, would hopefully alleviate some of the awkwardness that would surely surround them as soon as he stepped inside and they were alone once again.

He'd been gone over three hours and had no more answers now than he had when he set out to check the fence lines. He needed a shower, he could use a drink, and he wanted his wife. If he could multitask and have all three at the same time, well, he'd call this day one of the best in a long time.

The shrieking alarm echoing through the open patio doors had Nolan charging inside, the fantasy ripped away.

Why the hell was his smoke alarm going off? Where was Pepper? Was she okay?

As soon as he stepped into the kitchen, he quickly realized she was indeed okay…but their dinner wasn't. Pepper had a towel and was smacking the hell out of a casserole dish on top of the stove. Nolan couldn't help the laugh that escaped him.

Pepper spun around, met his gaze, then saw that her towel was on fire, so she beat the casserole once again. With a sigh and a muttered curse, she tossed the towel into the sink in the center island and doused it with water. When she leaned her hands on the smooth granite countertop, Nolan crossed the room.

"There's always takeout."

Pepper narrowed her eyes. "If you tell Winnie that I burnt her casserole, I will tell her about the time you used her favorite pan to make me dinner and ruined it because you burnt the bottom and she never could figure out who did it."

Nolan mimicked her actions and rested his palms on the island opposite her. "She'll never hear it from me. But tell me, was it the chicken-and-broccoli casserole? Because that's my favorite and I'd hate to cry in front of you."

"Actually, it was. I guess I owe you one." Pepper wrinkled her nose. "I'm really sorry. I wanted to have a late lunch all planned and I wasn't sure when you'd be back. I was getting hungry and I figured I'd heat this up, but then I called the doctor and got sidetracked—"

"What doctor? Why?" Immediately, he came around the side of the island and gripped her shoulders, turning her to face him. "What's wrong?"

"I just had some minor bleeding, but I wasn't cramping or anything and it stopped almost as fast as it started. I just wanted them to know."

"I'm your first call if something is wrong," he commanded. "I could've taken you to the hospital to get checked out. Matter of fact, let's go. We'll get an ultrasound and listen for the baby's heartbeat and—"

"I'm fine," she assured him. "I've felt the baby move and my doctor promised that this was normal and most likely from intercourse. Every pregnancy is different, so there's no textbook case. He said as long as I feel fine and I still feel the baby, there's nothing to be alarmed about."

But there was everything to be alarmed about. When she'd miscarried before, she'd felt fine. Everything had been going great with the pregnancy, their child had been healthy...and then suddenly out of the blue she was gone.

The fear of years ago slithered through him, squeezing like a vise around his chest.

"Go up and lie down. I'll make something and bring it to you."

Pepper tipped her head to the side. "I'm perfectly fine. I know what my body needs and right now it's just food. I've been sitting all day talking with Annabelle. I went down to their house and met the twins. They are absolutely adorable, by the way."

Nolan slid his hands down her arms, feathering his touch until he stepped back for distance. "You probably overdid it, then. Those girls are a handful."

Pepper smiled and patted his cheek. "They're twins under a year old. Of course they're a handful. That's pretty much their only job right now."

"Still, you don't need to be doing too much."

Pepper glanced to the stove, where the dish was still smoking. "Apparently, I can't do anything. I could probably whip up a grilled cheese. I'd say that's safe."

Nolan pulled his hat off and swiped his forehead with the back of his arm. "I need a shower in the worst way.

I was going to have you join me, but I don't think that's a good idea with hemorrhaging."

Those bright eyes widened. "Nolan, I'm not here to scratch your itch or be at your command. Yes, I want you and I'm not sorry for last night, but I also can't pretend this is real."

Well, the way she said it made him sound foolish.

"I won't apologize for wanting you, Pepper." And he wouldn't look coldhearted, either. "Our feelings are mutual and you can't deny that you want more. We may be a paper marriage only, but there's no reason to play the game and dance around the sexual attraction. We already proved that doesn't work."

"Maybe you're out of my system now."

When she cocked her hip and quirked her brow, Nolan took that challenge and opted to call her on it. He snaked his arms around her waist and pulled her flush against his body. Torso to torso, pelvis to pelvis. Her eyes widened with surprise. Then they betrayed her as they darted to his mouth.

"You were saying?" he murmured as he leaned in to slide his lips over hers.

"You're going to at least rest on the couch," he told her, his lips hovering over hers. "I'm going to work on dinner and grab a quick shower. You're not to move a muscle. For the rest of the day, I'll be doing everything for you."

She let out a slight whimper, one he knew she meant to hold in. He couldn't help but smile. The amount of willpower she had was no match for him. He'd bust down every barrier she tried to put up, because his need for her wasn't even close to being sated. Last night only served as a reminder of all he'd missed with her and all he wanted to explore again and again.

"I don't need to be pampered," she muttered.

Nolan gripped her backside. "Maybe it's time I showed you that's exactly what you deserve."

"You're going to make me want." She closed her eyes and rested her forehead against his. "I can't, Nolan. I can't want you."

"Keep telling yourself that."

He covered her mouth with his, and she melted against him. He didn't need to use words to prove her wrong. She couldn't deny the pull between them any more than he could. Their physical attraction had never faded, even with the gap of time they'd lost.

Nolan ended the kiss as abruptly as he'd started it, pleased when Pepper leaned forward and had to stop herself.

"I'll get that shower and have lunch for you in no time, babe."

He turned and headed out of the room, but not before he heard her mutter, "I'm not your babe."

That stopped him. Something snapped inside him. After what they'd been through, all of it up to this point, she was his and damn it, he was going to prove to her that she couldn't lie—not to herself, not to him.

Nolan turned back around, crossed the space and enveloped her in his arms. He claimed her mouth as he arched her backward, completely consuming her. He craved this woman like nothing else and the way she gripped his biceps, moaning as his lips crushed hers, only proved she wanted this, too.

He slid his mouth along her jawline, down her throat. Pushing the strap of her tank and bra aside, he continued to trail his mouth along her heated skin. Pepper's fingertips glided through his hair as she panted his name.

"Never say you're not mine again," he growled against her lips as he released her breast.

"Nolan…"

That's right. His name would be the only one on her lips. He might not be able to make love to her now because of her tender state, but he could damn well stake his claim and have her coming apart in his arms.

He yanked her skirt to the ground to puddle at her feet. Then, stepping back, he took in the sight of her hair in disarray, her tank half hanging on her body and her standing before him in only her panties. The round belly had him reaching out, placing his palms possessively on her as he met her gaze.

Pepper's breath came out fast, her lips wet and swollen from the proof of his desire.

He fisted a handful of her hair and guided her head to the side as he went back in for another taste. Easing his fingertips along the edge of her panties, he nearly lost it when she moaned and widened her stance.

Nolan rubbed her, teasing her mercilessly, and had her jerking her hips against him. In no time she went over the brink, tearing her mouth from his as he watched her squeeze her eyes shut and cry out in pleasure.

This was the most erotic sight he'd ever seen and he damn well wasn't ready to give it up anytime soon. As long as Pepper lived in his house, legally carried his name, she was his.

"Of course. I'll be right there."

Nolan hung up his phone and shoved it back in the pocket of his jeans. Pepper had just finished her grilled chicken and salad. She wiped her mouth with her napkin and sat up in her seat.

Their intense make-out session nearly an hour ago had left both of them ravenous. He'd wanted nothing more than to take her upstairs and lay her out on his bed and finish what they'd started. But he worried it might be too much. Soon, though. He just wanted to follow up with the doctor himself and hear that she was okay.

"What's wrong?" she asked.

Nolan grabbed his keys off the counter and headed toward the garage door off the kitchen. "It's my dad. He fell and the nurse thought I'd want to come assess him before they decided what to do."

Pepper knew his father lived in an assisted-living facility. She came to her feet. "I'll go with you."

"Stay here. Dealing with my father isn't part of our agreement."

Pepper reeled back as if he'd slapped her. "You're right. It's not, but I thought…forget it. Go on."

Nolan took a step toward her. "Pepper—"

"No." She held her hands out. "You're right. This isn't a real marriage and I'm not part of your life like I used to be."

Emotions threatened to consume her, so she spun around and headed for the living room. She didn't want to see Nolan's look of regret, because she was coming to realize the only thing he regretted was the fact he was stuck with her…or at least that was how it felt.

"Come with me."

Pepper froze in the wide doorway. Nolan's boots shuffled against the hardwood as he moved in behind her. She took a deep breath.

"Just go, Nolan. This is ridiculous to argue about. I'm going to go into the shop and paint. I also want to see how the renovations are coming." Ready to face him, she shifted around. "We don't have to do things together— your family isn't actually mine, I know. I don't need the reminder."

Nolan shoved a hand through his hair, still damp from the shower. "I have to go. I want you with me."

Pepper forced a smile. "No, you don't. Your first instinct was to close me out. There's no need to apologize for being who you are."

Now Pepper did leave the kitchen and went to compose herself in the privacy of her own room. She'd change her clothes and go into the shop. The sooner her apartment was ready, the sooner she would be that much closer to getting back to the life she'd planned. All she needed was her baby…not the reminder that she and Nolan were only pretending to be a fairy-tale couple.

Pepper walked through her apartment, admiring the new touches that were being added as well as how everything was blending with the old charm of the building. The kitchen had custom white cabinets now as opposed to the old dated oak. The backsplash looked like something out of a magazine. She leaned over the open cabinet. She had no idea what the countertop would look like once installed, but as she ran her fingertip over the backsplash, she marveled at the smooth glass finish in a pale blue.

If the half-done kitchen was looking this modern yet cozy and chic, she couldn't wait to see the final product. She'd definitely have to paint some new pieces to be added into her new space.

Careful to step over tools and materials, Pepper made her way down the hall. The room she planned on using for the nursery had the door closed. The last time she'd stopped in, it had been open, and she'd gone in and done a little fantasy decorating.

Pepper eased the door open and stood in shock as she took in the sight of a nearly finished nursery. The far wall with two windows had been painted navy. A silhouette of a horse with two colts was painted in a pale gray between the two windows. The other three walls were the same pale gray and had various rustic touches. There was a cluster of wood slats with horseshoes hanging at an angle as if to be used for hooks. One wall had a cowboy hat and in cursive font curving around the brim it said Future Cowboy.

Pepper noted the new hardwood floors in a dark wood that went with the male theme. Everything was perfect. She hadn't told Nolan or even the contractor she wanted this room done, and she actually wasn't a bit upset that she didn't get to paint it. This was exactly what she would've wanted for her son. Something simple yet very much part of the lifestyle that would embrace him here in Stone River, Texas.

There was no way the contractor had done all of this on his own, or even at all. And there was no doubt who was the mastermind behind this decision.

One minute he was shutting her out, the next he was going out of his way to make sure she had everything she needed. How could she keep up with her already jumbled emotions?

The shifting in her belly had her placing her hands over the movement. In a few months she could welcome her son into this room. She could already imagine a rocker in the corner where she'd cuddle him to sleep. She'd always heard about that special bond between a mother and her son, and Pepper was convinced now more than ever that they would be tight. After all, who else did they have?

They would be a team and she would protect him from all harm. And that included letting strangers raise him. Pepper would be absolutely gutted if she had to hand over her child. To lose a child in any way was something no parent should have to go through—didn't the Wrights see that?

Pepper's cell chimed from the pocket of her maxi skirt. She reached in and frowned at the display. Why would the attorney be calling on a Saturday?

This couldn't be a good sign, could it? Was something wrong? Had there been a crimp in the case?

With a shaky hand, she answered.

"Hello?"

"Pepper, I tried calling Nolan, but he didn't answer. I hope this isn't a bad time."

Of course he hadn't answered. He was with his father and he was off work for the next few days.

"No. This is fine. Is something wrong?" There seemed to be so many ups and downs lately, she didn't know how many more she could handle.

"Nolan had hired an investigator to dig into the Wrights," he stated.

Pepper gripped the phone. She'd been completely unaware of any of this. Why hadn't he told her what he'd done? How much more had that cost? She refused to be any more indebted to him than she already was, but part of her was thrilled he'd thought to have them investigated. That was brilliant, especially because she needed to know everything about the couple who could possibly take her son from her.

Still, why hadn't Nolan told her? Sure, they were married just for pretenses, but this was a big deal and he'd kept vital information from her.

"Their attorney has been notified of the findings and the Wrights want to know if you would consider settling out of court. They've offered one generous sum to compensate you."

"What the hell does that mean?" she all but yelled.

"They want to buy my child? They offered money once and I don't care what they're offering now. I won't take it."

Pepper's heart kicked up as fury bubbled within her. "What were the findings from the investigator?"

"Apparently the Wrights owe quite a bit of back taxes and their financial state isn't as glossy as they like to portray."

Pepper considered exactly what this meant. "How would they pay me, then?" she asked.

"I have no clue," he replied. "But I think they're going to tell you anything to get custody at this point. They've lost their son and they desperately want to hang on to him in any way possible."

Pepper understood that need. She'd do anything to hang on to her son, as well. Hadn't she married the only man she'd ever loved? Wasn't she living in his home, playing house, just to make sure her son remained with her?

Already she was that parent who would go to any length to make a secure, stable environment for her child. And she wasn't the least bit sorry. Her emotions, her worries about her own life, didn't matter.

"I have my store to run, so any meeting would have to be in the evening and Nolan goes back to work next week," she explained.

"I'll get it set up and let you know. We're going to win this, Pepper. It's almost over."

She could only nod as emotions threatened to overtake her. Damn pregnancy hormones.

After disconnecting the call, she gave a final once-over to the nursery. Inspiration for new paintings flooded her mind and she was eager to get downstairs. To have her own artwork in her son's room was an absolute must.

She needed to do something creative—that was the only way she'd calm her mind. Not to mention that seemed to be the only thing she could control right now. Her emotions were out of her control, this case was out of her control, and her marriage was out of her control. Coincidentally, Nolan occupied real estate in each of those areas.

She'd let his words hurt her earlier and she knew better than that. For a moment, she'd let that guard down and her heart had suffered the fallout. She wouldn't make that mistake again.

Fifteen

By the time Pepper got home, she was definitely relaxed. So much so she felt as if she could fall asleep at any minute. She'd painted three pictures, all with her son's room in mind, but she wasn't sure how she'd arrange them. Once she had the furniture placed, she'd get a better idea of how she wanted all of the wall art.

She came through the garage door that led to the kitchen. The four globe lights suspended over the massive island were on, but Nolan wasn't in here. His vehicles were here, but he could've taken the four-wheeler down to one of the stables.

Her stomach growled and she nearly groaned. The pretzels and banana she'd shoved in her purse and devoured two hours ago had already worn off. She wasn't about to attempt to make something, and most likely Nolan had already had dinner, so she figured she'd go for the mature peanut-butter-and-jelly sandwich.

Pepper slipped her sandals off by the door and dropped her bag onto the kitchen table. Her bangle bracelets jingled with each movement. She'd put on her favorite set earlier, the one with the newest charm of a silver baby rattle. It was just one of the many pieces that had been waiting for her in her new closet when she'd come to Nolan's house.

"Hey."

Nolan came through the wide doorway and strode toward her. With a smile lighting his handsome face, those well-worn jeans hugging his narrow hips and a fitted gray T-shirt showing off his muscles, he didn't look like a master surgeon...he looked like every woman's fantasy.

"How's your dad?" she asked.

"He's all right. He fell trying to get into bed and he's bruised his hip pretty good, but thankfully, nothing is broken." Nolan crossed the room, his eyes raking over her. "You look exhausted."

"Ironically, I feel exhausted." She yawned, unable to hold it back. "I'm ready for food and bed. In that order, but hopefully within the next few minutes for both."

Nolan laughed and reached out. Before she realized his intent, he'd scooped her up and cradled her against his chest. Pepper didn't have much choice, so she looped her arms around his neck.

"And what are you doing?" she asked breathlessly as he carried her out of the room.

"Apologizing for being a jerk earlier and showing you that you deserve to be pampered. I wasn't sure when you'd be home, but I knew you'd be hungry and probably tired."

When he stepped into the living room, Pepper gasped at the spread on the floor. Laid out over the dark hardwood floors was a thick blanket. Random takeout boxes were set off to one side, bottles of water and a small bouquet of wildflowers next to the boxes.

"Are you apologizing or seducing me again?" she asked coyly. Suddenly her hurt from earlier disappeared, replaced by an emotion she refused to identify because that would cross that line into opening her heart.

"Both." He looked down into her eyes, and for a moment Pepper forgot this was all a farce. "Maybe I want to seduce my wife, to show her that even though this is all temporary, I still care for her and want her to be happy."

Temporary. Yes. She'd do well to remember that.

Nolan set her on her feet. "I have a variety of tasty offerings, and I promise you won't leave here hungry."

Pepper took a seat on the blanket and crisscrossed her legs in front of her. Nolan sat across from her and opened the basket. As he pulled out dish after dish, Pepper was utterly stunned. Fruits, cheeses, crisp veggies. He even had fried chicken that instantly hit her senses and made her mouth water.

"This is Winnie's fried chicken," he explained as he settled all the food between them. "I actually just got back from getting it. I was afraid you'd get home while I was gone."

And there went those emotions. Pepper couldn't control the tears; she didn't even try. "Damn it. Why do you do this to me?"

Nolan leaned forward and swiped her cheek with the pad of his thumb. "Because you deserve it. I keep telling you that. One day you'll listen."

Why couldn't he see what a perfect husband he'd be? Well, he was a great husband now, but for the long term, for real, Nolan would be every woman's dream.

His cell chimed and he groaned. "I'm not on call, so I

know it's not the hospital. But I need to answer that because it could be about my dad."

Pepper waved her hand. "Go. I don't expect you to drop everything for me."

"Why not?" Nolan's eyes held hers as the phone continued to intrude on their moment. "You should always come first."

Pepper wasn't quite sure how to respond to that comment, so she reached for a plump strawberry. She popped it in her mouth and surveyed the rest of the spread.

"I suppose I have you to thank for the nursery in my apartment," she stated softly, ready to move on to another topic, something less to do with feelings and this new territory they'd ventured into.

Nolan nodded. "I know you'll want to decorate your way, so I told the decorator to keep it to a minimum and if you weren't pleased, she'll come back and do what you want."

"It's perfect. How did you pull all that off?"

Nolan grabbed a piece of fried chicken. "I paid her extra to come when you weren't in the shop. I didn't want you to know. Whenever you're ready, we can haul all of your baby things to the apartment and I'll help you set up his room."

Pepper's heart squeezed, but she faked a smile. "Already counting down the days until you're rid of me?"

His intense blue eyes came up to lock on to hers. "I figured you were ready for your own space and to move forward with your life when this case is over. You're more than welcome to stay here as long as you like."

He didn't mean that. Because as long as she liked would be forever, as man and wife, till death do them part.

Pepper analyzed each piece of chicken and chose the

perfect one. She tore off the crispy skin and popped a bite into her mouth, nearly groaning when all those flavors hit her at once.

"You always loved Winnie's fried chicken."

Nolan was watching her, a hunger in his own eyes that was all too familiar. This *entire setup* was all too familiar.

"The first time I had her fried chicken, you set up a carpet picnic for me," she recalled. "You surprised me and I think that's when I fell in love with you."

She didn't look away; she wasn't sorry she'd told him. He knew how she'd felt when they were together before. But this was completely different. In the time they were spending together now, they seemed to be forging a deeper bond than ever before.

"We were in love," he said gruffly, still holding her gaze. "I just…couldn't be what you wanted."

And he still couldn't. The words hung in the air between them just the same as if he'd said them aloud.

"No matter how grief stricken I was, I should've been there for you when you miscarried." He shook his head and glanced down to the blanket. "That was my child, too."

"I mourned for our baby for so long—part of me still does," she admitted.

"I mourned." His words were so low she was almost convinced she hadn't heard correctly. "After you left, I wondered what the hell I'd done. I thought of the baby that I would never see. I couldn't describe my feelings. My family was furious about how I'd treated you. It was a dark time for me."

Up until she'd lost the baby, she'd been convinced they'd marry and live happily ever after. But that was a foolish fantasy of a young, guileless girl who thought love could carry them through life.

She knew better now.

"Well, we can't go back." Pepper attempted a smile, but she hurt. Her heart literally hurt for that young couple they'd been, for the dreams she'd thought they shared but that had been only one-sided. "Thanks for everything you've done. Whether out of guilt or because you are genuinely concerned, I know this will only help my case."

Nolan leaned across the blanket. His hand gently cupped the side of her face as his lips grazed hers. Pepper closed her eyes, giving in to the moment. Letting him have his way, because she was just as eager for a taste of him.

Every time he touched her, kissed her, looked at her like he wanted to devour her, Pepper had a hard time reminding herself this was all temporary.

Sixteen

Nolan slid his fingers through Pepper's silky, dark hair. He'd always had a thing for her long hair, how it glided over his hands, over his body.

He wasn't even going to deny that he wanted her now, but he had to prove to her that even though the marriage had an expiration date, he wasn't interested in any other woman.

Pepper eased back, reaching up to grip his wrist. "I seriously need to eat. My little guy needs his nutrients."

"And you're going to need your energy."

Her eyes flared at his vow. There was no need to pretend this was all just a nice friendship when it wasn't.

"When the case is over, are you just going to divorce me?" she asked. "I mean, I don't expect a commitment from you, but I know for me, this is getting more difficult. When I'm with you, I want…"

Nolan shouldn't have felt relieved, but he did. He

didn't want her to finish that sentence. If Pepper was wanting more from him, what could he say? She was vulnerable right now and the last thing he wanted to do was hurt her.

"I want you," he told her matter-of-factly. "While we're married, I want you and only you. We're adults. We have a mutual passion. Why deny it?"

Pepper shook her head and let out a soft laugh. "You make things sound so simple when they obviously aren't."

"For now, we will make them simple." He added more fruit to her plate and a few slices of cheese. "Eat. Take care of that baby and yourself. Then we'll talk."

She quirked a brow. "Is that code for strip me naked and have your way with me?"

Damn if she wasn't sassy and so perfect. "That's exactly what it's code for. Now hurry up and eat."

They ate without speaking for a few minutes. Nothing awkward, just a comfortable silence, and he was thankful they were on the same page. He truly didn't want to cause her any more grief, but he also wanted her to know exactly where he stood.

"Tell me about Hayes. I know he's coming home, but I haven't seen him since I left."

Nolan peeled another piece of meat from his drumstick and popped it in his mouth. "Honestly, the last time he was home, he looked, I don't know, haunted. I thought he was done with the military then, but he said he couldn't leave his men. Now, though, I worry something has happened. That he won't be the same guy we once knew."

Nolan hated that his younger brother had seen so much ugliness in this world. Hayes had a big heart—he wanted to save everyone and had been convinced he could make a difference. Nolan shared those same qualities, but he'd chosen a different path.

"I'm sorry," she said. "Hopefully, being back home on the ranch, surrounded by family, will help him."

Nolan nodded. "I sure as hell hope so. I worry how he and Dad will be when they see each other. We never know what type of day Dad will be having and we won't know Hayes's frame of mind. They've both changed drastically over the past few years."

"Maybe they need each other," she replied, hope lacing her tone. "Sometimes one broken person just needs another to forge a new bond and become renewed."

Nolan considered her statement. As a doctor, he'd seen that exact thing happen between family members and friends. But when the circumstance involved his family, he wasn't so quick to believe it. A part of him knew, from a medical standpoint, that his father wasn't going to be cured. He was a prisoner in his own mind, and Nolan wasn't sure Hayes would be much better.

"I just want Hayes to understand that he can talk to us when he gets home, but he's the most stubborn of all the Elliott boys." Nolan paused to eat a grape. "I wish he had someone in his life. He doesn't need to be alone with his thoughts every night. At least with Colt moving forward with the dude-ranch plans, maybe Hayes will jump on board."

"He'll be fine," Pepper assured him. "He has a great support team here. If he wants to talk, he will. Just don't crowd him and don't treat him like you're afraid he'll break."

Nolan stared into her dark eyes. For a woman who'd had hurdle after hurdle placed in front of her, she was surprisingly optimistic. She was always optimistic, always proving that life wasn't going to get the better of her. He sincerely hoped she and Hayes could talk.

"You're pretty remarkable," he murmured. "I've always known it, but I guess I didn't realize just how determined you are to see the bright side of everything."

Pepper shrugged. "There's not many options but to move forward, are there? I mean, it would be easy to lie around and feel sorry for yourself or think of all that has gone wrong in your life, but that won't accomplish much and you'll only feel worse. I admit, though, when I left here, I was so depressed. I'd lost a baby, lost you. My entire future, my dreams were just…gone."

Pepper glanced down at her swollen belly. "I wasn't sure I could move on, but then I knew if I ever did have a child, I certainly wouldn't tell them to ever give up."

When she looked back up to him, she offered a sweet smile. "Hayes will be fine. He'll take time to adjust, but I'm confident you all will be just fine. Perhaps wait until your dad is having a better day to take Hayes to see him."

Nolan nodded. "I'm going to check with the facility. I want to bring Dad here for a day, but only if we're all in agreement that he'll be fine once we're here. I don't want to confuse him even more."

When she reached across and gripped his hand, Nolan stilled. She'd never initiated any contact since they'd been married.

"You know, when I left, I was convinced you didn't have a heart." She squeezed his hand. "I hated you for making me fall in love with you. I see now that fear drives you. You were afraid of being a father, of being with me and raising a family. You're afraid of your brother coming home because you're worried about getting entangled in his living nightmare."

Nolan had no idea how she'd managed to dissect him so perfectly when he'd never once thought that about himself. But she was dead-on. He *was* afraid. Staying detached was the best way to avoid those damn emotions.

"You're a great doctor because you care," she went on. "But you can keep your heart at a distance because you don't know the patients personally."

Nolan flipped his hand over and laced their fingers together. "Don't start analyzing me, babe. I'm not the man you used to know."

She tipped her head back and those gray eyes seemed to penetrate straight through to his heart. Damn it. No. His heart wasn't involved. It wasn't.

"You're not the same man," she agreed. "You've put these walls up that weren't there when we were together before. It's almost as if…"

He cringed, gripped her hand even tighter as he watched the truth dawn in her eyes. But he didn't look away, as much as he wanted to. He held her gaze, willing her to say nothing, knowing she'd reveal exactly what had happened to him. She was too smart, too in tune with him even after all this time.

"What happened to you when I left?" she whispered, tears filling her eyes.

Oh, no. He wasn't going to get into this.

Nolan started to release her hand, but she squeezed and held him in place. "Nolan. Before I told you I was pregnant, we were so happy, so perfect. Then the miscarriage tore us apart. You started changing before my eyes. You're hardened now," she added with a slight shake of her head. "It's like you refused to let anyone in after I was gone."

That was exactly what happened, but he sure as hell wasn't about to keep going with this prodding. There were more interesting things he wanted to do tonight, and other plans he had for that mouth of hers.

"I thought you were tired," he stated, coming to his feet. He reached down for her hands and tugged her up and against his chest, pleased when her eyes widened. "You seem wide-awake now."

Her rounded belly between them had become so familiar. This might not be his child, but he loved seeing how Pepper's body transformed. She was even more vibrant and sexier than ever.

Nolan slid one hand on the side of her abdomen. "How are you feeling? Be honest. I'm a doctor, I know when people are lying."

She covered his hand with her own. "I feel great. I obviously needed to eat something."

"No more problems?" he asked.

Pepper shook her head. "None. I promise to tell you if anything at all happens."

Nolan picked her up once again with his arm behind her knees and the other supporting her back. "Time for bed."

Her laugh sent a jolt of arousal pumping through him…as if he needed another reason to want her.

"I'm not tired anymore," she stated, throwing her arms around his neck.

Nolan paused at the base of the steps and looked her in the eyes. "I don't plan on sleeping."

Her gaze dropped to his mouth and Nolan took off up the stairs. If she kept looking at him like that, he'd take her right in the hallway, and she deserved a bed. He might desire her with a need even greater than he could comprehend, but he wasn't going to be a complete savage. He'd already taken her on his couch among packages. It was time to step up his game.

Only this wasn't a game. This was Pepper. The only women who'd ever truly held a piece of his heart. The only woman he'd ever temporarily marry to get her out of a bind.

"Are you doing this because I was getting too close to figuring you out?" she asked softly, laying her head on his shoulder.

"I planned on seducing you anyway. Your analysis of me may have accelerated the plans a bit."

Her fingertips slid through the hair on the nape of his neck. Just the slightest touch from her could get his body stirring. There was something so incredibly special about Pepper, beyond their past. She was…

No. Now was not the time to get into his head. He had a sexy woman ensconced in his arms and he'd just stepped over the threshold to his bedroom…*their* bedroom.

"We still need to talk," she informed him. "But it can wait."

Nolan smiled triumphantly as he made his way toward his king-size bed. Carefully, he laid her on top of the duvet and looked down at her. Something twisted inside his chest, something he refused to take the time to identify.

But seeing her in his bed, all spread out and her body lush from her pregnancy, Nolan knew he wasn't in such a hurry for this marriage to end. He rather liked seeing her in his bed.

Pepper extended her arms. "I've wanted to be here… with you…ever since I moved in."

"You denied it." He started ripping off his clothes, his ego boosted just a bit more when her eyes raked over his bare chest.

"I didn't want to let myself feel." Raising herself up on her elbows, she stared at him through those heavy lids. "You understand all about guarding your heart, don't you?"

Enough talk. Nolan reached for the elastic waist of

her long skirt and yanked it down her smooth legs. Before he could reach for the hem of her tank, she'd already whipped it up and over her head and tossed it to the floor.

With Pepper in only her simple white bra and panties, Nolan took in her perfect body. Placing a knee on the bed, he put a hand on either side of her face and leaned down to nip playfully at her lips.

"You won't sleep anywhere else," he commanded. "This is your bed as long as you're here."

"I don't want to be anywhere else."

He took his time peeling off the rest of her clothes. The turmoil swirling around inside him had no place in this moment. Whatever doubts he had, any fears or unknowns, would not join them in this bed. Their marriage was one big question mark as far as the future, but the end was coming. And he wasn't quite ready to say goodbye just yet.

When he joined their bodies, Nolan made the mistake of gazing straight down into her eyes. There was no denying the emotions staring right back up at him. A heady feeling he recognized all too well. But the pressure of what that entailed wasn't something he was ready to face right now.

Nolan closed his eyes and slid his lips over hers. As he started to move, she clutched at his shoulders and kissed him with so much passion and, damn it, love that he was having a difficult time differentiating his own deeper feelings from the physical ones.

He tried to focus on her tiny whimpers, her warm breath on his shoulder. He made sure to balance his weight on his forearms beside her head, keeping most of his torso off hers.

The moment her body tightened all around him, Nolan

increased the pace and kissed her one last time as he followed her over the edge.

For now, she was in his bed…but soon that would come to an end. Then he'd move on just like he'd always wanted. The unwelcome pang in his chest irritated him. He'd made his decision and he was happy.

Damn it. He wasn't going to revisit the past.

Nolan wrapped Pepper in his arms and rolled to his side, tucking her firmly against him. Stick with the plan, he reminded himself. When this case was all over and Pepper was back in her newly renovated apartment, Nolan would return to that perfect life that suited him so well.

Then something shifted inside him as he protectively rested his palm over his wife's belly. How many times could he tell himself he was happy alone until he finally believed it?

Seventeen

Pepper had just unlocked the back door to her shop when her cell rang. She juggled her purse, her small lunch bag, and her cell, all while trying to turn the key and not drop anything.

"Hello," she finally managed after pushing the door open.

"Pepper, I have some news."

She closed the door behind her as the attorney's words gave her heart a mild attack. "Is something wrong? I thought we were meeting later this week."

"That won't be necessary anymore," he informed her. "The Wrights' attorney called and they've decided to drop the case."

Pepper's knees nearly gave out. She crossed the back room to put her stuff on her worktable before sinking down into her old metal chair.

"What? Why? I mean, I'm thankful, but what caused the sudden change?"

"Money talks and they needed it. They'd like you to consider letting them see the baby, but they've given up the idea of custody. They've been well compensated."

Nolan. There was no other way to explain it. He'd done this. She didn't even need to ask. He'd done so much for her and he was making sure she had the life she'd always wanted.

Pepper absolutely hated that her child had been basically used by the Wrights for less-than-altruistic reasons. But if they were that quick to drop the case over money, then they weren't fit to be guardians and raise her child anyway.

Relief swept over her. Pepper rested a hand on her belly just as her little guy started to kick. Tears pricked her eyes, but she swallowed back the emotions. She didn't want to break down over the phone.

"Have you told Nolan they officially dropped the case?" she asked.

"I wanted to tell you first."

Pepper drew in a deep breath. "Okay, then. I'll call him. But first I have to thank you. It sounds so simple and not nearly adequate enough, but you don't know how much I appreciate what you did."

"It was my pleasure," he told her with a smile to his voice. "But if you want to thank anyone, that would be Nolan. He was checking in with me constantly, following up with the investigator, making sure we knew to stop at nothing, and to put your case first."

Pepper's heart flipped. She'd made love to her husband every night for the past five nights. She'd not once told him her feelings had evolved into something so much more than she'd ever thought possible. And now hearing just how diligent he'd been in getting this case dropped, she knew for a fact she'd fallen in love with him all over again.

No, not again. What she felt now was so much more intense than what she had before. And if she was honest, she'd have to admit she never stopped loving him. All the hurt she'd built up had just pushed that love to the back of her mind, but it was always there, just waiting to be given new life.

"Well, I still want to thank you," she reiterated. "I'll call Nolan right now."

"Congratulations," he told her before they disconnected the call.

Pepper got to her feet, suddenly feeling lighter than she had in weeks. Then a sense of melancholy washed over her. She'd been Mrs. Nolan Elliott for less than a month and it was already coming to an end.

She glanced down at the ring that had been his mother's. Pepper didn't want to take it off, didn't want to put this chapter behind her. She wanted to write the rest of their story and she wanted Nolan in her life permanently and for real.

But he'd made it clear they were over once the custody battle was resolved. Was that why he'd been so forceful with his lawyer and investigator? Was he that eager to get back to his old lifestyle? He'd been all too anxious to have her gone before—maybe he missed having his house all to himself.

Pepper started to call him when the back door swung open. She spun around, clutching her cell to her chest.

"I'm sorry." The contractor stared back at her, holding his hands up. "I didn't mean to startle you."

"Oh, it's okay. What can I help you with?"

"I just wanted to let you know that we should be finishing up today. We're just putting the trim back in place and cleaning up our mess and we should be gone by this afternoon."

Pepper blinked. "So, I can move back in?"

He nodded. "Yes, ma'am."

She swallowed a lump in her throat as her heart clenched. Her time at Pebblebrook really was coming to an abrupt halt. That was what she wanted, wasn't it? She wanted to get back into her apartment and start setting up for her baby. That had been the goal all along.

"Thank you," she told him, forcing a smile. "I'll let Nolan know and make sure he gets with you so you can be paid."

He waved a hand to dismiss her. "Mr. Elliott has already paid us enough. It's all covered."

The contractor left just as abruptly as he came and Pepper was left feeling such a mixture of emotions. She should have been elated that this time had come, but all she felt was that grip on her secret desires starting to slip once again. She'd been holding on to that dream, the dream she'd had years ago. Since she came back to Stone River, she hadn't realized she'd reached for it again, but she had...with both hands this time.

She wanted to continue to be Mrs. Elliott. She wanted to raise her child at Pebblebrook, and she wanted those things with Nolan as a loving spouse and parent.

If she thought he was even interested, then she'd fight for what she wanted. But he had done all of this only out of guilt, and out of primal attraction. That clearly wasn't enough to build a life on.

Pepper figured all of this needed to be done face-to-face. She'd wait until the end of the day and then go home. Hayes was coming back to the ranch today, so Nolan would be occupied. Then she could think of what to say.

How did she thank him or pay him back for such a sacrifice? How did she even find the right words for a goodbye such as this? Nothing about their reunion had been normal. She wanted to let him know how much she truly appreciated his help, but nothing was coming to mind... basically because she'd fallen in love with him again.

Pepper shook off her own heartache and decided to push forward. After all, she'd secured her son's future and that was all that had mattered since the beginning.

Nolan had been waiting on the front porch of Hayes's house for the past hour. Over the last several nights he'd grown even closer with Pepper. Their lovemaking had been so much more than just physical. They'd shared an intimacy that seemed to be intensifying, and there wasn't much he could do to stop it.

She'd woken him in the middle of the night to feel her son kick, and they'd ended up down in the kitchen for a snack...then he'd taken her right on the kitchen island.

Nolan crossed his ankles in front of him and rested his arms on the rocker. He and Pepper had settled into a dynamic of playing house so flawlessly he would swear she wasn't acting...and he wasn't so sure he was, either.

As the sound of Colt's truck rumbled nearby, Nolan came to his feet. The truck rounded the last bend and Nolan was off the porch and heading toward the drive. He couldn't wait to see his brother again.

Colt's truck came to a stop and Nolan crossed to the passenger side. Hayes's door flung open and his brother stepped out in his BDUs and combat boots. His military-short hair only accentuated his eyes. The light wasn't there like it had been when they were younger.

"Hey, man." Nolan wrapped both arms around his

brother and gave him a hard slap on the back before stepping away. "Good to see you."

Hayes nodded. "Good to be home."

Colt came around the truck and shot Nolan a look. Nolan wasn't sure what silent code he was trying to convey, but they'd definitely talk later in private.

"Your kitchen is stocked," Colt stated. "And I had some of my guys make sure everything was working fine. Water, electric. The air-conditioning has been on for a day to cool things off and you're good to go."

Hayes nodded and glanced around the portion of the property that belonged to him. His home had been the original house on Pebblebrook. Their grandfather had built it and their father had grown up there. Now with Colt and Nolan having their own homes on the spread, Hayes kept this one for himself.

And Colt's twin, Beau, was still out in Hollywood driving women crazy with his looks and making millions flashing his dimples and Southern charm on the screen. He rarely came home and when he did, he didn't spend more than a few days at a time.

"I missed this smell," Hayes said quietly.

"Manure?" Colt asked with a laugh. "We can put you right to work whenever you're up to it."

Hayes shoved his hands in his pockets and rocked back on his heels. "The sooner, the better. I'm not used to idle time."

Just as Nolan figured. His brother was going to have to stay busy. There was always plenty to do on a farm, so that was no problem. The real problem was that haunted look in his younger brother's eyes.

"Well, the dude-ranch plans are coming along," Colt said. "The engineer has finalized the plans and we're going to be building a few cabins back on the east side of the property."

"Dad would love that," Hayes replied before inhaling deeply and turning to Nolan. "How is he?"

Nolan released a breath. He wasn't going to sugarcoat things—Hayes would learn for himself soon enough. "He's not having as many good days as he used to. He's in the past more often than not and wants to know why mom isn't there. He fell the other night, but thankfully, nothing was broken."

"I want to see him."

"Of course. Do you want one of us to go with you?" Colt asked, tipping his hat to shield his face from the sun.

Hayes shook his head. "That's not necessary. I don't need you all hovering over me now that I'm home. I just need to get readjusted. It will take some time."

Nolan met Colt's gaze.

"Stop it," Hayes demanded. "I see the looks you two are throwing back and forth. Yeah, I'm not the same guy I was before I went over to that hellhole, but I'm still your brother and I'm still a rancher."

"We worry," Colt stated gruffly.

Hayes let out a dry, humorless laugh. "That makes three of us, but I'm okay. Well, I'm not exactly okay, but I'll be fine. Just…don't crowd me. Okay?"

Nolan and Colt nodded, but Nolan also knew there was no way they were going to let their brother deal with this darkness on his own. They might all be living their own lives, going their own ways, but they were still family and that was all that mattered.

"Just tell us what you need," Colt replied. "This is new for us, too, so we want to help but we don't want to make this more difficult, either."

Hayes nodded and reached into the truck for his bag.

His government-issued bag that had traveled through hell and back with him. Nolan watched as Hayes flung the large army-green sack over his shoulder and headed toward his house.

Colt shut the truck door and leaned back against it. "One of us needs to check on him pretty often until we see exactly what we're dealing with."

Nolan took off his hat and swiped the sweat from his forehead. "He'll be pissed if he thinks we're babysitting."

"I don't care what he thinks," Colt retorted. "It's better than having him suffer alone or worse. You know all those horror stories of soldiers who came home and couldn't handle the civilian life."

"Maybe seeing Dad will help him," Nolan said, propping his hat back on his head. "Dad may not know who he is, but this may be a simple case where Hayes will see someone is also struggling with identity. Or Dad may shock us and know exactly who Hayes is."

"I sure as hell hope so," Colt muttered.

His thoughts exactly. Nolan wasn't sure how these next few days, weeks or even months would play out, but he had to be aware of everything where his brother was concerned.

And not just his brother, but his wife. There were so many uncertainties with her, with their future. All he knew was he loved having her in his home, in his bed. He'd not wanted marriage, a family. But she'd come back into his life and thrust every bit of that into his face. He needed her, wanted her and planned on having her. Permanently.

"I have to go," he told Colt. "I need to get home."

Nolan hopped on his four-wheeler and headed for his house, ready to talk to Pepper.

Eighteen

Nolan came to an abrupt halt at the threshold of his bedroom. Lying out on the bed was a suitcase, clothes haphazardly piled all over it.

Pepper came out of the adjoining bath clutching her toiletry bag. As soon as her eyes locked on to his, she froze.

"I didn't know you were back." She worried her bottom lip as she held his gaze. "Um, how's Hayes?"

Nolan took one careful step in, as if any abrupt movement would shatter this already-fragile situation. "He's okay. Or he will be with time."

When she nodded and put her small bag on top of her existing pile, Nolan shook his head. "Care to tell me what's going on?"

Pepper turned, smoothing her hand over her fitted tank. "I have quite a bit of news, actually. The case was dropped, thanks to you and your investigator."

Surprised, Nolan smiled. "That's great news. Seems rather abrupt, though."

"Your money and power talked louder than I could, so I'm indebted to you." She crossed her arms over her chest and tilted her head. "The contractor finished up this afternoon, so my apartment is all ready for me. Looks like everything fell into place just when I needed it to."

When she needed it to. Those words were like a dagger straight to his heart...the heart he hadn't wanted to get involved in this marriage.

"You don't owe me anything," he managed after a moment. "You don't have to rush out, though."

Damn it, he didn't want her to leave at all, but apparently she couldn't get away from him fast enough.

"We agreed when the case was over, there was no need to be married." Pepper drew in a deep breath and dropped her arms, her bangle bracelets jingling. He'd become so used to hearing that sound he found even that simple gesture was something he'd miss. "I'm not going to drag this out any longer. We both have lives we need to get on with. I'm borrowing one of your suitcases since the clothes were here already. I'll pay you back for those, as well, once I get a solid income going. I'll let you contact your attorney regarding the divorce."

The divorce. Why were her parting words so damn soul crushing? He'd wanted this. He'd laid out the guidelines from the beginning. He'd just thought he'd have more time. This all seemed so sudden—there was no transition period. She was in his bed last night, all wrapped around him, and now she was hell-bent on making tracks to get out. And she'd laid out her speech so nice and neat as if she'd spent the past few hours rehearsing it. Was that so she could deliver it void of all emotion? If so, she'd nailed it.

"Sure," he muttered. "I can do that."

Her eyes darted back to her suitcase, then to him. "If

you don't mind, can you start loading my car with all the baby stuff we bought? Then I can get this."

He swallowed, hating how she seemed to be so distant and almost cold. His Pepper had always been so forthcoming with her feelings, but now, well, she had erected some wall between them that hadn't existed before. She was done—that much was evident.

Could she seriously just leave without caring? He desperately wanted to know what she was thinking. But from the hasty way she was tossing things into her suitcase—*his* suitcase—perhaps it was best he didn't know.

"I'll bring the baby stuff later," he told her. "Just concentrate on your things for now."

"Oh, right. Of course." She turned to the bed and quickly held the suitcase zipper together and forced it shut. "I'll be in the shop tomorrow if you want to come by then and drop it off."

She tugged the suitcase off the bed.

"Damn it, let me get that." He crossed the room and jerked the luggage from her hand.

"Why are you so angry?" she asked, looking up at him with those big, expressive eyes. "We agreed to this, and I can't stay here forever. You and I both know we have lives to get back to, and our time of playing house wasn't meant to be long-term."

Nolan hated how she tossed his own words back into his face. He hated that she was right because they were different people with different goals. Yet, somehow over these past couple of weeks, that line he didn't want to cross had become blurred. So blurred he had no idea where it even was anymore.

"This doesn't have to be difficult," she whispered. "You're off the hook. I mean, we're legally still married, but I don't expect you to remain faithful to me."

Her eyes darted away, but her words said everything. She was giving him permission to move on with another woman...and if that didn't speak volumes for where she stood, the loaded suitcase in his hand sure as hell did.

Nolan stepped aside and let her pass. "I'll take this down for you."

Pepper met his gaze once more. Biting her lip again, she nodded and eased by. As he watched her retreating back, he realized she'd never be in this room again. They'd never share a bed or late-night snacks in his kitchen. He wouldn't roll over in the middle of the night and feel her son kick.

Nolan swallowed hard and pulled the luggage behind him as he headed for the stairs. He'd never begged a woman to stay and he certainly wasn't going to start now. If Pepper wanted to go, then he had to set her free. He'd be fine—after all, he'd moved on the last time she walked out of his life.

But this time seemed so different, so final. And his heart hadn't felt this empty the last time.

She wasn't even officially gone and his house already had a void that he knew would never be filled.

Pepper left her suitcase in the car. She didn't care about her clothes, her toothbrush, her underwear. None of that mattered when her heart was in shattered pieces.

Nolan hadn't asked her to stay. He'd told her she didn't have to be in a rush, but he hadn't told her he wanted her in his home, in his life...his heart. Pepper had prayed he'd come home, pull her into his arms, and tell her he wanted her to stay. Convince her that the case and her apartment didn't matter. She desperately wanted him to tell her that her only home was with him at Pebblebrook.

But he hadn't and she had too much pride to open

up about her true feelings. She'd been burned before by this man. The only problem now was the flame was still burning.

Pepper walked around her newly renovated apartment and toyed with the ring still mocking her on her finger. She'd forgotten to return it, but she couldn't bring herself to take it off just yet. The marriage was over, but...maybe she could hang on in private just a bit longer.

The faint smell of wood and paint had her making a mental note to pick up some potpourri tomorrow. The laminate floor that stretched from the living room through the open kitchen and on into the bedrooms was perfect. She was so glad all the flooring was new. She'd find some bright rugs to put down and...

Tears filled her eyes as she covered her face and let the dam burst. She didn't care about rugs or flooring or anything else right now. She already missed Pebblebrook. In such a short time she'd made that place her home. She'd tried to remain detached, but how could she when she'd been staying in the home she'd helped design with the man she'd never stopped loving?

Now that she was alone, she planned on taking the rest of the evening for a good cry. The kind of cry that made the tip of her nose red, her skin splotchy, her eyes puffy. She'd just have to use extra concealer tomorrow for work.

Pepper headed to her fridge and realized with a pang of dismay that there was no food. Her new kitchen was perfect with the tiled backsplash and quartz countertops...but there was no emergency stash of ice cream in the freezer.

There was no way she was in the mood to go back out. It was getting late, not terribly so, but she'd had a rough day and she was emotionally drained.

Only another woman would understand this type of

need. It wasn't as if Pepper had made a bunch of friends since she'd been back. She'd been busy with her shop, busy dodging custody issues and busy getting married to the one man she loved but who didn't love her in return.

If only there were some reality show on screwing up your life in epic proportions.

Pepper grabbed her phone from her purse and shot off a text. There was one other woman who might actually know what Pepper was going through. Annabelle was the closest thing she had to a friend and she knew all about those Elliott boys. Annabelle had gone into all the mayhem that had surrounded her relationship with Colt. That woman definitely understood a frustrating, arrogant, sexy cowboy.

Pepper wasn't even sure if she wanted to talk about this—everything was still so fresh, so raw. But perhaps Annabelle could just leave a copious amount of ice cream on the stoop outside the apartment door and go.

In the bottom of her bag, Pepper found a packet of pretzels and a bottle of water. Better than nothing, but she was going to need real food. Hopefully, Annabelle would take pity on her and bring a pizza or something with that ice cream. If there was ever a time that called for junk, it was now.

Pepper waited for the reply, hoping Colt's fiancée would come through. Because the only other person Pepper had leaned on was now out of her life...and filing for divorce.

Nineteen

Four days had passed since she left. Nolan had gone back to work on the second day and had been there since. What was the point in going home? Colt had promised to check on Hayes while Nolan was at the hospital. The surgeries had been brutal on him—one right after another. He was more than ready to get home and have the next two days off because he planned on sleeping and then diving into ranch work with his brothers.

But on his way home earlier, he'd come across an accident. After working thirty-six hours, he was dead on his feet and wanted nothing more than to fall face-first in his bed...or a guest bed since he couldn't bring himself to sleep where the sheets still smelled like his wife.

The second he'd become a doctor, he'd sworn to help those in need and there was a definite need at the accident site. A woman was in full-blown labor and her husband had been in a hurry to get her to the hospital and run a red light, and their car had been hit in the side.

Nolan had helped deliver the baby girl while waiting on the ambulance. He'd held the mother's hand as they'd loaded her into the back, but he could tell that she probably wasn't going to make it.

The harsh reality of that entire scene gnawed at his gut and he nearly felt sick. When the father held on to his precious baby while praying for his wife to live, Nolan had known that man wouldn't get a second chance.

But maybe Nolan could. Hell, he'd had his second chance and he'd blown it. He'd let Pepper walk out of his house and he hadn't put up a fight. Why? Because of his stupid pride and hardheaded mentality. So what if she laughed in his face or told him there was no way she'd stay married to a man who was a workaholic? He hadn't even tried to convince her to stay. Since when did he just give up on things?

Risking grief and heartache was completely worth it if the ultimate ending was joy and a life with Pepper. He wanted all they could have, all they'd lost. They were both getting a second chance and he refused to walk away again.

As he headed to the kitchen to get a bottle of water, the ultrasound image of Pepper's son was the only thing stuck on the fridge door. Nolan slid his fingertip over the image and wondered if she'd left this for him on purpose to drive him out of his mind or if she'd legitimately forgot it in her haste to get out.

He grabbed the bottle and started to head upstairs to the shower. The piles of baby items in the living room caught his attention, though. All of the various things they'd shopped for. She'd been so excited that day, and he had to admit he'd had a great time watching her gather so many necessities for her son. He still needed to deliver all of that to her apartment, but he honestly had no idea how everything would fit in her living space. But it would all fit here in his home and he had plenty of bedrooms to spare for a nursery.

Pepper and the baby were so much more important than this ranch or his MD, and he'd fought like hell to make both of those top priority in his life.

Nolan wanted to call the hospital and check on the patient, but in his heart he already knew the outcome. Plus, if he didn't check in, then there was still that glimmer of hope that she'd pulled through.

And there was a glimmer of hope that he and Pepper could pull through, too. He just had to man up and go to her. He'd make her listen to what he had to say, to the reasons they should be together. If she chose to push him away, then he could live with it. He'd hate it, but at least he'd know he did all he could to get her to come back where she belonged…right here at Pebblebrook.

If Hayes was looking for a second chance at life after all he'd been through, why the hell couldn't Nolan? The only person standing in the way of what he wanted was himself.

Nolan was going to fight for his wife.

Pepper brushed the navy strokes over her stark white canvas. Once she had the background, she planned on free-handing a quote with her son's name. She'd opted to push forward with her thoughts, even if her heart hadn't quite caught up yet. So the past few days she'd devoted to all things baby and she'd finally come up with a name.

She touched up the edges, making sure all the white was covered, and took a step back to examine the even strokes. Someone pounded on her door, making Pepper jump and swipe the brush across her cheek.

With a groan, she dropped the brush into the cup of

water and wiped her hands on the towel before heading to the door. She'd deal with her cheek in a bit.

Her heart kicked up because she figured there was only one person who could be on the other side of that door. She assumed Nolan was finally delivering that baby stuff. Seeing him would hurt, but she was going to have to get used to it. They lived in the same town now and running into him was inevitable.

Drawing a steadying breath, Pepper glanced through the peephole. Her eyes immediately landed on his dark, disheveled hair. He'd turned his back and those broad shoulders were encased in a formfitting tee that made her remember exactly what those hard-packed muscles had felt like beneath her hands.

Rubbing her fingers together, she took another breath before flicking the lock open. Nolan turned as she swung the door open.

"If you have the baby's things—"

"I don't." He moved into the doorway, crowding her until she backed up. "I came to talk to you. You don't have to say anything. Just give me five minutes."

He didn't give her a chance to reply as he skirted around her. Realizing she didn't have much choice, Pepper closed the door. Whatever he wanted, she prayed he made it fast. Five minutes with Nolan was cruel when she knew he didn't reciprocate her feelings. And if he hadn't brought the baby things, what did he want?

Crossing her arms, Pepper spun around and remained in place. Nolan was at the art table she'd set up in the living area. He stared at the navy canvas, then looked back to her.

"What's this going to be?" he asked.

"For the nursery." When he continued to stare, Pepper let out a sigh and threw her arms wide. "If you came for small talk, I'm busy."

Nolan raked a hand over his jawline, the stubble scraping beneath his palm. She finally took a moment to study his appearance. His eyes were puffy and dark, as if sleep had not been his friend for quite some time. The finger marks through his hair were evidence of his frustrated state. Yet she didn't feel sorry for him. He could've had everything—she would've given him everything—in exchange for love. Was that too much to ask?

"What do you want, Nolan? Because you look like you're about to keel over."

He met her gaze across the narrow space. "My thirty-six-hour shift ended a few hours ago. I was caught behind a wreck and delivered a baby. I managed to run home and shower before coming here because I was a total mess."

Pepper gasped and took a step toward him. "Why on earth aren't you in bed? How's the baby? Did you have to deliver in the car?"

She couldn't help firing off questions, because she had so many, but most of all she wanted to know why he was here when it was obvious he was a zombie.

"The baby is fine. I delivered a healthy baby girl on the side of the highway while we waited on paramedics." Nolan shook his head and glanced down to his cowboy boots. "I'm almost positive the mother didn't make it, though. I couldn't call and find out. I just… I didn't want to know."

Pepper's heart clenched. She fisted her hands at her sides and waited for him to continue. Maybe he'd come because he just needed someone to talk to. If that was the case, she'd listen. She loved him too much to turn him away, even if he didn't love her in return.

"I've been a doctor for years," he went on as he brought his haunted eyes back up to hers. "I try not to get emotionally attached, but this case…"

The pregnant woman. The possible loss of life. It was all making sense now. Pepper slowly took a step forward, then another. Dare she hope he'd had some epiphany? While her heart literally ached for the family of the woman who'd just delivered, if that instance brought Nolan to her door, back into her life, she had to believe he was at that scene for a reason.

Nolan watched her as she neared. When she came toe-to-toe with him, he reached for her arms and pulled her close.

"Not everybody gets a second chance," he whispered into her hair. Pepper trembled as she wrapped her arms around him. "I don't deserve a second chance, but I let you walk out of my life once. Then you walked out of my house. I can't let you go, Pepper."

Instant joy and relief flooded through her as she gripped his shirt and rested her forehead against his chest. "Are you here to ask me to come back?"

Nolan eased away but kept his grip on her. "I'm telling you that my life has been empty since you left ten years ago. I'm telling you that Pebblebrook is lonely and everywhere I look in my house I see you. The paintings, the ultrasound image you left. There's even a pair of flip-flops by my back door. They're waiting on you, Pepper. I'm waiting on you. Come home."

Pepper's eyes burned as tears welled up. "Why?" she couldn't help but ask. "Why do you want me to come back? I'm pregnant with another man's baby, our marriage was a farce, and—"

"I love you."

Those three simple yet life-changing words had her stilling. "You…love me?"

He framed her face in his large hands, swiping the blue

paint from her cheek with the pad of his thumb. When he held it up in front of her face, he smiled.

"I love this. I love the free spirit inside of you. I love the creativity you have to make something from nothing." He took the blue and wiped it on his own cheek. "Make a life with me, Pepper. Make something from nothing with this heart of mine."

Oh, that did it. She sobbed, falling into his chest as her emotions completely overtook her.

Nolan's arms enveloped her as he smoothed her hair down her back. "I was hoping for a better response," he rasped.

Pepper laughed through the tears. "I just wanted you to love me as I love you. I had no idea you'd be so eloquent and perfect when you told me."

"I should've told you long ago." He leaned back and brushed his mouth tenderly over hers before pulling away. "This marriage isn't a farce. It's very real and it's forever. Come back to Pebblebrook. I'll give you all the babies you want and I'll raise this son as my own."

Pepper nodded, letting out a hiccup with her tears. "I'm a mess," she muttered. "I didn't expect you to do this. I dreamed of it. I'd hoped you'd come to see that we deserve this second chance, but I really thought you'd pushed me out forever."

"I'm a fool for letting you go. I'll never make that mistake again." He kissed her hard, a promise of a lifetime together poured into that kiss. "Come home and we'll make a nursery and an art studio. We'll make the life we deserve. Together."

Pepper smiled and returned the kiss. "Together."

Epilogue

Hayes stared at the bottle of bourbon. He'd pulled out the unopened bottle from his cellar and had been eyeing the damn thing for the past hour.

Drinking would be the easy part. Getting lost in that bottle would be the coward's way out. But he wanted anything to dull the ache in his chest of being home. He'd known coming back would be difficult, but he hadn't expected the guilt that came along with being back at Pebblebrook.

He had all the money a man could ever want. He had a five-thousand-acre ranch, so work would definitely keep him busy. And he loved it here…but he'd left so many of his brothers overseas.

Hayes shut his eyes and tried to push his demons aside, but nothing helped. When he had his eyes open, all he saw was the life he had here in Stone River. The perfect life, some would call it. Money, power, family. Yes, he did have it all on a certain level.

He'd give it all up if he thought he could save his friends on the other side of the globe. Hayes grabbed the bottle and headed out onto the back porch. He'd inherited the original Elliott homestead and he loved this old two-story farmhouse. There was some work to be done, but he was ready to dive into a project that would keep his hands busy and his mind occupied.

Hayes sank into one of the old rockers on his porch. Clutching the bottle like some warped sense of a lifeline, he stared out at the darkened sky. There was nothing as peaceful as Pebblebrook. With a river running along the back of the property behind his house and a brook running through the front of the property where Colt's house was, there was so much beauty and tranquility here.

Quite the polar opposite of where he'd spent the last several years of his life. Coming home every twelve to eighteen months for a brief time wasn't the same as coming home for good. Other than farm life, what else did he know? What else did he do? Because with the way his heart and soul had been battered, he figured it best if he stayed on the ranch as much as possible until he got acclimated to civilian life again.

Colt and Nolan had both found love. Nolan and Pepper were married and blissfully in love. Both of his brothers seemed so happy. There must be something in the water because both of his brothers were going into ready-made families. Hayes wanted no part of kids. Hell, he wasn't even sure he could handle a regular relationship with a woman, let alone a child. He had too much darkness inside him, had seen too much to be a father.

But Colt had always wanted that large-family lifestyle, and Nolan had finally come to his senses where Pepper was concerned. Who knew love could last across a decade and time apart?

Hayes had no sweethearts in his past. He didn't do relationships because he'd been in the service and always traveling. Hell, he'd been married to the army, and just because he was getting out, didn't mean that he could simply turn off his feelings about the life he'd lived.

The bottle in his hand mocked him and he wanted to throw it to get rid of the temptation. He didn't know how long he sat and rocked, replaying his career in slow motion in his mind. A muscle ticked in his jaw. He knew his brothers were worried about him, and they had every right. But he meant what he said when he told them he needed space. If they started hovering, he wasn't sure he wouldn't lash out at them—and they were the last people on earth he wanted to get angry with.

Tomorrow he'd go see his father. He wasn't sure he'd be strong enough to see his formerly robust, vibrant father now in a nursing home not even knowing his own name at times. Hayes didn't care, though. He wanted to be there, to sit by his dad's side and do absolutely nothing. Hayes wanted that simplicity.

Hayes knew his father would be proud of Colt for pushing ahead with the dude ranch. Opening Pebblebrook to the public had been a dream of their father's for some time, but he'd never fully gone ahead with the plans. Then dementia had stolen everything and the project had gotten pushed to the back of everyone's mind.

Hayes didn't recall the last time he'd seen Beau, other than on the big screen. Now that he was home, he wondered when they'd have an old-fashioned Elliott gathering. Hayes wanted everyone together—he wanted to go back to that time when they all hung out in the stables talking about nothing and everything. When they'd drink beers late at night, go for early-morning rides to check the fence lines... Hell, he just wanted an existence that didn't involve fearing for your life every single day.

Hayes set the bottle on the porch and leaned forward on his elbows. Resting his head in his hands, he sent up a prayer. He'd done quite a bit of that recently. He wasn't sure if anyone heard his thoughts, but he figured it didn't hurt.

He was home. All that mattered was that he was here now and he was going to heal. With the help of his brothers and his soon-to-be sisters-in-law, he wouldn't be alone.

Maybe, over time, he'd get back into the realm of socializing and perhaps even dating, but he wasn't going to plan too far ahead. One day at a time: that was how he had to live.

He got to his feet, crossed to the railing and rested his hands on the wood beam. Tomorrow he'd start renovating his home.

Home. He liked the sound of that, even if he would live in this big house all by himself.

He was home and that was more than some of his comrades had. Hayes would be happy with the life he'd been given and he'd push forward. Alone...just like he wanted.

* * * * *

Pick up these other sexy romances
from Jules Bennett!

TWIN SECRETS
TRAPPED WITH THE TYCOON
FROM FRIEND TO FAKE FIANCÉ
HOLIDAY BABY SCANDAL
THE HEIR'S UNEXPECTED BABY

Available now from Mills & Boon Desire!

* * *

If you're on Twitter, tell us what you think of
Mills & Boon Desire! #Mills&BoonDesire

Beckett stepped into her personal space.

Her heart bounced off her rib cage and her stomach felt like it was taking a roller-coaster ride, but she'd be damned if she'd let Beck see how much his hot, hard body affected her.

Beck smiled, lifted a hand and rested the tip of his index finger in the V of her throat. "Your pulse is trying to burst through your skin."

Dammit. Damned pulse. *Heart, stop beating.*

Beck's hot fingertip ran up the side of her throat until he reached her jaw. "God, your eyes. My memory didn't do them justice. Silver and green all contained in a ring of emerald."

Cady swallowed and shook her head. "Don't do this, Beckett."

"I think I have to," Beckett replied, the heat of his hand scalding her jaw. His other hand grasped her hip and he pulled her into him.

Beck's lips were pure magic as his mouth took possession of hers. Cady felt his hand cup her right butt cheek and he launched her up into his muscular body. She closed her eyes, not quite believing that he was holding her, that his mouth was on hers. It felt like it belonged there, as if she'd been created to be kissed by him. Beck kissed like he owned her, like she was—just for this moment in time— still his.

* * *

Reunited… and Pregnant
is part of The Ballantyne Billionaires series:
A family who has it all… except love!

REUNITED...
AND PREGNANT

BY
JOSS WOOD

First Published in Great Britain 2017
By Mills & Boon, an imprint of HarperCollins*Publishers*
1 London Bridge Street, London, SE1 9GF

© 2017 Joss Wood

ISBN: 978-0-263-92824-2

51-0617

Our policy is to use papers that are natural, renewable and recyclable products and made from wood grown in sustainable forests. The logging and manufacturing processes conform to the legal environmental regulations of the country of origin.

Printed and bound in Spain
by CPI, Barcelona

Joss Wood loves books and traveling—especially to the wild places of southern Africa. She has the domestic skills of a potted plant and drinks far too much coffee.

Joss has written for Mills & Boon KISS, Mills & Boon Presents and, most recently, the Mills & Boon Desire line. After a career in business, she now writes full-time. Joss is a member of the Romance Writers of America and Romance Writers of South Africa.

To the reader: thank you for spending your precious time with my characters.

Prologue

In Bangkok International Airport, Beckett Ballantyne, his booted feet resting on his backpack, looked across the row of seats to Cady and smiled. Her eyes were closed, her lips moving as she silently sang along to whatever she was listening to via the new pair of earbuds she'd bought in Pantip Plaza yesterday.

A light green bandeau held her long, deep brown hair off her face and turned her wintry eyes a light green. Sitting with her heels on the seat of her chair and wearing denim shorts, a white tank and beaded bracelets, she looked exactly like what she was: a sexy backpacker seeing the world.

With that half smile on her face, the flirt of a dimple in her cheek, she would make anyone looking at her envious of her freedom, jealous of her next adventure.

She was young, gorgeous and adventurous and, no one, Beck was certain, would suspect that she was utterly miserable.

Not with him. They were, as far as he knew, perfectly fine for a couple who'd met and run off to South East Asia together within a month of meeting at an off-campus party in New York. Technically, since his trip was planned, she'd run off, choosing to spend the long summer holidays after freshman year traveling with him.

Her staid, conservative, churchy parents had freaked.

Beck glanced at the phone in her hand and he wondered how many emails and voice messages they'd left, begging her to come home. How many tears would she shed this time? How long would it take her to come out of the funk their recriminations tossed her into?

In Beckett's mind it was psychological torture, and her parents just kept up the pressure. She was wasting her life; she was a disrespectful daughter; she was living in sin with him...

Her father had an ulcer; her mother was depressed. How could she be enjoying her trip when they were so miserable? They missed her and worried constantly about her—what if she was kidnapped and sold into the sex trade? They'd heard there was a bomb blast in Thailand—what if she was caught up in an explosion?

He'd told her to ignore them, to only check in once a week, but Cady couldn't disconnect. Their mind games turned her into a conflicted mess. She wanted to be with him but her guilt over disappointing her parents was eating her from the inside out.

He knew that she felt stuck in the middle. He thought her parents were narrow-minded and they thought he was a spoiled rich kid, the spawn of Satan because he lured their innocent daughter overseas with the sole intention of corrupting her.

If one could call worshipping her body at every opportunity corruption...

Beck felt the action in his pants and tipped his head back to look at the ceiling, readily admitting that he couldn't get enough of Cady. At twenty-three, he'd had other lovers, so he couldn't understand why he was utterly addicted to making love with her, being with her.

If he believed in the emotion, he might think that he was in love. But since he didn't, wouldn't allow himself to, he did what he always did and pushed those uncomfortable thoughts away.

Her parents' disapproval would've been easier for Cady to handle if she genuinely loved traveling, loved experiencing the hugely different cultures they stepped into. But having been protected and cocooned, she'd cried at the poverty and slums she saw in India, been shocked by the sex trade in Phuket. The crowds, the sounds and strange food threw her, and the lack of English disoriented her. He couldn't fault her for trying, and she didn't whine but she wasn't enjoying the experience. It didn't help that she'd had her wallet lifted, her butt touched and had to spend four days in a grungy bathroom, her arms wrapped around a cracked toilet bowl.

He'd thought she'd enjoy the clear sea and white-sand beaches of Phi Phi, the island they'd just returned from. But Cady was miserable. And because Cady was miserable, he was, too. He'd thought that their desperate need to be with each other could conquer anything.

He was so wrong.

With his ridiculously high IQ, being wrong was not a concept he was very familiar with.

God, these last two weeks together would be torture. Every time he thought of her leaving, his stomach knotted and his lungs seized. They had a plan, he reminded himself; they'd agreed to three months together and then she'd head back to college and he'd continue his travels.

But after two and a half months together, he knew that he could no longer take her, and his feelings for her, lightly. And that realization made him feel like his life was spinning out of control. While his little brain was already mourning her departure, his big brain was insisting they could do with some distance, some time apart. He needed a lot of space and quite a bit of time apart because he was starting to suspect that she might be the beat of his heart, the breath on his lips, the reason the sun rose in the morning.

He had to let her go because, if he wasn't careful, he could love her with a fierce, crazy, forever type of love. Love like that meant taking a very real risk, a huge leap of faith. It made him feel lost, exposed and far too vulnerable—all the emotions he'd been trying to avoid since he was eight. Love meant pain, and he was too smart to put himself in harm's way.

Love meant losing control.

Love was also, it was said, supposed to make you feel happy and complete. He didn't deserve to feel happy and he'd never feel complete. How could he when he was the reason his parents' remains, and those of his unborn sibling, were scattered on a mountain in Vermont?

Beck felt his cell phone vibrate in his back pocket and pulled it out. He smiled at the name on the display. He had two older brothers, Linc through adoption and Jaeger through birth, and he loved them equally.

They were also equally annoying in their belief that he needed looking after. The fact that he was taller and bigger than both of them didn't stop them fussing over him and his younger sister, Sage.

This time it was Jaeger calling.

"Jay, what's up?" he asked after answering the call.

"Just checking up on you. Any trouble?"

Beck rolled his eyes. He wasn't that stupid; he wasn't stupid at all. "Actually, I was just about to call you. We're sitting in a Thai jail. They found some coke on us."

There was long silence before Jaeger released a harsh curse. "That's not funny, Beck."

Beck grinned. "I thought it was."

"You are *such* an ass."

Beck tapped Cady on her knee and pointed to his backpack, silently telling her to keep an eye on his stuff. She nodded and Beck stood up to walk toward the window looking out onto the busy tarmac.

"Where are you? Bangkok?" Jaeger asked. "And are you still heading for Vietnam?"

"That's the plan, why?"

"I'm heading there day after next. I've had a tip about a new rustic mine in Yen Bai producing some very high quality rubies. Want to come with me and see what we can buy?"

Beck felt a spurt of excitement, the kick of adrenaline at the thought of hunting gems with his brother to supply the demands of Ballantyne's rich and demanding clients. "Hell, yes."

Then he remembered that he wasn't traveling alone. "Can I bring Cady?"

"I'm not sure of the area, Beck. I wouldn't," Jaeger replied. "Can't she stay in Hanoi by herself for a couple of days?"

Beck ran his hand over the back of his neck. The backpackers they'd met on Phi Phi were heading to Hanoi, as well, and they were all staying at the same backpacker's hostel. Maybe they—and their new friend Amy especially—could keep an eye on Cady for a few days. He was fairly certain she'd be okay.

Then the disapproving faces of Cady's parents jumped

onto the big screen of his mind and he instantly felt guilty. He was responsible for Cady, not Amy.

"Let me think about it," he told Jaeger. But he knew he couldn't leave Cady in Hanoi by herself.

"No worries," Jaeger replied. "I'm glad that you've reconciled yourself to traveling. Connor was worried that you wouldn't but I knew that our parents' adventurous spirit was still in you, albeit deeply buried."

"It's not like I have a choice, Jaeger. That was the ultimatum Connor and Linc gave me, supported by you, I might add."

Yeah, he enjoyed traveling but he was still pissed that his uncle and his brothers refused to allow him to join Ballantyne's until he'd taken a gap year or two.

"You know why, Beck," Jaeger said, his deep voice low and concerned. "You've been operating at warp speed since you were a kid. You finished school early, partly because you're brilliant, but mostly because you worked your tail off. You made the national swim championships because every moment you weren't studying you were in the pool. When you gave up competitive swimming we thanked God because we thought you might finally get a life. Date some girls, have some fun, get into some trouble. Not you. You went off to college and got your master's in business in record time. You're twenty-three years old and you've spent the past ten years working your ass off. If you come back to Ballantyne's, you'll do exactly the same thing. So we don't care if you sit on a beach for the next eight months or if you enter an ashram, but what you aren't doing is going straight to work."

Beck gripped the bridge of his nose with his thumb and forefinger. He'd heard this lecture a hundred times before.

"Anyway, this is a stupid conversation because we all know that you love traveling."

He did. He loved the freedom it gave him, loved the anonymity. While traveling, he was Beck, no surname attached. For the first time in fifteen years he felt marginally free, a little at peace, a lot chilled.

"Do you think that tying yourself to Cady while you travel is a good idea?" Jaeger asked.

"What are you talking about?"

Beck glanced at Cady, who met his eyes and gave him that quick, sunburst smile that always jump-started his heart.

"According to her social media posts, she's ditching school and spending the next year traveling with you."

What the hell…?

"She's going back to school," Beck said, forcing the words up his tight throat.

"Uh…not according to Sage, who follows both of you on social media. It was girl speak…something about her loving you enough to continue traveling with you."

A large bead of sweat rolled down his temple and into his heavy stubble. A loud bell clanged in his ears, and his stomach felt like it had taken a ride on a death-defying roller coaster.

That wasn't the plan. He needed them to stick to the plan.

"That's not happening." He managed, through his panic, to push the words out.

"Look," Jaeger said, impatient, "I've got more important things to do than talk about your love life. Just let me know about ruby-hunting in Yen Bai."

Using his phone, Beck pulled up her social media account and yep, Cady had posted something about not returning to college and extending her trip with him.

Beck pocketed his phone and gripped the railing separating him from the floor-to-ceiling windows. He dropped his head and stared at his grubby boots. Fear, hot and acidic, burned a ring of fire around his heart, up his throat and coated his mouth in a bitter film.

She was supposed to be a three-month fling. This wasn't supposed to get this intense, this quickly. He'd been banking on her going home, heading back to college. Her leaving had been his safety net, the way he stopped himself from falling all the way in love with her. If she stayed with him, he doubted he could resist her and then he'd be up crap creek in a sinking canoe.

He wasn't prepared to go there. If he loved her and lost her...

Hell, no. Not happening.

Why hadn't she spoken to him first before blabbing online? He knew that her choosing him over her parents was her way of making a statement but hell, hers wasn't the only seat on this train. He had a right to decide whether he wanted to keep traveling with her. He couldn't bear to see her go but he couldn't risk his heart by her staying.

Devil, meet the deep blue sea.

The only rational option, his instinctive reaction, was to stick to the plan they'd decided on back in New York. She needed to go home, go back to college and he'd see her at Christmas. The only deviation he was prepared to make to that plan was to send her home as quickly as possible. They were in an airport and that could be accomplished right now.

Because if he didn't walk away today, he knew that he never would.

His decision made, Beck walked over to her and picked up his backpack with one hand and grabbed hers with another.

Cady pulled out the earbuds and slung her smaller backpack over her shoulder as she stood up. "What's up?"

When Beck gestured to the familiar logo of an American carrier at the neighboring gate, her eyes flashed with joy. "Oh, my God, we're going home?" she squealed, dancing on the spot.

He just looked at her, wanting her to understand without having to say the words. After a little confused silence, the light faded from her eyes and color leached from her face. "You're not coming with me?"

Beck shook his head.

He dropped the backpacks at his feet and slapped his hands on his hips. It took him a while to find the words he needed. "Jaeger wants me to meet him in Vietnam to look for rubies with him, and you can't come with, and I can't leave you on your own."

Cady's bottom lip trembled and she rocked on her heels, looking like he'd sideswiped her with a stick, but he continued. "It's only two weeks early, Cady, and it's not like you were enjoying yourself."

"I love spending time with you! In fact, I had just decided that I want to stay, to ignore my folks' disapproval, to get into the hang of this. I want to be with—"

Beck jumped in before she could finish that sentence. "You're going back to school, Cady. That was always the plan. I'm just sending you home two weeks early."

Cady took a step back and her eyes filled with tears. "You're *sending* me home?"

Oh, damn, bad choice of words. "I'll be home for Christmas. We can reevaluate then."

"You're sending me home?" Cady repeated his words, emphasizing each one.

"Christmas is in three months—"

Cady's lips firmed and she folded her arms across her torso. "Do you love me, Beck?" she demanded.

Ah, no. Not this question. He could love her, he silently

admitted, and that was why she needed to go back to the States. Falling in love with Cady, with anyone, wasn't something he was prepared to do.

When he didn't answer, Cady grabbed his arm, her nails digging into his skin.

Beck jerked his arm away and forced himself to meet her eyes. Oh, damn, he wished he hadn't because, as long as he lived, he'd remember the betrayal he saw within them, the pain he'd caused. Cady lifted her hand to grab the fabric of his shirt just above his heart, twisting it in her fist. "Don't do this, Beck. Don't throw us away, don't toss me aside. We can fix this."

"That's the thing, Cades, I can't be fixed."

It was a special type of hell, Beck thought, to watch a heart break. It was even worse when you were responsible for it breaking.

One

Almost a decade later

Sitting at one of the many high tables in Bonnets, a swish cocktail bar just off Fifth Avenue, Cady Collins had to physically stop herself from appropriating the massive salt-rimmed margarita delivered to the table next to her. The taste buds on the back of her tongue tingled as she imagined the perfect combination of salt and the sugar-tinged tang of tequila.

It had been a tequila type of day and week. Year.

The waiter turned to her, lifted an eyebrow at her empty glass. "Another virgin Bloody Mary?"

God, Friday night and she was in the most reviewed cocktail bar in the city—the joke was that Bonnets had the license to serve cocktails to the angels—and she was drinking tomato juice.

How sad.

Cady saw the screen of her phone light up, saw the display say The Boss and sighed as she lifted the device to her ear. "Hi, Mom."

"Cady, where are you?" Edna Collins asked in her best I'm-the-preacher's-wife voice.

Cady resisted the urge to tell her that she was in a bar tucking dollar bills into the tiny thong of a muscled, oiled male stripper. *You're an adult. You don't need to try to shock your parents anymore.*

"What's the matter, Mom?"

Edna called her at precisely 8:00 p.m. every second Sunday. A call outside that time meant that something had rattled The Force.

"You might have heard that the preacher at our sister church in Wilton is retiring and the church has been looking for a suitable replacement."

Not really. She didn't keep up with what was happening in the exciting world of church politics in upstate New York.

Cady sent another look at the icy margarita and felt her mouth tingle. One little sip... How much damage could one sip do?

"Your father is being considered."

"Good for him," Cady replied because she was expected to say something.

"We need you to come home in two weeks," Edna stated, her voice suggesting that an argument would not be tolerated.

"Me? Why?"

"Your father is undergoing a process of rigorous interviews. I will be interviewed, as well. As you are our only child, they want to meet you, too."

Cady wanted to tell her mother that she wasn't an only child, that she'd had a brother, that his life mattered, but as always she refrained. Will wasn't someone they regularly discussed. Or at all.

"Mother, what possible bearing could I have on the proceedings? I live in New York City, and I rarely come home."

"You never come home," Edna corrected.

That might be because home was the place where she had no wiggle room, where there was no room for error. Home was a place of pressure, with a lot of interest shown but little love. After Will was sent away, she'd lived in constant fear that she would be, too.

Home was hymnal music and stockings, religious books and piety.

Cady shuddered. "Well, sorry. That's not going to happen."

Cady heard her mother's shocked gasp. "But you have to! Not meeting with the interview committee would reflect very badly on your father and his chance to secure this position. It's a big church, Cady, with a lot of resources. Since you put that traveling nonsense behind you, you've been a model daughter, a credit to us. Highly educated, with your own business. I have no doubt you are an example to others in that sin-filled city."

Yeah, Cady Collins, the beacon for clean living. Oh, God, her mother was going to die when she heard her latest news. As for that traveling nonsense, her time in Thailand with Beck was the only time she felt completely herself. Free.

Loved. For a brief moment in time, she'd felt so loved.

"It would be a huge step up for him," her mother droned on. "And when they meet you, they'll have the proof that we have raised a God-fearing, smart young woman who has her feet firmly on the ground."

If the statement wasn't so sad, she'd roll on the floor

and wet herself laughing. "Mom, trust me, you really don't want me there. Find an excuse and we'll save a lot of trouble."

"I have no idea what you're rambling about and I don't have the time to argue with you. We have guests for dinner. Do not disappoint us, Cady," Edna snapped before she disconnected.

Cady gently tapped the corner of her phone against the tabletop. She'd left home more than a decade ago, but the urge to please her parents was still strong. In their small rural town in upstate New York, she'd been the popular pastor's kid. Honor student, cheerleader, student council president, homecoming queen. Pretty, popular, nice. As perfect as she could possibly be.

She said "please" and "thank you" and "excuse me" and ran errands and never missed church. She didn't smoke or drink or party or date because she was an "example." She'd never had the chance to be a regular kid, to mess up, to fail.

The pressure to be perfect was immense and it was generally accepted that she became an overachiever because that was what her parents expected. Sure, that was part of the reason, but no one knew that she was terrified of messing up, of doing or saying the wrong thing.

Of being banished like Will, her older brother.

As a result, her desire to please her parents still lingered. They wouldn't be very impressed with her now, she thought, reflecting on the trouble she'd landed herself in. Then again, she was fairly sure that Edna and Bill Collins had been expecting her to mess up again since she'd run off to Southeast Asia with Beck Ballantyne nine years before. She'd wanted to be with Beck more than she'd wanted to please her mom and dad and... *boom*! Fireworks.

This latest bombshell would rock their world again. Cady pushed the tips of her fingers into her forehead and held back a whimper. And that was without telling them that her business was rocky and she was running out of options to keep it on the rails.

"Cady?"

Cady jerked her head up to see a small blonde and a tall brunette standing next to her table. The blonde looked familiar, but she instantly recognized the classic good looks of Julia Parker, a Fortune 500 business consultant who socialized with the great and good of New York society. Cady would never forget Julia, especially since the woman had recently convinced Trott's Sports— a corporate sports store that was one of two clients that paid Cady a hefty monthly retainer—to not renew their contract with Collins Consulting.

Thank God she was still contracted to Natural Fuel, Tom's company, a chain of health food outlets, to handle their media releases and promotions. Without that contract, she'd be sunk.

Losing Trott's had left her with a sizable hole in her business bank account. And without her biggest client. Cady resisted the urge to toss her tomato juice over Julia's pristine white dress and instead held out her hand to shake. God, sometimes being an adult sucked.

"Cady Collins, Collins Consulting."

Julia immediately made the connection.

"Trott's… They couldn't afford to renew," Julia murmured, and wrinkled her nose. "Sorry."

Cady shrugged.

"Are you doing okay?"

Julia's question surprised her; she didn't expect her to ask or to sound like she cared. Cady lifted her hands up in a "what can I do" gesture. "It's tough."

"For what it's worth, I like your work," Julia stated, and Cady heard and appreciated the sincerity in her statement.

"Thank you."

"You don't recognize me, do you?" the blonde demanded, pulling their attention back to her, her smile bright and big.

Cady shook her head.

"I'm Amy Cook. We met on Phi Phi island when you were traveling with Beck years ago."

Beck. Funny, she'd just been thinking about him. *Like that's a coincidence,* Cady mocked herself. *You've been thinking about the man, pretty much constantly, for the best part of the last decade.*

Cady cocked her head and peered at the woman. The image of her with waist-length blond hair and a thong bikini popped into her head. "I remember you. You flirted shamelessly with Beck."

"She flirts with everyone. Don't take it personally," Julia said, a rich chuckle following her words.

"Do you live in Manhattan?" Amy demanded. "What do you do? Are you married? Do you have children?"

Cady didn't know which question to answer first. Work was easy, the other questions were a tad more complicated. "Um... I live in Brooklyn and I have my own PR company."

Amy's eyes widened. "Really? Seriously?"

Millions of women worked in PR and many owned their own companies. Why was this such a surprise? Speaking of business, she desperately needed to drum up some, and it wasn't every day that she bumped into one of the best business consultants in the city, so Cady reached into her tote bag and pulled out a business card.

She handed Julia the card with a small shrug. "I'd be

grateful if you kept me in mind if any of your clients need PR or any marketing help. I'm good, efficient and reasonable."

Julia took the card from her and nodded. "I'll do that."

Amy cocked her head, and her dark brown eyes connected with Cady's. "You didn't tell me if you're married or if you have children."

Yeah, right. She was not discussing any of those thorny subjects with a woman she'd exchanged ten words with nearly ten years ago.

Cady looked at the entrance of Bonnets and faked a smile. "Ah, the person I'm waiting for has arrived. It was interesting running into you again, Amy. Nice to meet you, Julia."

"But—" Amy protested.

"Come on." Julia placed a hand on Amy's back and pushed her away. "Let's find someone else you can practice your CIA interrogation skills on."

Cady rolled her eyes. Of all the people in the world she'd thought she'd never see again, and whom she never wanted to see again, Amy was at the top of her list. Nearly a decade ago, Beck had tired of Cady and he'd sent her home so that he could sow his wild oats all over the Asian subcontinent. Once Cady left, she was sure Amy had stepped right on into the space, in bed and out, that Cady had occupied in Beck's life.

Beck had been and still was the honey that female bees flocked to. She watched his subtle flirting, heard him laughing with Amy, and she'd felt like she couldn't compete with the blonde bombshell.

Cady was long, lanky and not overly blessed, as her boyfriend, Tom, told her often enough, in the "boobage" department. But it was more than that. Beck, Amy and the other backpackers they'd met had been just so to-

gether, so effortlessly confident. Of course, there were
the stoners and weirdos and the lost, but many of the trav-
elers had their lives sorted. They were street-smart and
confident and knew where they were going and what to
do when they got there.

Thanks to her protected, insulated childhood, she
would've been utterly lost without Beck making the decisions for her. Was that why he'd ditched her, because
she'd been lacking in self-confidence and because she'd
become more of a responsibility than a girlfriend?

Who knew? He'd been long on termination and short
on explanations. He'd just handed her a ticket and stood
in line with her at Passport Control. When she'd cleared
that, she'd turned back to look at him through the glass
walls and saw him walking away, taking a fair share of
her shattered heart with him.

"Cady."

Cady looked up and accepted Tom's quick brush of
his lips against her cheek. He sat down opposite her and
immediately glanced at his watch. "I have about a half
hour before I need to be back in the office. Can we make
this quick?"

Wow, nice to see you, too, Tom. "I thought we were
having dinner together?"

"Can't. I have some problems at work, so I need to get
back to my desk."

She was sleeping with her client, and the fact that she
was still embarrassed her. Tom dismissed her concerns
of their lack of professionalism, saying they were both
single and it wasn't a hanging offense. She'd tried to be
okay with it but she'd finally made the decision to call it
quits. Fate, however, had other ideas.

"You look like hell, Cady. What's up with that?"

Tom's jerk quotient always went up when he was

stressed, Cady thought. It wasn't personal, she reminded herself.

But it sure felt pretty personal. Beck had hurt her when he tossed her away, but he'd never talked to her like this. Then again, Tom Steel wasn't Beck Ballantyne. Nobody could be.

Gorgeous, super-smart and highly successful, he'd set the bar pretty high and no man could reach it.

Let's get some perspective here, Collins. Beck kicked you out of his life; he sent you away. You expected it from your parents, but not from the man you loved to distraction. Who you thought might love you.

That had been a very erroneous assumption.

Tom's flat hand hitting the table jolted her back into the present. "Cady! Just say what you have to say, will you?"

Sure.

"I'm pregnant."

Tom's low, vicious curse hung in the air between them. "Get rid of it."

She'd somehow expected him to say that. "Not an option."

Her parents had rid themselves of Will by sending him to live at a residential home when he was thirteen, and Beck had sent her away, too, but she was not prepared to do the same to her child. Sure, a pregnancy wasn't convenient, but neither had Will's autism or her falling in love with Beck been convenient.

You didn't just erase the problem because you didn't like the outcome.

Tom's face turned paper-white. "I need a drink."

Cady watched Tom walk to the bar and hoped that her baby didn't inherit his knock-kneed walk. Or his lack of height. Or the cowlick just above his right ear.

He isn't Beck...

Damn him for being the entire package, both smart and sexy. A blue-eyed wavy haired blond, Beck looked like he belonged on the cover of a surfing magazine. Long-limbed and muscular, he looked as good in a tuxedo as he did in a pair of swimming shorts. Unlike Beckett, Tom didn't make her head swim or her heart race and she liked it that way. It was an adult relationship with no teenage hormones and irrationality to cloud her thinking. She certainly never felt short of breath or felt the need to rip Tom's clothes off.

She'd been careful with Tom; she hadn't given him any of her heart. She'd given Beckett everything—including her virginity—only to be dismissed when he'd had enough of her.

So, yeah, Tom never set her panties, or her heart, on fire and walking away from him was going to be easy. She'd just prefer not to be pregnant while she did it.

Single and pregnant. Her parents were going to be so proud.

Cady rested her hand on her stomach. There was only one fact of which she was certain: she was keeping her baby.

Tom banged his tumbler of whiskey onto the table and sat down again. He lifted his glass to his lips and sent her a long, cold look.

"Is it mine?"

Cady lifted her hands in the air. "Are you crazy? Of course it's yours. I haven't slept with anyone else but you since we started dating."

Tom shrugged. He turned his head toward the bar, leered at a new female arrival and turned back to her, looking supremely disinterested.

"The baby is yours, Tom," Cady repeated, enunciating the words.

He pouted. "So you say."

"Tom, we've been seeing each other for the best part of a year."

"I didn't think we were dating *only* each other."

Cady blinked, utterly astounded. What the hell?

Wait, hold on a second… If Tom thought that they weren't exclusive then that meant that he had colored outside the lines, so to speak. "Have you cheated on me?"

"Since I didn't think we were exclusive I don't consider it cheating."

"You bastard!" Cady stopped herself from banging the table. "Who?"

"Does it matter?" Tom asked, his voice cool. He motioned to her stomach, and his next words catapulted this exchange from a bad dream into a nightmare. "Get rid of it or you're fired."

"You can't fire me. I have a contract with you!" Cady stated, not recognizing the cold, heartless man sitting opposite her. God, if she lost Tom's business, as well…

"So sue me." Tom shrugged, unconcerned. "I'll win. Cady, I'm not interested in having a baby. If you want child support you're going to have to sue me for that, as well," Tom stated after draining his glass of whiskey. "But I should warn you that I'll sic both sets of lawyers on you—mine and my wife's."

What? His *wife's* lawyers? He was divorced; he'd been divorced for a little over a year. He'd divorced her because she'd refused to date him until he was free.

Oh, dear God…

"You called Gretchen your wife." Cady forced the question through her now-numb lips. "Have you been cheating on me with your wife?"

Tom's cold look pushed ice into her bones. "Cady, I never divorced her. I've been cheating on her…with you."

* * *

After sending a text message to the group name "family" on his phone—telling them he was fine and enjoying his trip—Beck sat down at the desk in his luxury hotel room to Skype Amy.

His computer did its thing and then Amy's pixie face filled his screen. She scowled at him. "It's about time you called."

"Hello to you, too," Beck said with a faint smile. Beck wondered, not for the first time, who was the boss in the relationship. He might be a Ballantyne director, but Amy, the PA he shared with Linc and the person he and his siblings entrusted with the most confidential information, was the power behind the throne. "What's up?"

"So much," Amy answered and held up her index finger. "Don't go away. I'm just going to get my wine."

Beck laughed when Julia hung her face, upside down, over the screen to blow him a kiss. Amy's long-term partner and soon-to-be wife was a goofball, and around her loved ones, she rarely acted like the cool professional the financial world knew her to be.

Beck picked up his laptop, walked toward the bed and placed the device on the bedside table. He tucked pillows between his head and the headboard of the massive bed and stretched out his legs. He liked beds to be big enough to accommodate his six-four frame.

Beck placed his laptop on his knees and reached for his beer. He sipped it as he watched Amy's cat, Lazy Joe, jump with great effort onto her chair and curl up into a gray-and-white ball. Amy returned, picked up the cat and resettled the feline on her lap.

"God, look at you with your messy hair and your stubble, wearing only a pair of track pants. So hot." Amy tossed a quick look over her shoulder. "Julia, I'm thinking of going straight."

"Stop lusting over Beckett, you pervert. He's your boss." Julia's voice drifted over from the kitchen, sounding perfectly relaxed.

"And you're not my type. Even if you were straight we'd have no chemistry," Beck said mildly.

"True. So, I'm now going to ignore that fabulous chest and six-pack abs."

"So kind," Beck murmured.

"You look like you're having a miserable time on your forced break," Amy commented.

After his first year of working for Ballantyne International, Connor had insisted that, because he was a driven, relentless workaholic with a habit of working sixteen or more hours a day, he take a week off every four months. Initially, he'd felt like Connor was punishing him for working too hard, but he eventually realized that it was his uncle's way of looking after his health. Connor knew that he couldn't force Beck to stop working but he could at least manage him.

No one did that now. Connor's death had leveled the playing fields between him and his brothers and he no longer took orders that he not work so hard. His siblings didn't understand, and he'd never explain, that he liked to work insane hours, that his devotion to Ballantyne International was his way of showing them that he was an asset to the company, his way to earn and keep his place in his family.

It was the kid's fault. He asked them to come home. He'd broken his wrist and he needed to have it pinned and made a big deal about them coming home to be with him.

"Which one is he?"

"Can't see him right now. But he's the middle child, the one who had a panic attack in church."

"Two lives and a baby on the way—a hell of a price to pay for a broken arm. I wonder if he'll ever know the damage his whining caused."

Because Beck was under the table, hidden by the long tablecloth, and listening to the whispered conversations of the mourners invited back to the family home after the funeral, he heard the comments and understood perfectly. His parents' deaths were his fault.

It was a conclusion he'd already come to. Hearing it spoken aloud just confirmed what he already thought. From that day on, he'd always felt like the outsider looking in and he'd made himself as independent as he possibly could be. He'd emotionally distanced himself from his siblings and, really, it was better that way. Distance allowed a buffer against the hurt that emotional connections always created. Distance allowed him to keep control.

He'd come close to losing control once and he'd paid the price for it. Over two months and on a continent across the world, Cady had snuck under his skin and into his heart and he'd lost himself in her.

She was just a young man's stupidity, Beck told himself for the millionth time. Every guy had that one woman he idolized in his head. It didn't mean anything.

He'd been trying for nearly a decade to believe his own BS. At the time she'd meant *everything.*

"Where are you this time?" Amy demanded, pulling him out of his thoughts. "Please, please tell me you're lying on a beach somewhere reading a book."

Not his style. Admittedly, all his breaks were action based and full of physical activity, but at least his brain slowed down from constantly operating at warp speed.

"Saariselkä, Finland."

"Of course you are. Heli-skiing?"

Beck smiled at her concern. Amy hated it when he indulged in his love for high-risk adventure sports. "Not this time. Cross-country skiing."

"Dangerous?"

"Not at all," Beck lied. There had been a couple of hairy traverses this morning, but he was here in one piece, wasn't he? What was the point of upsetting her?

"Liar."

Beck smiled and took a sip of his beer. Since meeting Amy in Thailand, she'd been his closest friend. He was reasonably sociable but the reserve he cultivated meant that he didn't have many close friends. Amy had ignored his "keep out" signs and had barged her way into his life. He'd flown to Hanoi after saying goodbye to Cady in Bangkok and Amy had immediately sensed that he was hurting. She'd plastered herself to his side and traveled with him as he hauled his dented heart over the soil of various Southeast Asian countries.

You couldn't BS a person who'd witnessed your heart bleed.

Amy had been a kind and consistent presence, a true friend. And because of her sexual orientation, they'd never complicated their friendship with sex. He and Amy had quit traveling at the same time and he'd joined Ballantyne International, knowing that it was time to put his MBA to work. Amy had needed a job and he'd arranged for her to do some temporary secretarial work at Ballantyne International. Within three months, she'd made herself indispensable, not only to him, but also to his ex-guardian and uncle, Connor Ballantyne. Amy, irreverent and hip but brutally efficient, became Connor's eyes, ears and right hand and she'd been devastated when Connor was diagnosed with Alzheimer's.

It was Amy who'd made all the arrangements to transport Jaeger back home when he was involved in that car accident in Italy, and Amy who'd held Beckett's hand at his brother's hospital bed and at his uncle's funeral.

"So, what's happening at work?" Beckett asked her, tapping his finger against the neck of his cold beer bottle.

"The usual. I sent out the briefs to various PR firms today to bid for the rebranding strategy."

A small frown appeared between Beck's eyes. "Which firms did you send the brief to?"

Amy named a few firms Beck was familiar with and he nodded his approval. "Linc instructed me to send them to smaller firms, too, ones that think outside the box," Amy added.

"Hard to find."

"Jules had a suggestion or two."

"Who?"

Amy shrugged. "You wouldn't know them."

Beck couldn't identify the emotion flashing in Amy's eyes and he frowned at her uncharacteristic reticence.

"Well, let's see what they come up with. Email me their bid documents and I can go through them."

Amy shook her head. "Linc told me that that he'll run through them and pick the top four to do detailed presentations. You'll be back for their presentations, so you can weigh in then."

Amy had her stubborn face on and he knew he'd lost this round. To be honest, he really didn't want to plow through the bid documents. It was tedious work and if Linc wanted to do it, he'd let him.

"Listen, Beck…"

Amy bit the inside of her lip and Beck knew she was

about to say something he didn't want to hear. Worse, she had the same look on her face when every year or so she suggested that he track down Cady, that he see where she was and what she was doing. That he find a real connection, like the one she and Julia had.

And every year he told her he wasn't interested, that he was perfectly happy as he was. Well, not happy, but content.

"Guess who I saw today?" Amy asked before he could tell her not to go there.

Beck tensed. He didn't need her to say the name; he heard it in her voice. "Where?"

"At Bonnets, a cocktail bar off—"

"I know it." Beck felt hot then cold. He stared down at the patterned comforter, the blue-and-white pattern rising and falling.

He forced his tongue to move. "New York is in so many ways a small town. Listen, I have to go."

"No, you don't. You're just trying to avoid talking about Cady. I need to tell you—"

"Bye, Ames, I'll talk to you soon." Beck slapped his laptop shut on her annoyed squeal.

He ran his hand through his wavy hair and flipped the laptop open again. He quickly accessed a file, opening the one photo he'd kept of her. She was lying on the sand at Maya Bay on Phi Phi island, her bright pink bikini a blaze of triangles against her tanned skin. She'd turned her head to look at him and her long and silky hair dropped into the sand. Her startling eyes brimmed with laughter. And love.

They'd been apart for nearly ten years and would be apart for a lifetime more. He knew that, accepted that. That was why he never thought about her, said her name, discussed those first few months of his trip. They were completely, solidly over. So why was he looking at a photo of her, wishing that things had turned out differently?

Because he wasn't busy and he had time to think. And to remember.

But mostly because he was, despite his high IQ, a moron.

Two

Beck exited the private elevator that only he, his siblings and Amy had access to and stepped into the corridor of Ballantyne International. The corporate offices were situated above their flagship, and oldest, jewelry store on Fifth Avenue. Unlike the classic decor of the store below, the Ballantyne offices were light, airy and modern. Beck, as director of finance and the group's troubleshooter, saw an intern walking down the hall to the copy room and struggled to remember his name.

"Cole, Cody..."

The kid turned and offered a tentative smile. "Charles, sir."

He had the *C* right and he was only in his early thirties, far too young to be called sir. Beck shrugged out of his leather jacket and laid it across the top of his suitcase and pushed the bag in the intern's direction. "Put this in Amy's office and bring me a very large cup of coffee. I'll be in Linc's office until further notice."

"Mr. Ballantyne—Linc—is in the boardroom with the other Mr. Ballantyne and Ms. Ballantyne."

Beck nodded, holding back his smile at the mouthful of *B*s. "Thanks." He turned and headed in the opposite direction, greeting the odd person he encountered on his way. Monday morning and thanks to his flight being diverted to Newark because of an anticipated emergency landing at La Guardia, he was late. He'd picked the least aggressive cab driver in the city and his trip from New Jersey had taken forever. He hated being late.

Beck opened the door to the conference room and pushed his shirtsleeves up his elbows. As Charles said, his siblings were all in the room, but Amy wasn't.

"Driven is back," Jaeger stated, leaning back in his chair.

Jaeger had given him the nickname shortly after his thirteenth birthday when he graduated at the top of his class and made both the state swimming and track teams. They thought that he was an outlier, one of those kids who was gifted in both sports and academics. They never suspected that he'd always felt the need to prove himself worthy of being born a Ballantyne.

"How was Finland?" Linc asked, standing up to give him a one-arm hug. Linc was almost as big as he was and a couple of years older. Beck stepped away and bent down to drop a kiss in Sage's black hair. Like him, his brothers were big and brawny but Sage had the body of a ballerina.

"Good," Beck replied, slapping his palm against Jaeger's. "How's Ty? Flu gone?"

Jaeger nodded. "He's fine. When are you going to find a woman and bake yourself a kid, Beck? They are a blast."

Oh, no, not this again. Beck noticed the glint of mischief that appeared in Jaeger's eyes and did an internal eye roll. Since reconnecting and falling in love with Piper, Jaeger was determined to pull his siblings into his sparkly, loved-up world. Beckett had no objection to being loved up; he just didn't need the emotional connection. He had no intention of flirting with that hell again. After Cady, it had taken him six months to feel halfway human and another six before he'd felt relatively whole again.

He refused to think of her, not now, not ever. He hadn't been able to discuss her with Amy; couldn't bear to even hear her name.

"I've had a nightmare morning so don't start," Beck said as a hesitant tap came from the half open door. He pulled the door open, took his cup of coffee from Charles, said thanks and took a reviving sip. "So, this looks like a meeting. What's on the agenda?"

"Only one thing," Linc told him.

"And that is?"

"Deciding who we are going to appoint to oversee our new PR and rebranding campaign."

Linc dropped into the chair at the head of the conference table and Beck sat to his right. "A lot has happened lately. At the beginning of last week, I met with eight PR companies, including Jenkins and Pale, who's always done our PR and advertising."

As the Ballantyne finance director and all round troubleshooter, this item for discussion was in Beck's wheelhouse. Jaeger sourced magnificent gems and Sage was their head designer, but Beck and Linc ran the business side of Ballantyne International.

"We decided that we needed to rebrand a while back, but I moved it higher up our priority list," Linc said. "As we know, Connor was the face of Ballantyne. He had the personal connections and brought charisma to the brand. Without him the Ballantyne brand is...staid, stuffy."

Linc leaned forward, clasping his hands on the table and looking at Beck. "The day you left town Sheik Abdul Ameen went to Moreau's and bought a diamond bracelet for his mother instead of coming to us. I did a sales audit and I noticed that other long-term, super-rich clients have also moved on."

Their clients' loyalty was to Connor, not to them, Beck realized.

"But we have the same quality of gems we always have had," Sage protested.

"Yeah, but we don't have Connor selling them," Linc pointed out. "Connor knew his clients inside out. They liked dealing with him and only with him."

"And our younger, rich clients want sexy and they want hip." Beck sipped his coffee, agreeing with his brother. Linc was brilliant at managing their staff and dealing with their shareholders. He was a hands-on manager, but Beckett was their strategist, able to see the big picture. He and Linc worked really well together with each of them playing to their strengths.

He looked back to Linc. "So you met with these PR firms and...?"

"And I isolated four who, I think, have some idea of what we want. They aren't perfect by any means, but their ideas have potential. One of them is better than the others."

"Who?" Sage asked Linc.

Linc shook his head. "Listen to their pitches and make up your own mind."

Beck glanced at his watch. "When are we due to start?"

"Fifteen minutes," Jaeger replied.

"Good, I have time to change. Where's Amy?" Beck asked, standing up, his coffee cup in his hand.

"She should be out in the reception area meeting and greeting the company representatives," Linc replied.

Beck nodded. "I just need to say hi to her and I'll see you back here in fifteen."

"Beckett," Linc said as he reached the conference door. Beck heard the note of concern in Linc's voice and turned around to look at his brother.

"Yeah?"

"Remember that we're making the right choice for the company. That might not be the right choice for you."

Beck looked from Linc to Jaeger and to Sage's worried eyes. "What the hell do you mean by that?" he demanded.

"You'll see."

Beck heard Linc's ominous words and felt a shiver run up his spine. He looked down the hall to the bank of elevators and wondered why he had the instinctive urge to run.

What in the name of all that was holy was she doing here?

Saving her business, Cady reminded herself. No more, no less. Sitting on one of the low, tangerine-colored ottomans in the reception area of Ballantyne and Company, she placed her hands under her thighs and ordered her knees to stop knocking. God, there was Gayle from Jenkins and Pale, Ballantyne's long-term PR partner. And was she talking to Matthew from Anchor and Chain Consulting? They were at the top of the PR food chain. She was plankton. Or the stuff plankton ate.

Cady fixed her eyes on the large, abstract painting on the wall behind the receptionist's head and begged her queasy stomach to settle down. *Yes, baby, it's been a hell of a week, but I had no choice. If we want to eat and have a roof over our heads, I have to work and not sleep, as I so want to do.*

Ten days ago, after her disastrous meeting with Tom, she'd doubted she could pull herself out of this hole. Accepting that her baby's father was a cyanide pill, she'd headed back to the office that night, knowing that she had plans to make. When dawn broke that Saturday morning, she realized that she had three months to turn her business around. If she didn't she would be single, pregnant and broke.

Not knowing how to do that, she'd fallen asleep on the sofa in her office and was jerked awake later that morning by the ping of her computer, informing her of a new email. Congenitally unable to ignore a communication, whether it was an email, a text message or a smoke signal, Cady opened the email from pr@ballantynes.com.

Ballantyne International is seeking to appoint a specialist PR agency to work with us to reinvent our century-old brand. We require a passionate and creative firm/individual to develop and install a range of external communications and media activities.

The brief attached sets out our objectives and requirements, together with a range of background information on Ballantyne International. Interested agencies are asked to respond in full by 9:00 a.m. Monday January 3 at the latest.

Somehow, somewhere, the PR person at Ballantyne's had heard of her and she was invited to the party. Late, but still invited.

Given the choice, she would've avoided doing work for Beck's company but she didn't have that luxury. Winning this project would keep Collins Consulting afloat. Sure, she was a minnow competing with the sharks and she didn't have that much of a chance, but if she didn't submit a proposal she didn't have a chance at all.

Basically, it was a choice between telling her parents she was pregnant, single and could support herself and her child or that she was pregnant, single and could they help her out until she found a job?

Yeah, when she broke it down like that, it was no contest.

But first, she needed to face Beck.

At the thought of him, she resisted the urge to grab her laptop and run. She had no other option. She had a business to save, a baby to raise, money to earn. Unlike Beck, she didn't have endless family money and hefty trusts as a backup plan.

Not fair, she chided herself. Beck never used his position as a Ballantyne heir as an excuse not to achieve. If anything, it spurred him on to prove to the world that he would be successful whether he was a Ballantyne or not. Even though the Ballantynes were practically American royalty, Ivy League schools didn't hand out MBAs just because you were rich.

But she didn't want to be fair. Beck's actions in Thailand, his playing loose and fast with her feelings and her love, had devastated her. And she wished more than anything there was something she could do to never lay eyes on him again.

"Cady?"

At the sound of her name Cady looked up and saw Amy standing over her. Amy? *Beck's Amy?*

"Hi. I'm glad you made it through the selection process." Amy smiled at her, effortlessly confident.

Cady quickly realized Amy must have sent her the

pitch documents and the brief; the timing made sense since she'd given her card to Julia Parker on Friday night and she received the email on Saturday morning. Well, the how made sense but not the why.

"You emailed me," Cady said as she stood up. "Why?"

"Take a walk with me," Amy suggested and Cady fell into step with her as she proceeded down the hallway that led to the glass-walled offices of Ballantyne International.

Amy stopped under another large, expensive art piece. "Linc asked me to contact a range of PR firms, both big and small, to bid for this job. Julia said that you did good work for Trott's, so I gave you a chance to pitch, just like I gave seven other companies the same chance. Linc liked your ideas and you're one of the final four."

"So this has nothing to do with you feeling guilty about taking my place with Beck?"

Cady felt like a twit the second her words left her mouth, and Amy's laughter deepened her embarrassment. God, she sounded like a sulky teenager.

When she stopped laughing at her, Amy said, "That's the funniest thing I've heard for a long, long time."

"Hey, Ames."

Oh, damn. She recognized that voice; she heard it in her dreams often enough. Dark as sin, rich as butter, warm as hot chocolate after playing in the snow.

Cady looked over Amy's shoulder and watched him walk down the hall toward them, dressed in battered jeans, boots and a navy, long-sleeved T-shirt the exact color of his eyes. The shirt was tight across his chest, skimming his muscled stomach. Blond stubble covered his cheeks, and his wavy hair brushed his collar. He looked rough and hot and fifty times better-looking than the Greek god she'd traveled with so many years ago.

His hair was a lot shorter than she remembered; the man bun was gone and so was the heavy beard. His eyes, a brilliant dark blue, seemed harder and his face thinner. His mouth, that clever mouth that had once dropped hot kisses all over her body, was a slash in his face. He looked hard and tough and every inch the smart, determined, sometimes ruthless businessman he was reputed to be. He looked like he could handle any and all trouble that came his way.

Her knees buckled and air rushed out of her lungs as she remembered those brawny arms around her, the way he used to easily lift her off her feet to kiss him. Cady tasted him on her tongue, could feel his heat, and smell his citrus and cedar scent. She was back in Thailand, the air was muggy, the sky was blue and she was turned on.

Breath short, mouth dry, panties damp...so turned on.

Oh, dammit!

Beck didn't pay her any attention as he scooped Amy off her feet and dropped a kiss on her lips. He hugged her again before he allowed her feet to hit the ground, his hands on her hips.

"Before you ask, no, I didn't bring you a present," he told Amy, that open smile flipping Cady's stomach up and over. She shivered, remembering the sexy phrases he'd muttered in that same baritone as he'd taught her how to give and receive physical pleasure.

Amy mock pouted before half turning away from him. Cady saw her suck in a deep breath before she placed her hand on Cady's bicep. "Obviously you remember Cady, Beck."

Color drained from Beck's face as he looked from Cady to Amy and back again. The warmth in his eyes faded and she watched, fascinated, as his eyes raked her from head to toe. She saw his eyes deepen with... God, could that be desire? But when they met hers again, they were the dark, cold blue of a winter's ocean.

"Cady. What are you doing here?" His voice held no emotion as his words whipped across her.

Before she could answer, Amy flashed him a bright smile. "Cady is in PR. Julia knows Cady's work and she suggested that Cady take a stab at developing a proposal to rebrand Ballantyne's. Since Julia is one of the most respected consultants in the city and since she rarely makes recommendations, I thought her advice was worth taking."

Beck didn't drop his eyes from hers as he leaned one big shoulder into the wall. God, he was still so sexy—no, scrap that. He was even hotter than he used to be. And so remote, disinterested.

His eyes finally moved to Amy and as he narrowed them on her, Cady realized that he was pissed.

So Beck wasn't happy to see her.

She couldn't do this; she absolutely could not be around him. He'd sent her home, tossed her away. She couldn't stay here and be constantly reminded that she wasn't enough.

Cady started to turn to walk away and then she remembered what was at stake. Her business was her only source of income and she needed that income. If she wasn't pregnant, she would leave but she was now responsible for another life, and walking away wasn't that simple anymore.

She needed this damned job.

Cady planted her feet and turned her attention back to her ex-lover and potential client and to Amy, who obviously had an important position in his company.

"Linc asked me to source proposals from new, hungry firms as well as the established companies we've worked with before. Cady made it through the first round and she's about to do her presentation," Amy explained, still sounding cool and composed.

Cady could see the tension in his body, see his fist clench. "You've gone too far, Amy."

"I have not. This is a business arrangement, a job. She's creative, hungry and needs work, and Ballantyne's needs someone creative, something different. You're making this personal, not me," Amy retorted.

How could it not be? What they had had been very personal indeed. She allowed this man to do things to her that still made her blush. And she'd returned the favor…

As she remembered hot mouths, desperate hands, labored breathing and mind-shattering orgasms, she had to place her hand on the wall to keep her balance. Beck's eyes slammed into hers and she caught a flash of awareness, a lick of fiery heat, and she knew that he knew exactly what she was thinking. For an instant he was there with her, holding himself above her, about to slide into her.

His eyes always turned that particular shade of cobalt-blue when he was turned on. Cady licked her lips and dropped her eyes to his crotch…

Nope, nothing. No action at all. Mortified, she lifted her hot face to see the ice in his eyes. So, she was alone in that little fantasy, and Beck was definitely not taking a walk down memory lane.

But Beck was giving her another once-over, his gaze starting at her nude heels, moving slowly up her skinny black trousers to her blush-pink silk blouse. She'd pulled her long hair into a severe braid, which she twisted into a low knot at the back of her head, and her makeup, while minimalist, was flawless. With black, heavy-framed glasses, she looked every inch the New York businesswoman and nothing like the free-spirited girl he used to know.

While he inspected her like she was a car he was considering buying, she thought that Beck was now bigger and broader, harder, and he exuded power from every sexy pore. Even dressed casually, he emitted a don't-mess-with-me vibe that dried up the moisture in her mouth and sent it straight to that special spot between her legs.

Damn.

Amy broke the tension by poking Beck with her red-tipped finger. "You need to change. You can't listen to presentations looking like you've just walked off a trail."

Beck grabbed her finger and held it, just enough for Amy's eyes to widen and for her to realize that Beck was still pissed off. "Do try to remember who the boss is."

Amy, utterly indefatigable, just grinned. "I do. It's me. Let's get back to work, people."

Cady spun around and walked back to the reception area and ignored the curious looks she received from her fellow competitors. Beck, she presumed, went to clean up.

Neither of them saw the gleeful expression on Amy's face or heard her whispered words. "Watching them is going to be so much fun."

Three

Keyed up and tense after her ninety-minute-long presentation, Cady left the conference room feeling like a washed-out rag. Needing a comfort break, she headed down the hall to the ladies' room, thinking that she'd wash her hands and face, reapply some war paint and try to catch her breath. The Ballantyne siblings—with the exception of Beck, who had just sat there, as immovable and silent as a rock—had bombarded her with questions, most of which she'd deftly answered.

She'd done her best in the limited time she'd had, putting together a mammoth strategy for a global company, but she had no illusions. She was up against the best in the business. If she got the contract then she'd earn herself a get-out-of-bankruptcy card. If she didn't, in a month or two she'd be packing her bags and throwing herself on the mercy of her parents.

They'd take her in; there was no doubt about it. But

she'd have to learn to live with disapproving looks and the what-were-you-thinking lectures. And the image of the perfect family, the one her mother tried so hard to project, would be shattered. The pastor's daughter, single and pregnant, the one who had so much potential, would be hot, hot gossip.

Her mother was going to *kill* her.

Cady felt a big hand wrap around her upper bicep and she spun around to look into Beckett's deep blue eyes, the exact color of the navy-and-white polka-dot tie he now wore over a finely striped light-blue-and-white shirt. Walking into the conference room earlier, the last company to present, she'd immediately noticed that he'd changed and couldn't help thinking he should always wear blue. The cuffs of his shirt were folded over the sleeves of his trendy cardigan, and both sleeves were pushed up to his elbows, showing his thick, muscled forearms.

Beckett was a snappy dresser.

"Beckett, I need to use the facilities," she protested as he walked her past the ladies' room.

"I have a private bathroom adjoining my office," he growled and Cady had to half jog to keep up with his long-legged stride. He ignored Amy's startled face as he walked past her desk and into the office on the right. Through the glass walls, a feature of the Ballantyne offices, she could see that Linc's office was empty. Cady wondered if they ever felt like they were working in a fish tank.

Beck pushed her through the glass door into his messy office.

"The bathroom is through there." He nodded to a door at the other end of the large space. "When you're done, we're going to talk."

That didn't sound good. Cady kept her face blank, not wanting Beck to see her flinch. Nodding once, she placed her laptop bag on one of the two bucket chairs facing his ridiculously large desk and headed for the bathroom.

After using the facilities, she took her time washing her hands and touching up her makeup. Beckett could wait until she got her galloping heart under control.

Cady gripped the counter of the vanity and stared at herself in the mirror. Severe hair, white face, bands of blue under her unusual eyes. Two stripes of color on each cheekbone, saving her from the need to apply blush.

She looked like what she was: a stressed-out woman trying to hustle a job. She didn't look pregnant but she did look flustered, and a little unhinged. She was older and more experienced, so why did she feel like she was nineteen again? Her palms were damp, her panties, too. He just needed to touch her and she'd go up in flames.

She might be older, but she wasn't any wiser, Cady thought, washing her hands for the second time.

"You're stalling, Cady. Get out here. I don't have all day."

"Yes, Your Lordship," Cady muttered, yanking the door open and stepping back into his office.

Beck stood by the floor-to-ceiling windows, his hands jammed into his pockets, every square inch of his long body taut with tension. Cady walked over to the window and stopped next to him, her arms folded across her chest. She felt equally uptight herself.

Cady looked down to the iconic Manhattan street below and watched the pedestrians navigate the busy intersection, their chins and noses tucked into scarves or coat collars, their faces ruddy from the icy winter wind.

"Why are you doing this, Cady?"

She turned to look at him. This was, at least, a question she could answer.

"It's my job, Beckett. Like you, but on a far smaller scale, I am running a business, a business that I'd prefer not to see go under. I need new, bigger clients. Ballantyne International is a new, big client." Cady shrugged, knowing that her edgy attitude wasn't conducive to good client–service provider relationships.

Beckett rolled his head on his shoulders and rubbed the back of his neck. "I would've liked some damn warning that you were going to drop back into my life."

Why? She didn't mean anything to him. He'd broken up with her by sending her home. He'd gone on to Vietnam, hooked up with Amy there and then God knew where. She was the one who had the right to feel caught off guard. Then again, she had had days to prepare herself to see him again. He'd only had a few minutes.

But since she meant nothing to him, why should it matter?

"This is just business, Beckett. I was a teenager and that was a lifetime ago. I have real problems to worry about—" like pregnancy and poverty "—and I really don't have the time or the energy to spend thinking about something that lasted a millisecond a million years ago."

She needed this contract and that meant putting her and Beckett on a very firm this-is-business footing. A cynical smile touched the corner of his mouth as his eyes dropped from hers to her mouth and back again.

"Are you really trying to tell me that the chemistry between us has disappeared? That you weren't remembering Thailand, hot nights and sweaty bodies? The way I'd kiss you?" His eyes dropped to her crotch, and Cady thought her panties might burst into flames. "How it felt when I sank into you?"

So he had been with her earlier, thinking of the way they'd made love to each other. She had seen the desire in his eyes and it wasn't her imagination.

Right now if she took one step she'd be up against his hard chest. If she pushed herself onto her toes, she could touch her lips to his.

God, she wanted to kiss him, touch the hard muscles she'd once known so well.

Job. Money. Contract. Baby. Glass walls.

The words cut through her haze of lust and she remembered why she was here and what was at stake. Cady sucked in a breath, tossed her head back, lifted her chin and borrowed her mother's you're-on-the-path-to-hell look. "We're going to go there, *really?*"

"Yeah, really."

Beckett slapped his hand on a switch panel and the glass walls turned opaque and Amy, and her curious face, disappeared.

Cady had to smile. "Now that's a cool trick."

"I think so."

Beckett stepped into her personal space and Cady's folded arms brushed his rock-hard abdomen. Her heart bounced off her rib cage, and her stomach felt like it was taking a roller-coaster ride, but she'd be damned if she'd let Beck see how much his hot and hard body affected her.

Beck smiled, lifted a hand and rested the tip of his index finger in the V of her throat. "Your pulse is trying to burst through your skin."

Damned pulse. *Heart, stop beating*, she ordered.

Beck's hot fingertip ran up the side of her throat until he reached her jaw. "God, your eyes. My memory didn't do them justice. Silver and green all contained in a ring of emerald."

Cady swallowed and shook her head. "Don't do this, Beckett."

"I think I have to," he replied, the heat of his hand scalding her jaw. His other hand grasped her hip and he pulled her into him.

Cady tried to keep her arms folded, she really did, so she had no idea how her hands ended up being splayed onto his chest. And why was she tipping her head up, watching his mouth as it slowly descended to hers?

Beck's lips were pure magic, Cady thought, as his mouth took possession of hers. She felt his hand cup her right butt cheek and pull her up into his hard body. She closed her eyes, not quite believing that he was holding her, that his mouth was on hers. It felt like it belonged there, as if she'd been created to be kissed by him. Beck kissed her like he owned her, like she was still his. He kissed her with unreserved passion, unafraid to show her how turned on he was. His mouth, lips, tongue...all hot, silky, sexy.

Underneath the fabric of her trousers, Cady felt the heat of his fingers pushing into her skin and she wished that he would use his hands to do something interesting. Touching her breasts and swiping his thumb over her nipple sounded like a really good idea right then. But Beck did neither. He continued to kiss her, his tongue tangling with hers until she didn't know where she started or he ended.

The strident ring of her phone in the side pocket of her tote bag had Beck pulling away from her. He cocked his head and nodded at her bag. "Want to get that?"

Cady couldn't form any words so she just shook her head, her hands gripping his clothing to pull him back to her. She needed more kisses, more of him... It had been so damn long.

"Just business, huh?"

Beck's sarcastic comment had her eyes flying open and she immediately noticed the sarcastic glint in his eyes, the muscle ticking in his jaw. Cady released her grip and took a decisive step back. "Was that a test?" she demanded, annoyed to hear the shake in her voice.

"Sure. And we failed." Under his shirt Beck's biceps bunched as he folded his arms and widened his stance. He looked big and tough and intimidating, but Cady knew that he was as deeply affected by that kiss as she was. It was cold comfort.

"I don't mix business with pleasure, Cady," Beck told her, his tone non-negotiable. "And I will do anything and everything to protect Ballantyne's."

"I'm working with you and not against you, Beck," Cady protested.

"This rebranding strategy is the most important marketing project of the last twenty years and I do not want my business performance affected because we can't keep our hands off each other."

"We're adults, Beckett. If we decide to keep it professional, we can," Cady told him.

Pfft, her inner voice mocked. *Just like you did with Tom? What a liar!*

"It always blows up and we're pretty combustible as it is," Beck stated.

Cady released a frustrated sigh and at her sides, her hands pulled up into fists. *Do not react, do not react.* "It's unlike you to put the cart before the horse, Beckett. Why don't we see if I am awarded the contract first? I have some pretty strong competition."

Beck sent her a long, hard look. "I'll give you twenty thousand dollars if you walk out that door and forget all about us, and Ballantyne's."

Cady felt her knees buckle and she dropped down to sit on the edge of his visitor's chair, unaware that she was sharing the space with her laptop bag. "Sorry... *What?*"

"I'll pay you twenty K for you not to take this contract."

That was what she thought he said. Cady lifted her head to look at Beck, conscious of a throbbing pain underneath her rib cage. Were those three months in Thailand such a bad memory that he couldn't stand to be around her, couldn't wrap his head around working with her? Okay, she hadn't loved traveling, mostly because her parents had been so dead set against the notion. She'd been pulled in two directions by her parents and by Beck, but they'd had some fun. Hadn't they?

Cady didn't understand any of this and her first impulse was to tell him to take his offer and stick it. She opened her mouth to blast him and then she remembered that this wasn't just about her. She had a child on the way and if she refused his offer, and wasn't awarded the contract, she'd be broke and soon homeless. If she took the money, she'd buy herself a hell of a lot of breathing room.

First prize would be landing the contract, of course, then all her money hassles would be solved.

"Well?"

It was tempting to take the cash and run. She opened her mouth to agree, struggling to think past the feelings of inadequacy and confusion. But if she took his money she'd be dancing to someone else's tune, to Beck's little ditty. He'd be putting her on a metaphorical plane again and sending her away because once again she was inconvenient.

She'd done that once and it took years for her to patch her heart back together, to regain her confidence.

She'd be running away, taking the easy option.

Have faith in yourself, Cady. If you don't get this project, you'll make another plan.

Beck no longer had the power to dictate her actions. She wasn't a teenager anymore.

Cady stood up, straightened her spine and sent him a death stare. "That's not going to happen, Beckett. I either get the contract or I don't. That's business and that's life. If I do get it, you're just going to have to deal with whatever problem you still have with me. If I don't, I will sort myself out. I've done okay on my own for a long time and I don't need you or your money."

Cady picked up her laptop bag, slung it over her shoulder and grabbed the strap of her tote bag. "I think we're done here."

Cady walked to the door and placed her hand on the doorknob. She looked at Beck, still standing at his desk, his eyes on her. "My pride and my self-respect are not for sale, Ballantyne."

Cady left the door open behind her and because Beck didn't want to see or speak to anyone for, oh, a hundred years, he hurried to the door and slammed it shut. He banged his head against the jamb, wishing he had a punching bag to plow his fist into.

From the moment he met her, Cady had the ability to turn his life upside down and inside out. And when she was awarded this PR contract—and she would be, since her presentation and strategy were creative, innovative and interesting—he wouldn't be able to avoid her.

Damn. He liked his life as it was. Drama free.

He also liked the fact that he was firmly in control of it. Since Connor was no longer here to hound him about being unemotional, to demand that he open up and communicate, he was able to stay on the fringes of the family group, present and supportive but not emotionally engaged.

He loved his family, intensely, but he still felt that deep down his siblings blamed him for his parents' deaths and if they didn't, then they should.

If he hadn't begged them to return home...

Feeling responsible and unable to rectify the problem, he'd realized that the only way to redeem himself was to show them that he was worthy of being a Ballantyne. At eight years old, under a table at the post-funeral reception, his drive and ambition were born.

The only time he'd taken a break from feeling responsible, from feeling like he had to prove his worth, was when he was traveling with Cady. Despite her family issues, he'd relaxed around her, and the freedom to be himself was intoxicating. She didn't care that he received his MBA when he was twenty, that he'd been a nationally ranked swimmer, that he was an heir to the Ballantyne fortune. To Cady, he was just Beck and he'd loved being just Beck.

He acknowledged that was the real reason he sent her away. For years he'd justified his actions by reminding himself that she was miserable, but in truth, the longer he spent with her, the less important his ambition and drive became. What Cady thought or believed about him started to become more important than what he believed about himself, and he couldn't have that.

Years later their attraction burned hotter and brighter than before—just being in the same room as her set his nerve endings on fire—and Beck worried that, if she stuck around and if he spent any time with her at all, history would repeat itself.

He had an obligation to his family, to Ballantyne's, to help Linc steer this mammoth ship of a business in a global economy. Ballantyne International, and all its many subsidiaries, including the high-end jewelry stores that were the face of the business, were his top and only priority, and he had to guard against anything that threatened his duty to Ballantyne's.

Cady had, and if he wasn't careful, she might again. He couldn't take the chance.

Beck lifted his head off the doorjamb and as he did so, the door flew open and smacked him in the forehead. He groaned and stepped back, placing his hand over his forehead.

"Why the hell are you standing behind the door?" Linc asked, unsympathetic.

"Crap! Why didn't you knock?" Beck demanded, dropping his hand to check for blood.

"Problems," Linc said, stepping inside and closing the door behind him.

"It's been that type of day," Beck said, walking back to his desk, conscious of his throbbing head. He dropped into his leather chair and placed his ankle on his opposite knee. "What's up?"

Linc paced the area in front of Beck's desk. If there was one good thing to come out of his parents' deaths, then it was Linc, and his mother, Jo. Unable to cope with three kids, Connor hired Jo as his housekeeper and nanny, and she and her son moved into the brownstone with the rest of them. A few years later, Connor formally adopted his nephews and niece, and also Linc, thereby legalizing their emotional bond. As he had been then, Linc was still the person they ran to when their wheels fell off.

He was their brother, not by blood, but by choice.

Linc placed his hands on Beck's desk, his gray eyes worried. "So, Tate Harper just called me."

Now there was a name he hadn't heard for a while. "Harper? Kari's sister?"

Linc nodded, anger flashing in his eyes. Beck didn't blame him. When their son, Shaw, was six weeks old, Kari up and left Linc and their son. After another two months, Linc's PI friend tracked her to Austin. Reame returned with a message from Kari telling Linc that she wasn't coming back and a document signing over full custody of Shaw to Linc.

Kari's sister, a travel presenter, seemed as flaky as her sister.

"What does she want?" Beck asked.

"She has something urgent to discuss with me." Linc shrugged. "No idea what but, knowing the Harper sisters, it can't be anything good."

"Have you met her?"

"No."

"If she's anything like Kari then she'll be very easy on the eyes," Beck stated.

"And, if she's anything like her sister, as cracked as a sidewalk," Linc said, looking and sounding tense. "We're meeting in an hour, at the brownstone."

"It's that important that it can't wait until the end of the day?" Beck asked, surprised. Like him, Linc was rarely distracted from his work at Ballantyne's.

"So she says. Kari probably sent her to try to sweet-talk me into sending her some cash," Linc said, sounding bitter.

"Just say no, dude." Beck dropped his foot and looked at the piles of paper on his desk. A quick glance at his monitor showed that he had a slew of emails he needed to look at. Taking a break was good for him, but the recuperative effects were quickly negated by the avalanche of work that hit his desk in his absence.

Linc started to leave, then he turned back around to Beck. "We need to make a decision about the PR consultant."

Beckett tensed. He prayed they'd choose someone else, anyone else, just not Cady. Was he allowed, just this one time, to put his interests above those of Ballantyne's?

"The three of us want to hire Cady."

Of course they did.

"Can you live with that? Jaeger says that you can, that whatever happened between you and Cady occurred a long time ago and that you're adults now and not kids. Sage isn't so sure."

Sage was a wise woman.

What was he supposed to say? No, don't hire her because she threatens my calm, controlled world? He'd rather bang a rock against his head than admit to that.

"Sure, we're adults. Anyway, I'm not going to deal with her, Carol is. She's our in-house PR person."

Linc pulled a face and Beck's stomach dipped and flipped.

"Carol's asked for a three-month sabbatical. Her father is terminally ill and she needs some time to be with him. I thought that, with a new PR person coming in, she could take that time." Linc perched on the edge of Beck's desk and tapped his finger against the frame of the photograph of Connor and his adopted kids. "I need you to work with Cady and be her go-to person within Ballantyne's."

Oh, hell, no. "Ah, come on, Linc! Are you trying to torture me?"

Linc smiled. "Not deliberately, but torturing you is always a pleasure." His face turned serious. "You understand best of all what we need in terms of this rebranding strategy because you have the type of brain that sees the big picture. You also know more of the family history than any of us. Besides, Jaeger is leaving for Thailand on a buying trip, and Sage is heading to Hong Kong for a jewelry show. And I have my own fires to put out."

Something in his brother's voice caught his attention and Beck frowned. "Like?"

Linc stood up and shoved his hands into the pockets of his suit pants. "I've been hearing rumors about someone buying up massive blocks of Ballantyne International stock."

Beck rubbed the back of his neck. "It can't be a hostile takeover. The four of us own controlling shares so we'll never lose the company."

"Yeah, but why would someone want so many shares? I want to know who's behind this and why."

"Don't you think it makes better sense for me, as finance director, to do that and you deal with Cady?"

Linc shook his head. "I have a better relationship with the shareholders than you do."

That was true. Beckett scowled at his brother. "Do I have a choice about working with Cady?"

Linc grinned. "No."

Crap. There went his calm, controlled life.

"Just try to keep your hands off her, Beck. Or, if you can't, keep it tidy until you're out of the office, dude."

Beck sent him a hard look. "You should know better than to accuse me of that."

Linc raised his eyebrows. "Then, I'm really interested—and not just a little worried—as to why you've decided to start wearing lipstick. And, FYI, that shade of pink isn't your color."

Busted.

Four

Two weeks later, Cady checked her email for the final time that night and reluctantly tapped the red X to close the program. For the last two weeks she'd done market research and before she moved on to the next phase of the project, she needed to speak to Beck. His lack of response meant that she had the weekend free. The thought of not working over the weekend made her feel twitchy. At least when she was working she didn't have time to think of him and remember that kiss.

Cady walked past her wine rack on the way to her kitchen—wishing she could indulge in a glass or three—and opened her fridge to remove a carton of fruit juice. It was Friday night, she was alone and pregnant, wearing an old pair of yoga pants, thick socks and a long T-shirt of Tom's he'd failed to reclaim.

He'd taken everything else when he visited her a week ago—his CDs, the ceramic kitchen knives he'd given her for her last birthday, the abstract painting of red and yellow globs she'd never liked. While he'd been gathering his possessions, he'd intimated that he'd be prepared to resume their relationship if and when she freed herself of her "responsibilities."

He might even throw some business her way.

Since she didn't have the slightest intention of either aborting her baby or talking to him again, Cady marched to the door, opened it and told him to get out. She'd considered yanking one of the ceramic knives from its holder and stabbing him, but she didn't want to waste the little money she had on bail.

Cady sipped her juice, walked over to her kitchen window and stared at the street below. The sleet-tinged rain fell steadily and the streets were deserted. Loneliness, cold and heavy, fell over her and she wished that she could pick up the phone and call someone. Anyone. Building her business had taken all her time, and the few friends she'd had slipped away. Then Tom came into her life and she'd convinced herself that she wasn't lonely, that someone with a lover and a business couldn't be lonely.

But she had been. She was.

She wished she had one good friend she could call and say, "I'm scared and I'm lonely and I'm not sure I can birth a new campaign and a baby."

Amy, Beck's personal assistant and possibly his lover, jumped into mind. Cady was sure Amy had never felt lonely in her life; with her ebullient and feisty personality she could talk to everybody.

Unfortunately, the person she most wanted to call was Beck.

Back then she'd been able to tell Beck anything and everything. Well, everything besides the truth about her autistic brother. That her parents had sent him to live in a residential home because they hadn't wanted him to live with them anymore. Beck wasn't a fan of her parents, and that knowledge would've amplified that dislike. Neither had she told him that she'd lived her life wondering if her position within their home was equally tenuous.

All her life she'd tried to be perfect and she'd sacrificed relationships in her effort to win the trophy, the election, the prize. Beck had been her first real, intense friendship and she'd loved talking with him, being with him as much as she loved kissing him and making love to him. She'd reveled in his attention and, for the first time since Will was sent away, felt that there was no pressure to be anything other than who she was.

She now realized how little Beck told her about himself. He'd been happy to listen to her ramble on but he'd never opened up to her. She knew his body intimately but nothing of what drove him.

What she thought they'd shared had been very one-sided. And why did that still hurt?

Shaking off her melancholy, she told herself that the power to change was always one decision away. Tom and her business had been her focus for the last while. Her boyfriend was a married, insensitive asshat, and her business was in intensive care, but she was rid of one and the other was recovering. Once this campaign was finished, when the ground under her feet felt a little more solid, she'd make an effort to be more sociable, to make some new friends.

Or maybe not. People had the habit of turning out to be someone or something you never expected.

Cady heard the rap on her door and frowned. Visitors to her Sunset Park, Brooklyn, apartment needed to be buzzed in. Tom was the only person who'd come to her place in more than a year. Her buzzer hadn't sounded and Cady felt fear lurch up into her throat. Who was at her door so late on a freezing night and what could that person want?

Cady crossed her tiny apartment to the front door and looked through the eyepiece to see the distorted image of Beck on the other side.

Beck? She immediately looked at the clock on her kitchen wall and frowned at the time. Ten-twenty on a Friday night? She expected him to be on a date, eating dinner in a four-star restaurant, in a club or at a party, the things that normal, filthy-rich Manhattan bachelors did on a Friday night.

"I'm growing old here, Collins. Open up."

Through her thin door Cady heard Beck's growly words, so she flipped the three dead bolts open. She yanked the door open, realized that the chain was still on, shut it again, removed the chain and opened the door to Beck.

Calm the hell down. There's no need to feel so damn excited at seeing him.

"You're in Brooklyn? Did you get lost?" Cady asked, leaning against her door frame so that he couldn't step into her teeny, tiny apartment. God, his bathroom was probably bigger than her whole place.

Beck grabbed her elbows, lifted her up and walked her into her apartment. He placed her on her feet, shut the door behind him, shot the bolts and shrugged open his coat.

"Amy said that you need to see me," Beck said, ignoring her annoyed squawk.

"Yes, during *office* hours."

Beck sat down on her black-and-white-striped couch and rested his forearms on his thighs. "I'm here now. Got a beer?"

Cady frowned at his bent head and watched him as he rubbed his forehead with his fingers as if he was trying to massage a headache away. He looked frustrated and exhausted, like the week had kicked his ass to hell and back.

Cady waved her hand at her small wine rack. "I have wine. Nothing special, but I can offer you a glass."

Beck stood up and it took him two strides to reach her galley kitchen and the small wine rack next to the fridge. He started pulling out bottles to check the labels and Cady waited for the disparaging comment at her shoddy taste in wine. Instead he just picked a bottle of Cabernet and opened it.

He lifted two glasses off the shelf next to the rack, pouring the ruby liquid into the first glass.

"I don't want any," Cady quickly told him.

Beck lifted an eyebrow. "Why not?"

She couldn't tell him that she was pregnant, so she opted for a quick shrug. "Not in the mood."

After a sip of his wine, he brought his glass and the bottle back to where she was perched on the single chair and resumed his seat.

After a long silence, during which Beck examined her apartment, Cady linked her hands around her knee and spoke. "Why are you here, Beck?"

"Two reasons. The first is that I need to apologize." He stared down into his glass, his mouth tight. "I was wrong to offer you money for you not to take the job. It was insulting and, well…" He looked at her, his eyes troubled. "I didn't like the fact that we got that hot that fast. It was a quick, get-out-of-the-fire-fast reaction."

She understood. She'd felt as disoriented, as shattered as he had obviously. And she couldn't forget that she'd come very close to taking the money and bolting out of there. "Um…okay. Thanks?"

Beck's mouth held the hint of a smile. He sipped his wine and kept his compelling eyes on her face. "The second reason is that Amy told me to give you some time because your begging her for an appointment is driving her nuts."

"Begging is a strong word," Cady replied. "But I do need to talk to you about the campaign."

"Yeah, I know. I'm sorry, I've had a hell of a week." He leaned back and placed an ankle over his knee. "Can we do it now?"

Cady glanced at her desk, tucked into the corner of her tiny apartment, and saw her meticulously organized files, her laptop. She'd brought home everything she needed from her office, but she never liked discussing business in a ratty T-shirt and yoga pants. Still, Beck was here now... She nodded her agreement and then she saw the yawn he tried to hold back, saw the tension in his neck, the exhaustion in his eyes. It was the end of a long week and they were both played out.

"You look tired, Beck."

Beck scrubbed his hand over his face. "It's been busier than usual. Linc has taken a few weeks off. He's dealing with his own personal crisis, so I'm holding down the fort."

As his hands fell, she saw a different Beck from the handsome playboy the world saw online and in the society column. She didn't see the man who was always ready with a smart-alec comment, the well-dressed, ripped, swoon-enticing Bachelor Ballantyne. She saw a man who looked like he'd worked an eighty-hour week. The Ballantyne director with far too much responsibility on his plate. Someone who hadn't had a decent night's sleep or a good meal in far too long.

"Have you eaten?" Cady asked him.

"Lunch, a lifetime ago." Beck took a moment to answer. "I was planning on nuking a frozen pizza when I got home."

Cady wrinkled her nose. She wasn't a great cook, but even she knew that frozen pizzas were nothing more than refined sugars and MSG. "I have some frozen homemade pasta sauce and I can boil some linguine and put out a salad, if you'd prefer real food to fake pizza."

Enthusiasm flickered in Beck's eyes, but it was quickly replaced by regret-tinged determination. "Don't bother. I just came over to see what it was you wanted to discuss with me."

She needed his answers and approvals, but he needed food, decent food. Besides, her brain was so fried she didn't think she could have a clear and detailed conversation about the campaign if he put a ticking time bomb under her butt. And she suspected that Beck wasn't at his best, either.

"It's far too late to discuss business, so we're not going to do that. Pasta and sauce, last chance to say yes."

Beck reluctantly nodded his head.

So, Beck didn't feel comfortable with gestures of kindness and thoughtfulness. Was this something new, or was it something she'd never known about him before? Beck had never really shared himself, so for all she knew he could've come out of the womb walking and talking and trading shares on Wall Street.

And she'd been so caught up with juggling her parents' disappointment in her and her own rebellion, that she never considered he might need to lean on her occasionally.

Shame on her.

In the kitchen, Cady took out the frozen sauce and put it in the microwave to defrost. She placed a pot of water on her small stove and dashed in some salt. "Where is home, by the way?" she asked him after she pulled a ready-made salad from the fridge.

"SoHo."

Of course he lived in the most expensive, trendy area of Manhattan. Where else?

"In a warehouse-converted loft apartment or in a new development?" Cady asked.

"I own the top floor of a warehouse that was converted into apartments in the nineties." Beck slid down so that his head rested on the back of the sofa. "It's a lot of space, but I'm a big guy and I don't like feeling like I'm living in a teacup."

"Then you must feel like this place is a thimble," Cady commented.

Beck looked around. "It is tiny but very you. And those framed mirrors on the wall make it feel a lot bigger than it actually is. And, although I don't think both of us would fit into your kitchen, it has charm."

"Yeah, this is as charming as I can afford."

When it was ready, Cady took the heated sauce from the microwave before moving the pot of pasta to the sink. Using a tiny colander, she drained the pasta, added olive oil, tossed in the sauce and wished she had some Parmesan to grate over the top. When she had a regular income, and time to shop, she promised herself she'd always have cheeses and sauces and herbs in her fridge.

Cady placed a fork and a placemat on the coffee table in front of him, put the plate down and gestured for him to eat. Beck scooted forward and quickly pulled his tie from around his neck. He tossed it in the general direction of his jacket before picking up the fork. "This smells great."

"It tastes better."

Cady curled up into her chair, tucking her feet beneath her bottom and watched Beck eat. He'd always loved food and he'd never hesitated to try something different while they were traveling.

"So good," Beck muttered between mouthfuls.

Cady smiled and rested her head on the back of the chair. Beck was in her apartment, eating her food and looking so hot it made her ache. She wished that she could crawl into his lap, rest her head on his chest and feel his muscled arms around her. He'd always made her feel so protected, like nothing could hurt her. But if she did that, she knew that his big hands would skim her from butt to knee and she'd lift her mouth to nuzzle his throat. He'd sigh, look down at her and she'd drop her head back and two seconds later his mouth would be on hers.

Within another two seconds she'd be naked. And she was not going to get naked with Beckett Ballantyne again! He was her client and she'd learned her lesson with Tom. Naked and business and client were words that shouldn't occur in the same sentence.

Add pregnant to the melee and bad went directly to terrible.

It didn't bear thinking about.

Yawning, Cady tucked a cushion under her head and rested her hand on her still-flat abdomen. Good idea, she told herself. Think about the baby and not Beck. Come to think of it, she needed to make an appointment with a doctor to have a checkup.

Thinking of the baby made her think of her parents. Her mother had given her a pass on coming home and meeting the church interview committee, but sooner or later she had to inform them that they were going to be grandparents. But she wasn't ready to tell them…she wasn't ready to tell anyone, and especially not Beck.

What, exactly would she say? *I've just broken up with my married ex-client and I'm pregnant with his child.*

Married man. Who was also her client. Who made her pregnant. Strike one, two and three. Professional she was not.

But she was determined to be professional with Beck. She'd made enough mistakes confusing business and pleasure, and no matter how sexy Beck was, it would only be business between them. To prove her point, she'd show him how dedicated she was and run through her ideas for the campaign with him at nearly eleven on a Friday night. She'd just wait for Beck to finish his food and then she'd open her eyes and tell him.

Beck looked up and smiled at Cady's open mouth. Her long lashes were smudges on her too-white face. He'd thought she looked tired when he first arrived, but now, her face relaxed in sleep, he could see how exhausted she really was. Her face was thinner as were her arms and thighs, he noticed now as he let his eyes roam down her slight frame.

Cady looked like she needed to go on a month-long diet of hamburgers and milkshakes. Beck placed his fork on his plate and rested his forearms on his knees, happy to take the time to really look at Cady. Thailand Cady had been open and chatty, but this Cady was quieter, stronger, somehow even more attractive. She was mysterious, an enigma, a puzzle he wanted to solve.

And he knew, beyond a shadow of a doubt, that he wanted her under, on top of him, any damn way he could get her.

That hadn't changed.

Beck ran his hand over his jaw and pushed his plate away. How the hell was he going to work with her and be around her without stripping her naked and taking her on the nearest surface or up against the closest wall? And that was the real reason he'd ignored her request for an appointment this week. He'd wanted time to wrap his head around the kiss that they shared, and around the fact that she was back in his life and fifty times as likely to turn it upside down.

He'd needed time to get his need for her under control. To get his life back.

He needed that control.

He'd been in her apartment, in her presence, for less than an hour and he was thinking about picking her up, walking the five steps to her bedroom and, after placing her on the bed, exploring every inch of her skin, kissing her mouth, sliding into her hot, moist channel. He'd dreamed of her for so long and here she was, back in his life.

God, resisting her was torture. Plain and simple. Since time hadn't dulled the attraction between them, he'd been right to push her away all those years ago.

Beck found himself reaching out to push a dark curl off her cheek. He yanked his hand back and shot to his feet, picking up his plate and taking it to the kitchen. He rolled up his sleeves and filled the small sink with hot water, finding the dish soap in a tiny cupboard to his left.

He was bone tired, he thought as he washed her dishes, but after a visit to Cady, sleep wouldn't come easy tonight. It never did. He'd tried meditation and acupuncture and massage, but his brain refused to shut down. Exercising to the point of exhaustion was one of the few ways he could obtain a few hours of sleep.

To this day, making love to Cady was still the only activity that relaxed him enough to fall asleep and stay asleep for any length of time. After she returned to the

States, insomnia had quickly become his best friend and he'd assumed sex was the answer. He was an okay-looking guy and sex and backpacking went together like popcorn and beer, so finding someone to share his bed, or tent, or hammock had never been difficult.

When his sleep patterns didn't improve he had to admit that it might've been sex with Cady that relaxed him and not plain sex.

And speaking of sex, he couldn't remember when he'd last had that pleasure, either. Three months ago? Maybe.

He wanted to make love to Cady, and sleep would be a fantastic side benefit. Beck tossed the dish towel onto the counter and looked across the room to her still-sleeping form. This wasn't all about reliving their past. He also wanted to make love to her because she was still the most fascinating woman he'd ever met. At nineteen, she'd been young and in need of his protection, a role he hadn't minded taking on. But this Cady, fast asleep and breathing deeply, was tougher, stronger and far too compelling for his piece of mind.

She was Cady 2.0, fascinating and so sexy that his breath caught in his throat every time he looked at her. He wanted her.

In his bed.

But not, per se, in his life.

Cady was dangerous, he reminded himself. She had a way of crawling under his skin and digging in. He couldn't allow that, couldn't lose control of this situation. He'd sent her away because she'd become a threat to his self-sufficient, lone-wolf lifestyle, because she made him dream of things he had no right to have. A love of a good woman, happiness, a family, kids. All the stuff he was not entitled to.

He had no intention of allowing Cady Collins to slide under his skin again. He was smarter than that.

And the best way to do that was to keep his distance... especially physically. If he touched her, kissed her, then he'd want to make love to her. So he'd just have to stay at least six feet away from her at all times.

Play it safe, dude.

But damn, he really wanted sex. And sleep.

Five

On Monday, clutching a pile of folders and her tablet to her chest, Cady made her way down the hall to her appointment with Beck. A few feet from Amy's office she stopped when, through the glass walls, she noticed Sage Ballantyne perched on the corner of Amy's desk. The two women were deep in conversation. Not wanting to intrude she turned away, thinking that, since she was ten minutes early, she'd wait at Reception.

"Cady!"

Damn. She couldn't exactly ignore Sage Ballantyne, who was as much her boss as Beck. Cady retraced her steps and stood in the open doorway to Amy's office, feeling uncomfortable.

"I can come back in ten," she stated as she flicked a look at Beck's office and saw that his glass walls were opaque.

"No, come on in," Sage said on a welcoming smile. "Amy and I were just about to have coffee. My brothers are still in there," she said with a nod to Beck's office. "We've just had a quick partners meeting."

Sage pushed her hands into the back pockets of her faded jeans. She wore a gypsy top and her dark hair was pulled into a messy knot on top of her head. Sage wore no makeup—not that she needed it with such expressive eyes and flawless skin—and she looked nothing like the polished woman who'd politely grilled her at her presentation yesterday.

"That was director Sage, this is artist Sage," Amy said, seeming to read her mind.

"How do you do that?" Cady demanded, placing her tablet and folders on Amy's desk as Sage picked up her desk phone and quickly ordered coffee to be delivered to Amy's office.

"You have a very expressive face." Amy shrugged before pushing her chair back from her desk and crossing her legs. She gestured to the chair on the other side of her desk. "Take a seat. Sage has a million questions."

Oh, God. Cady lifted an eyebrow at Sage. "You do?" she asked, hoping that her cool tone would make her reconsider that decision.

"Honey, I have three older brothers. You need more than an unfriendly look to deflect me," Sage replied with a grin. "So, question one… You are the girl Beck went to Thailand with."

Cady shrugged. "That's not a question, but yes…"

Sage's eyes narrowed. "And you were the one who broke his heart."

Now that was a crazy statement. She wasn't even sure Beck had a heart.

"I went to Thailand with Beck, but Beck sent me home. He broke *my* heart. Besides," she said as she sent

Amy a measured look, "I'm presuming he found some willing company as soon as I left."

Amy grinned. "He did. Me."

Yeah, she got it. Beck moved on quickly, proving that he didn't give a fig about her leaving and that his heart hadn't been affected by her departure.

Sage frowned at Amy. "But you said he was miserable for months after she left."

"He was," Amy answered. She flashed a mischievous grin. "But Cady thinks that I comforted him in the tried and tested way."

Sage's eyes widened as laughter crossed her face. "No! Really?"

Cady didn't think any part of this conversation was amusing and she sent a longing look at the door. "Can we talk about something else?"

"She thinks you slept together?" Sage asked Amy, totally ignoring Cady's question. "She doesn't know?"

"Apparently not." Amy's eyes met hers and she smiled. "I'm gay, Cady. Julia is going to be my wife. We've been together for nearly seven years."

What?

Amy exchanged a quick look with Sage and the naughty expression reappeared on her face. "Actually, you caught my eye in Thailand, not Beck."

Again...*what*?

"Stop it, Amy," Sage said. Then she turned to Cady. "Ignore her. She's a chronic flirt. And a world-class troublemaker."

"I am not," Amy protested, placing her hand on her heart in protest. Sage frowned at her and she lowered her hand and shrugged. "Okay, I am. And I was, sort of, joking about eyeing you in Thailand."

Cady stared at her. "But I thought he moved on from me to you."

"Nope. I'm not saying that he didn't move on eventually, but I was his buddy. I still am."

Okay, well… Wow. Cady shook her head, trying to assimilate what she'd just heard. She stared down at her hands, totally confused. If Beck hadn't wanted to move on to a new relationship, then why did he force her to leave?

"Why did you leave Thailand, Cady? You were good together. Anyone could see that." Amy gestured to the intern who entered her office. Once he put down the tray holding a coffee carafe and they were alone again, she looked at Cady. "Well?"

"I didn't leave. He sent me away. He bought me a ticket back home and said it was time for me to go."

"That doesn't make sense," Sage said, frowning.

"Of course it does," Amy scoffed. "It's classic Beck behavior." Amy looked at Sage. "He pulls back when—"

Amy stopped abruptly and she shared a long look with Sage. Cady caught the flash of warning that arced between them. Cady mentally begged one of them to finish that sentence but Sage busied herself with pouring coffee, and Amy glanced at her computer monitor.

Cady knew that they felt like they'd said too much, that they were being disloyal to Beck by discussing him.

They were and always would be protective of him and she was not, and never would be, part of their inner circle. She was just someone they'd hired and, speaking of, maybe it was time to do that job.

What happened so long ago had absolutely no bearing on her work with Ballantyne International, and she was wrong to discuss the past with Beck's sister, and his employee and friend. It didn't matter that they were being as unprofessional as she was. Sage was a director and Amy a long-trusted employee. It was up to her to apologize. "I'm sorry. That was unprofessional of me, and I shouldn't have brought up the past."

"You didn't. We did," Sage said, flicking a glance over her shoulder. "And we really shouldn't have, either. Beck would skin us alive if he knew."

He would. Beck had no time for office gossip. "Yeah, maybe we can forget this conversation," Cady replied.

"Done," Amy said. "I'm really glad you got the job, Cady. Sage said your presentation was fantastic."

"I'm glad you liked it." Cady took her cup of coffee from Sage and took a sip.

"I love the idea of trying to meld Ballantyne tradition with something new and hip and cool."

Cady looked down at her lap, took a breath and looked Amy in the eye. "Thank you. I am very conscious of how much I owe you."

Amy pulled a face. "No worries. As I said, if Julia hadn't said you were any good, I wouldn't have suggested you pitch. The fact that Beck lights up like a Christmas tree whenever you are around is just an added bonus."

Before she could utter a denial, Beck's voice rumbled out of the intercom on Amy's desk. "Sage, get back to work. Cady, get your ass in here. Amy, is there any point in telling you to do anything?"

Cady's jaw dropped and the cup in her hand wobbled. She sent an anxious look at the still-opaque walls.

Amy grinned as she hit the intercom button to speak. "Nope, you can try, though, boss. You might get lucky."

"Did he hear us?" Cady demanded, not realizing that Sage took her cup from her hand.

Amy shrugged and grinned. "I hope not. I'm going to

the ladies' room." She stood up and gestured to the door leading to Beck's office. "Go on in when you're ready."

Cady nodded but stayed in the chair, fighting her urge to bolt.

She couldn't face Beck right now. She needed time to assimilate the fact that Amy wasn't anything more than his friend, that both Sage and she seemed to think that he'd been miserable when she left.

If that was true, then why did he send her away?

Cady shook her head. It didn't matter; none of this mattered. What was important was that she did a sterling, professional job for Ballantyne International, so that she would be able to parlay this one job into more. This was her way to resuscitate her company. And to put cash in the bank.

She was not going to jeopardize that by taking a fruitless stroll down memory lane.

Cady stood up and touched the knot at the back of her hair, conscious that Amy and Sage were staring at her.

"It'll be okay, Cady, I promise." Amy walked out of her office and tossed Cady a sincere smile over her shoulder. "I'm glad you're here. Welcome to Ballantyne International."

Amy closed the door behind her, and Cady turned at Sage's low chuckle. "Sometimes I think that Amy should just change her name to Ballantyne and be done with it."

"And you don't mind that?"

Sage smiled. "Being a Ballantyne is about heart, not name. We became a family when Connor adopted the four of us. We don't get hung up on DNA around here." Sage placed her elegant hand on Cady's forearm and squeezed. "But from me, welcome to our world. I'm glad you're back."

Cady watched Sage walk away and reminded herself that she was just a visitor to their world. Despite her previous relationship with Beck, she wasn't part of their inner circle, and there was no chance that she ever would be.

What she and Beck had was possible in Thailand, a million miles away, where he was just Beck and she was just a girl he'd met at a party. But things were different now. Despite their raging chemistry, the ridiculous physical attraction and the fact that they both didn't want to work together, they had no choice.

He was her client, the man who paid her invoices, her boss.

Nothing remained of the backpackers they once were. This was business.

And that was all it could ever be.

Cady walked over to Beck's door, lifted her hand up to knock and lowered it again. She hadn't seen or spoken to Beck since she'd fallen asleep on him Friday night. It was now Monday and she was still embarrassed that her boss had picked her up from her chair, tucked her into her bed, and washed and dried the dishes she'd used to make him supper before leaving her apartment. And she had just snored on. She knew she snored because he'd left her a note, penned in his strong hand on a bright pink Post-it note from her desk.

You still snore.
Thanks for supper.
—Beck.

Cady didn't think she could be any more embarrassed.

But she had to face Beck right now. And she had to open the door to do it.

Cady knocked and when Beck told her to enter, she did, smiling at Linc and Jaeger. Linc was lounging in Beck's leather chair and Jaeger stood across the room, his shoulder pressed into the wall. She turned to look at Beck and her heart bounced off her rib cage. He stood by the window, the weak sun turning his dark blond hair to gold. A baby boy, who looked to be about a year old, was slapping his hand against Beck's mouth, yanking it away when Beck tried to nibble his fingers. Both of them, man and baby, were laughing.

Cady had to remind herself to breathe. She hadn't seen Beck smile like that, that heart-stopping, heartbreaking smile, since Thailand. It changed his entire face and he looked both ten years younger and ten times sexier.

It was sensory overload, Cady thought. Looking at him was like looking into the sun. If she didn't stop soon, her eyes would melt.

But try as she might, she couldn't pull her eyes away. Watching Beck play with a baby turned her heart to mush. All those years ago, her teenage heart had imagined a scenario like this, Beck playing with his baby, the baby she carried for him. Her life had taken a three-sixty from then. She was back in Beck's life, as his PR person, and she was carrying a baby. But it wasn't his.

It was Tom's… Actually, no. Cady straightened her spine. This baby was hers.

A masculine cough broke the silence and yanked her back into the here and now. She blinked and she was in Beck's office with Linc and Jaeger and a baby who could only be Jaeger's newly discovered son, Ty. Amy had filled her in on the Ballantyne family dynamics and Cady had listened, astonished. Jaeger had recently reunited with Piper, who he'd had a fling with in Milan eighteen months ago. Piper got pregnant then but Jaeger only heard about, and met his son a few months before. Jaeger and Piper, Amy gleefully told her, had wasted no time in expanding their family and Piper was newly pregnant. Linc was a single dad of a four-year-old, having raised Shaw since his mom, Kari, abandoned both of them when Shaw was six weeks old. And, Amy divulged, Kari had done it again and dumped her baby daughter with her sister, Tate, and run off again. Tate was currently living in The Den, working temporarily as Shaw's nanny, but Amy was certain that there was a lot more to that story!

Lives of the rich and famous, Cady thought, intrigued.

"Hand my boy over, Beck," Jaeger said after she'd said a general hello. "We're keeping you and Cady from working."

Beck held Ty like a football and shook his head. "No worries. We're going to discuss the PR campaign and I'd welcome your input."

Linc looked at his watch and shook his head. "Sorry, I have a conference call in five."

Jaeger looked at his own watch and crossed the room to take Ty from Beck. "And Piper just sent me a message that she's downstairs and she's taking Ty home."

Cady smiled as Ty shouted his displeasure at being removed from his uncle's arms. Beck didn't look that happy about it, either. "Are you enjoying living in Park Slope?" Cady asked him, Ty wiggling in his arms.

"Love it." Jaeger flashed his heartthrob smile. "But I'd live in a tent in Prospect Park if that's where Piper and Ty were."

Aw. Sweet guy.

"You are such a sap," Beck muttered, but Cady heard the affection in his voice. He looked at Ty and gently pulled his foot. "Remember our deal, little man. Your first word is going to be Beck."

"Like hell," Jaeger muttered and Cady laughed.

Linc, on his way to the door, bent his knees to look into Ty's face. "Better yet, make it Linc. Anything but Dad, okay?"

"You guys suck," Jaeger muttered as they left the room. Cady heard the door click closed behind them and looked at Beck, who was still standing by the window, sunlight glinting off his hair and his two-day stubble.

"Take a seat," Beck said, walking over to his desk and pulling back his chair so he could sit down. He pushed it away from his desk and placed his ankle on his opposite knee. Cady sat down, crossed her legs, linked her hands around her knee and tried not to squirm under his direct and penetrating gaze. "You still look tired."

Cady felt the heat in her cheeks. "I'm sorry I fell asleep. That was so rude."

"It's not like you fell asleep at the boardroom table, Cady. It was late, and I was in your place, so relax."

"You should've just left me there or shaken me awake. You didn't need to put me to bed." She saw the heat flare in his eyes so she jumped off that subject. "And you definitely didn't need to do the dishes. Though that was probably a novelty for you," she added, teasing him.

Beck's mouth tipped up in a half smile. "For your information, I washed dishes last Sunday night, after our family dinner at The Den."

She knew that was how they referred to their family brownstone. "Have you Ballantynes not heard of a wonderful invention called a dishwasher?"

"Oh, Jo has one, but she doesn't see why we should waste power using it when she has minions to do it for her," Beck stated.

"I always liked her," Cady said, looking at her hands. "Is she still the housekeeper at The Den?"

"No, she retired after Connor died. She stills lives at The Den and she helps Linc with Shaw, his four-year-old."

"Although I only met them once, I liked both her and Connor."

"He liked you," Beck replied, his voice gruff and growly. Their eyes clashed and memories whirled and swirled between them.

Don't do this, Cady told herself. *Don't get sucked in.*

Whatever it was that existed between her and Beck, it was over and if it wasn't, then it should be. He'd pushed her away once; he'd do it again. Beck was, possibly, more unavailable than he'd been at twenty-three. And there were two of them in the game now. Beck wouldn't want to start anything—even an affair—with a pregnant woman just out of a relationship with her married, ex-client boyfriend.

"We should work." Cady dropped her hot, desperate words into the charged silence between them.

Beck blinked, looked down at his desk, and his shoulders rose and fell. When he lifted his head again, his face was blank and his eyes emotionless. Her old lover was gone and the Ballantyne CFO was back.

Good. She needed the here and now, and didn't need to remember the there and then.

Cady pulled her tablet from her bag and put it on her lap. As she consulted her notes she forced her attention off Beck's wide chest and muscular arms and onto her job. Occasionally she looked out the window but she didn't see the traffic and pedestrians below; she saw magnificent gems, Ballantyne gems, and told him how she intended to reintroduce them to the world.

Cady told Beck about her market research and the results of her brand audit. She touched on the company's weak spots and pointed out areas for innovation and growth. When she finished her report, she tossed out a seemingly random question.

"Of all the pieces of jewelry you've seen pass Ballantyne's, what is your favorite?"

"Wow, change of subject." Beck rubbed his jaw. "I have no idea. I've seen so many valuable stones and exquisite works of jewelry art that it's a hard question to answer."

"What piece of jewelry did you feel most connected to? What makes your heart beat faster?"

"Why are you asking this?"

"Bear with me."

Beck shifted in his chair, looking a little on edge. "Real or imagined? Or lost?"

"Anything. Don't qualify your response. I want your gut reaction."

Beck shifted in his chair and she thought she saw a touch of sadness pass through his eyes. "My mom's engagement ring. It was a magnificent, five carat red beryl stone. Fantastically rare."

Cady saw the pain flash in his eyes and wanted to reach out to him, wanted to offer comfort, but she didn't dare. She maintained her professional demeanor. "Okay, that's your special stone. The Kashmir sapphire Jaeger gave to Piper in her engagement ring is his. Linc, apparently, loves Alexandrite because the stones can be different colors under different light. And Sage has an affinity for red diamonds."

"Because they are so damn rare. And incredibly beautiful," Beck said. "Where are you going with this, Cady?"

"I want to do a series of print ads around each Ballantyne and the gems you love. I would suggest we start with

Jaeger and Piper, and ride the wave of interest around their engagement. I want to get those ads out in time for Valentine's Day."

"That's less than a month away."

She was aware of that. She was also aware that pulling this off would require long days and longer nights. "In addition to Piper's ring, Linc has, according to Amy, a magnificent Alexandrite ring he inherited from Connor Ballantyne, and then there's the one I can't wait to see—a red diamond, platinum and diamond flower ring that's in your uncle's private collection that Sage loves."

Cady tapped her finger against her tablet and brought up the mock-up she'd put together. "I'd feature each of you in an ad—relaxed and accessible, white shirt, blue jeans, bare feet—and holding your priceless jewelry. The public will have to go online to read up on why that piece in particular speaks to you. We'll advertise Sage's new, modern designs on those pages, as well. And when the ads launch, I want to do a function to exhibit those jewels and others in the Ballantyne collection."

"That's not possible," Beck said through gritted teeth.

"Why not?" Cady demanded.

"First, those gems are worth a freaking king's ransom and they'd need extraordinary security measures if they're going to be shown to the public."

"Not the public. Only rich, hip, hot, young celebs will see the exhibition," Cady told him, enjoying herself. "And I've already contacted a company specializing in jewelry exhibitions. They haven't lost a gem yet. Speaking of, where's your mom's ring?"

Beck didn't crack a smile. "Somewhere on that mountain where they crashed."

She heard the pain in his voice and again Cady wanted to wrap her arms around him. Such pain. There was nothing to say so she sent him a sympathetic smile. But that meant she'd have to find another piece of jewelry to connect to Beck. "I'm sorry, Beck. Is there another piece we can use that you feel strongly about?"

Beck linked his hands around the back of his head. "I like the idea, the connection between old and new. Could we use a paste copy of my mom's ring?"

"You have one of those?"

"Every time an important piece comes through here, a copy—and an excellent imitation—is made for our records."

"We'd have to explain that it's the copy, but it'll work. Great." Energized by his reception of her ideas, Cady stood up. Her mind was reeling with plans as she walked to the window, resting her palm on the thick glass as she envisioned the exhibit. Then she sent him an uncertain look. "It might dredge up some memories for you and your siblings."

"The memories are always there, so there's nothing to dredge up," Beck said as he walked toward her. When he stood in front of her, he ran his hand over her hip and skimmed his knuckles across her abdomen. "Animation and excitement suits you, Cades."

Cady saw the heat in his eyes and she shook her head. "Don't do this, Beck."

"I want you."

"It's not a good idea," Cady told him, sucking in a deep breath as his knuckles skimmed the underside of her suddenly sensitive breasts.

Beck placed his palms on the glass, bracketing her head. He looked down at her, desire on his face and, Cady ascertained with a quick glance down, in his pants.

"Beck...please."

"What are you asking me to do, Cady? Kiss you?

Touch you? Let you go? You're going to have to be more specific."

Damn, what did she want? Him, same as always. She shouldn't, Cady thought, but she lifted her hand and brushed her fingers against his rough jaw. She didn't want to say the words. If she did, she couldn't take them back, couldn't rewind. Couldn't blame him for taking the decision out of her hands.

He was leaving the decision to kiss him up to her. If she asked him to let her go, he would. Conversely, if she asked him to kiss her, touch her, taste her, he'd rock her world. So much time had passed, so much had happened, but she was still inexplicably drawn to him. Cady knew it was smarter to walk away, but how could she ignore the flash of masculine appreciation in his eyes, the catch in his breath when they touched? When it came to Beck she'd never been smart and nothing, it seemed, had changed.

They'd always had the ability to spark off each other and she knew that if he kissed her, they'd both go up in flames. They were that volatile.

God, she wanted to burn under his touch.

"Ask me to kiss you, Cady." Beck clasped her face in his hands, his thumbs rubbing the arch of her cheekbones.

Cady meant to push him away, but instead her hands ran from his wrists to his biceps, enjoying the power in his muscles. "Kiss me, Beck. Properly, intensely, like you mean it."

His eyes flashed and when she touched her bottom lip with the tip of her tongue, he swooped down. Beck slanted his lips over hers, and time and space and thought rolled away as she lost herself in his arms. Or had she found herself?

Her fingers curled into his hair and she pushed her

breasts against his chest. Beck was more powerful now than he'd been at twenty-three. Cady could feel it in the arms wound around her butt and back, in the hands pulling her into him. His mouth was sweeter and hotter than she remembered, his body bigger and harder, and her response more fervent and insistent. How was she going to step away, to get back to business when her heart and mind and body demanded more?

Beck groaned, jerked his mouth off hers and rested his forehead on the top of her head. "I wasn't going to do this. I really wasn't."

Cady pushed her hands against his chest to put some distance between them and when his hands fell from her body, she took another step back. "Me neither. We can't go back, Beck. Not to that."

Beck shoved a hand into his hair and looked irritated. "You talk as if we have a choice."

"We're adults, Beck. We always have a choice." All her mistakes up to this point had been because she'd made some stupid choices and she couldn't take any more chances. She felt like a cat on number eight of her nine lives.

"I cannot, I will not, jeopardize this job and my relationship with Ballantyne International because we have something bubbling between us."

"Those are two totally separate issues."

She'd lost Tom's business because she'd slept with him, because she was stupid enough to think that she could mix business and pleasure.

"That's what you men always say until pleasure and business collide and someone—usually the woman and the one needing the business—gets screwed." Cady winced at the bitterness in her tone.

Beck gripped her chin and forced her to look up into

his hard, unyielding face. "Don't judge me by someone else's yardstick, Cady. I'm my own man and if I say that what happens between us physically won't impact on business, then you can believe it."

Yeah, she didn't think so. She'd learned that lesson and learned it well. "It's better not to start anything that might blow up in our faces." Cady pushed her hair off her forehead and placed her hands on her hips. "I need to get back to work. I also need to convince Jaeger and Linc that these ads will work. They really don't want to get in front of a camera."

"I'm not fond of the idea myself," Beck replied. "But I can see why it will work. It's a good concept. Come to dinner at The Den on Sunday night and we can all discuss it then."

Dinner at The Den, the family brownstone, was a Ballantyne tradition. She remembered him telling her that it was a time for the family to reconnect, to wind down, to talk. Her presence there would be an intrusion; Beck could talk his brothers into doing the shoot, he didn't need her.

Besides, being around the Ballantynes as a group reminded her of the family she'd always wanted but knew she'd never have. The kind of family she wanted for her baby.

"I don't think so."

Beck sent her a long look and Cady struggled to keep her face blank. When he turned those piercing, smart and questioning eyes on her, she wanted to hurl her deepest fears and most secret desires at his feet. *Not a good idea*, Cady told herself.

She knew from past experience that she was the only one who could, and should, shoulder her baggage.

Cady injected starch into her spine and picked up her

mind map. "You said that there are paste copies of all the important pieces. Can I look at them, including the one of your mom's engagement ring?"

Beck gave her a sharp nod. "Ask Amy to get them for you on the way out. The copy of the red beryl ring is in my safe at home." He glanced at his watch. "I have a business lunch at Sam's but I can stop at my apartment before I go to lunch. I'll be done by two-thirty. If you can meet me at Sam's then I can give it to you."

Sam's was only the finest restaurant in New York City. A haunt for the rich and famous, where a booking had to be made six to eight months in advance. And this was where Beck conducted business lunches? She was so out of his league.

"Sam's at two-thirty. I'll see you there."

Six

After a punishing routine followed by a half hour swim in the private gym in the basement of his apartment building, Beck let himself into his apartment and toed off his trainers at the front door. Dumping his gym bag next to the hall table, he walked across the expansive loft to his gourmet kitchen and grabbed a bottle of water. After gulping it down, he looked out the tinted windows at the incredible view of the city skyline.

He had another crazy day ahead of him trying to keep on top of both his and Linc's work. Linc, thanks to the arrival of Tate and baby Ellie—Kari, Linc's ex, had dumped her baby girl on Tate and done another runner—was running himself ragged, so Beck was picking up the slack. In between running a billion-dollar corporation with offices all over the world, he was also trying to make sense of Cady's dropping back into his life.

He was still insanely attracted to her. And he didn't

like feeling this off balance, like he was trying to navigate the rapids of a treacherous river in a leaky bucket. He wasn't used to feeling so out of control, so unsure. The women he dated—okay, slept with—were smart, gorgeous and, well, forgettable. There was only one woman he'd never been able to forget. Who, like a burrowing bug, had crawled into his brain and stayed there.

And she was back.

Cady.

Back then and now, Cady made him want something more than the life he had. Oh, his life was good, he knew that—he was strong, smart, wealthy and successful—but Cady made him want more. Friendship, companionship, having someone to come home to at the end of the day. Someone to fill this empty space with laughter, conversation, music. Someone who made him want to slow down, to chill.

Sex on tap would be great, too.

But a relationship like that wasn't in the cards for him. His parents had a fantastic marriage; they'd been crazy in love with each other, like Jaeger and Piper. Beck hoped that Sage and Linc found the person they could be that happy with. But he didn't deserve that sort of happiness himself.

Intellectually, he knew that he was being hard on himself and that his request for his parents' type of love was normal, even expected. But his neediness had such massive consequences and that was what he couldn't wrap his head around. That was where he stalled. If he started to need someone again, what would the consequences be? If he fell in love and that person was hurt or, God forbid, killed, he wouldn't be able to live with himself. He'd survived his parents' deaths by keeping busy, and he'd earned his place in his family by being smart, hard-working and responsible.

Falling in love, exposing his heart, was irresponsible. And it was simply not happening. So he needed to stay away from Cady. He needed to keep a physical and, most important, an emotional distance from her.

Beck drained the last of the water and tapped the rim against a pane of wet glass. Maybe he'd escape New York, Cady and this cold weather by visiting the Hong Kong and Tokyo branches of Ballantyne's. Both managers had issues that he needed to resolve.

He could take a week, get his head on straight, and maybe even do a surprise visit to the Dubai store on his way back. Or the LA store if they flew in the other direction. Either way, it would put thousands of miles between him and Cady.

Beck heard the chime that informed him that someone was leaning on his buzzer and he frowned. His brothers and sisters had the code to open the front door but none of them would be at his door at six forty-five in the morning. Jaeger would be snuggled up to Piper, Sage needed a bomb to get her out of bed in the mornings and Linc was out of town.

Beckett walked to his front door and pushed the intercom button. "Yeah?"

"Beck, it's me, Cady. We have a problem."

Judging by Cady's stressed-out tone, he knew it was a big one. Beck released the lock on the front door and told her to come on up.

Cady at the crack of dawn. Yeah, this had to be a big-ass problem.

When Cady stepped out of the elevator and saw Beck standing in his doorway she had one thought. Someone dressed in an old, sweat-stained T-shirt, athletic shorts and worn trainers had no right to look like he stepped off the cover of a men's health and exercise magazine. The old jeans and college sweatshirt she wore under her thigh-length coat didn't look half as good on her as ratty clothes looked on him. She wore no makeup, had pulled her hair up into a lopsided ponytail and had just remembered to brush her teeth.

That was what happened when you found out, online, that you were engaged to one of the most eligible bachelors in the city.

Beck stepped back and gestured for her to come into his apartment, so Cady did. He hung her coat up on a metal coat stand that looked like it cost more than the small car she wanted but couldn't afford. Cady jammed her hands into the pockets of her sweatshirt and looked around his loft conversion. She liked the large windows and the exposed red brick walls. The laminated floors were stylish and contemporary as were the oversize, minimalistic, L-shaped, oatmeal-colored couch and the armless leather chairs. The large ornamental lemon tree in the corner needed water.

It was stylish and it was rich, but it didn't have much soul, Cady decided. Apart from a large photograph of Connor and the four Ballantyne siblings, there was little in this apartment that told Cady who lived here. A large wooden door led to what she thought might be a second bedroom, and a steel, spiral staircase led to the suspended master bedroom.

Yeah, rich. Contemporary. She preferred her colorful rabbit hutch in Brooklyn.

Beck stepped into the kitchen area and took a mug from a cupboard above his coffee machine and held it up. "Coffee?"

Eeew, no. Morning sickness had her stomach churning and she was a hairsbreadth away from tossing her cookies. Coffee would send her right over the edge.

"I don't suppose you have any tea? Something with ginger in it?" Cady asked, knowing that her chances weren't good.

Beck opened a narrow cupboard and she saw a large range of herbal teas. "You drink tea?" she asked, incredulous, as he pulled a tea bag from a yellow box.

"I spent enough time in the Far East, I should," Beck said, turning on the luxury coffee machine to make hot water.

It was the first time he'd mentioned traveling and she wondered if he'd ever thought of the time they'd spent together. He probably remembered being frustrated because she was always checking her phone, always crying after speaking to her parents.

Maturity and hindsight made her admit that she hadn't been the best traveling partner, and Beck had been incredibly patient.

From this vantage point Cady could see more decoration on the wall to the left of the front door. A series of enlarged black-and-white photographs. Immediately she recognized the stunningly beautiful bay, encircled by huge cliffs. Looking at the photographs, she could almost feel the silky soft white sand and feel the tropical warmth of the exceptionally clear water.

"I remember you taking these pictures. You got up at some ridiculous hour so that the beach would be empty of people," Cady commented, pleased to hear that her voice was steady. "Later that morning I decided to keep traveling with you and the next day I was on a plane home, my life turned upside down."

Beck gripped the edges of the counter and looked at

her, his face expressionless. "That was always the plan, Cady. I never asked you to stay."

"You're right. You didn't and I assumed too much." Cady shrugged. "My bad."

She perched on a very uncomfortable, stainless-steel bar stool on the dining room side of the sleek counter.

"We were young, Cady, and crazy attracted to each other. It couldn't last," Beck said slowly, his voice emotionless.

Lust didn't explain why her world stopped turning, why she'd cried for three months straight and felt hollow for another six. It was fear of trusting and being hurt again that had her avoiding men and relationships for years, dating occasionally but never inviting a man back into her bed and her life. Tom had been the only one she'd taken a risk on, and that decision just reinforced her belief that her choice in men wasn't to be trusted.

Beck filled her cup with hot water and pushed it toward her. He leaned against the counter. "I'm sorry if I hurt you, Cady."

"You did hurt me."

Beck stepped forward and touched her hand with the tips of his fingers. "I really am sorry but I wasn't ready for a relationship with you then."

Then? What did that mean? Was he ready for one now?

Beck shook his head in answer to the question he must've read in her eyes. "I'm not relationship material, Cady. I don't do relationships and I don't do long-term."

Cady made herself ask the question. "What do you do?"

"Sex." Beck's answer was as blunt as her question.

After Tom's lies, his honesty was refreshing. "Fair enough."

"And you, what are you looking for?" Beck asked, his lips thin and his eyes wary.

Cady stared down at the hot tea, inhaling the ginger aroma and praying it would settle her stomach. Once upon a time she wanted to be married, have a family, be happy. Her teenage dreams were all so airy fairy, so intangible. She was older now and a lot more practical. She wanted to reemploy the handful of staff she'd had to let go, renew her office lease, put some money in the bank and stop feeling like she was constantly fighting nausea and losing.

Having a relationship, falling for someone—Beck—was out of the question. Apart from the fact that she'd just ended one relationship, she couldn't forget that Beck had emotionally slaughtered her heart and then tossed the pieces into what felt like a cold, dark, continuous blizzard. Cady felt a shiver run through her and remembered what it felt like to have ice in her veins.

Not again. Never again.

"I'm not looking for anything, Beck. From you or from anyone else," Cady stated, her eyes meeting his. One heartbreak a lifetime was more than enough.

Beck nodded once, abruptly, but his shoulders dropped a notch and she thought she saw him exhale a relieved sigh. Cady wanted to roll her eyes but resisted.

It's okay, Beck. I'm not here to complicate your life.

Oh, wait, she was.

"Congratulations," she said without any preamble, "we are, apparently, engaged."

Cady smiled at the panic that hit his eyes. "I haven't had any caffeine yet, so I'm a bit slow. Would you like to explain that?"

She supposed she should. Beck pushed a button on the state-of-the-art machine and Cady heard the sound of beans grinding and then the distinctive smell of coffee wafted over to her. Once again, her stomach twisted and her throat closed. *Oh, God, morning sickness, go away!*

Cady took a sip of her hot tea and breathed through her mouth. "I woke early and I couldn't sleep, so I thought I'd get a jump on my day. When I started working on this campaign, I set up numerous internet alerts on Ballantyne's, because I wanted to know what was being said about the company. I had fifty messages in my inbox this morning, directing me to websites with breaking news."

Cady rested her elbows on the granite counter and placed her chin in the palm of her hand. "Sam's is a favorite hangout for the paparazzi to find photos of celebs. Yesterday one of those bottom feeders caught the exact moment when you handed over the copy of your mom's ring and I—"

Beckett put down his coffee cup and groaned. "You put the ring on the ring finger of your left hand and held your hand up to look at it. And the photographer assumed he saw an engagement."

Well, nobody could ever accuse Beckett of being slow on the uptake.

"Essentially," she said. "A little research added the details to that scenario. Your mom's ring was well documented and it was immediately assumed that you were giving her ring to me."

Beck gripped the edge of the counter and let loose with a curse.

"Adding depth to the story, they know exactly who I am and that we spent two months traveling together years ago," Cady told him.

Beck's head jerked up. "How the hell would they know that?"

"We were kids. We used the social media sites, and those photos of us together are probably still out there," Cady said, trying to keep calm. One of them had to.

"We need to decide how we're going to manage this," she added, switching into PR mode.

"What do you suggest?" Beck asked. "Are we going to deny it, run with it, ignore it?"

He was a smart guy and Cady wanted to know how he would manage this crisis. "What would you do?"

Beck sipped his coffee and took some time to answer her. "I'm usually pretty decisive but I'm actually not sure. If we deny that we're seeing each other, then we'd have to explain why we were meeting at Sam's, why I was showing a PR person my mom's ring. That would raise questions about why Ballantyne's needs PR. The press might start speculating about whether the brand is as strong as it once was. That, in turn, might have an impact on the price of Ballantyne shares. That's something we don't need, especially since we have concerns about someone who's snapping up large blocks of Ballantyne shares."

Beck's expression indicated that he wasn't going to discuss that any further, so Cady returned to the original problem.

"An astute journalist might ask those questions. I'd prefer to keep the rebranding a secret until the last possible moment. The campaign has more impact that way," Cady said.

Beck pinned her to her seat with a hard look. "Are you suggesting that we stay engaged and keep the rebranding a secret?"

Oh, hell... Cady closed her eyes and hauled in a long, deep breath. "It's not that simple."

"Oh, God, what now?" Beck demanded. He held up his

hands, gesturing her not to answer. "Wait, I need more coffee to continue this conversation."

Cady was happy to delay the inevitable, to take a moment to gather her courage. She had to tell Beck that she was pregnant, that if they pretended to be engaged, the world would assume that he was the father of her child. Pretending to be engaged was one thing but his assuming responsibility for her pregnancy was another.

Beck placed his refilled cup of coffee next to her tea, and the smell of coffee traveled up her nose and hit the back of her throat. Cady felt her stomach lurch. She slapped her hand across her mouth and swallowed it back. She wasn't going to be sick. She wasn't.

Cady felt a strong hand on her back and opened her eyes to see Beck holding a small trash bin below her. She grabbed the stainless-steel bin with both hands, ducked her head and threw up.

Cady sat up and took the napkin Beck held out to her and wiped her mouth. Mortified, she hugged the bin to her side and looked at him through teary eyes.

"So, there's a reaction to getting engaged I hadn't expected," Beck said. "Trust me, Cades. It would be a fake engagement. I'm the last person in the world who intends to marry."

"I know that!" Cady told him. "There's just one complication…"

"What?"

"I'm pregnant. And you, obviously, are not the father."

"Oh, crap."

Beck stared at himself in the bathroom mirror, his eyes bleak and his face a shade paler than normal. His hands gripped the edges of the vanity as he tried to assimilate the news he'd just heard.

Cady. Pregnant. Which, the last time he'd heard, meant that she was going to have a freakin' baby.

Dear God in heaven.

Beck lifted his hand up and saw that it was trembling. He shook his head and had to wonder why he was feeling so gob-smacked and sideswiped. He hadn't seen her for nearly a decade and they'd shared a couple of hot kisses so he wasn't entitled to feel pissed off, disappointed or judgmental.

He had a relationship with her almost ten years ago and, whether he was attracted to her or not, he had no right to feel... Exactly how did he feel? Jealous. The thought of someone else loving her, touching her, tasting her fabulous skin, kissing her luscious mouth, made the content of his stomach bubble and boil.

Jealously was not an emotion he was familiar with.

They'd been apart for almost a decade and he'd had other women, lots of women, so he had to accept that she would've had other men in her life. He could accept it... but he didn't have to like it.

Stop emoting and start thinking, Ballantyne!

Forcing his emotions aside, Beck started to think. Before he excused himself to take a shower, she'd briefly explained that she'd been in a relationship, that her ex had no interest in being a father and she no longer wanted to be with him. Getting pregnant hadn't been her intention. It just happened.

Beck picked up his toothbrush to brush his teeth for the second time that morning, needing any excuse to stay in the bathroom for a little longer. Cady's face, her big eyes and her sexy mouth popped up in his brain, and his junk stirred to life. Huh. So the news that she was carrying someone else's kid didn't affect his attraction to her. He still wanted her in the worst way possible.

Beck rinsed, spat and admitted that if this was any other woman handing him the same news, there would be skid marks from him running out of her life at a hundred miles an hour. He would not, for one second, be able to be with, sleep with or date a pregnant woman. It was a perfect recipe for disaster—too many hormones and emotions and physical changes. It was also natural for a woman to look for a mate when she was pregnant, to look for someone to hold her hand, to feel a little less alone. To have someone to nest with.

He wasn't a nesting type of guy.

But this was *Cady*, who was unlike every other woman he'd ever met.

When he pushed away his jealousy at the thought of some cretin making love to her, he realized that her being pregnant didn't fundamentally change his opinion of her. He didn't want to bolt out of her life and, yeah, he still wanted to sleep with her.

He tested his forehead to check if he didn't have a fever.

Beck left his bathroom and walked into his closet, pulling out the first hanger he laid his hand on. Dropping his towel, he quickly dressed and ran his hands and then a brush through his wet hair. How should he handle her surprise announcement?

With the truth, he thought, as he knotted his tie. Nothing, really, had changed. He still didn't want a relationship with her, or anyone else, but her being pregnant didn't change his desire for her.

Sure, sleeping together was complicated. She was just out of a relationship, she was pregnant, he was her client, after all. But she was still a woman and he was still a man and they were still attracted to each other.

Desire didn't stop to read the warning labels.

He'd play this by ear, Beck decided, stepping out of his bedroom. He'd take it day by day, week by week, if he had to. But he was adult enough and experienced enough to know that pregnant or not, Cady would, at some point, be in his bed again.

Seven

While Beck took a shower, Cady sat on his couch, clutching the cup of ginger tea. Thankful for some time alone, she thought back to his expression when she'd made her announcement. To say he looked shocked was an understatement, but she couldn't blame him for the string of curses he'd let fly.

He was a guy who wasn't into commitment or relationships, only quick flings, and she was damn sure that having a quick fling with a pregnant woman was not on his bucket list. Even if they did share a history and were madly attracted to each other.

Beck was too into control to be caught up in such an unstable, potentially highly dramatic situation. As for her, she was borderline nuts to be even thinking about Beck in this way. She had enough emotional, physical and financial problems without adding the complication of sleeping with that delicious slab of muscle.

Man, her life was so messed up. For someone who'd

always tried so hard to do the right thing, who pursued perfection, she was surrounded by chaos.

Cady stared at her fingers and wished that Beck would come down from his room. Sitting here, wondering what he was thinking, hoping that he wasn't judging her too harshly, had her palms sweating. Cady knew that she shouldn't care what he thought of her. She was an adult and she should be over wanting anyone's approval. But Beck wasn't just anyone. He was an important part of her life.

She still respected him and he was her client. And, dammit, when she pushed her lust away, she still liked him. He was, and always had been, a good man.

Cady heard his footsteps and watched Beck walk down the spiral stairs, freshly shaved and his hair damp from his shower. She watched as he shoved his arms into a navy blazer, perfectly complementing his white dress shirt worn under a thin berry-colored sweater. Slim-fit wool pants in dark gray covered his long legs, and his trendy sneakers added a hip touch to his outfit. Between Thailand and now, T-shirt-and-cargo-shorts-wearing Beck had morphed into a clotheshorse, Cady thought. She looked down at her baggy sweatshirt and thought that she really had to up her game.

Beck walked over to her and sat on the backless leather chair facing her. "So, pregnant, huh?"

Cady couldn't see any judgment in his eyes or distaste on his face.

She nodded glumly. "Yep."

"Are you okay? Any problems?"

"Apart from the puking and the tiredness that I understand is normal, no." Cady gripped her teacup with both hands. Thinking that he might think she was whining, Cady straightened her back. "I'm perfectly able to manage this campaign, Beck."

"I never doubted that for a second," Beck replied, his voice steady. "I just need to know that you're healthy."

Cady nodded, touched by his concern. "I'm fine. I haven't seen a doctor yet but I will."

Beck nodded and stood up. He walked over to the window and leaned into the red brick wall. "And the father? Is he out of the picture?"

"Very. I was going to break up with him before I found out about the baby, but his insistence that I have an abortion nailed that coffin closed."

"Is he an utter moron? You're a pastor's kid."

Cady smiled at his understanding. "My decision to keep my baby goes deeper than that." Should she tell him about Will? Would he understand? "Do you remember that I had a brother?"

A small frown appeared above Beck's nose. "Yeah, he died when you were fifteen, right? From something... Sorry, I can't remember that part."

"I'm touched that you remember that much. Yeah, he had Lupus and he got pneumonia. The virus attacked his lungs and he passed away."

"I'm sorry, Cady."

Her smile just touched the corners of her mouth. "What I never told you is that he was autistic and disabled. I adored him, and he was my best friend, despite his limitations. When I was ten, I came home from school and my grandmother was there instead of Will and my mom. She told me that they'd taken Will to live in a residential home and that it was best for Will that there weren't any long, drawn-out goodbyes. He was, as my grandmother put it, becoming 'difficult to handle.'"

"What did she mean by that?"

"I have no idea. The Will I knew was funny and kind and...good."

Beck looked empathetic and interested, unlike Tom who'd just yawned his way through her story. "I was devastated. I've never understood why my parents shipped him off, but that's another story." Cady placed her hand on her stomach. "This child didn't do anything wrong and he or she shouldn't be disposed of because it's more convenient for me."

"Is that what you believe your parents did? Made life more convenient for themselves by sending your brother away?"

Cady stared at him, his words rolling around her head and then crystallizing. That was exactly what she thought and never been able to verbalize. Unwelcome tears burned her eyes. Trust Beck to put his finger on the essence of the problem.

And that was why his words at the airport in Thailand scoured her soul. Sending her away had been so convenient for him.

Beck sat down next to her and, with the pad of his thumb, wiped a tear from under her eye. "Then good for you, for keeping this baby, for taking the harder, less convenient path."

Cady gripped his wrist, holding on to his strength, his warmth. "I'm scared, Beck."

"Raising a kid is a scary thing. But you should also remember that you are bright and capable and so much stronger than you think you are." Beck tipped her chin up. "You can do this, Cades. I promise."

Cady let out a small laugh and felt his strength flow into her. She could do this. After all, it wasn't like she had a lot of choice.

"Thanks," she said, leaving her hand on his wrist. It felt good to touch him again.

"Have you told your parents about the baby?" Beck asked.

Cady sent him an "are you friggin' insane?" look that he quickly and correctly interpreted. His mouth twitched with amusement. "Let me rephrase that… Are you going to tell them?"

Cady shrugged and sighed. "They're going to hit the roof. Dad is also up for a promotion, so hearing that I'm pregnant and single will not be well received." Cady shook her head and made a quick decision. "I don't think I will, not yet. After all, this baby isn't going anywhere."

"Or you can tell them that we're engaged and that you're pregnant. They'll assume it's mine and we don't have to correct them."

"You'd do that for me?"

"Listen, I am one of the few people who know how over the top your parents can be. What's worse, being engaged and pregnant or single and pregnant?"

When he put it like that, Cady was tempted to agree. But using Beck as an excuse would be like taking the twenty thousand dollars he offered her to walk away from Ballantyne International. It would be taking the easy route. If she was old enough to have sex and get pregnant then she was old enough to be truthful about it.

"Delaying telling my parents is one thing but I can't flat out lie to them."

Beck nodded. "Fair enough."

"Speaking of lying…" Cady wrinkled her nose. "What are we going to do about the engagement?"

"Nothing," Beck stated, his tone suggesting that she not argue.

"What? Why?"

"If we deny it, we look like we have something to hide. If we confirm it, we step into the scamming-the-public-for-publicity territory and that makes me feel uncomfortable. So we do neither and let people think what they want. They will anyway."

It went against every instinct she had as a public relations expert. Situations like these had to be managed, steered, directed. "I don't know if I agree with you, Beck. It could blow up in our faces."

"Whatever scenario we choose could blow up. By not commentating, confirming or denying, we give ourselves room to move."

Cady could see that he'd made up his mind and that there was no point in arguing. "Okay, well, then I suggest that you call your family and give them a heads-up."

"Don't need to. If I was engaged for real, they'd know about it before the news hit the public space. Would your parents hear about this?"

Cady shook her head. "I very much doubt it. They live an insular life." She glanced at her watch and seeing the time, told herself she needed to get going. She had a long day ahead of her, and Beck, she was sure, was anxious to get to work. "Okay, we'll play it by ear. I should go."

Beck placed his hand on her knee to keep her seated. "It's been a pretty intense morning but there's one more issue we need to address."

There was?

"Okay. What?"

"The fact that every time we're together we're only a heartbeat away from stripping each other naked and doing what we always did best."

Cady looked at him, her mouth half open. What the hell was he talking about? "Beckett, I'm pregnant."

"I heard. I understood."

"I'm pregnant, so you can't want me anymore," Cady stated, comprehensively confused.

Beck rubbed his hand over his jaw and she saw frustration and annoyance flash in his eyes. "I wish I was that shallow. It would be a lot more convenient. But... I still want you, and I probably always will."

Cady placed her palms together and rested the edges of her fingers on her mouth. He was being open and honest and she should be, too.

"I feel like it's wrong to be this attracted to you, that I should have absolutely no interest in the opposite sex, that all my mental focus should be on my baby," Cady said, confused.

"But it's not?" Beck demanded.

She shook her head.

He rubbed the back of his neck. "I think that's a societal expectation, that you should put your life on hold for this child. But the fact is that you are a sexy woman and we've always had a combustible chemistry. That doesn't go away just because you're pregnant."

Before she could respond, Beck continued. "Don't look so worried, Cady. I'm not about to jump you." He smiled. "Not that I don't want to...and that's what I'm trying, with very little finesse, to say. Whatever this craziness is between us, you're in control of it. I want you but I also understand that your life is crazy at the moment. I know you're stressed and that you have enough to deal with without me trying to coerce you into bed."

Cady looked at him, trying to make sense of his words. Beck was putting her needs above his, and her heart thumped at his sensitivity. And his generosity.

"And when you decide that the time is right for us to make love, just say the word," he added with a small smile.

Cady tipped her head to the side, smiling. "Which particular word is that, Beck?" she teased.

He touched her lower lip with his thumb. "It won't matter what you say. I'll see it in your eyes, Cades. I always could and that hasn't changed."

The air between them felt charged with electricity, and Cady knew that it would be so easy to step into his arms, to allow him to make toe-curling love to her. But it wasn't a good idea, and sleeping with him might be another mistake. It had been an emotional, roller-coaster morning and it was smarter, safer, if she stepped back and thought before she acted.

She wanted Beck but damn, there was a high probability that he would be just another in a long line of blunders.

Beck must've seen her decision in her eyes because he lowered his thumb and he stepped away. Cady felt disappointed and immediately second-guessed her decision.

She didn't want to be an adult anymore. It wasn't half as much fun as they'd told her it would be.

When Cady made the arrangements for Jaeger's photo shoot at his home in Park Slope, Brooklyn, she'd expected it would be just her, Jaeger, the stylist and makeup artist, the photographer and his assistant, and maybe Piper and Ty.

She hadn't expected his siblings to head for Brooklyn after work. Linc and his son, Shaw, arrived first and then Sage arrived and with her, Amy. Thank God they were nearing the end of the shoot because Piper's apartment was now full to overflowing. Linc found Jaeger's liquor stash and was handing out drinks while she and the photographer tried to placate the increasingly impatient Jaeger.

When Ty escaped from Sage and bolted across the floor into the picture frame, Jose, the photographer, threw up his hands and eagerly reached for the bottle of red wine Linc left on the mantel. And that, Cady quickly realized, was the end of the shoot.

Her feet ached, her head was on fire and all she wanted to do was go home and have a long, long soak. She was exhausted.

"Cady, these are amazing!"

Cady looked at Sage, who was standing next to Jose looking at the screen of his camera. Judging by Sage's enthusiasm, the shoot wasn't a complete bust. Maybe there was a photo or two they could use for the campaign.

Cady walked out of the study and into Piper and Jaeger's living area and dropped into the corner of the sofa. She really enjoyed the Ballantyne bunch but, God, they were loud! Shaw was chasing a just-walking Ty around the apartment, weaving their way in between adult legs and laughing like loons. Linc was teasing Jaeger about one thing or another and the others were discussing a photography exhibition they'd apparently all seen.

She'd been raised in a quiet, ordered, disciplined house, and the noise and laughter felt like a red hot poker was being repeatedly jammed in her ear. She just wanted to cry. Pregnancy hormones, she told herself. Perfectly normal.

It was and it wasn't, Cady admitted, resting her forearm over her eyes. Yeah, she was a hormonal stew but there was more to this melancholia than a little noise and exhaustion. Working with Beck and fighting her attraction to him was taking its toll. They'd spent a lot of time together lately, both at work and at his apartment—using work as an excuse. They always did *some* work, but they spent more time talking, reconnecting.

And she remembered how much she liked him, how much she simply loved being with him. Since that morning he'd told her that she would have to make the next move, he hadn't once tried to kiss her but she knew he wanted to.

And, God, how she wanted him. She wanted to feel his muscles bunch and move under his hot skin, taste the slight tang of his manly skin. She wanted to nibble the long cord in his strong neck, run her hands through the light layer of hair on his chest. She wanted to feel his hands on her body, his weight on her as he settled over and into her, listen to him gasp in pleasure, sigh in sleep.

She wanted him. She needed him. She couldn't have him.

Because she couldn't afford to forget that he'd once had her heart and broken it, that she'd felt like this about him once before and he'd tossed her out of his life and moved on. If she and Beck slept together, she knew her feelings for him would deepen but his wouldn't. He didn't want what she did and she'd be the one to end up hurt. She'd have to pick her beaten and battered heart up from off the floor.

He'd love her, physically, but she knew the day would come when it would end and she had to protect herself. She could not allow herself to fall in love with him. If she did, and he stabbed her heart again, she feared that she would never recover.

No, it was better that she keep her very desperate hands to herself.

"Hey, Cady, where's Driven?" Linc demanded from across the room.

"Who?" Cady asked, lowering her arm.

"Beck," Sage explained, taking the spare seat next to her. "Linc and Jay have called him that since he was a kid. Because he works so damn hard."

The nickname was apt, Cady admitted. Beck did work ridiculously long hours.

"Oh. I don't know," she told Linc.

"I'll call him," Jaeger said and whipped out his phone. He walked through the front door and into the hallway and laughed. "Hey, we were just talking about you."

"And don't you look like a pretty boy with your perfect stubble and styled hair."

Cady heard Beck's drawl, and her stomach tightened. She turned her head to look over the back of the couch and sent him a small smile. A frown appeared between Beck's eyebrows as he took off his coat. "Hi. You okay?"

Cady started to answer but Shaw hit his knees with the force of a tiny tank, so she just nodded. Beck tossed Shaw into the air, and the noise level increased again. Cady thought her head might explode.

The mayhem continued as Jose and his crew said their goodbyes. After they left, Cady sat down again and closed her eyes. She felt Beck's hand on her shoulder and when she opened her eyes, she saw that he held two pills in his hand and a glass of water. She lifted her eyes to his and shook her head. She couldn't explain that she couldn't take anything because of the baby. Not in front of everyone.

"These are safe," Beck assured her, his voice pitched low enough so that only she could hear him. "Trust me."

She did. And that was the problem. She couldn't afford to.

Cady swallowed her pills and turned her head as Piper sat down next to her. "The boys are ordering pizza. Stay and eat with us."

"I should get home," Cady said, although she didn't have the energy to move.

"Stay," Piper urged her. "It'll be here in twenty minutes. Have a slice and I'll order a cab to take you home."

She could be home within forty-five minutes. A bath, her bed. Bliss. But for now she had to try to be sociable.

She thanked Piper for the invitation and nodded at the gorgeous sapphire on Piper's ring finger. It was the same ring that Jaeger had held and posed with all afternoon. "It's a stunning ring."

"I love it," Piper said, her voice full of emotion.

"I designed it," Sage said from across the room. There was pride in her voice and Cady realized that the Ballantynes, for the first time that evening, were all tuned in to the same conversation. "It's one of my favorite designs," Sage added.

"It should be since it was a special commission and you charged me through the nose for it," Jaeger grumbled. "Linc stiffed me on the cost of the stone and you wiped out my bank account with the price of your design."

Piper laughed at him. "Good thing you live rent free with me. I'd hate to see you homeless and begging. And, as you keep forgetting, Sage said that the design was our engagement present."

"Is it?" Jaeger's face brightened. "Cool."

"Actually, it was my way to thank Piper for taking you off our hands," Sage teased. "But if you want to pay me, you can."

"I can't afford you." He continued the joke by looking at Linc and raising his eyebrows. "How about giving Piper the sapphire as a thank-you for marrying me, too?"

"I love Piper but not that much," Linc replied, his tone dry. "Nice try, though."

Sage raised her eyebrows at Cady. "As you can see, I'm happy to pay the price to be rid of my annoying brothers. Are you interested in making a deal?"

Oh, God, yes, right now. She'd take Beck off her hands, into her hands. She really wanted him in her hands... God knew how much longer she could resist him. A day? An hour? Ten more minutes?

An awkward silence fell over the room, and Cady wondered if her thoughts were on her face. Blushing, she decided the only way to defuse the tension was to crack a joke. "Sure, I'll take Linc off your hands." She grinned at Beck's scowl and nodded at Sage. "Let's negotiate."

"Let's not," Beck muttered, placing his hand on her shoulder as if to stake his claim.

Sage and Piper exchanged a long look and they both nodded. "Quick and smart," Sage commented. "We like you. If you stick, I'll up my offer."

If she stuck... No chance of that happening.

Eight

An hour later and back in her apartment, south of Jaeger and Piper's red Victorian in Park Slope, Beck took Cady's coat and hung it up, trying to suppress the urge to jump her. It had been hell trying to keep his mouth, hands and other parts of his body to himself and he was running out of patience. Tonight he didn't think he could.

Maybe it had something to do with her fitting into his family, her easy banter with his sister, the way she looked at him across the room. It might be one or all of the above but mostly it was because she was all feminine heat, creamy skin, desire and deliciousness, and he couldn't go one more night without finding out if she was as good as he remembered. He had to have her.

"Shall I make coffee, Beck? Would you like some?"

Beck turned to face her and noticed that she'd slipped out of her heels, holding them so that they dangled by their ankle straps. Her lipstick was gone and a curl had escaped from the bundled, sexy mess on her head and she looked glad to be home.

Her sexy factor nearly dropped him to the floor.

Beck just stared at her, knowing that his eyes, the look on his face and the rod in his pants would tell her exactly what he wanted, and it sure as hell wasn't coffee.

Cady's eyes darkened, her nipples tightened and she shifted her weight from one foot to the other as if trying to escape the heat between her thighs. There was no escape, they had to go there and it was inevitable. It had been since the moment he saw her in the hallway at Ballantyne International.

"I'm *pregnant*, Beck," she reminded him, as if that had any bearing on the situation.

He shook his head and jammed his hands into the pockets of his suit pants to keep them from reaching for her. "So? I look at you and I stop breathing and all I can think about is getting you into my bed, hearing your moans, slipping inside you to see if you feel as good as I remember."

"Beck…"

"Tell me that you want me, Cady." He wasn't going to move toward her until he heard her say the words.

Cady dropped her shoes to the floor and moved toward him, as graceful as a prima ballerina. She pushed her hand under the lapel of his suit jacket and through his cotton dress shirt, her hand burning his skin. "I've thought of you, imagined touching you. You are so hard, Beck. Your chest, your stomach…" Her eyes dropped to the tent in his pants. "Everywhere."

Cady pushed his jacket off his shoulders and he allowed it to fall down his arms and onto the floor. It was designer but hell, who cared? Cady was touching him and that was all that mattered. She pulled his tie off and undid the button at his neck, and resting her hands on his chest, she rose on her tiptoes and placed a warm, open-mouthed kiss at the base of his neck. Beck felt heat and electricity shoot down his spine and tighten his balls.

"Tell me, Cady."

"I want you, Beck."

That was what he wanted—no, needed—to hear. He yanked her into him, pressing her breasts against his chest. He dropped his head and at the same time, she lifted her mouth and they fused together, their mouths clashing and tongues dueling. Her tongue swirled around his and memory collided with reality. What they shared now was even better than he remembered. Cady made a sexy sound in her throat, and her fingers dug into his chest.

She tasted of the crisp winter air and longing, and kissing her was both a comforting memory and a fresh pleasure. Her perfume swirled up from her heated skin and her scent, lemongrass and jasmine, took him back to the hot Thailand nights by the sea.

He hiked up her shirt so he had access to her creamy skin. Still kissing her, unable to pull away, he placed one arm below her butt and yanked her up and into him. Her legs, as he knew they would, opened and curled around his waist. But that contact was not enough. Still needing more, he pushed her down so that she brushed his erection with her mound. When her kisses turned fiercer and she ground against him, he realized that the passion between them was hotter than before, deeper, all grown up.

Beck walked her over to the kitchen counter and set her down on the cool surface, still standing between her legs and feeling her heat radiating from her core. He cradled her face, tipping her head to change the angle so that he had easy access to every part of her mouth.

Cady's moans of approval sent the last droplets of blood from his brain to points south and he strained the fabric on the front of his pants.

She was sex and heat and sweetness and softness and he needed her. So much more than he should. He couldn't stop, didn't want to stop. This train had left the station but he had to slow it down. He didn't want to take her on the kitchen counter. After so long, he needed to be in a bed. He wanted to take his time to rediscover her, to explore every inch of her endlessly sexy skin.

Although he didn't want to, Beck pulled his mouth from hers to rest his chin in her hair. "Cady."

She muttered something unintelligible as he felt her lips flutter against his skin.

"We need to slow down," he told her. "Find some more room."

"Trust me, my bed is not much bigger than this counter," Cady muttered. "Don't stop, Beck."

"I want to take it slow."

"Next time."

She'd barely finished her sentence when his mouth captured hers. Her words gave him permission to lose control, the control he was so famous for. With Cady, his brain shut down and biology took over. As her tongue met his swipe for swipe, he lifted her shirt over her head and immediately noticed that she wasn't wearing a bra. He thumbed her already hard nipple and Cady pushed her breast into his touch, silently demanding more. She ran her fingers across his taut stomach, stopping now and again to make a swirling motion as she let them drift lower before settling them on his erection.

He couldn't wait much longer. He needed her, needed to be inside her.

Beck wrenched his mouth off hers and attacked the

button of her pants, sliding her zipper down. "Lift up," he ordered her and Cady lifted her butt, allowing him to pull the slacks down her slim thighs. The garment dropped to the floor and he kicked it aside.

He leaned back and sucked in a breath, taking a moment to appreciate her rosy nipples, her endlessly creamy skin, the barrier of pale pink lace over her feminine mound. He lifted his eyes to her flushed face and his voice was low and harsh when he spoke. "Here? Now?"

"Here. Now."

Beck used one hand to pull his shirt over his head and the other to pull his wallet out of the back pocket of his pants. He tossed it into her lap. "There's a condom somewhere in there."

While Cady searched his wallet with trembling fingers, he stepped out of his shoes and hastily undressed, till he stood naked between her warm thighs.

He put on the condom she held out to him, then hooked his hands under the backs of her knees and pulled her to him so that his tip probed her entrance. She felt so good.

He really wanted to take her to bed, or the floor, somewhere where he could really look at her, feel every inch of her as he entered her. "Cady, we are not doing this on the kitchen counter."

Cady touched her mouth to his before speaking. "If you make me move, I swear I will punch you. I need you, Beck. Make me whole," she murmured against his lips.

Beck groaned and pushed into her, sighing when her tongue echoed his action and slid into his mouth. An inch, then one more, and another and he was inside her. Cady pushed her heels into his back, asking for more, and within seconds Beck was buried to the hilt.

Yeah, he missed this. He missed her.

"God, Beck, you feel so good," Cady said, burying her

face into his neck. "Take me over the edge, Beck. You know how. You always did."

Beck surged into her and slid a finger between them, stroking her, and around him he felt Cady tense. He could feel her orgasm hovering, so he rocked into her one more time and she shattered around him.

Then, with a hoarse, relieved cry, he followed her into that fireball.

Another day, another photo shoot. Another day of trying to work out what, exactly, was bubbling between her and Beck. Since she'd barely spent any time with him since her amazing night with him four days ago, she couldn't take her cue from Beck. Panty-dissolving sex aside, Cady thought, nothing, essentially, had changed. He was still her boss; she was still pregnant; she had a job to do, a business to save, to grow.

Cady watched Emma, the photographer's assistant, carry a small ladder out Beck's door and Beck closed the door to the loft behind her. A dozen people had filled this space an hour before—stylists, makeup artists and creative directors. Now only she and Beck remained. Cady sat on the third step of Beck's wide spiral staircase, her computer on her knees, looking through the photographs Jose wirelessly transmitted to her device.

Like his siblings had in their photos, Beck wore a designer white dress shirt, collar open and cuffs rolled up his arms. His jeans were faded from years of washing, and the fabric clung to his narrow hips and long legs, and he wore no shoes. She scrolled through the shots, pleased that they conveyed the exact image she was going for in the campaign: the rich, successful, super-sexy Ballantyne siblings at ease in their homes or, in Sage's case, in her studio.

They looked young and smart, aspirational and accessible. Cady knew that the print ads would make the rich millennials sit up and take notice.

She stopped on a photograph of Beck sitting exactly where she was, his knees apart and holding the fake copy of his mom's ring between his finger and thumb, looking at the camera, his eyes deep and mysterious. His broody attitude, wide shoulders and the brilliance of the pink-red stone screamed class. And cool.

As with his siblings' ads, consumers were encouraged to read the story behind the piece of jewelry on the website, and that would link them to Sage's latest hip and sleek collection. They'd already released Jaeger's and Sage's ads, and Linc's was due to be released tomorrow, Beck's later in the week. The Ballantyne website had never received so many hits.

Cady felt a flutter of excitement as she marked the photo. She looked up when Beck, holding a cup of coffee, took his seat next to her. "Can I drink this here next to you? Or are you going to bolt for the bathroom?"

Her morning sickness wasn't a constant presence, just triggered by sights and smells. The smell of chicken sent her running, as did vanilla. Sometimes coffee was her friend, sometimes her foe. Cady took a tentative sniff, waited a little while and when her stomach didn't react, she smiled. "Today is a good coffee day."

Beck pressed his shoulder into hers and looked at the screen. "Is that the shot you want to use?"

Cady nodded. "But you can look through the others if you'd like to."

"Hell, no, I trust you. Damn, this thing is poking a hole in my skin." Beck leaned back, pulled the copy of his mom's ring out of the front pocket of his jeans and rested it on his knee. Cady moved her laptop to the floor and picked up the ring, examining it in the fading light of the late afternoon.

"It's so beautiful, Beck."

"And it's only a fake. The real one is deeper, more vibrant, the color more intense." Beck sipped his coffee. "Her ring is my first memory, that and her smell."

"Tell me about her." Cady twisted to face him, her knees against his thigh.

Beck put his hand on her knee and kept his eyes on the ring she held. "I remember her hand over mine. I was holding a crayon. We're both left-handed so that's why I remember the ring. I was so young but I remember being fascinated by the color."

"American rose," Cady murmured, allowing the stone to catch the light. "It's a shade of red, between red and magenta...and it's called American rose. I wished I could've seen the real deal," Cady murmured.

"Yeah, I wouldn't mind seeing the ring, and them, again," Beck said, his voice threaded with pain. "Unfortunately both are in pieces on that mountain in Vermont."

Cady changed position so that she could thread her arm through Beck's and hold his hand. "I'm sorry, Beck. God, you were all so young."

"Yeah. Ten, eight and six." Beck's coffee cup shook as he lifted it to his lips. "I still miss them."

"I think you always will," Cady said, keeping her voice low. This was the first time Beck ever talked about his past and his parents, and she didn't want to break the spell by talking too much or by saying the wrong thing.

Beck stared at his bare feet, pale against the laminated floor. "My siblings missed out on so much. Their parents weren't at Jaeger's games, their graduations, Sage's ballet concerts. My father won't walk Sage down the aisle. Ty and Shaw won't go with my dad to find semiprecious gems like we did." Beck rubbed his jaw and pushed his hand to the back of his neck.

He never once mentioned himself, what he'd like to do with his parents, she noticed. "And what did you miss out on, not having your parents there?"

Silence, hot and heavy, hung between them, and Cady wondered if he would reply to her question. She saw him pull in a deep breath as he turned his eyes to her. They were saturated with pain. "It doesn't matter what I missed out on. It never did."

Whoa. What?

Cady frowned, opened her mouth to loudly object to his statement and saw the misery on his face. He hadn't said that lightly. He meant every cruel and bitter word. After squeezing his hand, she carefully chose her next words. "Beck, why would you think that? You lost your parents, too."

"But it was my fault they died."

Cady felt the words slam into her, stopping her breath and paralyzing her vocal cords. When her brain restarted, she noticed that Beck was in the process of rising to his feet, intending to walk away. Oh, hell, no. He was going to sit here and talk this through. He'd been eight, for God's sake; no eight-year-old was responsible for his parents' deaths. It was sheer luck that Cady managed to snag a belt loop through his shirt but she did and she pulled him back down. "Sit down."

Beck shook his head. "I have a report to write, some financials to go through."

"You need to sit here and talk to me," Cady hotly replied. Beck sighed and sat and looked mutinous. She stared at his stone-like profile and shook her head. "Why would you think that, Beck?"

"Because that's what happened. Cady, I don't want to talk about this."

She ignored the second part of his statement. "No, that's not what happened! I know that you were at The Den with your uncle and your siblings so you didn't do anything to cause their deaths. So what do you mean?" She wished she could reach into him and yank his words out.

Beck cursed and muttered something about him having a big mouth. He raked his hand through his hair and sighed, then eventually, reluctantly, he answered her. "I broke my wrist skateboarding and it wasn't a straight break. It needed to be pinned and I had to have an operation. I was petrified. I'd watched a horror movie that took place in a hospital and I was convinced that the zombies would get me, and Jaeger was egging on my fears. I asked my folks to come home, to be with me. I was crying on the phone, practically hysterical, and they decided to fly home right away. The weather was bad and my dad took a chance. The weather closed in and he didn't have enough height to clear that mountain."

His dad took a chance, she wanted to point out to him, not him. He'd just been a kid asking for his parents. Why would he think he was at fault? "I still don't understand why you think their crashing is your fault. Your dad gambled and lost."

"At the reception after the funeral, I heard a conversation between two people I knew. They said it was my fault, that a broken arm is a hell of a price to pay for the deaths of two amazing people."

"Oh, Beckett."

"And they also mentioned that my mom was pregnant. We had a sibling on the way so I was responsible for the loss of three lives."

Swamped with anger for the young boy Beckett had been, Cady moved to stand between his open legs and wrapped her fists in his shirt. She waited until he looked into her eyes and when he did, she took a breath and then another, to get her temper under control. When she spoke she heard her burning fury in her words. "The insensitive bastards! What they said was *wrong*, Beck! Wrong and *ugly*!

"Who were they?" she demanded, her anger bubbling in the back of her throat.

"Why?" Beck asked, confused.

"Because I swear I will track them down and strip fifty layers off them. How dare they say that? How dare they!"

Beck pulled on her wrists and she realized that his shirt was tight against his chest and a good portion of it was wrapped around her hands. She released the fabric and placed her hands on Beck's shoulders.

"Cady, I appreciate your anger on my behalf but it was a long time ago."

Cady shushed him to keep quiet and closed her eyes in an attempt to harness her anger. It wasn't often that she lost her temper. It didn't matter that they were two faceless, nameless people whom he'd last seen almost twenty-five years ago; they'd hurt him to the depths of his soul. Nobody hurt Beck, not like that.

She waited a moment until she thought she could speak again then opened her eyes. Beck was looking at her, looking awed and confused.

"You okay?" he asked her.

"Yeah," Cady replied. She felt him start to move and she pushed her hands down, trying to keep him in place. "Where do you think you're going?"

"I was going to take my cup to the kitchen and then

I was going to do some work, since I lost the afternoon staring into the camera."

"Oh, hell, no, you're not." Cady shook her head. She pushed his legs together and straddled him, taking his rough, stubbled, beautiful face in her hands.

Beck managed a small smile but his eyes reflected only desolation. "Or we can go to bed. I vote for that."

"That's not in the cards, either, or at least not right now." Cady swiped her thumb across his bottom lip. "Right now I am going to talk and you are going to listen."

Beck narrowed his eyes and she felt him pull away from her. His fingers on her hips pushed into her skin as if to warn her to change the subject. He could glower and glare at her all he liked; he needed to hear what she had to say.

"I can't force you to listen to me, Beck, but I hope you will."

Beck muttered a curse and she saw his resentment and under that, his fear. To his credit, and her surprise, he stayed where he was.

"Beck, you are not responsible," Cady told him, keeping her voice low but allowing her sincerity to be heard. "You were a scared kid and you had every right to ask your parents to come home to be with you. And they, being the parents they were, heard your plea and made their way home. That's what good parents do."

"But—"

"Your dad took a chance, and it worked out badly. It wasn't your fault," Cady insisted.

"She was pregnant, Cades!"

"And they could've died in a car accident and her being pregnant and them dying wouldn't be your fault either. You were eight. You wanted and needed your parents, and there is no need for you to feel guilty. None, Beck." Cady's eyes filled with tears. "Intellectually, you know this."

"Yeah, but—"

"No buts." Cady felt a tear roll down her cheek and she sniffed. "Please don't do this to yourself."

Beck's hand moved from her hip to her face, tracing her jawline with his fingers, his touch sparking wherever he touched. "My siblings still don't know that she was pregnant. Should I—"

"Tell them?" Cady finished his sentence for him. "I don't know, Beck. But maybe it's a way to start dismantling that suit of armor between you and your siblings, you and the world."

"I don't—" Beck started, half laughed and shook his head. "Yeah, I do wear that armor. You always had the ability to find my weak spots and sneak on in. Cades, you…this…"

Cady stopped his fumbling words with her lips on his. She didn't want him to say more, to make promises he couldn't keep just because he was feeling emotional. This entire interlude was too intense and she had to pull away now because she couldn't fall any deeper into whatever was building between her and Beck.

Too much had happened lately; too much was at stake. She was, for the second time, sleeping with a client and although Beck said that he could, and would, separate the two issues, she'd been burned in this situation before. She was pregnant and Beck wasn't the father and they didn't have a future.

She wasn't going to fall in love with Beck again. It didn't matter that he was the best man she'd ever met, that she thought he was sexy as sin, that she adored him.

This. Was. Not. Going. To. Happen.

She was not going to fall in love with Beck. Not again.

"Let's go to bed." Beck's hot chocolate voice rumbled over her.

She shook her head and stood in front of him.

Beck frowned at her. "Problem?" Beck asked, concern in his voice.

Cady shot steel into her spine and told herself to be sensible. "Having sex after such an intense conversation is not a good idea."

"Having sex is always a good idea," Beck argued.

Such a man answer, Cady thought. "No, it's *not*. Emotions get jumbled up with physical pleasure, and everything gets turned upside down. We're emotionally connected at the moment and that could deepen if we sleep together. It's better that we take some time, put some space between us."

Beck took a minute to answer her. "And that would be a bad thing?"

"Of course it would be a bad thing! Beck, you broke my heart and I'm not prepared to give you another chance to do that. I'm working for you and I am being so damn unprofessional. I hate myself for not being able to resist you. And, for God's sake, just to add to this pile of crazy, I'm pregnant!"

"Your being pregnant isn't a problem for me," Beck said, his eyes hot but his voice calm.

"It should be!" Cady threw her hands up in the air at his stubborn face. "I'm hormonal, emotional and I know myself well enough to know that sex with you, right now, would not be good for me." Cady couldn't blink away the tears in her eyes. "I need some distance, Beck. From you, from us, from how you make me feel."

"Why?"

Cady picked up her laptop, shoved it into her tote bag

and did a quick scan of his loft for anything she'd left behind.

"Because I don't want to get too used to something I know is temporary. Because one of these days you're going to get scared and bolt and I can't allow you to break my heart again. I can handle sex with you, I can handle being friends with you, I can work for you—but I can't be emotionally attached to you. I can't let you break my heart again, Beck."

Cady walked to the door and put her hand on the knob and pulled it open.

"Cady."

She looked over her shoulder to see him standing there, hot and a little bewildered. "Yeah?"

"My heart broke, too."

Cady lifted one shoulder in a sad shrug. "That was your choice, Beck, not mine."

Nine

"Come on, guys," Beck complained as he stepped out of the taxi in front of The Den, the brownstone he'd grown up in. He scowled at the paparazzi standing in front of the steps leading up to the front door. "Isn't there someone else for you to stalk?"

A bearded man in a combat jacket shrugged and lifted his camera to his face. "You and Cady are the current fascination. When are you going to admit or deny your engagement?"

"When hell freezes over," Beck retorted, holding his hand out to Cady. Her bare fingers slid into his hand and he felt the same buzz he always did when they connected. They'd been sleeping together for more than two weeks and the electricity arcing between them seemed to be intensifying. As if by mutual agreement they kept the sex between them hot, the conversation light. Damn him for, occasionally, wanting the sex to be fun and the conversation deep. But, he acknowledged, it was safer this way.

Cady climbed out of the cab and immediately buried her face in her voluminous scarf. A hat covered her dark curls and she looked mysterious and sexy, and Beck knew that the media's interest in her was fueled in part because she was an unknown and because she looked liked Audrey Hepburn with light eyes and long hair.

"When is the wedding?"

Beck ignored the question and pulled a shivering Cady to his side as they walked up the steps to the imposing front door of The Den.

"Cady isn't wearing your mom's ring. Why not?"

Because it's fake, you moron, and no fiancée of mine is going to wear a fake engagement ring.

"None of your business." Beck tossed the words over his shoulder. Nobody outside the family knew what happened to the original ring, the real one. He'd looked but he hadn't found another stone to match it. Red beryl was incredibly rare and stones above two and three carats were even rarer. Finding another five-carat beauty was impossible.

It didn't matter; he was never going to offer it to a woman—Cady or anybody else.

He unlocked the door and ushered Cady inside, inhaling the familiar smell of fresh flowers and beeswax polish. He took off his coat, hung it up on the rack next to the door and watched Cady unwind her scarf.

She looked nervous and he couldn't blame her. His family would all be present tonight, including Amy and Tate, who'd moved into The Den with her sister's—and Linc's ex-fiancée's—ten-month-old baby. What was with all the babies suddenly? Up until three months ago there had only been Shaw, Linc's four-year-old, but now they were being overrun with the smaller species. Ty was new, Linc's ex's baby was living with them, Piper was pregnant and Cady was pregnant.

Was there something in the water?

Beck took Cady's coat and scarf and noted how beautiful she looked She wore a tight-fitting blue sweater over a blue-and-white-checked shirt, equally tight camel-colored jeans tucked into brown, knee-high leather boots. She didn't need designer clothes to look stylish; she had a way of putting together outfits that just worked. Unlike him. He needed a stylist to buy his clothes. Stefan even packed his closet, hanging all the items together so that Beck couldn't go wrong.

Cady jumped at the shout of laughter coming from the living room, and Beck took her hand. "It'll be okay, Cady. This is a safe place. You don't need to pretend here."

"Then why am I here?" Cady asked. "I don't need to be here."

Her lack of enthusiasm about spending time with his family shouldn't hurt him but it did. These were his people, dammit, and he wanted her to like them. And them to like her. But why? he asked himself. It wasn't like she was going to be a permanent part of his life.

Irritated with his irrational thoughts, Beck said, "You haven't had time to brief Linc, Sage and Jaeger about the response to the campaign. They don't know what a success it's been. I thought you could do that tonight."

"But you try not to talk business at these dinners," Cady replied.

"We try not to but we always do. It's a hazard of running a family business." He grabbed her hand and pulled her to him. "What's the matter, Cades?"

Her eyes skittered away from his. "Do they know I'm pregnant?" she asked.

"I haven't told them."

"Why not?"

"Because it has nothing to do with them. But if you want to tell them, feel free."

Cady shook her head. "No, I just thought you would've—"

"I didn't," Beck assured her. When she still wouldn't look at him, he asked, "What else is bugging you, Cady?"

"I'm not usually intimidated by people, regardless of how rich they are, but this—you—" Cady waved her hand around the hall "—this is serious, Beckett."

Serious? What was serious? "You've lost me."

"The Ballantynes are old money New York, one of the most influential families in the city. I'm from a middle-class family in a tiny upstate town. This house, the business... It's all a bit intimidating, Beck. The chandelier, the staircase, the fancy furniture."

"The hall table is eighteenth century. French, I think, but my grandmother found it in a junk shop and restored it herself." He looked up at the massive chandelier. "If you look carefully, there are still tiny spitballs on it. It was a prime target when we were kids. Yeah, the staircase is imposing but hell, you can get some serious speed when you slide down the banister on your butt. It's just a house, Cady."

"Cool! Can I do that, Uncle Beck?"

Beck turned and saw blonde-haired and blue-eyed Shaw standing next to him. The kid had skills that ninjas didn't, Beck thought, hoisting the kid up and over his shoulder to dangle him down his back, his hand gripping both his ankles.

"Beckett!" Cady gasped, shocked.

"Don't worry, he always does this," Shaw told her, laughter in his voice.

Beck fumbled his grip, trying to scare the boy, but

Shaw just giggled. "Nice try, Uncle Beck. I know you won't drop me, because if you do my dad will fry your gizzards in hot oil."

"Do you even know what a gizzard is?" Cady asked him, amused.

"Nope. I'm Shaw, who are you?" Shaw asked as Beckett started to walk in the direction of the living room.

"I'm Cady."

Beck stood back to gesture her into the room that held the crew. Jo, Linc's mom, held a cute biracial, blue-eyed baby, and Ty, Jaeger's son, was sitting between Jaeger's feet on the floor and dropping biscuit crumbs on the rare Persian carpet. Piper was talking to Amy, and Linc was watching Tate, who stood apart from the family, looking like she was ready to bolt.

Fun times at The Den, Beck thought on a wry smile.

As his brothers stood up, Shaw wiggled his way into Beck's arms. The boy stared at him, clearly puzzled. "The storks must be really busy at the moment, hey, Uncle Beck?"

Storks? Had Shaw moved on from his train craze to birds? "Why do you say that, bud?"

"Well," Shaw said into the silence that had fallen over the room, "storks bring babies and there have been a lot of them lately. There's Ty and Ellie, and Piper has a baby in her tummy and Cady said she's pregnant—that means she has a baby in her tummy, too, doesn't it?"

Oh, dammithellcrap. All the curse words Jo banned from this house came rushing through his mind as one.

Thanks, Shaw, Beck thought as Cady turned pale and bolted for the powder room.

Thanks a lot, buddy.

Beck turned back to his family and sighed at their raised eyebrows, their cocked heads. He also caught the resignation on his siblings' faces, the expectation that he would refuse to discuss this any further. It was what he did, as Cady had pointed out to him the other night when she'd cried tears for the little boy he'd been.

He'd thought long and hard about what she'd said, and her belief in his innocence melted some of the ice around his heart, the guilt he'd lived with all his life. For the first time in forever, he thought that maybe it was time to forgive the child he'd been. Oh, he wasn't there yet but maybe, with a little work, he could get there one day soon.

But he did know that it was time to really start reconnecting with his family, that he needed to start opening up to them on a deeper level. These were the people he trusted and it was time he showed them that he did. He took the glass of whiskey Jaeger poured for him and shrugged. "It's not my kid."

He thought he should clear that up, just in case anyone had their doubts.

"We kind of figured that," Linc drawled.

"Yeah, you work fast but not that fast," Jaeger added.

Piper smacked her fiancé's shoulder and sent him a "be serious" glare. Beck tossed her a look of gratitude. Opening up and talking was hard enough as it was without having to deal with their sarcasm. "How far along is she, Beck?" Piper asked.

Beck shrugged, embarrassed that he didn't know. "I'm not sure."

"Beckett, really?" Jo asked, shocked.

"Has she seen a doctor?"

"Is she taking vitamins? Getting enough sleep?"

Amy, Julia, Piper and even Tate looked horrified at his lack of information. But, in his defense, every time he raised the issue of her pregnancy, Cady changed the subject. He hadn't pushed and if the looks he was receiving from the females in his life were to be believed, he'd messed up, big-time.

"Is her being pregnant a problem for you?" Amy demanded.

Beckett frowned. "What do you mean?"

"If you're developing feelings for her, will her pregnancy put you off?"

He looked down the hall to make sure that Cady hadn't left the powder room. "I'm *not* developing feelings for her, Ames."

Or was he?

She was the only one he'd ever told his whole story to, the only one who knew about his mother's pregnancy. She occupied far too many of his daytime thoughts and his nighttime dreams. Being with her, making love to her, was the closest thing to heaven on earth.

Or maybe it was just the residual feelings from years ago seeping their way back into his psyche. It didn't mean that he was in love with her.

He couldn't be. It wasn't part of his life plan.

A life plan he'd made for himself at eight? How reasonable was that?

Beck frowned at that rogue thought and shook his head, quickly turning back to the conversation at hand. He'd rather take grief from his family than consider that he'd based his life on a lie.

"You didn't answer the question." Sage leaned forward, her eyes on his. "Would Cady being pregnant with someone else's child be a problem for you?"

If he decided to be with Cady, would a baby be a problem? He didn't think so. He liked kids, babies didn't scare him and he could, thanks to babysitting Shaw more times than he could remember, do what needed to be done. And yeah, he wasn't thrilled that she was pregnant by someone else, but if the choice was between Cady and baby or no Cady, he knew that he'd chose her and the child.

But that wasn't a choice he was going to make.

He lifted his glass in Linc's direction. "Linc's not blood but we seem to like him enough. If I decided to take on a woman with a child who wasn't mine, I'd probably feel the same."

"Are you thinking of taking her on?" Linc demanded. "Because if you're not, then you've got to let this go, Beck, before she gets hurt."

Beck shook his head. "Whoa, hold on. I'm not the only one who has his foot on the brake. She's equally wary, equally not willing to start something we can't finish."

"You really hurt her before, Beck. Please don't do it again," Sage begged him.

Beck heard the door to the powder room open and he made a slashing motion across his face to silently order his family to change the subject. As he watched Cady walk back toward him, he thought it ironic that his family was so damned worried about her.

Not one of them thought of the emotional danger he was in. None of them considered that his heart was on the line, as well. Was he that removed, that blasé, that they thought he couldn't be hurt?

They really didn't know him at all. And whose fault was that? His. They'd tried; he hadn't. He was the only person to blame.

Right, that had to be changed.

Waking up in Beck's bed the morning after the dinner with his family, which she'd enjoyed more than she should have, Cady heard the shower going in the en suite bathroom. Scooting up, she leaned her back against his leather headboard and pushed her tangled hair off her face. They'd made love last night and she'd fallen into a deep, dreamless sleep, wrapped in Beck's arms. She loved spending time with him and, because her place was the size of a shoe box and Beck was a big man, they tended to gravitate to his place. As a result, Cady was starting to feel far too at home in his loft and his life.

She just had to get through the cocktail party and exhibition of the Ballantyne jewelry collection and then her contract would be over. She had some money in the bank and better yet, a contract to do PR for a minor-league baseball team and another for a celebrity chef who was launching his own line of cookware. Between Julia's recommendations and the fact that the Ballantyne International campaign was a huge success, she now had clients knocking on her door. With the money she earned from Ballantyne's and these new contracts, she could re-hire some of her staff and run a functioning office again.

She was back in business.

The Ballantyne contract would end next week and neither she, nor Beck, had broached the subject of whether they would continue to see each other after that. It was better if they didn't, Cady admitted.

She could no longer pretend that she wasn't pregnant. Her stomach and breasts were rapidly expanding, and it was time for her to walk away from Beck before she started to show. Her being pregnant would raise a lot of interest in the press and she'd have to admit that the baby wasn't Beck's, which would make her look flaky at best, or, at worst, like someone who bed-hopped from one boss's bed to another.

An even better reason to walk away from Beck was because she wanted this; she wanted him. Oh, not the luxurious loft or the designer furniture but what it represented. Security, companionship, acceptance…

Love.

She wanted him to love her. She'd thought she wanted him at nineteen but it didn't come close to the depth of what she now felt. Back then she'd a vague idea of life with Beck but that was a life on the road, slightly unreal. Life with Beck, grown-up life, meant early-morning coffee after he came in from the gym, sex in the shower, arguing about politics—she was a little conservative, he a tad too liberal—sharing meals, time, memories and their bodies.

With Beck she felt alive, like the real, genuine Cady she'd always wanted to be.

But she was pregnant, he was her boss and he didn't want her the way she wanted him. One of these days, when the bloom left the rose, he'd realize that he was in too deep and he'd back off, all the way off. And he'd let her go. Could she live her life wondering whether this was the day, the hour, the minute he'd decide that it wasn't working, that it was time for her to go?

If he left, she couldn't crawl up into a ball and sob. She had a business to run, a child to raise.

This time her heart wouldn't break, it would shatter. And she'd have no hope of patching it together again.

It would be better if she gently, quietly, put some distance between them. She'd spend less time with him and in a month or two, they could issue a quiet press statement saying that they'd parted amicably and were still good friends.

Cady's head snapped up as the bathroom door opened and Beck stepped out, a towel wrapped around his waist and droplets of water still on his chest and arms. His eyes widened in what she thought might be pleasure at seeing her still in his bed. "Hi. You're awake. Sleep well?"

Cady nodded. She watched as he dried his hair with a small towel and slung it around his neck.

He walked to his closet and within seconds he was back, with a hanger holding a complete outfit. Tawny-colored pants, a white shirt and a dark gray jacket. He tossed the outfit on the bed and she saw a tag showing a complete list of every item, including shoes. She recognized the logo on the card as that of one of the city's best and most discreet men's stylists.

Cady grinned. Beck did not have fabulous taste as she first suspected; he just had a great stylist. Thinking that she could mess with him, she tipped her head to the side.

"I think a navy jacket would look better than the gray."

Beck looked at the outfit, looked at her and back at the outfit. Panic crossed his face. "Uh... I don't think so."

"The gray is a bit dull. I think it needs some punch, a red pullover, maybe orange?" She couldn't help her grin and Beck caught it.

He grabbed the wet towel from his neck and threw it with deadly accuracy right at her face. "Brat."

Cady pulled the towel off her face, laughing as she threw it back at him. "You are so spoiled! I thought you had great taste in clothes but it's Stefan's."

"It is my taste, sort of." Beck flicked the towel at her leg. "Initially, for every ten outfits Stefan chose, I'd only wear one, the most conservative one. He now knows what I will and will not wear."

"Why don't you just choose your own clothes?" Cady demanded.

"Shopping?" Beck shuddered. "Shoot me. Besides, I really do have crap taste. I'd go to work in faded jeans and flannel shirts if I had the choice."

He sat down on the edge of the bed, his butt next to her thigh, and placed his hands on either side of her body, caging her in. He looked serious, his jaw tense. "We need to talk."

Cady nodded. Maybe this was it; maybe he was about to tell her that it was time they walked away. He'd be gentle with her; he wouldn't be as abrupt as last time. He'd explain why he thought it better that they part and she'd agree and she wouldn't cry.

She wouldn't. Okay, she'd try not to.

"We've avoided the subject of your pregnancy, mostly because you've ducked the subject every time I've raised it."

Pregnancy? He wanted to talk about that? Cady pulled her head back to look at him, utterly confounded. "You want to talk about my baby?" she clarified.

"Yeah. And you're not going anywhere until you answer my questions."

Oh, God, he wasn't breaking it off! Her relief made her feel light-headed and she grabbed Beck's thigh to ground herself.

"How far along are you, Cady?"

Flustered, Cady had to think hard to answer that question. "Twelve, thirteen weeks?"

"Have you seen a doctor?" Beck asked.

Cady shook her head. "I've been meaning to but I've been quite busy, you know, trying to run a successful campaign."

Beck didn't react to her peevish tone. "And the father? Will you tell me who he is?"

"Does it matter?"

Cady saw impatience in Beck's eyes at her evasive response and she sighed, lifting her hand from his thigh. "He's not interested in me or the baby."

"Is he going to pay any of your medical expenses, support the kid when it comes along?"

"No." Cady snapped the word out.

"Cady, I'm not the enemy and I don't want to pull this out of you. Talk to me."

She lifted her arms and cradled her head. "It doesn't matter, Beck," she cried. "I'm doing this solo."

"It does matter. Talk."

Cady dropped her arms and stared past Beck's shoulder. She'd talk, but she'd keep it short. "He's married. I didn't realize until I told him I was pregnant. He lied to me, told me he was divorced. He wanted me to have an abortion. He's not prepared to pay child support."

"Douche."

Cady's eyes flew to his face and she saw his anger, not at but for her. Underneath the anger, she saw support and empathy and understanding. If she was going to tell him everything, now was the time. "It gets worse."

Beck lifted an eyebrow and waited for her to continue.

"He was a client and he fired me and my company when I told him about the baby."

A muscle jumped in Beck's jaw and his lips thinned. "Double douche."

"I promise you that sleeping with my clients is not what I do. He was the first guy since you and then there was you and I slept with you both. I've worked for you both!" She covered her face with her hands. "God, it's just so not me! I'm not the girl who does this!"

Beck pulled her hands from her face and rested his forehead on hers. "Did you know he was married? Did you sleep with him to get the contract?"

Cady slapped his shoulder. "No!"

"Then you didn't do anything wrong, Cades. With him or with me. So just let it go." Beck gripped the back of her neck and used his thumb to push her chin up. "You need to see a doctor and make sure everything is okay with the baby."

Cady grabbed the sheet and twisted it in her hand. "I'm scared, Beck. My mother miscarried a few times between Will and me, and Will was autistic. I'm scared they're going to find something wrong with the baby and—"

She hadn't really realized that was the way she felt until the words flew out of her mouth. She was scared and so very tired of being alone.

"I'll go with you, Cades."

"You don't have to," she said, not realizing that she'd wanted him with her. But now that he'd offered, she was desperately hoping that he would.

"I'll get Amy to find a decent OB-GYN and she'll make an appointment for you."

"Not this week. I'm crazy busy trying to finish the arrangements for the cocktail party and the exhibition and I have an industry awards dinner on Friday night. I don't suppose you'd—" No, of course he wouldn't be interested in accompanying her to one of the most boring functions on Planet Earth.

Beck smiled. "Are you asking me to come with you? As your date?"

"Yeah, sort of."

Beck kissed her once, his smile against her mouth. "Then I accept. And if we can get you a doctor's appointment, you're taking it, busy or not. But right now I want you naked and begging."

"You'll be late for your breakfast meeting," Cady breathlessly said, her hands skimming across his shoulders, down his hard pecs.

"They can wait."

Beck stared into her eyes, his mouth a breath away from hers, and he saw it on her face—desire—right before he kissed her.

At the first touch of his lips, she opened up and let him

in. She ran her splayed hands against him, trying to make as much contact as possible with his hot, masculine skin.

His mouth snacked on hers, suckled and teased and she followed his lead, thinking that there was redemption and forgiveness in his kiss. His mouth on hers assured her that she was okay, that she was redeemable, that she was allowed to be imperfect and make mistakes.

Beck's hands moved under her T-shirt and pulled it up and over her head, dropping it to the floor. Then they slid up her sides, his thumbs brushing the undersides of her breasts. Cady murmured insensible words of encouragement, silently demanding him to touch her. His thumbs finally brushed her nipples as he dropped hot, openmouthed kisses along her jaw.

"More, more, more," Cady chanted.

"Not yet," Beck growled. "I want to see you, every beautiful inch of you."

He stood up, yanked away the covers and, with little ceremony, grabbed her ankles and pulled her so that she lay flat on her back, her legs slightly spread. She felt shy and exposed and her hand came up to shield her groin. Beck picked up her hand and lifted her knuckles to his lips. "Don't be shy, Cades. Not with me."

"I'm not nineteen, Beck. I'm pregnant, and my boobs are bigger."

His smile touched her fingers. "Bigger boobs are never a problem."

Cady jerked her fingers away. "Beckett! I'm being serious here."

"So am I." His hot, dark glance moved down her body, lingered on her breasts and then her crotch, and heated the skin on her tummy and thighs before returning to her face. "You're exquisite and I can't wait to touch you, taste you. Every inch of you."

Cady knew that he was struggling to keep himself from reaching for her, flabbergasted by the heat and passion in his deep, dark eyes. Under his hot gaze her inhibitions disappeared and she lifted her hand to touch her nipple, sliding her fingers down her abdomen to flirt with the small strip of hair at her thighs. "I'd much rather have you touch me and me touch you," she murmured.

"Oh, we'll get to that," Beck assured her.

Yet he still looked at her, seemingly content to enjoy the view. Frustrated with his lack of action, Cady kneeled on the bed, dug her fingers between the towel and his six-pack and tugged his towel away. His erection jutted out from his groin, fantastically hard. Cady ran the tip of her index finger up his length and smiled when his erection jumped and his eyes closed. "I think you're beautiful, too, Beckett," she murmured.

She needed to taste him, to take him into her mouth, but she only managed a quick taste before Beck's strong arm banded around her stomach and he pulled her up his body. Her legs circled his hips and her ankles crossed just above his hard butt.

His penis probed her opening, hot and insistent, and Cady pushed down, feeling him slide inside her.

Cady smiled. He felt so amazing. "Love me, Beck." She pushed down, taking him inch by inch, and she groaned as he pushed his way into her, filling her.

Nothing felt as good as Beck loving her. Wanting more, wanting *everything*, she placed her mouth on his and lost herself in his kiss. It was kissing with no start or end point. Sure, sexy strokes of his tongue that echoed the action below.

Cady felt herself climbing, losing track of the here and now and what was real and not. Beck took her into another dimension where only they existed, two bodies intent to give pleasure. It was a battle of the best kind, both determined to give not receive, knowing that their lack of selfishness would result in their pleasure being redoubled.

Beck used his height, power and muscles to pick her up and he walked her to the wall next to his bed. Cady felt the cool wall on her naked back, a perfect contrast to the hot man pressed to her front. Anchored to the wall, he allowed his hands to roam free and his hand trailed lightning down her back, over her hip, across her stomach. His hand moved up to cover her breast and he rubbed the center of his palm across her nipple then pulled it into a harder peak before dropping his head and laving it with his tongue.

He wanted all of her, she realized. He wanted her mindless with passion, feeling him on every inch of her skin. She did and Cady let out a deep, demanding moan, grinding down on him to take him farther into her, if that was at all possible. She wrenched her mouth off his. "Now! Dammit, Beck, now!"

Beck responded by slamming into her, pinning her to the wall, and when his hand pushed between their bodies to find her, she screamed and splintered into a million shards of pure orgasmic pleasure.

His entire body stilled and she clenched her inner muscles once, then twice, and her big man, so in control, lost it and followed her into oblivion.

Perfection, Cady thought, her forehead on his shoulder.

He was her first and, she thought, her last. He was the place she always, and only, wanted to be.

Feeling like this terrified her, the thought of walking away lifted the hair on her neck and arms.

Staying with him petrified her the most.

Ten

Feeling like he was about to jump out of his skin, Beck paced the small waiting room outside the technician's office and pushed his sleeve back to look at his watch. Dr. Bent was an OB-GYN and a friend of Amy and Julia's. She'd agreed to see Cady after her last patient of the day. Beck appreciated it but wished she'd hurry up. He wanted to get out of here, and fast.

Beck glanced at Cady, paging through a magazine on her lap. He'd left work to accompany her to this appointment, mostly because she might, accidentally-on-purpose forget the appointment. Her fears that there could be something wrong with this child weren't unfounded but being an ostrich wouldn't help her or the baby.

It was better, Beck thought, to face life head-on and deal with whatever problems arose. Yeah, maybe he had bullied Cady into seeing Dr. Bent but he needed to know that she was okay, that everything was as it should be.

He had a million things to do and a thousand fires to extinguish but Beck was rapidly coming to the conclusion that he'd do anything and be anywhere for Cady. What he felt for her ten years ago was not a fluke. She was just the adult version of the girl he'd loved so long ago.

Taking care of Cady was just something he did, something that was. Like the air he breathed, it was just there.

That didn't necessarily translate into living happily-ever-after. Like their vacation a decade ago, living and sleeping together was something that wouldn't last. She was gun-shy, and a permanent arrangement wasn't part of his master plan.

Neither was standing in a waiting room with a pregnant woman!

"Will you please go back to the office, Beckett?" Cady demanded. "You're making me nervous."

"No, if I do that you might leave without seeing the doctor."

Cady lifted her chin. "That would be rude after all the effort Amy and Julia went to to get this appointment."

Beck narrowed his eyes at her. "But you'd do it if you thought you could get away with it."

Cady slapped her magazine shut and threw it onto the table next to her. "This just makes it all very real."

"I thought you puking was pretty real. And not being able to button your pants this morning makes it pretty real," Beck said, sitting down next to her and covering her hand with his. "I'm sure everything will be fine, Cades."

"Autism can be hereditary, Beck."

Beck pushed the palm of his hand under hers to link their fingers. "But it's not something that you diagnose early, so why avoid a doctor's appointment?"

"How do you know that?" Cady demanded, pulling back to look at him.

"I did some reading." Beck didn't bother telling her that when she moved in, he realized that what he knew about pregnancy could fit on a pinhead. He didn't like feeling ignorant so he ordered some books.

Okay, he ordered a lot of books and read most of them. He was now convinced that having babies was not for the faint of heart.

A tiny Asian woman appeared in the doorway and sent them a bright smile. "Cady Collins? I'm Dr. Giselle Bent. Come on through. Let's see what's what."

Cady stood up and Beck noticed the tremors in her fingers, her suddenly white face. Dr. Bent turned her megawatt smile on him. "Beck Ballantyne, I've heard a lot about you."

Beck shook her hand and sent her a wry grin. "Do not believe anything Amy and Julia have said about me."

The doctor laughed and motioned them down the hall.

Cady stood up, wincing as she did so. "Are you okay? What's the matter?" he demanded, walking over to her and placing his hand on her back.

"She has a very full bladder," Dr. Bent casually said.

Beck frowned. "I hate to state the obvious but—"

"We see the baby better with a full bladder," Dr. Bent said, opening the door to a small dark room containing a bed and, what Beck presumed, was the ultrasound machine.

Dammit, he'd forgotten about the full bladder thing. Typical Cady, she fried his brains.

Beck hovered in the doorway but the doctor motioned him into the room and told him to stand on the other side of Cady. "I'm going to do a quick ultrasound, then we'll head back for an exam and some blood tests. Lie down, open your pants and pull your top up."

Beck kept his eyes on Cady as she lay on her back,

her eyes wide in her face. She quickly readied herself, rolling up her top under her breasts so that her belly was exposed. He'd kissed that skin last night, swirled his tongue around her belly button, traced a path down to between her legs.

He'd made her scream and cry and beg him for more.

Cady met his eyes and she raised an eyebrow. When he returned her stare with a bold look, she blushed and looked away. He knew that she'd flashed back to his bedroom and the explosive sex they'd shared.

He wanted more of that, wanted more of her. But he was balancing on a precarious pile of rocks and they were going to skitter out from under him at any minute. He had to take control of this situation. If he could corral his emotions, stop these flights of fancy, that would be a very good start.

Dr. Bent squirted gel on Cady's stomach and Cady cried, "That's cold!"

"Sorry." Dr. Bent pressed a wand on her stomach, and a picture flashed up on the monitor.

"Here we go," Dr. Bent said. Using her free hand, she pointed to the kidney-bean shape on the screen and flashed Cady a grin. "There's your baby. See that constant flash? That's the baby's heartbeat. We like to see that."

Neither Beck nor Cady reacted to her joke; they were both staring hard at the screen. Beck flicked Cady a look and saw tears in her eyes. He felt a lump form in his throat and when Cady held out her hand for his, the lump hardened.

As Dr. Bent turned up the volume on the ultrasound machine, he heard the *boom, boom, gurgle, boom* of the baby's heartbeat and wondered how he could describe something so elemental, so incredible. He felt both humble and blown away, in awe and ridiculously overexcited. The baby's heartbeat told him that he was utterly real, growing and on his way.

In a perfect world, that little blob should be his baby. Cady would be permanently his, rather than a temporary fling, the fiancée the world thought she might be. In a perfect world his parents wouldn't be dead, and he'd have another sibling. His parents would be playing with and spoiling their grandchildren.

Feeling this connected, this overwhelmed, this emotional, caused his throat to tighten and his heart to bang against his chest. Sweat pooled at the base of his spine and he felt disconnected from his body, like some unknown entity had its hands around his throat and he was battling to breathe. Panic attack, he realized.

He hadn't had one since standing in that crowded airport in Bangkok, watching Cady walk out of his life. Before that, he'd had a couple and usually handled them by diving into his training or into his books. Anything that was a distraction. As he grew up, they disappeared entirely.

It didn't escape his attention that Cady seemed to trigger these attacks, that she overwhelmed him, made him feel out of control. He swallowed, fighting his tight throat. He couldn't do that, couldn't go back to feeling so off balance. Being in control comforted him, made him feel like he could cope with the world and the demands it made on him. If he kept his life tightly controlled then he'd never feel like he was spinning off into an unknown and terrifying place.

He couldn't do this... He'd worked too damn hard to find this place where he didn't feel like fear was constantly nipping at his heels.

Cady terrified him. The attachment he felt to her, and

to that half-formed blob on the screen, scared the crap out of him. He was fit, wealthy and successful but this woman had the ability, with one look, word or touch, to cut him off at the knees.

Beck held up his hand, stepped back from the bed and shook his head. He had to get out of here...

Now.

There had only been one woman for him and she was it. But, like ten years ago, he couldn't take a chance on her, couldn't allow himself to be happy.

Cady looked from the screen to him and raised her eyebrows. "You're looking a bit pale. Are you okay?"

"Fine." Beck pushed the word out through gritted teeth. It was the biggest lie he'd ever uttered. "I just need some air."

Cady nodded and he saw her face tighten, her eyes dull. "I'm going to be a while, so why don't you head back to work. I'll see you back at your apartment."

Beck started to walk toward the door but then he stopped and looked back at the screen. He couldn't do it. Beck just stared at his lover, her eyes on the monitor, his mouth half open. Yes, he was scared and yes, he wanted to run, but if he quit this, if he quit them, he'd regret it for the rest of his life. He was terrified, and he felt like his heart was on a rope swing in his chest, but if he walked away from Cady for the second time, he wouldn't get another chance. Life only handed you a certain amount of opportunities to walk through the door. If you didn't, the door would eventually be permanently sealed.

Beck was self-aware enough to know what he was doing: he was scared spitless and he was pushing her away. His first instinct when someone got close to him was to run them off but he'd wanted Cady enough that he'd allowed her to come closer than most. She'd sliced right through his emotional armor, and his internal alarm bells were ringing loudly. Habit screamed that he should retreat, that he should return to that place of safety where he needed no one and cared little for much beyond work and the occasional date.

He wasn't going to do it. He couldn't do it.

Beck walked back and placed his palms on the bed, staring hard at the screen. He wanted that baby to be his—oh, it was an irritation that the genes it carried weren't his but he believed in nurture versus nature. A passing on of DNA made a man a father, but time and effort made him a dad. He wanted to be there for Cady, be there for her child who would become his. He'd be there for his family, every step of the way.

He loved the baby's mother to distraction and he'd love her child as if it were his own. He wanted to take on the responsibility, and joy, of loving her and her child, and he wanted to be loved in return.

Maybe he didn't deserve love and a family. Maybe it was wrong for him to be happy. But he wasn't going to let those thoughts stop him from grabbing this chance to be with Cady. He wasn't going to miss out on another chance to have a family with her. Because they were meant to be together.

Whether he deserved it or not.

"Beck."

He jerked his head up and looked at Cady. Her face held no expression and he could see that she was biting the inside of her lip, a sure sign that she was nervous or worried. He reached out for her hand and when she jerked it away to avoid the contact, he frowned. What was that about?

"Go now, Beck," Cady said. Her voice was low but he heard the plea.

"Why?"

Her chest rose and fell and she looked to the monitor, her attention captured by the images there.

"I just need to be alone. Just me and my baby."

Now she wanted to be alone? What was that about? Beck, feeling hurt, looked at the doctor, who was pretending not to listen to their conversation. "But…"

"Beck, please. Just go."

Okay, he didn't understand but he wasn't about to have a fight and cause a scene. Cady was emotional and stressed and he'd just reached a life-changing decision. Maybe a little time apart would be a good idea. He could get his bouncing heart and careening emotions under control. Later he would tell her how he felt and they could discuss where to go and how to get there. All he was sure of was that if he walked away he'd be leaving everything that made his life joyful behind.

Not happening. Not again.

"We'll talk later," Cady told him, her tone resolute.

Beck quietly closed the door behind him. Yeah, they'd talk. But he wouldn't walk.

Cady stood in front of the door to Beck's apartment and waved her hands in front of her face to dry her tears. She blinked rapidly and pressed her fist to her sternum, trying to ease the burn.

Find your courage and open that damn door, Collins!

She knew this day was coming and she'd tried to prepare for it. She'd told herself over and over that she was living a fairy tale, that this was not reality, that she and Beck would end.

But she didn't expect it to happen in front of her eyes in a small dark room five minutes after looking at the blurry images of her baby.

She'd seen his retreat in his eyes, had read his thoughts as clearly as if he'd spoken his goodbyes. He couldn't cope with the emotion that was bubbling between them, their fierce attraction. With a baby on the way, she was just too much to cope with. Beck was overwhelmed and he was doing what he did best: distancing himself. She knew what would happen when she walked through this door. He would push her away.

The best predictor of future behavior is past behavior, Cady reminded herself. She wasn't going to let the past happen to her again. She'd walk away before he could toss her away again.

Still, the little girl inside her, the one so desperate to be loved, wanted him to make the grand gesture, to verbalize the words she most needed to hear.

I love you.

I will always love you.

I will always be at your side.

But Beck valued his freedom and his lone-wolf status more than he valued her, and she couldn't change that. Neither could she alter the fact that the people she most needed love and support from were the ones who were destined to disappoint her. It was better, easier and safer to walk this road by herself. She had her business and she had her baby. It would be enough. It had to be enough.

Cady felt a touch on her shoulder and then Beck was standing next to her, in front of the door. She'd been so lost in thought she hadn't heard him walk up to her. Cady straightened as he unlocked the door.

"Let's go inside," he said.

Cady walked into his apartment and headed straight for the stairs. Words, at this point, were superfluous so she headed for the master bedroom focused on what she needed to do next—pack her clothes that had accumulated over the past week. She remembered a suitcase in Beck's closet, tucked behind his shoes. She hauled it out and swung it onto the huge bed, where they'd loved and laughed, held each other through the night.

Beck appeared in the doorway to the room, his arms folded across his chest. "What are you doing?" he demanded.

"Packing."

Cady walked to the closet and grabbed the clothes he'd handed over to his cleaning service to take care of. She tossed them into the suitcase.

"Why?"

"Because this isn't working. You know it and I know it," Cady retorted.

"I thought it was," Beck replied, his words slow.

"Oh, come on, Beck. I know you have doubts about us. You always have! And we agreed that this was temporary."

Beck pushed an agitated hand through his hair. "It's natural to have doubts, Cady. It's a part of being in a relationship."

"We're not in a relationship! We're having a fling and I'm pregnant with another man's child."

His jaw tensed. "I consider that baby yours, not his. And, as I've said before, I don't have a problem with you being pregnant."

Cady snorted her disbelief. "That's just because you're getting fabulous sex."

Cady winced as hurt flashed across Beck's face. "That's not fair."

God, he sounded so calm. How could he stay so calm?

Cady returned to the closet and, fighting tears, picked up another pile of clothing. She threw it into the suitcase and stared down at the jumbled mess. "Please don't do this, Beck. Please don't give me hope that this can go anywhere."

"Maybe it can."

Cady shook her head. "I saw the doubts on your face before. You were this close." She held her thumb and forefinger slightly apart. "You were this close to bailing on me. You fought it this time, possibly because we're still really enjoying each other. But what happens when I'm fat and miserable and you decide that it's time to run? Will you stay or will you go? What happens when the urge to run becomes stronger than the urge to stay? I can't do that! I can't live like that. I can't—I won't—be tossed away again."

Beck walked over and held out his hand to her. Cady looked at it, fought the urge to jump into his arms and backed away. "I loved you once, Beck, with everything I had and you threw me away. It's not only me now. I have a child on the way. I can't risk you doing that to him."

"What can I say or do to get you to stay?"

"Nothing." She wiped away her tears. "Beck, what you can't handle, you walk away from."

"I'm standing here, trying not to!" Beck shouted. "I'm *trying*, Cady."

"Until the next time when you can't. You're a lone wolf, Beck. You're comfortable in that space. You've been that way since you were a child and that's your default mode of operation. When we hit a tight spot, you back away. That's what you did today."

"Yet I am still here, asking you to stay."

"Today was supposed to be a happy day, Beck. We saw a new life, it was fantastic and you got scared. What happens when something else rocks us? How will you react then? Can I rely on you to be there? Would we stand together and deal with it or would you go off on your own?"

"We'd stand together." He said the right words but she couldn't believe him. If she believed him and she was wrong, she'd pay too big a price.

"You say that but that's not what you do. You dealt with your parents' deaths on your own and you kept the secret of your mom being pregnant from your siblings. That's you staying in your space, dealing with crap on your own."

Beck blanched and Cady fought the urge to touch him, to say to hell with it and take the chance. But it wasn't wise and it damn well wasn't smart. "Somebody very wise once said, 'There's nothing worse than being lonely with the person you love.' I'd rather be lonely on my own, Beck."

Cady zipped her suitcase, not sure if she had everything but knowing that she needed to leave while she still could. Before Beck talked her into staying.

She lifted the suitcase off the bed and placed it on its wheels.

"What about the campaign, your contract?" Beck asked, his voice and face tight.

"We're professionals, remember? We can communicate via email." Cady sighed and rubbed her forehead with her hand. "From a business point of view, we're in a good place. We never admitted to being engaged, so if we stop seeing each other, the attention will fade without any major repercussions. Sage's new line is a massive success and the ads are making an impact. After the exhibition and cocktail party, where Sage will reveal even more new designs, I have no doubt you'll capture that new, young, rich market you're after. It's all good, Beck."

"But you're still walking."

"I'm still walking."

"Don't go, Cady."

She looked at him. God, she was going to miss him. "I have to. We have the ability to rip each other apart. I survived that once. I won't again. The stakes are too high, Beck."

"If we close this door, it stays closed, Cady."

Cady forced her feet to walk over to him. She stood on her toes to drop a kiss on his cheek. "I love you, Beck, but my love isn't enough. I need to know that you'll stick. But sticking isn't what you do."

Eleven

Cady rested her hand on her abdomen as she heard the click of her mother's low heels on the wooden floor on the other side of her door. This wasn't going to be a pleasant conversation but she was tired of lying—to herself and to her parents. Last night, with Beck, was the first time in years that she'd been completely authentic with the people she loved.

He'd just stared at her, shocked, and let her leave. Underneath all the sadness, in the odd spaces that weren't totally devastated, she felt…cleaner. There was a freedom in truth, in being honest, in dealing with what was, not what you wanted it to be.

The front door opened and Cady caught her mother's surprise before her how-nice-to-see-you expression crossed her face. Edna leaned forward so that Cady could drop the briefest kiss on her cheek and stepped back into the house. "I wasn't expecting you."

Cady heard the undertone of "how rude of you not to call" and stepped into her childhood home. She shouldn't need to call, shouldn't have to give her parents advance warning of her visit. Her child would be raised knowing that there was a key to their house under the mat, that there was food in the fridge, a warm bed in the spare room. Her home would always be her child's home, his refuge, his soft place to fall.

"Your father is in his study. Let me call him," Edna said, her fingers playing with her fake-pearl necklace. It was late afternoon but her mom's makeup was perfect, her white blouse spotless.

She was so concerned with looking the part, she never lived.

"Why don't we take this chat to Dad's study, Mom?" Cady suggested, dropping her leather bag on the hall table. She smiled when her mom picked her bag up and hung it over a hook behind the door.

Edna waved at the formal room just off the hallway. "But we always meet our guests here."

"But I'm not a guest, Mom, I'm your daughter," Cady stated as she walked down the hall toward her father's study. At the door, she hesitated, thinking that she could count the times on one hand that she'd entered this hallowed sanctum. There was no way that her father and mother had made love on his desk the way she and Beck had in his office the other night. It had been fun and hot and raunchy and exciting...

Beck. Dammit. Tears welled and her stomach knotted and she wanted to sink to the floor. Instead, she hauled in a breath and ordered herself not to think about him. She'd cry later, when she was alone.

She knocked once and turned the handle on the door. "Hey, Dad, I'm invading your man cave!"

Bill Collins looked up at her over the tops of his glasses. He sent Edna a quick look and raised his eyebrows. "Were we expecting you, Cady?" he asked in his formal voice.

Cady walked over to the corner of his desk, moved a couple of books and hopped up onto the desk, her feet dangling. "You see, Dad, that's part of what I wanted to talk to you about. Why do you need advanced warning? Shouldn't you be happy to see me?"

Edna exchanged a long look with her husband before walking up to Cady and lightly resting her fingers on Cady's shoulder. "What's this about, Cady Rebecca?"

"It's about your expectations of me." Cady jumped down from the desk and walked to the bay window, pulling the drape aside to look at her mom's now barren garden. A light dusting of snow covered the paving stones and the angel statues and the roof of the birdhouse.

"Beck and I broke up," Cady said, stating the fact without emotion and waited for them to detonate. When her statement was met with silence, she turned around and threw up her hands. "Oh, right, you didn't know that Beck and I have been seeing each other again."

"Why didn't you tell us?" Bill asked.

"I thought you'd freak," Cady admitted.

"I'm sorry that it's over and I'm sorry you didn't tell us," Bill said, placing his elbows on his desk, his eyes steady on her face. "I know that you love him very much and that it must hurt."

"It does." Cady frowned. "Why do you think I love him?"

"Cady, you always have." Edna perched on one of the leather chairs and linked her hands. "From the first moment you saw him, I knew he was going to break your heart."

Cady shrugged. "It wasn't for the first time."

Edna nodded. "We suspected that's what happened after you returned from Thailand."

Cady pushed her hands into the kangaroo pockets of her sweatshirt. "That wasn't the first time my heart broke, Mom. It broke the day you sent Will away, and it broke again when he died. It broke a little every time you told me I couldn't play with a Barbie doll or look at a fashion magazine or watch a program on TV."

Cady heard her parents' swift intake of breath but trying to hold back her words was like trying to use a cork to hold back a flood. "When you try to fix something that's not broken, you end up breaking it. In your quest for a perfect child, by sending a perfect child away from his home, without explaining why, you broke...me."

"Jesus God."

It wasn't a blasphemy, more like a desperate plea from her father's mouth to God. Cady saw the horror on their faces and she felt a quick spurt of sympathy. They were like two balloons, full of hot air, and she'd just jammed a red-hot poker into them. She didn't want to hurt them but she also realized that, until she stood up for herself, she couldn't stand up for the child growing inside her, the child she would be raising alone.

"I didn't come here to criticize you but to explain a few things." She looked at her dad. "Congratulations on the promotion to the big church, Dad, but maybe you should tell them that your daughter is going to be a single mom raising a married man's child."

"Beck is married?" Bill shouted.

"No, of course not. Beck isn't the father. I was in a relationship with a guy who I thought was divorced but he wasn't."

"Cady!"

Cady whipped around and met her mother's shocked eyes. "Yeah, Mom, I know, I messed up. But you know what? Real people mess up! They wear jeans and get bad marks at school and run away with their boyfriends to Thailand! They get pregnant and they fall in love and get their hearts broken." Cady felt the hot slide of tears down her face. "I just wanted to tell you the truth. I'm tired of lying and I am so tired of trying to be the pastor's perfect kid. I'm not a kid anymore and I'm not perfect. I'm just human."

Cady wiped the tears off her cheeks. Her parents looked shell-shocked and her mother was doing a fantastic impersonation of a goldfish. Her dad removed his glasses and tapped them against the desk.

"So, I'll go now. Next time I'll call." Cady pushed her hair back from her forehead as she walked to the open study door, the space behind her heavy and loaded with tension.

"We sent Will away because we thought he could hurt you."

Her father's words stopped her in her tracks. Not sure if she'd heard him correctly, she slowly turned. "What did you say?"

Bill stood up and folded his thin arms across his narrow chest. "His behavior took a turn for the worse when he hit puberty. For some reason he never acted up around you but when you were at school, he became impossible."

Cady felt anger bubble in her chest. "I don't believe you."

"Do you remember that day you came home from school and the fire department was here?" her mom asked.

"Yeah. You told me that you were ironing in Will's room and you left the iron on and somehow the room caught fire."

"Will found a lighter and set fire to the curtains. He also started punching me. The last straw was when he tried to stab me with a potato peeler," Edna said, her voice coated with pain. "You never saw it but he was starting to hurt you, too."

"He was not!" Cady protested, not quite able to believe what she was hearing.

"The hair-pulling, the playful pinches that made you cry?" her mom shot back. "He was getting so much bigger, stronger. I couldn't control him or his rages. Dammit, why do you insist on seeing me as the bad guy, Cady?"

"He was uncontrollable, Cady," her father said, "and we thought a residential home was best for him. And you." He looked at her and she saw the truth in his eyes.

Oh, God. Her parents were right. If she pulled the rose-colored glasses off and looked at the past clearly, she could see how her brother had changed, had become meaner and bigger.

"You were trying to protect me?"

Bill nodded and Cady pushed her hair back from her face in sheer frustration. "Why the hell didn't you talk to me? I thought that if I colored outside of the lines I'd be sent away, too."

"Oh, God," Bill muttered.

"Seriously, for a pastor and a pastor's wife, you both suck at communication!" Cady cried.

Bill walked over to her and gently, hesitantly wrapped his arms around her. It was the first hug she'd had from her father in too many years to count. "I'm so sorry."

"Me, too." Cady laid her head on his chest. "I'm sorry if my being single and pregnant causes you trouble in your new job."

"Screw them."

Cady let out a strangled laugh and tightened her arms

around her father. He gave her an awkward pat on her back and led her out the door. "Now, my girl, you and your mom and I are going to have a chat. A real, no-holds-barred, soul-deep conversation."

"I don't need a preacher, Dad, and I don't need counseling."

"Maybe you don't," her father agreed. "Maybe you just need to talk to your mom and dad."

Sitting on the edge of his sofa, Beck watched as his siblings walked across the laminate floor toward him, their faces somber. Sage sat down beside him and wrapped her arm around his bicep, her head on his shoulder. Linc headed to the kitchen, grabbed a bottle of wine from his enormous wine rack and handed it to Jaeger to open. He pulled four wineglasses down from the cupboard and returned to the living area.

His brothers sat, wine was poured and sipped, and no one spoke.

They were all waiting for him to start. After all, he'd summoned them here.

Beck loosened the tie strangling him and encountered his burning skin beneath his open collar. Still no air. So he couldn't blame the tie for his constricted throat.

God, how was he going to do this? He had to, he knew that, but how? He wished Cady was here, sitting next to him, his hand on her thigh, encouragement in her eyes. Beck ran his hand over his face, trying to push away the image of her stricken expression, her eyes reflecting her soul-deep pain.

She'd walked away and he now knew how it felt. But it was the right thing to do, Beck assured himself. Because he knew it couldn't last; nothing that wonderful did. The connection they shared was magic, a mirage, an illusion. It wasn't real.

It couldn't be. And, because he'd started to believe in those concepts, to fall in love with being in love, with the normality of having a partner and child on the way, they'd hurt each other. Again.

"You're starting to scare us, Beck," Jaeger said, his voice low but concerned.

Sage squeezed his arm. "Are you sick?" she demanded. "Whatever is wrong, we'll get you the best medical help, fly you wherever you need to go."

Beck briefly touched her knee. "I'm not sick, Sage. Not physically, anyway." Beck made himself look at Jaeger. "I'm sorry that I asked you to come alone, to leave Piper at home, but I just wanted the four of us here. The siblings."

Jaeger nodded his understanding.

Beck hauled in a sharp breath and looked at Linc. "What I have to say was before your time but you're our brother, so here you are."

Linc mirrored Beck's body language and rested his forearms on his knees, holding his wineglass in a loose grip between them. "And you're our brother and whatever the hell this is about, we stand by you."

He'd see if that held true after he'd told them what he had to say. He knew he had to release the truth; he couldn't keep this secret anymore. It was too heavy to carry anymore. Cady was right about that.

Beck sat up straight and looked at each of his siblings. "Our parents were killed in that plane crash because I asked them to come home to be with me because I was having that operation to put a pin in my wrist."

Their expressions didn't change from wary expectation, so Beck plowed on. "What you don't know is that

Mom was four months pregnant when they died. She was expecting another child. We would've had another sibling."

Beck waited for the shocked surprise, the hot outrage. Linc looked sympathetic, Jaeger thoughtful, and Sage's eyes filled with tears.

"Oh, man, that's horrible," she said. "Poor Mom and Dad. Poor little baby."

Jaeger stared into his wineglass for a long time before lifting his head and pinning Beck to his seat with his penetrating eyes. "How do you know this, Beck?"

"After the funeral, I was hiding under a table in the living room. Do you remember Dr. Blaine?"

Jaeger frowned. "Vaguely."

"Maybe I knew him better because he treated me for my arm. He was also Mom's doctor and I heard him talking to his wife—his nurse—about Mom's pregnancy."

"God, Beck." Through his cotton shirt Beck felt Sage's lips touch his shoulder. "Why didn't you tell us?"

Beck shrugged. He stood up abruptly and walked over to the closest window, keeping his back to his siblings.

"Beck!" His name was like a bullet on Jaeger's lips. "Why didn't you tell us?"

He couldn't answer that, not without cutting his heart open and allowing all his fears and guilt to gush to the floor.

"Because he thought you'd blame him for that, too," Linc said in his calm, measured voice.

"What the hell do you mean by that?" Jaeger demanded. "We've never blamed him for anything!"

Beck turned slightly to look at Linc, his brother through choice and not blood, and tried to push the ball of emotion down his throat. Linc understood, he realized. He'd understood far more than Beck gave him credit for.

"Tell them, Beck," Linc said. "You need to."

Beck turned and pushed his hands into the pockets of his suit pants, rocking on his heels. *Now or never, Beck. Just spill it and get it done.*

"I've always felt guilty for our parents' deaths and I blamed myself. I've always thought that you might blame me, too, just a little bit."

"But why?" Sage cried. "Why would you think that?"

"Because I asked them to come home! I was the whiny, needy kid who needed his mommy to hold his hand when he went into the hospital. I was the reason their plane flew into a freakin' mountain, killing them and the baby!"

Silence, pure and saturated with emotion, filled the space between them.

"Are you friggin' nuts?" Jaeger finally roared as he jumped up and stormed over to him.

Beck braced for a punch but Jaeger just gripped his neck in his hand and pulled his head down so that their foreheads touched and their eyes were level.

"You did not do this," Jaeger stated. "This was not your fault."

"But—"

"Not your fault," Jaeger reiterated, his eyes boring into his. "Jesus, Beck! How could you think that I would blame you for that? You were a kid!"

"I never blamed you, either."

Beck pulled his head away from Jaeger to look at Sage, who was in Linc's arms, tears running down her face. "Really?"

"You lost them, too, Beck. We all did," Sage said, between sobs.

"But the baby—"

"It happened, bro." Jaeger dropped his hand and stepped back, his eyes suspiciously bright. "Yeah, it's sad and yeah, we've missed them, but why you would take this on yourself, I have no damn idea."

"Why don't we have some wine and talk about that?" Linc suggested. He sat down in the chair and Sage, like she'd done when she was little, sat on his lap, her arms looped around his neck. Beck felt the slap of a memory: Sage sitting in Linc's arms, him sitting at his feet, Jaeger standing behind them, a unit, a team. Them against the world.

He bit his lip, desperate to keep the tears from sliding down his face. He'd done them a disservice not talking to them about this, not talking to them about the wounds that hadn't really healed.

"I called them home. It was my fault they ran into bad weather," Beck said, picking up a glass of wine from the table and taking a fortifying breath.

Jaeger lifted his hand. "Stop! Dad was reckless. We know that. He took chances. He should not have flown if there was a chance of the weather turning."

Point taken, Beck thought, feeling the pressure start to ease off his chest.

"It was their job to be with you, Beck," Linc said. "It's what parents do. Your kid calls and no matter what you're doing, you run. I'd do that for Shaw. Jaeger and Piper would do that for Ty."

"Do you get that?" Jaeger demanded.

"It's starting to sink in," Beck admitted.

"Keep going, Beck. Get it all out," Linc ordered.

He didn't want to but he knew that this was an emotional abscess that needed to be lanced. And he was halfway there...

"Because I felt guilty, I thought I had to prove my worth to you, to this family. I had to show you I was worth loving." Beck felt like every word was being dragged up his throat.

"So that explains your constant studying, constant training. God, you were a pain in the ass," Jaeger commented, a hint of amusement on his face. He looked at Linc. "It was hell standing in the shadow of our younger brother."

"It really was. Then you grew taller and bigger and we really started to hate you," Linc agreed and Beck saw the mischief in his eyes.

Sage ignored their teasing and climbed off Linc's lap to walk to him. She took his hand. "Connor worried about you, more than he worried about the rest of us." She tossed a saucy look at her two older brothers before continuing. "Connor said that God would protect the stupid, so he didn't worry that much about Dumb and Dumber over there. But he worried about you. I think he knew that you blamed yourself."

Linc nodded. "He was always telling you to go easy, to not work so hard, give so much. That you were perfectly okay, being who you were."

"That's why he made you travel after college," Sage added. "Why he insisted you take a break every few months. It was his way of protecting you from burnout. You give too much of yourself to work, too little of yourself to life. And love."

Beck met Sage's vivid blue eyes and realized that she knew that he and Cady were over. He saw her frustration. "You shouldn't have pushed her away, Beck. She's the only one who's ever really got you."

"She left me this time," Beck replied.

"She left before she could be hurt again," Sage told him, her eyes worried. "She loves you, Beck. Anyone can see that."

"I don't—"

"I swear to God, if you say that you don't deserve her, I'll punch you!" Jaeger shouted. "You don't find love twice and push it away, you moron! You fight for it, you hold on to it, you do everything you can to keep it." Jaeger threw up his hands in disgust. "You're the smart one, so why am I spelling this out for you?"

Sage rolled her eyes at him and then Linc. "Was this the same brother who nearly lost his fiancée and son because he was being a moron? Or was that Jaeger's alter ego?"

"I think it was the other Jaeger," Linc murmured.

"Smart asses," Jaeger growled. "The point is—"

"I know what the point is," Beck said. And he did. The point was Cady. The point was that he loved her and wanted her in his life. He always had, always would.

"He's seeing the light…thank God and all his angels and archangels," Jaeger stated, sarcastically.

"I have to find her right now," Beck said. "I have to talk to her."

"That would be a very good idea," Sage said, smiling.

Beck patted the front pockets of his pants and then the back pockets. "I need my car keys. And my car. Where are my keys? My phone?"

Jaeger picked up his keys from the glass bowl on the counter and threw them at Beck. Beck snatched them out of thin air and picked up his phone from the coffee table. "Okay. I can go." He jerked his head up and looked at Sage. "What do I say?"

"Keep it simple, stupid. Say you're sorry for being a moron man, that you are a moron man and ask her to forgive you."

Beck frowned at her. That advice sounded a tad snarky. Like she had an ax to grind with his gender. But he couldn't think about that now.

"Right. Brooklyn. I've got to go to Brooklyn. Crap. That's going to take me forever." Beck moaned, now desperate to get to Cady, to be with Cady, to start his life. Then he remembered something else he needed to take and he ran into the kitchen and started yanking open drawers, sure what he needed was in one of them. He tossed random junk onto the floor and let out a victorious yell when his hand found what he was looking for. He shoved the item into his back pocket and looked around.

"This can work. I can do this," he muttered.

"He's looking a little green and a lot unhinged," Jaeger commentated, now openly amused.

"God help him when Cady goes into labor," Linc commented. "He's going to be a friggin' basket case. Get a grip, Beckett."

"Right." Beck pulled in what he hoped was a calming breath. "Cady, Brooklyn, ask for another chance."

"Oh, wait...she's not in Brooklyn," Sage told him. "She's in Chelsea, at that awards dinner you promised to accompany her to before you broke her heart."

Beckett looked at his watch, noticed the date and remembered that it was Friday. Also known as Day Four of Hell On Earth. It was also the date scheduled for the PR industry awards.

"Practice your groveling, dude," Jaeger suggested. "You're going to need it."

"You should know," Linc murmured and ignored the subtle middle finger Jaeger showed him but hid from Sage.

"Okay, let's go." Beck went to his door, held it open and gestured for them to leave.

Linc lifted his glass up to the light and swirled the red liquid around. "Fat chance. We're going to stay here and drink your wine."

Fair, Beck decided.

Twelve

Cady felt like the single girl at a wedding. Sitting alone at the table, she glared at the untouched place setting beside her. Two weeks ago she thought that she'd have a partner for this event, but looking from the crowded dance floor to the people milling at the bar, she was the only person in the room without a date.

How sad.

But even sitting here alone was better than returning to her empty, small apartment, to her cold, small bed. She hadn't been able to sleep in her bed since she left Beck's loft a few days ago, and the little sleep she'd managed was curled up in her chair by the window.

Cady rolled her head, trying to work out the knots her unorthodox sleeping position caused. She missed lying on Beck's chest, craved his big arms around her, missed rubbing her silky legs against his muscular limbs. She missed his deep breathing, his propensity to hog the covers…

She missed Beck sliding into her, emotionally and physically, filling up those deep, secret places nobody else could reach.

Cady stared at her glass of water, blinking away the tears in her eyes. Would this pain ever go away? She'd thought she'd experienced heartbreak when she was younger, but this, like their passion, bit deeper, burned brighter. This time around, the pain squeezed and pummeled, was a concentrated ball of agony. Cady felt Beck had whittled a hole into her soul and that it was irreparable.

It was something she suspected she'd have to live with the rest of her life.

Despite how much she loved him, she'd made the right decision to leave while she could. While she felt like half a person, she knew that this pain was better than hanging around, waiting for the day when Beck had had enough, when he ran out again. Living with that indecision would eat away at her, would slowly erode her soul.

A cracked, battered soul was better than none at all.

Her phone buzzed and she smiled when she saw the message from her mom.

I hope you're taking your vitamins and are getting enough sleep. Love you.

Her mother was trying and Cady couldn't fault her for that. She didn't know whether they would ever have a true mother-daughter relationship but she hoped so. She knew now that there were some things you couldn't force. Her parents were her parents. And Beck was Beck. She couldn't force any of them to give her what she needed.

Cady picked up her clutch from the table and pushed her chair back. There was no point in staying here any longer. She would go home, climb into her chair and fin-ish the rest of that carton of chocolate ice cream. Yeah, she was going to get fat but so what? She was pregnant and eating for two.

Okay, she was also overdosing on ice cream because she was miserable but nobody needed to know that.

Cady was about to stand up when a broad hand ap-peared in front of her, holding a tube of glue. She in-stantly recognized that hand, those fingers that loved her so well, the strong wrist and forearm, the cuffs and sleeves of his button-down shirt rolled back to reveal sculpted muscles.

Cady couldn't look up so she looked down, her eyes flying over his flat stomach and down his long legs, still wearing black suit pants.

She watched, astounded, as Beck hooked a chair with his foot and dragged it closer to her and then he was in her space, taking up her air. She lifted her gaze to his face, noticing his red eyes and heavily bearded jaw.

Beck took her clenched fist resting on her knee and gently pried her fingers open. When her palm was open he put the tube of glue in her hand.

Cady frowned, puzzled. "Glue?"

Beck nodded. "Super glue. Strong as hell."

"I don't get it, Beck," she said, holding the tube out to him.

"I'll stick, Cades. I promise."

Her eyes bounced between his face and the tube of glue and the seconds ticked by.

"I'll stick, Cades." He repeated the words. "I might get scared and feel like I want to but I won't run, I promise."

Cady felt her heart starting to defrost. "What will you do if you don't run?"

Beck lifted a powerful shoulder. "Talk to you, take you

to bed, kick my own ass and remind myself that you are the most important person in my life. I'll remind myself that I never want to feel the way I do now—lost, alone, a little crazy."

She wanted to believe him, she did, but she was terrified of reaching out and taking what she so desperately needed. "Why are you doing this, Beckett?"

His hands moved to the backs of her knees to capture her legs between his, to connect them together. "I love you, babe. I loved you in Thailand, I loved you while we were apart and I've loved you every second since we met again. It's always been you, Cady. Nobody else has ever made me feel the way you do."

Cady wanted to howl with joy but she forced that treacherous emotion away. Love wasn't enough...

"It is, Cady, if it's you and me," Beck said, and Cady realized that she'd spoken the words out loud. "But it's more than love between us. It's friendship, it's hope. It's trust. It's me believing that I deserve this, that I'm allowed to be happy, and it's you trusting me not to run and leave you behind. It's us—" he touched her tummy with the tips of his fingers "—raising this child and our other children with heart and humor, trying not to mess them up as we do. It's laughing together and loving together and living together."

Beck lifted his hand to cradle her face, his thumb rubbing her lower lip. "It's waking up and kissing this face for the rest of my life. It's your hand I want to hold, your body I want to love, your mind I want to explore." Beck's thumb glided over the wet skin beneath her eye. "Don't cry, Cades."

She didn't know that she was. Her heart was just so full of love it was leaking from her eyes. She curled her hand around his neck and fell into the love he was openly offering.

"Tell me that I can stick, Cady."

"God, yes," she murmured, touching her lips to his. "Stick to me, with me, by me, Beck."

He groaned, his lips tenderly tasting hers. "I love you so much. I always have."

"Me, too. Let's not do this again, okay?"

"Deal," Beck replied, pulling back. He looked around, looked down at his clothing and pulled a face. "You look like a million bucks. I love that dress and can't wait to get you out of it—but I think I'm slightly underdressed. I'm not even wearing a tie."

"I can't tell you how little I care," Cady told him, resting her hand on his knee.

Beck picked up her left hand to look at the bare ring finger on it. "This finger looks like it needs something on it."

"I like your mom's ring," Cady said, her voice breathless. She couldn't believe this was really happening.

"I do, too," Beck said, his voice full of emotion. "I'd give it to you if I could."

Cady rested her hand on his heart. His offer touched her deeply and if she had the slightest doubts about his staying power after his declaration earlier, they were now thoroughly banished.

"Ring or no ring, Beck, I'm yours. I always have been."

Beck held her face in his big hands, kissed her gently, reverently. "Then I am the luckiest guy in the world. I love you. Let's go home."

Cady allowed him to pull her to her feet, to tuck her into his side. Next to him, side by side, walking through life…this was what she was meant to do.

Cady placed a hand on his arm and Beck looked down at her, love in his eyes. When she couldn't push her words past the emotion clogging her throat, he squeezed her hand, silently encouraging her.

"Thank you for loving me, for loving my baby." Cady's voice broke on the words.

"That's so easy to do. It has always has been." Beck laid his hand on her rounded stomach. "Our baby, Cades. Our lives, our future, our children."

Cady nodded and felt the last vestiges of her tension drain away. How wonderful it was to feel like her life was clicking together instead of falling apart, she thought as she walked hand in hand with Beck toward her future. Their future, she corrected herself, on a huge internal smile.

She wasn't alone anymore. She'd never be alone again.

Epilogue

Cady looked around the exquisitely decorated ballroom, her eyes jumping from the bar to the security and from famous guest to famous guest. The gems were safe, tucked away in their pressure-sensitive, unable-to-be-shattered transparent boxes; the guests were behaving themselves and everyone loved Sage's new designs.

Ballantyne International was back, stronger than before. Talking about the Ballantynes, Cady looked across the room and smiled at the clan standing in the corner. Three brawny brothers looking rather yummy in their designer tuxes, and their black-haired, blue-eyed elf of a sister. Cady placed her hand on her stomach and felt tears prick her eyes.

They were her family now. Her baby would be raised a Ballantyne. Maybe, Cady thought on an internal smile, all her clean living as a child was paying off.

Beck caught her gaze, gave her a slow smile that

heated his eyes and the fabric of the minuscule thong she wore under her American-rose ball gown. Picking up the hem of her dress, she placed her fingers on top of the box holding Beck's mom's engagement ring and silently thanked her for the blessing of her son, promising her that she'd love him forever.

Cady quickly moved over to the Ballantynes and Beck held out his hand, pulling her into his side. They were joined by Tate, who looked fabulous in a vintage, boho-inspired ball gown. Judging by Linc's inability to keep his eyes off her, Linc thought so, too.

Standing with her back to Beck's chest, his arm across her stomach, Cady watched Sage, who was scowling at a sexy guy across the room. Cady immediately understood why Sage couldn't take her eyes off him. Nearly as tall as Beck, as broad-shouldered, he was a curious mix of Asian and European with dark, sultry eyes and a bright smile.

Cady watched, intrigued, as the man turned around, caught Sage's eyes across the room and gave her a look that said, "I know what's under that dress and I like it." He lifted his tumbler of amber liquid, took a sip and watched her over the rim of the glass.

Cady nudged Sage with her elbow. "Phew! That was hot. Like volcanic."

Sage broke their heated stare by giving him a kiss-my-ass look and when she turned her head, Cady saw the misery in Sage's eyes.

"Yeah, hot. And I got burned." Sage's shoulders rose and fell, and she turned her back on the guy to take both of Cady's hands in hers. "I am so happy that you and Beck are together. Welcome to the family, Cady." Sage briefly touched her rounded tummy. "And I can't wait to meet your and Beck's baby."

Their baby. Cady sighed and leaned into Beck. He was going to adopt her child and was going to raise him, or her, as his own. How lucky could she get?

"Thank you." Cady tossed a smile at Beck before looking back at Sage. "By the way, I thought you promised to pay me if I took another brother off your hands."

Sage laughed. "I did promise you that. And I always deliver. Jaeger has your payment." Sage tossed a mischievous look at Beck, who was now tuned in to their conversation. "And it's Cady's present, not yours, Beckett."

Beck stepped back but kept his hand, warm and loving, on Cady's hip. "What is?" he asked, puzzled.

Jaeger pulled a small white paper square out of the inside pocket of his tuxedo and tossed it at Beck. He snatched the packet out of the air and Cady watched excitement build in his eyes. "You got it?" he asked Jaeger, sounding like a kid on Christmas morning.

Jaeger looked seriously pleased with himself. "I did. I worked my ass off tracking it down and I did some very hard negotiating. Bribery and coercion might've been involved. You owe me, brother. Big-time."

Linc touched Beck's shoulder with his big hand and he smiled. "I'll send you the bill. I expect full payment right away."

Beck raised his eyebrows, laughter in his eyes. "No discount?"

"It's four carat, rare as hell and practically flawless," Linc retorted and then smiled. "Okay, five percent."

"Hey, I paid full price!" Jaeger complained, but everyone ignored him as they watched Beck open the small packet.

It's a Ballantyne thing, Cady told herself. She'd have to get used to the world stopping when the sibs found a rare and precious gem. She sent Tate a sympathetic smile as four heads obscured her view of whatever caught their interest.

Remembering that she was still there to work, Cady pulled the cuff up on Beck's wrist to look at his watch and thought that it was time for the dance floor to open. As she started to walk away, Beck grabbed her wrist to keep her at his side.

"Where do you think you are going?" he asked.

Cady gestured to the ballroom. "I have something to take care of."

Beck cast his eyes over the room. "Everything is fine. I thought you might like to look at what Jaeger found."

Cady nodded, thinking that a couple of minutes couldn't hurt. But she couldn't forget that they were paying the musicians by the hour and she needed to check on—

At the sight of the pink-red stone, resting on the white paper, her throat slammed closed. Oh, God, that was a red beryl, luscious, deep, sexy. It was a little smaller than the stone in his mom's ring but just as beautiful. Cady placed her hand on her heart and looked up at Beck, biting her lip as she noticed the depth of love in his eyes.

For her, all for her.

"It's beautiful." Cady touched the stone with the tip of her finger.

"Yeah, it is." Beck picked up the stone and placed it in the palm of her hand. He opened the paper it was wrapped in and held it up for her to see the ring design on the paper, beautifully rendered. It was his mom's ring but a little more modern, a little edgier. This was Sage's beautiful work.

"For me?" Cady whispered.

"Yeah," Beck replied, his voice husky with emotion. "Sage will make it for us."

"It's beautiful," Cady said, feeling overwhelmed. She blinked away her tears, gripping Beck's forearm to keep her balance. "I would've been really happy to wear your mom's ring. That one, over there." She glanced to the glass case that housed the copy.

"No wife of mine is going to wear a fake ring," Beck told her. A small smile touched his lips. "You are going to be my wife, aren't you, Cades?"

She smiled and cradled his face. "I really am. And I love the ring. But I'll always love you more."

Beck leaned down to rest his forehead against hers and his smile heated her from the inside out. "Welcome to the rest of our lives, Cades."

"Two down, one to go," Sage stated, sounding pleased with herself. "I'm making progress."

* * * * *

If you liked this story of billionaires in love,
pick up these other novels from Joss Wood:

TAKING THE BOSS TO BED
TRAPPED WITH THE MAVERICK MILLIONAIRE
PREGNANT BY THE MAVERICK MILLIONAIRE
MARRIED TO THE MAVERICK MILLIONAIRE
HIS EX'S WELL-KEPT SECRET

Available now from Mills & Boon Desire!

* * *

If you're on Twitter, tell us what you think of
Mills & Boon Desire! #Mills&BoonDesire

MILLS & BOON®

Desire™

PASSIONATE AND DRAMATIC LOVE STORIES